Dust Raiser
The Dominion Falls Series 7

Sarah Cass

Historical Romance
Romantic Suspense
Historical Western Romance

A Divine Roses Ink Book
Historical Romance
Romantic Suspense
Historical Western Romance

PUBLISHER
Divine Roses Ink
http://www.divinerosesink.com

Other Books in
The Dominion Falls Series

Independent Brake
Changing Tracks
Derailed
Dark Territory
Green Eye
Runaway Train
Home Signal
Red Zone

Coming Soon in
The Dominion Falls Series

Chasing the Red
Blizzard Lights
Dead Man's Switch
Bird Cage
A Highball Arrangement
Douse the Glim
Blood
Grave Digger
Bad Order

Books by Sarah Cass

The Tribe Series
The Tribe
The Wolf
The Chief
The Raven
The Lake Point Series
Santa, Maybe
Deep-Fried Sweethearts
Stalled Independence
Witch Way
A Thorough Thanksgiving
Eve's New Year
Heartstrings & Hockey Pucks
Luck of the Cowgirl
Stars, Stripes & Motorbikes
Free Falling
Love for Hire
Haunted Hearts
Stand Alone Novels
Masked Hearts
Leap

Dedication

To my family,
Who support me,
Even when they think it's weird.

Be proud. Be weird.
Be your unique selves.
Always

Table of Contents

The future is purchased by our present.
-Samuel Johnson

Jane poured a glass of beer with one eye on the clock. Under her breath she muttered, "And five, four, three, two, one."

"Lady Jane." Hammy's familiar greeting brought a smile to her face.

"Mr. Hamm. I could set our clocks by your daily lunch break." Jane set down the beer in front of him. She leaned on the counter. "One o'clock on the dot every day."

"Gotta get freshened for the rest of my day." He lifted his glass in salute. "Thank ya, kindly."

"It's my pleasure. Your daily visits are a bright spot in my day."

His cheeks grew ruddy as he slurped his beer. "Aw, gee, Lady Jane."

"How is my library coming along?" Hammy was well-known as many things, but being a fine carpenter was the highest of esteem among them. "I really hoped to have it open before the Centennial celebration next month."

Hammy finished the large gulp of beer he'd been taking. He wiped his scruff free of foam with his sleeve. "Almost done. I'll get my guys to move the books for ya in a day or two."

"Really?" Jane almost hopped with glee. They'd outgrown the old library nearly two years before, but it had taken some time to get the funding for the new building together, and even longer to plan. "I thought you were having trouble with the supports for the second floor?"

"We added lots more. Lost a little head room to cover 'em, but we got it figured. Ain't nothing but final touches now."

"I'm pleased to hear it. With help, I should be able to have the books shelved within a week, plenty of time for the celebration."

"Can't believe ya got that many books. Ain't no one that likes readin' that much."

"I do." Jane patted his hand.

Hammy took another large sip of beer. "Guess ya do."

Jane's attention was drawn by the large, bald man approaching the bar. "Graham Cooke. You look fit to be tied."

"Nah. Frustrated is all."

"How is that not the same?"

"I'm not ready to beat on anyone yet." Graham took a seat, rubbing his hand over his face. A large sigh pushed his lips out. "Close, but not yet."

"Is that so? What are you drinking?"

"Coffee." He grimaced at the word. Though he'd gone off the sauce a couple of years before, Jane knew he still struggled some days. She was impressed enough with his sobriety, she didn't bother to comment on the grimace.

Graham stared at the cup she set before him. "Sure could use a drink after that, though."

"After what?" She stepped in front of him. "Is Linh having trouble? Was there a problem at the doctors today?"

"No. No. She's fine. Baby's fine. Joshua is fine." Graham sipped his coffee slow, his gaze on the bottles behind her. He shook his shoulders and redirected his attention to a nearby game of poker. His wife, Linh, was having another baby. They'd received the news recently.

"If everyone is fine, then what has you so distracted?"

"Been trying to get us a house, what with the baby on the way and all."

"Makes sense. Your family is growing and I'm sure Linh doesn't care to keep a growing family in your undertakers office."

"With another baby we'd never fit. Besides, I wanted to make the undertakers bigger. More room for gathering in the front when people ain't got real homes to be seen in and such."

"Like a proper funeral home?"

"Yeah."

"Interesting. You'd need to expand or move to a new location."

"I'm right close to the mines. Long as they're running, it's still best."

"Hm." Jane absently wiped down a glass, pondering the problem. She shook off the thought. "We got off subject. You're looking for a new home. Where? In the settlement?"

"Nah. Want to do right by her, and she wants more kids." Graham jerked his thumb over his shoulder, though his next words meant the opposite direction. "On the hill."

"Snob hill? Some of those homes are a pretty penny." The hill west of town, north of the mines, is where the Daugherty's had first established their home. It was later turned into a monstrosity by the demagogue Jackson Krenshaw, who then sold off the bulk of the land piece by piece. Most of the wealthier denizens of town chose to live in those larger homes no matter the size of their families, over the more sedate settlement north of town. There many families and now quite a few miners lived.

"Trying to get Nickleby's, near the bottom of the hill. Not far from Main so Linh can get to the store easy, and wouldn't be far from work."

"Nickleby's? As in Silas Nickleby?" Now that Jane found interesting. The man was up to his eyeballs in debt with The Hangman's Inn. If he was trying to sell, he was either planning to clean the slate—or skip town.

"You know any other Nickleby's, Janey?"

"No. Of course not." She sMaced his arm with the towel when he kept chortling. "Stop it. I'm surprised to hear he's selling is all."

"Sure, sure."

"Behave."

"No fun in that." He released another sigh. "Man keeps changing the price."

"Why would he do that?"

Graham polished off his coffee, thanking her when she immediately poured another. "He's throwing in his gold claim. Says that's why he's raising the price."

By all accounts, Nickleby's claim had gone dry ages ago. It wasn't right to divulge information about their clients directly, certainly not the details of his significant debt. Perhaps there was a way for her to give Graham a clue.

"Figured I'd talk to Nick." He, of course, meant her brother Nick Young. A lawyer, the only one in town at present, actually.

"Good idea." Jane leaned on the bar to draw closer to him. "I will offer a word of advice. If you'll take it."

Graham picked his head up at full attention. She found it hard to believe with the earnest belief in his features that he'd once threatened to make her hanging longer and more difficult. Somehow these days she considered him a friend. Linh's return to his life had done him a world of good. "What is it, Janey?"

"I want you to think long and hard about this. If a man had a gold claim worth enough to drive up the price of his home—why would he put them together? Why not try to get good money out of the Daugherty's, who have much deeper pockets than a lowly undertaker? Use that tiny brain for a few minutes and see if anything comes to mind."

His brows rose. "Interesting poi—hey, what? Tiny brain?"

"That's what you get for teasing me earlier." Jane's laugh burst free for the briefest of moments. Cole stalking through the casino toward their apartment cut it off quick. Fists clenched, brows pursed, he didn't even bother to glance around the room or return any greetings. "Well, he doesn't look happy."

Graham turned in the stool a moment before Cole disappeared behind the back stairs. "He doesn't?"

The sound of a door slam barely cut over the general din of the few gamblers in the room. "You only saw the back of his head. Believe you me, ready to spit fire from what I could tell." She freshened his coffee again. "I'm going to see if I can soothe the savage beast before the bulk of the children return from their walk."

Graham shook his head. "Cole with all them kids. Never thought I'd see the day."

"Neither did he." Jane patted his hand quickly. On her way from behind the bar Edgar passed by before she needed to ask him to cover for her. She paused among the gambling tables to greet the handful of patrons. Though at one in the afternoon the place wasn't overly busy, she still liked to keep up with the lay of the land. At seven when the music started it would be difficult to keep up her friendly interactions as she liked.

Some days she almost wished they'd chosen to live off site to give more room for the stage and casino. Hindsight did little good, and they were happy as they were. Business might be bursting, but it kept things fresh.

With one last greeting to Zeb, she gathered her skirts to climb the steps out of the pit. By the time she drew close to the door of their apartment, the rapid notes of Vivaldi's *Summer* reached her ears. Cole's half-sister, Alma, only played the difficult piece when her nerves were particularly taut. The fact the notes came fast and hard meant she'd picked up on whatever mood Cole was in when he entered the apartment.

Jane pushed the door open to find Cole on the sofa, staring at Alma's back. His jaw set in a taut line, foot bouncing rapidly with the music. Jane circled around him to stare him down properly.

"What?"

"You're making Alma nervous."

"I'm not doing nothing."

"Then you are doing something."

"What?"

She set her hand on his foot to still the rapid bouncing. "You said you weren't doing nothing. By the default of the double negative, it implies you are in fact doing something."

"Jane."

"She's playing *Summer*, Cole. Whatever fit of temper you're in, Alma picked up on it. You need to calm yourself down." She sank onto the sofa beside him. Rather than face his continuing glare, she settled her own gaze on Alma's sharp movements. "Tell me what's happened."

"First, let's go calm down."

"No, sir. You tell me first. I will then decide if you need further calming."

"It's more fun the other way." The teasing of his tone drew her gaze back to him. At least he was finally calming. In fact, he wore a rather wicked grin. "Don't go all proper on me now, woman. Remember why I married ya."

"There's my man." Right in time with his boost in mood, Alma's song ended. Jane relaxed when the young woman switched to Pachelbel's *Canon in D*. "Much better. Would you care to tell me now what has you up in arms?"

"I was meeting the train." Cole's mood immediately soured again. He puffed on his cigar, glaring at the window. "New brothel came on the train. From the looks of them girls, he's a beater."

Jane sighed. "It's inevitable, Cole. You have to know this. Our old brothel closed years ago. Leanne is far too high priced for well over half of this town, especially in her new digs up on the hill. The miners want something they can afford. You can't keep running every brothel out of town. There'll be an uprising."

"I don't run them all out."

"The only one in town is Tully's. The saloon barely has 3 tables and four seats at the bar. He's only got 3 whores and they share a tiny room even when servicing."

"Least he don't beat 'em."

"It's not enough. The men are getting restless and rowdy. David is having a time keeping order. It's far worse when the cowboys come in. They won't come at all if they can't get their jollies." Jane leaned an arm on the back of the sofa. "You have to stop. You can't prevent the inevitable."

"I can control what riff raff comes in."

"If we could do that, Mac wouldn't still be in town." She leaned her head on her hand. Already he'd calmed a small amount. Not quite enough, though. His jaw still clenched tight. "What do you expect to do?"

"Ain't figured it out yet." Cole's rough vernacular seeped into their conversation. Though over the years with hers his speech had become more refined, the looser grasp on English slipped in now and then. Usually when his mind was occupied elsewhere. "But they aren't stayin'."

"We need a brothel we can trust."

"Outside of Leanne's ya mean."

"Of course. Unless you have any other madam sisters hiding around the country, we need to take another track with this one."

"I could. Bastard coulda." His features crumpled into fury. Alma's playing stopped.

She set her hand on his arm gently redirecting his attention to her. After a few minutes he nodded, his shoulders relaxing again.

"I won't have a beater bringing in a brothel." The tension lingered a smidge in his tone, but he spoke calm enough that Alma resumed playing.

Jane's mind spun over the problem. Brothels never lasted long so long as Cole kept doing all he could to run off the bad ones. Which, in truth, was most of them. "If you keep this up, you're going to have everyone in town believing you're opposed to brothels."

"Can't have that."

A laugh spilled free. "Oh goodness, no. Heaven forbid."

"You ain't even opposed to brothels as a rule."

"Not as such, no. As long as you don't partake, of course."

"Told ya long ago I don't need any whores. I got a crazy bitch right here."

She did her best to glare at him, but his amusement was written all over his face in a shit-eating grin. "Be careful, sir. You could offend my delicate sensibilities."

"Delicate my ass."

Jane walked to the window. Outside the butterfly garden Alma tended waved in the breeze. Horses were led around the paddock by stable hands. A recent conversation with Leanne about the loss of the brothel to the hotel fluttered to the surface. "I simply didn't want the brothel part of the Inn."

"I know. I get why, but…"

"You miss it."

"It was something I was good at."

"Even when you stopped sleeping with the talent."

"Some of the girls would disagree with that."

She chuckled softly. "No one could blame them for that. Least of all me."

"This ain't solving nothing."

"You were good to the girls. You never beat them. Your contract were fair, even before Nick helped. Best of all, you got them regular medical attention, let them have days off."

"Odds are this guy won't."

She leaned her forehead on the window. It wouldn't do to let this continue as it was. How could they solve it?

The idea took hold so fast she gasped at the ludicrous brilliance of it.

"What? Something wrong?"

"No. Not a thing." She turned to face him with her face schooled to hide the smile she wanted badly to set free. With his sharp gaze on her, she leaned against the window.

"Ya got that look."

"What look?"

"The crazy one."

That certainly wiped the smile away. "Excuse me?"

"Scheming."

She allowed a corner of her lip to lift. "Well, it has been quite some time since we truly stirred scandal around here."

"We just took in two Injun kids as wards."

"They aren't Indians, they were raised by them," Jane pointed out. "Be nice."

"They aren't here."

"Be nice."

He grumbled under his breath.

She drew closer, allowing her smile when he met her gaze again. "I mean scandal. We've been together for some times now. Quite devoted, even if people aren't aware how legally devoted we are."

He even grinned at that. The secret of their marriage had been a clandestine thrill for them both for nearly three years.

"Perhaps we should do something to give them all something to sweeten their tea with."

He tugged her forward until she leaned all the way over. "I like where you're going with this."

"I'm not talking about something like the back porch of Cora's."

"I am."

Jane leaned in to kiss him deeply. Once we was thoroughly distracted, she pulled free. She leaned close to his ear. "You should open a new brothel."

He became utterly still. Not even a hand moved to grasp her when she straightened. His jaw hung open, his eyes following her movement.

She tucked a finger under his chin to shut his mouth.

"You ain't serious?" His foot dropped from his knee as he sat taller. "Why would I do that? We got a good stake in Leanne's. We don't need the money."

"You wouldn't be happy with anyone coming in from anywhere. You'll run off anyone before they can get a good month in." She lifted the front of her skirts to straddle his legs. The puff of fabric between them became a buffer she'd rather be rid of. "This way you control the whole thing from beginning to end. The way the whores are treated, who's in charge when you're taking care of business with the hotel, or me."

A fire lit in his eyes at her last words. "It's crazy."

"It is. Still, we're doing well now." She rose again, pacing the floor. "From what I gather, our funds have seen a dramatic increase since the fire three years ago."

"You could say that. We bought out half of our investors."

"But only the smaller two."

"Cutler and them Armermann guys did right by us. Figured we'd let them reap the profits a while longer. That okay?"

"Wait." The meaning of what he was saying seemed impossible. She spun to face him. "Are you telling me we could buy them out as well?"

"Sure. Coulda six months ago, maybe longer. Thought you knew that."

"You are the numbers, I am the words."

"You know numbers."

Certainly she did, she'd done rather well on her own before buying out Graham Cooke to become Cole's business partner in the hotel. Still, he'd always been really good at handling the books, so she'd let him take over that part while she handled the people portion of it. "Not like you. You're the one that was smart enough to know you'd need a partner if you were going to take care of your family the right way. Of course, that led to Graham."

His nose wrinkled. "Yeah. Let's skip over that."

"Anyhow. I knew we were doing well, rather well. You're telling me we're…comfortable?"

"Daugherty level comfortable."

"With or without the mines?"

"Without. The mines kick them up quite a bit."

"Oh." Jane sat on the settee with a bump. "Goodness."

"Where ya going with this, Jane?"

"Right. The brothel." Jane shook her head to clear away the surprise of the new information. "That means we have the capital to open a brothel, bring in some whores, and someone to run the place, then."

"You really think we should?"

"I really think it's the only way to keep you from throwing fits of anger every time a brothel arrives on the train."

Cole studied her for a long minute. "People won't know what to think."

"I know. That's half the fun."

We are more wicked together than separately.
—Seneca

Jane lay curled against him. Her ragged breath a testament to the excitement of their coupling. For all the fun they'd had, her corset and chemise remained covering too much of her. Impatience had been Cole's folly there.

With time now, he slid his fingers down the laces toward the knot.

She grabbed his hand before he could tug. "No."

"You ain't near naked enough."

"I did that on purpose." She rested her chin on his chest. A wicked smirk settled in place on her tempting lips. "We have duties to attend to. Plus, the children will return shortly."

"Tom took Alma to—"

"The *other* children. Plus, Alma is hardly a child." She pushed herself to sit. When he reached for the ties, she swatted his hand. "Behave."

He groaned, flopping back to the bed. "We got too many little ones. You're no fun anymore."

"Balderdash. I used to turn you away to tend to duties plenty before we had any children or wards. You're just impatient."

"Impatient isn't what I'm feeling."

"I can see that." Her eyes flashed to the sheet where it tented. Despite her attempts to dissuade him, she bit her lip and sighed.

"Then come 'ere and let me—"

"Not right now." She slipped from the bed before he could grab her properly. All he managed to catch was her wrist, which held her in place well enough. She hovered beside the bed, but made no attempt to return. "Release me, you libertine."

"Not gonna." He shifted to crawl to her side. Her breath caught when he knelt on the edge of the bed, nuzzling the sensitive spot under her ear. "We got things to be doing."

"We do, and none of them are in our bed." The breathlessness of her protest didn't escape his notice. Once again he slid his hand toward the knot of her corset.

"Colton James Spencer," she scolded using his birth name. This time she ducked far enough away he couldn't reach her.

"Aw, come on Jane."

She tugged on her petticoats. The light dance of her laughter on the air eased some of his frustration. "I know you are excited at the prospect of a new scandal that doesn't involve children. However, we have duties to attend to."

He dropped back onto the bed. His deep groan filled the silence instead of a proper reply.

Jane didn't say a thing to help him, and she definitely didn't touch him. Fabric rustled as she put on her blasted layers of clothes.

Several minutes later delicate fingers danced up his chest. Hopefully, he opened his eyes to see if she'd forgone the clothes after all. The pearls wrapped around her neck in a tight necklace came into view as her lips touched his forehead. She hadn't stripped, she'd put on layers. Damn her. "Jezebel."

"What if I promise to make it up to you?" She got distracted by the bell on the wall, indicating there was someone at their door. They'd had the walls to their room constructed thick enough to block most sound in or out. The bells had been a necessity.

"Uh-uh." He used a finger to urge her gaze back to his. "Finish that thought first."

"After supper we will find a way to make some other scandal."

"Another one?"

"I'm certain we haven't lost our creativity under the weight of all this responsibility."

"Sounds promising."

Her lips danced along his for the briefest moment before she deepened the kiss. He tugged her back on top of him. Though she gave in easy as pie, he figured it was due to the layers between them. When she withdrew at a ring of the bell that came from the living room, her eyes were dark with lust. "Oh, I promise."

"I'll hold you to it."

"You'll hold me against you." She winked, freeing herself from his arms.

The second she hit the door, he got to his feet to dress. When she opened the door, screams of fury hit them both. "Damn it," he muttered.

Jane disappeared into the living room, closing the door to leave him in muffled silence. By the time he opened the door, the screaming had stopped. However, both Willow and Jay were speaking fast and angry at Jane. The words were a jumbled mass of foreign and English.

Jane stood calm. Arms folded across her chest, she didn't respond to any of the tirade. Rather, she stared down their two newest wards. The shrill protests in both English and Ute didn't seem to phase her a bit. Then again, there were flutters of her eyelashes and her fingers clenched tight to the fabric.

Cole turned to Sally, who also remained silent. The twins each held one of her hands. All three stared at the scene with wide eyes.

Sally tore her attention away from the scene at a nudge from him. She spoke low under the protesting children, "They fought me on coming back here, they wanted to swim longer."

"That made them scream like that?"

"It didn't make them happy. I think they like being outside as much as they can. Still, I reminded them that back here Jane let them wear what they wanted."

Willow and Jay had been raised by an Ute Indian tribe. When Leanne and Tommy had gone to Heber City, Utah to pick up more whores for Leanne's whorehouse, they'd been there to witness the two children dragged into town.

Though white by birth, the pair barely remembered their life before they were with the Ute. Jay didn't remember at all, Willow had been barely older than the twins. Jane had somehow convinced him to take in the new strays as wards. Though bringing in Sally as a ward had gone well, nearly every day was a struggle with the two children still all but yelling at Jane.

As a compromise to help them adjust, Jane allowed them to wear Indian clothes at home only. In public she ensured they wore the softest cotton she could find, much simpler outfits than even the twins wore. Jane thought it would make them more comfortable. Even Willow, though probably thirteen or fourteen, wore a simple cotton dress with no trappings. No corset as most young ladies in their teens wore. No boots for either of them, simple leather shoes Jane thought would emulate moccasins.

The transition was tenuous, rocky. At times the pair seemed almost happy, others were total chaos like this. One constant was that they never left each other's side. Stuck like glue.

"So why this?" Cole indicated to the scene that appeared to be calming. The children were losing steam in Jane's continued silence.

"On the way back, we ran into the Becker boys."

"Damn," Cole muttered. Not all of the town cared for Jane's new wards. Caleb Becker really went after them at every opportunity. His two boys were all too happy to join their dad's torment of the kids.

"You'd be impressed, though. Willow knocked Peter out cold."

Cole turned his gaze on the girl. From the start she'd done everything she could to protect her brother, even when he didn't need protection. "Peter went after Jay, then."

"Yeah."

Willow's tirade stopped suddenly. A wheeze rented the air. Willow sMaced away Jane's reaching hands and grabbed the pouch that hung around her neck all the time to breathe deep into it. After a few good breaths, the wheezing eased.

Jane crouched in front of Willow, brows pinched in concern. "I'd hoped you'd finish before that happened."

Willow continued to suck in air, her gaze stuck on Jane.

"Why don't you sit down? Come on." Jane led her to the sofa, trailing Jay along behind her. Soon as the girl sat, Jane turned to Jay. "Jay can finish telling the story while you recover."

"Shouldn't take this long to tell the story." Cole didn't balk under Jane's sharp glare. "What? Sally told me in about two seconds.

"Go on, Cole. I've got these two. Take the twins, please."

Cole frowned her way. "It's their nap time."

"I am painfully aware, but look at them. This has been quite some excitement for them. They'll never sleep now. Get them some cocoa to settle them down."

"Cocoa," Clara repeated. She squealed in excitement. Sally had to struggle to keep a grasp on her hand.

"Woah, there." Cole scooped up his daughter. Once settled on his hip, she pouted at him. He gave her as stern a look as he could manage. "I haven't said I'd take you yet."

"You will." Jane's laughter filtered through her previously terse tone. "You can't turn her down for anything."

"Conniving woman." He tried to glare at his wife, but the damnable woman's laughter proved far too infectious.

Clara smushed his cheeks between her hands before he could utter another word. "Cocoa!"

Cole did his best to speak through his squished cheeks. "Should I bring some for Jay and Willow when we're done?"

Jane turned to Willow. After a moment's thought, she nodded. "I think so. I don't believe Willow wishes to go out again today."

"No." Willow held her pouch of medicine close to her face. "Stay here."

Cole nodded to Jane. He managed to pry Clara's hands from his face. "Enough of that, you rotten beast."

"Rotten beast." Clara poked her finger into his nose. "You. Mama said."

"She sure did," Cole agreed. He carried her out of the apartment, with Sally and Colton following behind.

Sally chuckled under her breath. "Ma teaches them well, and early."

"Don't remind me." Try as he might to sound grumpy, laughter filtered into Cole's tone. Colton's small hand slipped into Cole's free one. "Colton, what do you say? Am I rotten?"

Colton shook his head. Always the quieter of the twins, he'd become almost serious despite being only two and a half. Most of the time Cole was convinced the boy was reading over his mother's shoulder when he snuggled with her. "Ma loves you."

"He's still despicable," Sally pointed out.

"Don't encourage them, Sally." Cole's further attempts at grumpiness were thwarted by Clara's incessant pestering. She kept alternately hugging him tight around the neck and trying to flip out of his grasp.

Soon as they entered the lobby, Tommy walked in with Alma.

"Tom!" Cole lifted the arm that held Colton's hand. The boy laughed as he was lifted right to his uncle. "Help me out. Jane is with the new strays."

Tom grabbed Colton without hesitation. His laughter boomed through the lobby. "You've got your hands full with Clara, I see."

"You're telling me." Cole caught Clara as she flipped nearly right out of his arms. He glanced at Alma. "What did you get?"

"Little Men," Alma said quietly. In the chaos of the young ones and the general din of the lobby she'd curled into herself as she always did in crowds. Still, she held the book out to him. "Jane ordered it."

"Ma was excited for that." Sally stepped forward to make it to Alma's side. Alma relaxed at Sally's familiar presence. Sally went so far as to tuck a supportive arm around Alma's wait. "Too bad she's busy. I'd love to start reading."

"Maybe tonight," Cole suggested.

Sally nodded to him, guiding Alma through the lobby to a table in a quiet corner of the eating area.

Right then Cora approached. She laughed outright as Clara clamored right over his shoulder. He caught the girl by the ankles, letting her dangle down his back. Through the girls giggles, Cole nodded to Cora. "We're supposed to get cocoa for them. Don't think Clara much needs it."

"Cocoa!" Clara squealed, pushing her way back up his back until she all but stood on his hands, her hands planted on his head. "Cocoa!"

"Cocoa I can do." Cora held out her arms. "Give her here."

Cole finagled the wriggling child into Cora's arms. He tried to look stern, pointing his finger at his daughter. "Cocoa only. No cookies."

"Cookies!"

Cora tsked Cole, holding out her other arm to Tom. The enthusiastic bouncing of Clara didn't seem to faze her one bit. "Give me Colton, too. I'll decide if they get cookies."

"In other words, they'll get them." Tommy handed off Colton. "You're a brave woman, Cora. Taking both of them on."

"I raised Isaac. I think I can handle a little rambunctiousness." Cora carried the twins to her kitchen.

"I think she misses raising her boys. Those kids spend a lot of time in her kitchen." Tom rubbed his hand over his face. "You say Jane has Willow and Jay?"

"They had some issues with the Becker boys on their walk." Cole filled him in on the incident quick as Sally had him. He led him to a table that had emptied.

"Glad she flattened him. He deserved it." Tom ordered a drink from the waitress. He waited for Cole to do the same before he leaned forward. "What were you and my sister scheming when I came to get Alma? I haven't seen you two so riled up since you started planning this place."

Cole grinned. "Oh, it's a story I have to wait to tell you until Jane is with us. She'd kill me if I told you before she could."

"Sounds like you are starting trouble."

"So? What if we were?"

"I'd say life was about to get interesting."

"When has it not been around Jane?"

"Fair point."

Happiness is like those palaces in fairy tales
whose gates are guarded by dragons:
we must fight in order to
conquer it.
-Alexander Dumas Père

Tommy sat quiet while Sally lay in the shallows of the swimming hole. She'd splashed about and made enough noise to scare off any fish, but he sat with his line in the water none-the-less. He had patience for her to become quiet.

Now that she was, he soaked in the silence he had no doubt was temporary. While Jane and Cole had managed to settle the twins into a nap despite cocoa and cookies, Jane was still pretty focused on calming Jay and Willow.

To that end, he'd taken Sally to the swimming hole with the intention of fishing, but she'd decided to swim instead. Eventually she'd do as she always did, ask him for stories of his time as a Pinkerton.

Since she'd saved his life several years ago to her own detriment, he'd taken a shine to the girl. He'd been glad he'd not had to push Jane to the conclusion that she needed to take her in as a ward. That had been solely Jane's idea, one he was relieved for.

The fire she'd pulled him out of had left scars along her hairline and down toward her chest. As she'd been a whore before the incident, her livelihood was at stake. That hadn't been what had made him think she should be Jane's ward, though it was a good enough point.

Something nagged the back of his mind about her. Something he couldn't quite yet grasp, which annoyed him to no end. He liked having the facts, all of them. Still, he'd not dug into her past at her own request. She hated speaking of her real parents, and avoided the subject at all costs, though he'd tried to poke and prod a few times.

Unfortunately, though he was an expert at digging up the truth about people, Sally seemed to have an instinct about what to hide. Only once in a blue moon did she ever mention her time before Dominion Falls, and the few breaches of her silence had simply been about Booneville, the little town outside Pueblo where Graham had found her.

He imagined his consternation centered around the fact she looked remarkably like Jane. It was disconcerting and made him wonder if she wasn't somehow related to their family. Their ma, Eunice, had quite a number of brothers and sisters spread out around the country. It wasn't out of the realm of possibility.

A deep sigh emerged from the figure resting in the shallows. Sally's lips pursed, her features twitching as though to speak or running through thoughts.

He wasn't about to make it easy for her to figure out what she wanted to say. The girl seemed to be in a constant battle with herself lately. Though he didn't doubt she was happy in the life she'd found for herself, he wondered if she was happy enough.

Tom was all too aware of the look she got on her face sometimes. When her gaze wandered to the mountains or lifted from a fantastical story. It was a look he'd likely worn many times himself. The look that said there was something else out there to be found or done. Something more. Always more.

At least until recently, he'd known that feeling deep in his soul. Dominion Falls had become a home he didn't care to wander too far from again. He'd had his adventures and was all too content to remain where he was now, with his job, his family, and his woman.

Sally, however, hadn't had any adventures since the one she undertook to come to Dominion Falls. In fact, since Jane had taken her under her wing, she'd been exceedingly well-behaved and sedate. The spark always lit when she read or listened to his stories.

The water sloshed when Sally sat up, her mouth open to speak. Just as quick, she shut it again. Her lips pulled together again, her gaze hard on the water.

Tom didn't push her to speak. He pulled back his fishing line before tossing it back in the water. His own feet hung in the water, but he didn't kick them about as Sally did. Though he could chastise her for scaring the fish, he hadn't expected to catch anything anyway.

Sally finally breached the silence. "My test is coming up."

"I'm aware."

"Been studying hard. I think I'll do well."

"Got no doubt about that." Tom knew Jane had set Sally with a task upon taking her on. Passing a teacher's exam well enough to achieve a second-grade certificate. The girl had been smart as a whip, though she'd had some trouble with learning and reading.

As though she was still Clara, Jane had managed to help Sally overcome that trouble until academically, Sally was top notch. Despite not attending the school in town due to her past, she'd learned at Jane's side until he imagined she could get a first-grade certificate.

"Then I'll be a teacher."

"You'll be qualified, yes." Being qualified didn't mean she'd be doing it. Tom couldn't see her as a teacher, no matter how good she was with her siblings.

"Ma wants me to be a teacher."

"Does she now?"

Sally's legs swung in the deep water, her shoulders slumped, hands resting inches below the surface on the rock ledge over the deeper waters. "Said so when she took me in."

"I remember something like that. It was a few years ago, though."

Her gaze fixed on the trees, yet quite beyond them, she sighed deeply again. "When did you leave home to be a Pink?"

"When did I leave home, or when did I become a Pink?"

"Both, I guess."

"Seventeen I left home. Deputied in Rochester, then in Illinois. Got married and moved back to New York. That's when I met Sam. He was a Pink, told me about the life. I'd always been nosy, or so Clara and Nick told me. Seemed real interesting."

"It does."

"Mysteries, travel, danger. Exciting. Not conducive to marriage, but I still started working for them. Did mostly guard duty, some investigating. Ended up guarding the President." Tom remembered all too clearly the first time he'd met Lincoln. "Before he was President, of course. Then again, after."

"You said when he died everything blew up for you."

"Or I blew it up. How ever you want to look at it. Wife was sick of my traveling and being in danger and doing things she likely didn't approve of in the name of investigating."

"Did you?" She turned her attention to him.

"Never once cheated on my wife. Had some folks thinking I had. Still, she didn't know me anymore. Hell, she wasn't wrong. I wasn't the kid she married anymore. Pinkerton was the life I was meant for back then."

"Not anymore?"

"I still take assignments from time to time, but nothing so involved. I like where I'm at. No more need to go on being the nosy bastard of a man." Tom pulled in the line again, only to toss it back out. "I'm not angry any longer, and while I'll always be curious like your ma, I've got enough keeping me busy around here."

"You mean Leanne."

"She's one factor."

"You love her?"

"Sure do."

"Gonna marry her?"

"Hell, no. Neither of us much want it. She doesn't have a better opinion of it than I do. People change, and they don't always grow closer."

"Ma and Cole haven't changed."

"They haven't?" He chuckled low. "I beg to differ. When you first came to Dominion Falls could you ever see either of them being parents? Much less parents to so many?"

Sally shrugged. "Ma was always like my Ma. Part of why I didn't like her. She was tough on me from the start, even when she didn't know how young I was. And Pa—I mean, Cole…"

He allowed a brow to raise at the comment. It wasn't the first time Sally had slipped up and called Cole Pa. It was a recent development, and he wondered if a couple years as their ward hadn't really changed not just Cole, but Sally. He let the slip slide on by. "What about him?"

"I didn't know him like the other girls did. He was with Jane, or sort of was, when I came. He stopped sleeping with the whores before I ever got there. He was—I don't know."

"You're perfectly good with words."

"He cared about us in a weird way. Protected us from bad john's. I'd been a whore before and never felt safe like I did at the saloon."

"You aren't the first whore to say that."

"Anyway. I could see it."

Tom nodded to himself, impressed. "That means you could see beyond the front they put on for the town. You've got a keen eye. You're good at reading people."

She flushed under the compliment.

"You thinking of leaving? Is that why you asked?"

"No. I mean, yes. No. Maybe?" Her blush deepened, and she laid back in the water as though hiding from his scrutiny. "Dominion Falls is my home. First real one."

"Home is always right where you leave it."

"I guess."

"What about your beau?"

"He's not—"

"I think Arthur would disagree with that." He eyed the young woman a moment before glancing at his pocket watch. It was nearing dinner, but they had time.

"I don't know what he is. He's good. Kind."

"That he is." He hid his smirk at the idea of how Jane would get so annoyed with him for being so evasive and vague with his replies. She always despised how he let people hang to dry on their own words. Then again, she hadn't room to talk, she did the same thing.

There was a splash of water when Sally slapped the surface. She grunted some frustration in the form of a curse before getting to her feet. She stomped out of the water, gathering her dress to her. As she threw it over her wet underlayers, she levelled a glare at him.

"What?"

"You aren't helping."

"Is that what I was supposed to be doing?"

"Yes!"

"How can I help you if you can't even say out loud the things you're thinking?"

She glared down at him, hands clenched at her sides, water dripping along her spiteful features. Without another word, she spun on her heel and stomped to her horse, Agatha.

He whistled to himself as the hoofbeats got more and more distant. Once Sally was far enough away he no longer heard the horse, he gathered his things.

The girl had a monster of hidden thoughts and feelings growing inside her. He didn't much care if she didn't tell him, but she had to get the gumption to tell her ma. Jane was worried about the girl, but also feared what the truth was underneath all the good behavior.

Tommy didn't fear what the girl was hiding, mostly because he had a good suspicion of what it might be. He'd not help her or Jane one lick until the truth came out, though.

Sally would get the gumption soon enough. Until then, he was happy to let them figure out their own path. He'd not help anyone along the path they laid for themselves until they admitted it. He'd done the same with Jane when he'd first met her.

He chuckled to himself at his own thoughts. They'd piss off his brothers something fierce. Unlike them, he didn't think Jane was their sister redressed. He'd watched for some time before meeting her face to face. He'd known from the start that it was the exact opposite.

Jane was a stranger in Clara's body.

It was fortunate for him, too. Clara had despised him. Jane actually liked him.

Voices interrupted his thoughts right as he gathered up the last of his things. First to come over the hill was none other than his nephew, Jesse. The boy lit up when he spotted Tommy. "Uncle Tommy! Are ya joining us?"

"I was actually just leaving." Tommy accepted the boys' hug. Following behind Jesse were his two best friends, Stephen and Isaac. Behind them came David and Arthur. "You boys swimming or fishing?"

"Swimming."

"Good. Not much biting after your sister was just splashing about." Tommy ruffled his hair before extending his hand to David. "Afternoon, Sheriff."

"Afternoon. We weren't expecting to find anyone here. I know Sally brought Jay and Willow by with the twins earlier." David returned his handshake heartily. "I got an earful from Becker about the incident on their way back."

"You aren't even on duty today." Tommy shook his head in exasperation. "That man just wants to rile up some trouble."

"Don't I know it? Why do you think he stopped me in the street?" A smile broke the man's face. "To that order, can I count on you to let Jane know he filed a formal complaint?"

"I tell her that and Caleb Becker will have a broken nose of his own, and you'll have to put Jane in jail again."

"Good point. I suppose I'll let it slide for now." David glanced over Tommy's shoulder. "Best get to watching the boys. Stephen's still not a great swimmer."

"All right. See you at the library opening? Jane says it'll be in a few days."

"Sure will. Jesse would be mad if we didn't go support his ma."

Since you are so well matched,
and so much alike –
a very bad wife, and a very bad husband –
I wonder that you do not agree.
–Marcus Aurelius

Cole ran his hand along Jane's leg. She had one foot on the floor, while the ankle she'd broken years ago propped across his legs. Whether her claim it eased the ache she never got rid of was true or not, he never minded. Then again, her assertions that it hurt more when a big storm was coming had proven true on many occasions.

Jane herself scanned the papers and ledger he'd gathered at her request. While she'd always been good with numbers and money, proving as much by the good amount she brought in through investments when she'd first arrived in Dominion Falls; when the new Hangman's Inn had opened, she'd taken a step back from the finances. She'd pointed out he was better with numbers, while she was better with people. Sure, they were both good at both, but he had to admit she edged him out with people by about as much as he edged her out on numbers.

Truth be told, the set up had worked well for them. Outside of occasionally suggesting a stock she'd read about, Jane was content knowing he'd let her know if things were tight. For that matter, she'd even agreed to let him set a budget on her clothing expenditures for herself and the kids. Of course, he kept the budget set pretty high, which kept her plenty happy.

Now that they'd agreed to open a brothel and in turn she'd learned how well they were doing, she'd been curious about what their worth actually was. Cole was more than happy to let her see. They'd done well in the two years since The Hangman's Inn had reopened. The casino alone helped fill their coffers to overflowing. For the time being, they wanted for nothing.

He trailed his fingers higher up her leg. Layers of skirt slipped forward to reveal smooth-as-silk skin. He managed to get as far as her knee before she tapped his hand with her pencil.

"Hey." The grin she sported told him she wasn't truly opposed. Before she could offer any argument, he slid his hand up her thigh. Gently his fingers danced along the sensitive skin inches from her core. A shaky sigh eased from her lips, her eyelids fluttering. "The numbers'll still be there tomorrow, ya know."

"Are you sure?"

"They're not going anywhere."

"Neither are you. Haven't you had enough today?" The ledger thumped to the table, her attention all on him now. "First this afternoon in our room, and then again during our walk after supper—right outside the livery in broad daylight, no less."

"It was dusk, ya liar." He pounced, capturing her lips in a slow kiss to cover any shriek that might wake the kids.

"I don't lie." Her words were low when he released her from the kiss. She licked her tempting pink lips. No protest to his pouncing came, rather the opposite. Her arms slid around his neck, body arched toward him. "You're full of vigor today."

"Every damn day. You always know how to get me going."

"Good to know that married life hasn't—um—softened you."

"Nothing soft here."

"Oh, I am quire aware." She pulled him into a deep kiss.

Footsteps on the stairs made them both freeze. Too heavy to be Alma or Sally, it had to be Tom coming down from his apartment for a visit.

"Aw geez, Lou. I told you I don't want to see that." Tom's protest proved Cole's suspicions right.

Jane groaned. "Your timing is horrendous, Thomas."

"With the pair of you, we could be in church and the timing would be horrendous."

Cole's dropped his head to Jane's chest in his laughter. Jane laughed just as strong under him. "Oh no. That is one sin we've never partaken in. In church is too much, even for me."

"Everywhere else in town is fair game, though." Tom grimaced at his own words. "As many have discovered at the oddest of times."

"We've slowed some in recent years," Jane protested.

"Not near enough for my liking." Tom waved a hand at them. "Get decent."

"You're the one that interrupted us in our home." Cole grumbled when Jane pushed him back to sit. "Without knocking or nothing. Middle of the night and all."

"Casino just closed, I knew you were up. Besides, you're the one that said you had something to talk about. As your siblings, we were curious."

Jane adjusted her skirts, but kept her foot on Cole's lap. "Siblings? Plural? I only see one of you here."

Cole frowned at the ankle still lying across his lap. "Storm coming?"

"Big one, based on the way it hurts all the way up." She rubbed her thigh. Not a whisper of argument came from her when he took over the task in earnest. "Who else would interrupt us by coming over at one in the morning?"

Tom rose again to pour himself a whiskey. At a gesture from Jane he poured two more. After he'd handed them to her, he took his seat. "Leanne. We had planned on her coming by anyway, but she was curious what had the two of you fired up as well. Said she saw you by the livery tonight."

A delicate blush lit Jane's cheeks. Her glass of whiskey got a sip that didn't quite cover the brief hint of embarrassment. She cleared her throat. "I see. Then the pair of you decided that Cole and I were up to something? As you pointed out, we tend to enjoy each other often."

"I know you're up to something." Tommy smirked at his sister. "You got that look, plus Cole all but confirmed it earlier."

Cole shrugged at the small glare she gave him. "Clara was playing tumbleweed on my head. I was too distracted to keep my mouth shut. Besides, we're gonna need his help. Probably Leanne's, too. I've been out of the game for a bit."

"What game?" The blonde that was Cole's other half-sister appeared on the stairs without warning. Somehow she'd descended nearly silent, as opposed to Tom's loud entrance.

Cole glanced toward her in surprise. "Didn't hear ya coming."

"Took off my shoes in Tommy's place. Didn't want to risk waking anyone." Leanne leaned in to hug Jane before dropping into Tommy's lap without ceremony. "Back to the subject at hand. What *game* are you talking about?"

"The brothel business," Jane filled in for him.

The reward for the suddenness of the declaration was instantaneous. Both Tom and Leanne's jaws dropped. Neither said a word, seeming to be unable to grasp what she'd said.

Jane leaned toward Cole, a wicked smirk on her features. "Oh, that was fun. Can we go back and do it again?"

"Cat's outta the bag now." He chuckled low. There was no doubt the moment was enjoyable. Neither Tom nor Leanne were often at a loss for words.

Leanne recovered first with a shake of her head. "Come again?"

"I plan to—soon as the two of you leave." Jane's raunchy comment stirred Tom out of his stupor as it sent Leanne laughing.

"Janey, stop." Tom glared her way. The use of the townies nickname for her proved he was still out of sorts. After a moment he seemed to recover himself as well. He gave a little shake, meeting Cole's gaze. "Now what's this about the brothel business?"

"We're getting back into it." Cole resumed his kneading of Jane's thigh. Still, he slipped his free hand under her skirts to find her flesh again. "Jane seems to think it's the only way to keep me from running every brothel that ain't Leanne's out of town."

"It's getting tedious, and the locals are getting restless." Jane drew her other leg onto his lap. She leaned on the arm of the sofa, relaxing under his ministrations. "And though we have a stake in your place, we aren't hands-on there. It's your place, we're silent partners. So, without the hands-on aspect and control, Cole is a little restless, too."

"He doesn't appear to be." Leanne eyed the area where Cole's hand disappeared under Jane's skirts. "Seems quite content, actually."

"I don't mean with me."

"Not even a little bit," Cole confirmed.

"Thank you," she demurred.

Cole propped his legs on the low table where Jane had deposited the ledger. "Plus, Jane thought it might bring back some of the scandal we were so popular for."

"Popular might be pushing it." Leanne took Tom's unfinished whiskey from his hand. "Renowned, perhaps. Popular? That's stretching the truth a little bit."

Tom shook his head, a low chuckle coming from the man. "In other words, there is boredom in being a loyal, devoted coupling that continually does good deeds, takes in strays, in general is well liked around town. You want to stir the pot."

"I do miss stirring the pot." Jane sighed heavily. "We haven't given the old crows much to sweeten their tea with this past year. At least until we took in Willow and Jay."

Tom stammered, his face growing ruddy. "You— opening a brothel? That's the way?"

"Cole was good at running his place." Jane smiled warmly at him. "His whores were happy, only one or two ever ran off in all his years."

"He slept with his whores," Leanne pointed out. She grimaced. "I'm painfully aware. I heard far more tales than I cared to, as his sister, about how happy that made them."

"True." Jane shrugged. "But he was also fair, didn't hit them. He made sure none of the clientele did either. All of that is good business."

"Can I talk?" Cole pinched her calf.

"Well, it was my idea." Jane stuck her tongue out at him.

Cole ignored her snark to face the other two in the room. "We have the capital to do it. The drive. We're just missing the girls, and someone to man the place. Tom, you're good at locating people, found most of the staff here. Think you can find someone trustworthy to man the brothel since I can't be there all the time?"

Tom stared at him so long, Cole couldn't be sure what the man was thinking.

A frown flickered across Jane's features at the silence. Even Leanne glanced at the man in confusion. In the lingering silence, Cole had stopped his teasing of Jane. Her leg nudged his hand in protest.

Tom turned beet red. First his neck, then his cheeks, right up to his forehead. The man flew to his feet so fast, Leanne toppled to the ground with an unceremonious thump.

Leanne emerged from the disheveled pile of fabric as Tom flew out the back door. She blew the hair from her face, in frustration. "What the devil was that about?"

All three of them clamored to their feet to follow him. Cole made it to the door first. When he wrenched it open, a loud braying laugh hit all their ears.

Jane followed Cole out, her arm laced through Leanne's. The laughter led them around the barn to find Tom. The man literally rolled on the ground in his laughter.

Leanne and Jane both set a fist on their hips to glare down at the man.

After a knee-slap, Tom rocked to his rump. His laughter continued. He swiped a hand across his face, but it did little to calm the continuing mirth.

"Thomas Eugene." Jane's tone lent to scolding, but her own features flickered with amusement. "What has gotten into you?"

Tom's laughter grew more subdued. He chuckled on. "This is a real trick. How perfect for the two of you."

"Glad you're amused." Jane pursed her lips.

"I had to come out here so I wouln't wake the kids." Tom laughed again. "Oh, you'll get tongues wagging for sure."

Jane shook her head at her brother. After another second she held out her hand to him to help him to his feet. "My goodness, you are a child sometimes."

"Takes one to know one, Lou." Tom took her hand but appeared to hop to his feet on his own. "This is going to be a riot—the two of you opening a brothel. Can't wait to see what the town thinks of this."

"Neither can we." Cole chuckled with his brother-in-law.

"Where are you looking for a location?"

"Closer to the mines," Jane started.

"Near the Inn," Cole said at the same time. He frowned at Jane. "It can't be that far away."

"Oh dear, the mines are all the way on the other side of town. Whatever shall you do?" Jane rolled her eyes. "Such a terribly long walk, and your legs all broken, and there's nary a horse to be found to ride there."

"We need to keep an eye on it."

"We don't need it that proximal to the Inn."

"Why the hell not? We got clients that want entertainment. It's not all miners that want affordable whores."

"If it's too close there'd be trouble. When the cowboys come to town, especially."

"That's what the damn sheriff is for."

"No, it isn't. The sheriff isn't working for *us*." By then Jane was in his face, hands full on her hips. "He works for the town."

He met her glare for glare. "Farther it is from us, less time I'm here."

"Maybe that wouldn't be a bad thing."

"Look, woman. You wanted me to do this because I'm good at it."

"That doesn't mean you have enough brains to plan the place."

"I planned this place."

"You fell into this place, you lunkhead."

They both stopped at renewed braying laughter. This time Leanne was equally in on the fun. Both her and Tom laughed outright at Cole and Jane.

Jane tugged on her bodice as if to straighten the smooth fabric. "Well."

"Oh-ho." Tommy pointed at them, doubled over in his laughter. "This is going to be fun."

"Shut up, Thomas."

Do not, as some ungracious pastors do,
Show me the steep and thorny way to heaven;
Whilst, like a puff'd and reckless libertine,
Himself the primrose path of dalliance treads
and wrecks not his own.
-William Shakespeare

Jane laced her arm with Kat's, leaning close toward her friend's ear. "Cindy has told me a secret. You must tell me if it's true."

"What secret would that be?" Kat's grin matched Jane's in amusement. "Would it be her crush on the Porter boy?"

"Jonah Porter? He's nearly thirteen. Cindy is a mere nine."

"Almost ten, as she'll remind you often."

"Not that near." Jane chuckled softly. "I believe she's jealous of Lizzie and Jesse. The pair have been thick as thieves since you took in Lizzie. I fear young love will fade all too soon."

"I don't know. The two of them are quite close. They wouldn't know how to live without the other in their lives these days, but you might be correct. She's growing up and getting interested in boys far too early for my liking. But where her sister leads, she follows."

"So it seems. That, however, is not the secret she told me."

"Then what, pray tell, has she told you?"

"That her darling Uncle Patrick is going to visit?"

"Told you that, did she?" Kat's gaze wandered toward the other side of the street. Whether avoiding Jane, or feigning innocence, Jane couldn't be certain.

"She did. Is it true that after nearly four years of hearing about this rake, I will finally meet the man you and Cindy speak so highly of?"

"Yes. I believe Cindy convinced him finally to come out for all the revelry this summer." A small flush lit up Kat's cheeks as if there were more to the story. "Between the Centennial celebration in a couple weeks, and our upcoming statehood I suppose he finally found our little town something worth visiting."

"I do believe you told me he had a difficult couple of years after the silver crash. That was reason enough. I'm simply rather excited to finally meet the man that you lived with before Norman. He seems an absolute scoundrel. My favorite sort of man."

Kat finally laughed at Jane's playful tone. "Oh, stop. You know he's a good man. Rake or not, he saved my life several times over."

"Maybe not your life, but definitely your soul and spirits. For which I am infinitely grateful. Should I plan to set aside a fine room for him?"

"Yes, please. Norman doesn't mind him visiting, but I doubt he would care to have him under the same roof."

"You haven't been lovers in a great many years. That ended far before you left his household. Before you left Chicago, even."

"Men are…"

"Men. To this day I still can't mention Al without Cole tensing up, and we were never lovers, nor did we live under the same roof."

"But the man did ask you to marry him."

"Fair enough." Jane slowed as they approached the new library. Men carried boxes back and forth from a wagon, loading her books into the newly finished building. Positioned on Third Street, right next to the pathway to her apartment for convenience, the new library was much larger than the original.

Rather than a false front, there was a full second story for the hundreds of books in the boxes. After she'd filled it with those, there'd be room for more as it struck her fancy to add to the collection. For the moment there were enough brand-new books in the boxes to keep her satisfied. She'd see how long it lasted.

"That's quite a lot of boxes." Kat's gaze was on the wagon being unloaded instead of the building itself. "We start unloading tomorrow?"

"We do. It shouldn't take more than a few days."

"Perhaps. If we work non-stop. Have you at least sorted them?"

"No. I didn't unpack them as they arrived, I merely had Cole put them in the kitchen of the old library. It won't be a problem. I'll organize as I unpack. Trust me."

"I do, but that is a lot of books."

"I've never known you to worry so much."

"I'm not worrying. Exactly." Kat chuckled when Jane cut her a look. "Fine. I just never realized quite how many books you had stuffed into that kitchen."

"It did look like less when they were stacked up tight in the room. We'll manage fine. I've got all hands on deck for this one. Michael is even coming out from his place to help. Charles said he'd come by. Millie won't be able to assist, but she may visit."

"Hasn't she had that baby yet? I swear she and Lee got pregnant at the same time, and little Marjorie is already several weeks old."

"Apparently they were a couple months apart. Millie still has a few weeks to go."

Kat sighed softly, her gaze once again, drifting away.

Jane squeezed her friends' hand gently. She alone knew that her friend had been trying since her wedding several years ago to have another child. Months, then years passed without success. "It will happen for you. I have every faith."

"I fear I'm losing faith." Kat shook her head, then her shoulders. "Let's choose another subject. Such as the numerous varied and outlandish activities we have planned for these celebrations. Mother may not be grasping for status as she once was for herself, but she certainly is for this town. She has a potential senator planned for the statehood."

"A potential senator coming here? Goodness. She is reaching."

"Always."

They both paused as a couple of cowboys tore down the street whooping and hollering on their way north to the camp they'd set up outside of town. Jane sighed. "Good for business though they might be, things always get dicey when cowboys come through."

"I heard David hired a couple new deputies to help with the extra load."

"He did. Simon Blackwell, and Bryan Kendrick. They both have other businesses but will only work as deputies sometimes. Bryan is a good man, if he didn't have the cooper shop, I know David would like him to come on full time."

"It seems like he'd need more. Mike has been so busy, and so has Tommy. Wouldn't hurt to hire a few more. The town is getting too big for David to handle without plenty of support."

"I agree, but I don't think he's ready to give up the idea we're still small and dainty. No matter that the settlement has grown to house hundreds now, and there's even two churches."

Kat's nose wrinkled. "Please, let's not speak of Glorious Valley. Pastor Eckles disturbs me. How does he get a following?"

"He has a powerful message and delivers it with aplomb. Unfortunately, it's a very unforgiving message that attacks so many good souls." Jane sighed. Reverend Greene had been talking of retirement and brought Eckles in as a possible replacement. The man's bold, unforgiving sermons had been too much for the kind Reverend's congregation and Eckles had left to start his own church south of town. "I do believe Mark regrets bringing him here."

"He couldn't have known. He said he came with high recommendations. Besides, in the end he brought in Reverend Lyons, who will continue his sort of sermons."

"Yes. Eli is wonderful. I think the Reverend asked for someone quite young so he might have a few more years of teaching before he truly retires."

"Much to Mabel's chagrin. I do believe she's the one who wishes him to retire."

"I've always wondered how two such different souls could be married, but it's clear that Mark loves Mabel."

"In recent years, with my sister gone, she's been known to show far more kindness. Perhaps she learned her lesson after the Indian business."

Years before the reverend's wife, Mabel, had helped Kat's sister take supplies to the Renegades that had been attacking the town. Those supplies included a load of dynamite used to blow up some businesses. Jane nodded. "She was rather repentant after that incident."

Gunfire echoed through town, interrupting the conversation effectively. Jane gathered her skirts, running toward Main to find the source of the ruckus. Kat ran right along beside her.

They both skidded to a stop when they immediately spotted the source of the trouble. Down the street the very man they'd spoken of, Pastor Eckles carried his bible, a small group of people behind him. They appeared to have been at the cowboy camp by the angry line of cowboys behind them with their pistols drawn.

"'But as for the cowardly, the faithless, the detestable, as for murderers, the sexually immoral, idolaters," Eckles loud, savage voice cut through town.

"Oh dear." Jane sighed. "Looking to call in more people."

"In the wandering souls of cowboys?" Kat's brow furrowed. "He's better served at the mines. That's where he gets most of his flock."

A series of gunshots had interrupted Eckles quoting of Revelations, but not for long. "'Their portion will be in the lake that burns with fire and sulfur."

Jane knew she didn't imagine the way Eckles stared her down as he passed them. She lifted her chin, turning her attention away to the cowboys trailing the Pastor. "Gentlemen!"

A few heads turned her way. The cowboy closest to her smirked. "Ain't often called that, ma'am."

"That's of no matter. You and your men are welcome in the casino. First round of the dime ante is on me. Leave that lot be, they won't learn to leave you alone, I'm afraid." Jane gestured toward The Hangman's Inn. "Come on in. I'll even offer each of you a whiskey for your disturbance to your day."

One of the men tipped their hat at her. "Sounds right good, ma'am."

"Wonderful." Jane squeezed Kat's hand. "I'll speak with you soon."

"Good luck, inviting them in. They're already riled."

"It's better than them firing off in the streets." Jane darted toward the porch of the Inn, gesturing the men inside. As the last filed in, David approached. She nodded to him. "Sheriff."

"Sure that's smart?" David glanced inside after the men.

"It gets them off the street where they've been firing blind in an attempt to scare Eckles. Keeps you from having to wrangle anyone, citizen or cowboy." She squeezed his arm.

"Go on now, find some real trouble. We'll keep this lot contained for a little while."

He nodded in return. "If they give you trouble, send for me or a deputy."

"I have a deputy working right now. We'll handle things." She rushed inside before anyone could protest the men's free drinks or round of poker. Once she had them set up, she moved to the stairs to leave the pit. At the top, she found Cole eyeing the group, a frown on his features. "They won't stay long."

"Why you giving away free booze?"

"Apparently Eckles was at the camp and got them all riled. They were marching him back through town, guns blazing. Wanted to get them settled."

"Whiskey won't settle them."

"Yes, well, we haven't a brothel yet. We haven't even selected a location. It's the best I could do. If I hadn't, someone was going to be arrested."

"That's not your problem. Now this is." He nodded toward where the group of cowboys had let out a boisterous yell.

"Our staff is capable of handling a few rowdy cowboys. It wouldn't be the first time."

He hummed his disapproval, gaze never leaving the group.

"Cole!" Alma's voice cut through the buzz of conversation. An excited edge to the near yell. "Cole. Cole!"

Jane turned to find Alma approaching, practically hopping in her excitement. The young woman hardly got quite so excited or vocal in public, so it was a sight to see.

The approaching figures of Sally and Arthur on Alma's heels were rather amused as well.

Sally shrugged at Jane. "It's all her idea."

Jane glanced between Sally and Alma, her curiosity rising. "What is?"

"Chickens!" Alma near-barked the word loud and clear. Then she squealed, the heel of her hand pounding against her thigh. "Chickens. Four chickens."

"Chickens?" Cole's brows twisted in confusion, even as he grinned broadly at his half-sister. His amusement wove through his tone. "What's this about chickens?"

"Four chickens," Alma repeated.

Jane chuckled low. "Why don't we go back to the apartment, and you can tell us what the deal is with chickens."

Sally said good-bye to Arthur before moving to Alma's side. "Come on. Ma and Cole will come and you can tell them all about the chickens and what Mrs. Mortell said."

Jane glanced at Cole with a wry smile. "Why do I get the feeling this means work?"

"I don't know what she's got in her head, or why chickens are so important." He laughed low, pulling her close. "I'll be right behind you. Want to make sure we've got the rowdy lot all set and plenty of eyes on them."

"Don't be long. Alma seems fit to burst."

"Won't be a minute."

By the time Jane got to the apartment, Sally had given up trying to settle Alma. Instead Alma took great rocking steps back and forth, grinning the whole time. Her hands twisted together before clapping rapidly, only to clasp again.

Jane smiled broadly, relieved Cole was true to his word and entered the apartment a moment later. "Goodness, Alma. You are excited."

"Chickens." Alma's skirts swayed with her rocking.

"We went by the Mortell's." Sally wore a flustered smile. "Alma likes to pet the cows' noses, I told her they're soft like horses, but she's still afraid of those so we settle with cows. She also likes the chickens."

"I'm well aware. She clucks at them when we pass, don't you, Alma?" Jane eyed Alma carefully. "What has got you all riled up about them now?"

"My chickens." Alma laughed brightly. "Four chickens."

"Your chickens?" Cole glanced at Jane in confusion. "We don't got no chickens."

"I'm afraid Mrs. Mortell made the offer." Sally grimaced. "She has quite a few hatching soon, more than she needs and she offered them to Alma."

"Oh." Jane did her best to keep her features neutral. "You want chickens, Alma?"

"Chickens make eggs. Cora buys eggs. I will get money." Alma had somewhat settled as Jane and Cole remained calm. Though she still rocked, the words were definitely coming clearer.

"Money? You want money? We got money." Cole's confusion was clear and seemed to match Jane's. "You don't gotta."

"My money. Butterfly money."

Jane set her hand on Cole's to keep him from protesting again. "It seems Alma has aspirations to be a woman of business. I hesitate to deny her, however chickens take some work, Alma."

"Garden is work, but only a few months. I like work." Alma's hand hit her thigh again. "Chickens. Four."

Cole smirked at Jane. "She likes work."

"Apparently so. Well, then. I suppose we need to talk to Mr. Hamm about building a proper coop. There are too many hawks in this area to leave chickens running amok." Jane chuckled at Alma's squeal. "Well, I guess we're going to have chickens now."

"Alma's gonna have chickens. They're not my problem."

"Oh, they will be if something happens. It's your head, not mine."

"How's that?"

"You caved first."

"Did not."

Good friends, good books, and
a sleepy conscience:
this is the ideal life.
-Mark Twain

Jane dug deep into the crate to pull free as many books in one swoop as she could. The whole way back to the desk, her ankle ached so deep she wished whatever storm was coming would break to ease the pain. There was far too much to worry about for such trivial matters.

"Why are you limping?" Kat returned to the desk, her arms empty.

"Storm's coming. Bad one, I think. My ankle is aching something fierce." Jane stacked the books one by one into their designated piles. She'd assigned everyone to an area to stack books more efficiently.

Despite her efforts to get as much help as possible, there was hardly enough hands for the task. Three to five more people working would increase her belief they'd get things done as expediently as she'd hoped.

"Where are Tom and Cole? We could really use their help." Kat flipped through the books in her designated stack.

"I don't know how you could have hoped for a reopening this week. There is a ridiculous amount of books here."

Jane hardly heard her complaints. She focused on the balcony above. Instead of putting books way, Sally had her nose buried in a book. "Sally Ann."

Sally jumped, the book slammed shut. A blush filled her cheeks. "Sorry, Ma. It's your own fault. You gave me the mysteries."

"My greatest error, apparently. I thought it would be safe since it's dreadfully small." Jane shook her head, turning her attention back to Kat. "What was that?"

"I asked where Tom and Cole were. More hands would speed this all up."

"It certainly would, I was just thinking the same thing. However, Cole and Tom are shopping." Jane grabbed another stack of books to sort. "Not that it would matter if Cole were here. He'd get bored and try to take me behind the stacks."

"He'll do that anyhow." Kat leaned on the edge of the desk. "What is it they are shopping for?"

"A building to purchase. Cole is hoping Alden is ready to sell. I'd rather we get Prescott's tannery. That building has a larger footprint than Alden's. That makes it easier to incorporate more rooms."

"Rooms? What would you need rooms for? Are you expanding the hotel?"

Jane set down the copy of *Bleak House* she'd been pondering simply giving to Sally rather than shelving it. "Expanding? Oh, no. Though I would like to, it isn't really necessary. No, they're shopping for a place to put our new brothel."

"Your what now?"

"Brothel." Jane met her friends' surprised eyes, and somehow managed to keep her laughter restrained. "You do know what that is, of course."

"I need more explanation than that."

"If you insist. A brothel is a place where women—"

"Jane!" Kat punched her arm lightly. "Stop goofing off and explain."

"Fine, fine." Jane laughed, guarding from another punch with a book. "I'll tell you. Cole and I thought we'd add to our revenue with a brothel of our own. None of the brothels that have come to town have been decent, save for that one."

"And most of them died in the epidemic those cowboys brought to town."

The year before a band of cowboys delivering cattle to the Edward's ranch had brought with them influenza. Before Charlie or Daisy had time to realize it had started, the epidemic ran rampant through the town.

Though the brothel in question, the only one in a string of them Cole didn't try to run out of town, had been run by a halfway decent man—in the end the owner and over half the whores were lost to the illness. The rest of the whores took off for parts unknown soon as the owner died.

Several men that refused to listen to the doctors, and a handful of cowboys had been lost to the epidemic as well. In all, nearly forty lives had been lost, even with Charlie and Daisy's best efforts. Of course, hundreds of lives had been saved thanks to their best efforts, too.

Jane shook off the reverie. "Right. We had a talk after the latest brothel arrived on the train the other day. In the end, we decided Cole was the best option to getting a good, safe brothel that's affordable for the average man. More importantly, he won't get grumpy every time another arrives. Nor will he be scheming how to run them all out of town."

"But…wait…" Kat set her hand on Jane's. "Are you two ending things?"

Jane's bark of laughter startled every person out of the stacks to see what was going on. "No. Not at all, Katherine. Why would you ask such a thing?"

"I know the new wards have been giving you trouble."

"Of course they have. They were stolen from the homes they'd always known, then shipped off far away from where the ma and pa they always knew are. Into a strange town, with strange people, people that want them to be as they were born rather than how they were raised."

"Of course, but it's been causing you strife. I saw you arguing the other day."

"Cole and I have always argued publicly. It gets tongue's wagging."

"Jane." Kat clasped her hand. "You told your man to open a brothel. Who does that?"

"I told him *we* should open a brothel. I certainly never told him to sleep with the talent."

"That's how he always ran it before."

"Before me, you mean." Jane squeezed Kat's hand. "Rest assured, there will be none of that. Now here."

Kat stared at the stack of books Jane dropped in her arms. "But, Jane."

"We'll hire someone to manage the place, and Cole will make sure the whores are trained up right."

"But he used to train them by—"

"There are other methods to train whores, you know." Jane met Kat's gaze. "I trust him. That's all that matters."

"Thought we were supposed to be working." Michael grabbed a stack of books from the desk. "Instead of gabbing. You're the one that said we're on a deadline."

"Your sister told Cole to open a brothel." Kat's words had the proper effect of stilling Michael's progress. "Exactly."

Jane glared at Kat when she receded into the stacks with a wicked smirk. "Tattle tale."

He stared at her for a long minute, then shrugged with a deep sigh. "Gave up trying to understand you a while ago."

She set her hand on top of the stack of books he bent to pick up. "Wait."

"What?"

"What is wrong?"

"Nothing. I'm trying to work. You're the one pressuring about getting this done."

"Michael, usually when you hear gossip you jump all over it like Mabel."

For that she received a harsh glare. "I do not."

"When it's about me and Cole, you do."

"Clarabelle." He rubbed his hand over his face. "I've got a lot on my mind."

"I've noticed. I've hardly seen you lately." She reached over to clasp his hand gently. "What is going on? Why do you seem miserable?"

"I'm not. I'm—"

"You can lie to me no more than I can to you."

"Would you believe me if I told you I honestly didn't know?"

"I actually do. Come." She circled the desk to take his arm. "Come sit with me."

"Your library…"

"Will still be here. I have good sized stacks waiting to be picked up. No more arguments, come. Sit." She pushed him onto the bench outside the door. "You never did say where Daisy was. I thought she was joining us today."

His eyes tightened the slightest bit, but then he blew out a gust of air. "At the clinic, I think."

"You think?" A rumble of thunder rolled through town. Jane lifted her gaze toward the darkening sky. Clouds rushed over the mountains in curling waves of darkness. Finally, the storm would come, and her aching ankle would be relieved. She pulled her attention back to her brother. "Are you two having trouble?"

"No. Yes. Maybe?" His nose wrinkled. "That was clear."

"As mud." She laughed, glad to have him join her. "Do you want me to be nosey Nellie and see how she's feeling?"

"You mean you'd actually restrain yourself if I said no?"

"I promise to do my best. Working in your favor is the very busy state of my life. Outside of weekly teas, I rarely have time to seek out the good doctor."

"Or me, of which I'm not complaining. You do get annoyingly pious at times."

"You take that back, you rotten brother!"

"What? You have this busy, full life with lots of kids. Feel like you can judge your brothers that aren't married and having more children than is right or decent."

"Michael Jacob Young!"

He laughed, ducking away from her beating arms. "All right, stop. Stop!"

She chuckled when he managed to grab her wrists. "Oh, you are rotten to the core. I'm going to tell Ma you said that

I had more children than was decent. I only have one more than she does, and at least one of them was technically grown when we took her in."

"If you count Lizzie, you have nine, dear sister. That's two more than Ma had."

"And less than she would have had without losing babies."

He frowned at the mention of their mother's miscarriages. "Fair enough point, I suppose."

"Now, back to you. Your nasty attempts to distract me didn't work."

"Damn."

"Do you want me to interfere, or shall you deal with matter like the adult you have just proven you barely are."

"I can handle my own—" He startled as lightning cut across the sky followed by an intense rumble of thunder that rattled the panes on the library windows. "Looks like it's going to be a bad one."

"If my ankle is any indicator, extremely bad."

"Maybe I should get back to the hotel, make sure all the guests are safe."

Jane rose with him. The wind picked up with such intensity, it knocked the breath clean out of her. She grabbed Michael's hand as she stumbled. "Shutters."

She flew into the library, barely acknowledging Mike's departing call. "Shut the windows. The storm is coming in fast. Close the shutters and head home quick as you can!"

Everyone rushed through the library to do as she'd asked. By the time she left the library with Sally at her side the streets were almost clear of people, though many huddled on porches to watch the sight.

Jane walked briskly back to the Inn with Sally. "It's going to be an ugly one. We'll have to distract the little ones."

"Yes, Ma."

Jane got them inside as the first thick raindrops hit the dirt outside. "Alma's room. The windows."

"On it." Sally took off at a run up the steps.

Cole burst into the room, a twin on each arm. "We got the shutters closed all over the hotel. Soon as we saw the clouds, Tom and I hightailed it back here."

"Thank you." Jane grabbed Clara. "Where are Willow and Jay?"

"On the porch with Tom. They wanted to watch it roll in. Tom promised to bring them in if it got real bad."

"We should have the staff get the guests into the casino pit. No windows there if the storm gets bad enough."

"Already handled." Cole pulled her close. "Relax."

"There are better ways to relax then with a storm bearing down on us."

"Good point."

"We'll relax after it passes."

"Promise?"

"Promise."

Storms make oaks take deeper root.
—George Herbert

Jane emerged onto the porch to a brutal blast of wind that knocked her breath away. To her right stood Tom, pressed against the wall. Jaybird stood beside him, a big grin on his face as he closed his eyes against the wind. "Tom."

He glanced her way, but his gaze immediately returned to the street. Willow stood in the middle of the street, arms spread wide. The wind buffeted her cotton skirt around her brutally. She leaned this way and that against the force of the wind. Through it all she laughed loud enough that the sound carried to Jane on the air.

Jane moved to Tom's side. "Are you crazy? She could get hurt."

"You try to contain that wild child." Tom chuckled low under his breath. Thick rain drops had begun to fall. Slow enough Jane didn't panic yet. Tom bumped her shoulder gently. "This is the most I've seen her smile since we got them. Besides, she promised to come back under shelter if I hollered."

She searched the skies, stunned at how dark the clouds were. To the west thick, black clouds tumbled over the mountains and foothills. To the east the same thing was happening. Though not as dark, the clouds to the east were no less rain filled.

For several minutes she watched the two, following the roiling clouds toward the north where the valley came together miles away. There the clouds crashed together and swirled about in a way that made concern lump in her throat. "Am I seeing what I think I'm seeing? Are there really storms coming from east and west?"

"You're the one that said it was going to be ugly."

In a sudden gush the thick drops of the initial rain turned into a torrent. Rain fell so hard and fast Willow flew under the cover of the porch of her own volition. Lightning streaked across the sky, followed immediately by a booming clap of thunder.

Jay spun to throw his arms around Jane's waist. Willow clasped onto her other side. Guests and employees filtered onto the porch. Townspeople emerged from their homes, staying in the shelter of their businesses to watch the show.

"This keeps up, we're going to have a flood." Tom stared north where the two storms crashed together in a violent tide of darkness. "Or worse."

"Worse?" Jane followed his gaze, that anxious lump lingering in her throat. "You mean there's worse that could happen?"

"Much worse." He squinted against the thick rain.

Jane followed suit as the downpour lightened again. Wind continued to whip through the streets with a ferocity that anyone attempting to stand or walk away from a shelter bent against the power. Her skirts lashed around her legs until they almost lifted.

Where the valley narrowed, the crashing clouds had begun to spiral into a whirlpool of condensation. Black and grey striations circled around a midpoint. Jane pulled the children closer on instinct. "Is that what you mean by worse?"

"It is."

Jane's duty to the children warred with her fascination over the scene. "Is it—"

"A tornado."

"But it mightn't form."

"Looks like it's trying pretty hard to do just that. Haven't seen one in years, definitely never seen one around these parts."

"Oh, no." She gripped the shoulders of the children clinging to her. "The settlement. Edwards and Keenan's ranches! They'll be right in the line of fire."

"It might not do anything, and there isn't much we can do at this point," Tom pointed out. His hands twitched at his sides as though he had the same desire to hop on a horse and rush to make sure everyone was safe. "We have to hope they get themselves to safety if the worst hits."

"Low ground could get drowned out by flooding. High ground if a funnel—"

Another huge clap of thunder interrupted her sentence. Lightning streaked across the sky in a rush of electricity. Green hues began to mis into the shades of grey.

"I didn't think such a thing happened here."

"Apparently it can—and will." Right then a funnel of clouds dipped from the center of the whirlpool toward the ground.

Jane held her breath until it slipped back into the clouds. "It's so far out, it won't hit the town. Right?"

"No telling. I've seen them travel far and fast before you know it. Get the kids inside. I'll keep a watch out. Make sure everyone is safely in the pit."

Jane nodded, but her feet wouldn't move from the spot. Another dip of clouds stretched so wide it seemed to take up the whole valley. This time it hit the ground in a puff of debris.

"What's going—what the hell?" Cole stopped short beside Jane. In a surprising move, Willow's tight grip around Jane's waist disappeared. When Jane glanced down, she realized the girl now clung to Cole. Foreign words erupted from her in a light whisper."

"You ever seen a tornado here, Cole?" Tom tore his gaze from the tornado.

"Not in the twenty years I've been here." Cole stared at the funnel as it moved south. In no time it raced toward town, covering the distance much faster than Jane thought possible. "Damn."

It seemed the whole town was fascinated by the odd event as nobody went running for cover, despite the speed with which the twister headed toward them. Some even stepped further into the street until the winds buffeted them against a building. Lightning flashed down from the swirling clouds. Smoke lifted from the ground after the strike.

Jane held Jay tighter. "Alma? The twins?"

"With Sally in the cage. Cuddy and Edgar are keeping the guests not out here in the casino and calm." Cole draped his arm across her shoulders. "Maybe we should get inside."

As he spoke, the tornado hitched west.

"The settlement," Jane cried. She took a step despite knowing better.

"Nothing doing for them unless they've gone for cover." Cole kept a firm grasp on her shoulder.

Jane followed the future path of the tornado with her eyes. Fear spiked through her when she realized the path it was on. "Oh my God. *Jesse*."

Two sets of hands circled her arms and yanked her back so hard her feet left the ground. She fought against their holds.

"Damn it, Lou." Tommy got her shoulder pinned to the wall. "You can't go running *for* that thing. You'll for sure get killed."

"Jesse." Panic seized the air straight from her lungs.

"David's got him. Lee's got him. He'll be fine." Cole's voice broke through the initial tidal wave of panic. "You know that."

"Right. Of course." Her heart felt torn in two. She had several children in the casino a fair deal less protected without a basement to get into. Willow and Jay, who'd been staring at her wide-eyed, flew back to her side when another crack of thunder rented through the town. "David will keep him safe. We have others to keep safe here."

Cole tore his gaze from the funnel cloud to take in the crowd staring at the oncoming horror. "What we gotta worry about is the town."

Tom followed Cole into the street. Both of them leaned against the increasing winds. Arms raised to cover their faces against flying debris, they crossed the street to approach the large bell used in emergencies.

Jane cringed against the clang. Still, she was relieved they'd done it. The action seemed to stir everyone to life. Figures darted for cover, many running toward the Inn. The funnel that had seemed so far away now loomed over the town faster than you could blink.

A sharp staccato beat hit the roof above her. Hail large as Jay's fist thumped to the ground, hitting far more insistent than the rain had.

Across the street Cole and Tom ducked their heads against the brutal icy assault. They didn't stop pulling the cord for the bell. The nearer the funnel came to town, the more Jane could have sworn she hard a train.

All too soon she couldn't hear the bell over the noise. The wind buffeted her and the children down the porch. She screamed for Cole and Tom, even though she knew they couldn't hear her.

Debris flew down the street. Leaves, sticks, then larger pieces of wood that appeared to have come from homes or fences. Panicked, Jane shoved the children through the doors. They tore through the lobby toward the casino.

When she hit the casino, the whole building seemed to jerk and tremble. She rushed the children around the pit to the back where they'd have easier access to the cage. Cole and Tom burst into the room at the same time as something shattered behind them.

They both ducked, but kept running. They caught up to Jane at the cage door. She unlocked it, pushing Willow and Jay inside. "There isn't room for us too. Sally, keep an eye on them for me."

Sally held the twins close, her wide eyes on Jane. Nearby Alma sat rocking, hands to her ears, fingers tapping her head.

"Cole." Jane grabbed his arm to shove him to the door. "One more can fit. Alma needs you."

Cole shook his head. "You go."

Another shatter of glass, and a rumble of the building sent everyone in the pit screaming. Jane shoved him to the door. "Go. Alma's too upset. It's you she needs."

Though he looked as if to argue, Cole went into the small caged office with the children. Jane slammed the door behind him. Tom grabbed her arm so forcefully she yelped. He threw her to the floor with him.

Screams continued to echo through the pit as the building trembled, glass crashed and loud thumps echoed through the building. Jane curled closer to the wall, ducking her head and pressing into the solid side of the pit. Tom took a protective stance over her, bracing his hands against the wall around her.

It seemed like forever, but then no time at all. The storm raged, glass shattered, heavy thumps and thunks carried on.

Then silence.

It stopped so quickly, Jane's ears rang with the sudden stillness. Bit by bit, everyone rose to their feet. The casino itself showed no evidence of damage. Jane gathered her wits about her to call out. "Is everyone all right?"

There were murmurs of assent, and confusion. Folks helped each other to their feet, checking each other over.

Jane peeked into the cage to check on her family. "Cole?"

He had Alma in a bear hug, a high-pitched keening carried on the still air. Over the top of Alma's head, Cole nodded. "I got her. Kids are fine."

"I need to check—"

"Go ahead. Be careful. Soon as I can get them to the apartment, I'll join ya."

Jane climbed from the pit, accepting Tom's help up the steps. Her legs were still a little wobbly. "We'll go check on the town. Why don't you all try to regroup. Have a drink if you need to calm your nerves."

Most of the group nodded their agreement. Cuddy and Edgar moved behind the bar to accommodate the requests for drinks from the men. The women didn't rush to get drinks, but most of them seemed content to remain for the time being.

Cora climbed the steps to join them, though. Jane didn't argue their new companion. Cora was her friend, and had her own restaurant within the Inn's walls.

Jane glanced her way. "Your boys?"

"Both fine. Over there calming down." Cora wrung her hands together. When they crossed through the doorway into the lobby and restaurant, a gasp slipped free. "Oh my."

The windows all across the lobby were shattered. Glass crunched under their feet with each step. Several tables and chairs were missing—the rest scattered about like kindling. The three of them stared around the destruction in absolute shock.

Tom was the first to move. He crossed the lobby toward Main. A low whistle blew from him as he stared into the street. "Damn."

Jane moved to his side as Cora rushed toward her kitchen. At the sight that met her, a whimper of a cry carried under her whispered, "Oh no."

Every building across the street, down to where the open-air café had sat were flattened. Every building gone, with only a few piles of lumber to prove they'd existed.

"Glad you moved the books a few days ago, Lou. Old library is gone."

"The bank, the laundry. The café. All of it." She gathered her skirts to climb out the window frame, but Tom grabbed her arm.

"Go through the doors, you'll get cut there." He pointed to the jagged remains of window.

Jane walked the few steps to where the doors had hung, though only one remained. She stepped onto the porch, or what remained of it as several planks had been torn asunder. With Tom's help, she stepped carefully across the uneven porch to descend the steps – the last two of which were missing. "Well."

Tom hopped down to the street, then turned to offer Jane a boost. Rather than risk slipping on the cobblestone, she accepted the help. Before she could take more than a step, Cora emerged from inside.

Cora sighed. "Kitchen has a few broken dishes, though that could have happened in the panic. Restaurant is missing about three tables and dozen chairs."

Jane paused mid turn, her attention caught by an odd sight. The side of the hotel had a bit of damage. Boards torn off, branches, planks and more stuck into the walls and windows. However, that wasn't what had caught her attention. "Make that eleven chairs?"

"What?" Cora straightened her skirts after Tom had helped her down. "What do you mean?"

Jane pointed down the side of the building. The chair, completely intact, stuck out of the side of the building by its four legs. As though someone had the idea to sit parallel to the street, twenty feet off the ground. "Found one."

"Well, I'll be." Cora chuckled softly. "Sorry, it isn't funny. Not with so much damage."

"It is a little funny," Jane acknowledged, laughing as well. "We seem to be none the worse for wear, cosmetic damage aside. I can't believe we were spared so well with such destruction right across the street."

"Me either, but I've seen stranger from tornados." Tom lifted his hat to scratch his head. "Hammy's gonna be busy for a while. Biggest worry is the roof and windows. We can do patchwork on everything else until Hammy's got time."

"We'll make do. We always have." Jane let out a long breath, taking in the damage across the street. "We'll need to take a census in town to find out if we lost anyone anywhere, especially over there. Then we'll need to send riders and a doctor to the settlement and ranches. Someone will have to gather Charlie and Daisy if they aren't already—"

"Here," Charlie supplied from behind her. "I can't find Daisy, but she may have been at the Sage Brush and it'll take her a bit to come to town. I'll need some help either way. My new doctor was supposed to arrive on today's train. I don't know if it—"

"Train. The depot!" Jane spun toward the south. Two businesses remained standing at the end of the road, which gave her hope that the depot, which sat beyond them, remained standing. "Norman! Kat!"

Jane gathered her skirts to dart down the street. If Kat hadn't emerged from her home with the children, that meant they'd all been at the depot. She skidded to a halt at the end of the road, relief flooding her when she saw Kat emerging with the children and Norman. "Kat!"

Kat waved, rushing off the porch toward her. "Thank heavens you're all right. We hightailed it into the cellar soon as Norman sent the telegraph to delay the train."

Jane hugged her tight. "I'm so glad all of you are safe. We were just talking about organizing search parties for here in town and at the settlement. We need a census to find out who was lost."

"*Ma*!" Jesse's cry broke through Jane's distraction.

She spun on the spot, relieved to see the group coming toward them.

Jesse tore down the street, the gangly limbs of his youth carrying him far faster than David or Lee, who ran behind. Lee had a small bundle in her arms. The newborn cries cut through the air wild and ragged. Lee's dainty features were wide-eyed and pale.

Jane caught Jesse when he bowled into her. She crouched to get him into a tight hug. Her son didn't disappoint, his arms tight around her neck. "Thank heavens you're alive. All of you."

"Jane." David nodded his gratitude, but his gaze carried over her head. "How's it looking?"

"The Inn stands, though the worse for wear. Most of the town has come out with damage, the worst being Main Street. Everything across from the Inn is destroyed. I don't know if anyone was in any of the businesses."

"We got into the cellar. It was a tight squeeze." Lee bounced the newborn in her arms. "We lost a corner of the house, and most of our furniture for it."

"At least you're alive. Thank the heavens for that." Jane kissed Jesse's cheek. "Your brothers and sisters are all fine. Scared like you, but we all made it."

"Ma." Jesse now flushed as he looked over her shoulder.

"Lizzie is fine, too." Jane rose, her hand clasped firm with Jesse's. "You and Lee can stay with Sally to help take care of our family. Cindy and Lizzie will probably join as well. Your pa, Kat, and myself will probably head to the settlement with Uncle Charles."

David glanced her way. "What about the town?"

"Tom and Cole can stay in town to help sort through the destruction. I imagine Graham will help too if he's uninjured. He's good for stitching. So's Lucky." Jane walked with the small group toward where she'd left her brothers. Kat and Norman had joined them.

"With Daisy?" David nodded. "We'll need one doctor in town in case of injuries and survivors."

"Daisy can't be located as yet. We're assuming she was at the Sage Brush and will be heading into town post haste."

Kat, Tom, Charlie, and Cole met them in the street outside the Inn. Jesse immediately went to Lizzie's side the second Jane released his hand.

Tom ran his hand along his beard. "Where to first?"

"I'd like to head to the settlement first," Charlie started. "When Daisy shows up, it'll likely be in town and she can remain here to help."

"Tom? Cole?" Both men turned to Jane when she spoke. "Why don't you both say in town to check on what was lost here. Hunt down Graham and Lucky to help with the injured. If the cowboy camp moved out of the way in time, we might be able to round up a few of them to help with stitching at the settlement."

"I'll talk to them." David nodded. "I know their point man. I can also find out if they lost anyone. They might not want help, but we'll do what we can."

"Great." Jane turned toward Lee. "You'll stay with the children, right? I'm sorry to assume, but I thought you'd want to stay with Marjorie."

Lee nodded. "You assumed correctly. I'll take the children now. Jesse, girls. Come along."

"Sally's at the apartment with Cora's boys," Cole said. "Damage is minimal. You should be safe enough."

After a kiss to David, Lee gathered the children and headed around back of the Inn.

"Cole, will you locate Charlie's new doctor when, or rather if, the train arrives?" Jane turned to Norman. "You did merely delay it's arrival, yes?"

"I did. I'll send a telegram out to let them know it's safe, so long as the wires are still standing." Norman pivoted, jogging toward the depot.

"What new doctor?" Kat eyed Charlie. "You got a new doctor?"

"Yes. Dr. Cross. He's a new graduate. Friend of the family." Charlie smiled sardonically. "He wanted to come out west for adventure. I think we'll be giving it to him straight off."

Jane chuckled. "We always do."

Happily in this community we all are bred and born to work; and this honorable mark, set on us all, shall bind together the various portions of the community.
—William Ellery Channing

Cole handed Leanne a pitcher of water. "Think we got everyone in town taken care of."

"It would seem so." Leanne dumped some water in the basin beside her. She turned her attention back to cleaning a cut on Hammy's forehead. The man blushed nearly as much as he did when Jane gave him any sort of attention. "Thank heavens we escaped with so few deaths here in town."

"Three at last count."

"And nobody missing?"

"Not that we can tell. We'll know better once we figure out what's happening at the settlement. All the miners that were working are accounted for, and everyone that was working on Main took cover. They all came out alive."

"It's a miracle." She dabbed at the cut, turning Hammy's head this way and that.

"Soon as the train gets here, I'll head out to the settlement to check on the progress out there." Cole scanned the crowded waiting room of the clinic. Daisy had finally arrived and was in a room with Graham. The man had been impaled in his shoulder by a knife from the tavern trying to get the widow Daub to safety during the peak of the storm.

Leanne tapped Hammy on the nose. "All cleaned up. I'll have Tom take a look to make sure you don't need stitches."

Hammy's ruddy cheeks darkened even more. "Aw, Tom ain't no doctor. I'll be fine."

Cole put a hand on Hammy's shoulder to keep him in place. "Tom'll know one way or the other. Wait until he or Mike comes by to check before you run off."

Leanne wiped her hands on a towel. She took her own turn studying the crowd in the waiting area. Across the room, Mike stitched up a cut on Isaac's arm. The boy had wounded himself leaving the Inn after the storm. He winced his way through the treatment, Cora at his side. Leanne frowned. "Where'd Lucky go?"

Luke 'Lucky' Carroll, the town barber, had made it through unscathed. They'd been using him as another helper for the stitching. Cole glanced around, though he knew the man had left a while back. "Said he was gonna head out to the settlement. Once Daisy arrived, and with Mike and Tom here, he figured we had it covered. The settlement probably needed more help. Since he's not back, I'm guessing he was right."

Leanne blew out a long breath. The train whistle sounded long and low in the distance, pulling both their attention. "Well, when Graham gets done being stitched up he will be of some use. The wound is on his left shoulder. With some assistance, he should be able to stitch one handed."

"Should get the quilting bee and their needles out."

"Don't joke. We might get that desperate."

When the train whistled again, Cole headed to the surgery room. He'd have to leave in short order to meet the new doctor. After a quick knock, he slipped into the surgery room.

Graham was pulling his shirt back over his shoulder. The man looked angry as hell, but it was likely the pain. The thought was confirmed when Graham nodded at Cole. "No bad damage. Just gonna smart like hell for a while."

"You good for stitching if you get a hand? Lucky headed to the settlement, and there's plenty more stitching to be done so Daisy can work on the worse ones."

"Long as I got some help, I got it." Graham hopped off the table. He clasped Cole's hand. "Glad your family made it."

"Same to you." Cole accepted the handshake easily. The animosity they'd gone through years ago over Jane's arrival had all but disappeared in the years since Graham's now-wife Linh had returned to Dominion Falls.

As Grahm left, Cole turned toward Daisy. "We put Vic in the next room for ya. Leanne'll clean up this room for the next one. Wagons will probably start arriving from the settlement soon. At least that was the last report we got."

"Right." Daisy dropped the tray she'd been carrying to the counter so hard the tools clattered and spilled over the edge. "She doesn't know how to clean my tools."

"Then she'll leave the tools."

Daisy spun on him. "Then the room won't be clean, will it?"

Cole held up his hands defensively. "Then tell us how to help proper so we can. There's lots to be doing, and I'm guessing Charlie's having it rough at the settlement so the new doc is going there. Best you got is Leanne, Tom, and Mike and anyone else you can wrangle."

Daisy let out a long breath as she washed her hands. The fit of temper seemed to leave her quick as it had risen. Over the past year, Cole had noticed it had been rearing its head more often. Along with something else. Something he couldn't put his finger on. She cleared her throat and nodded. "Of course. Add teaching how to deal with my equipment to my list of things to do."

"We're trying to help, Daisy."

"Of course."

When she moved to pass him, Cole grabbed her arm. She paused at his touch but refused to meet his gaze. He frowned. "Daisy."

After a few seconds, she lifted her gaze to his. The woman had been a whore in his saloon for three years. He'd gotten to know her pretty good, and the look in her eyes was oddly familiar. He couldn't place it, though. She pursed her lips at his silence. "What?"

"What's eating ya?"

"I'm very busy."

That wasn't it, not by a long shot. Still, he released her arm with a nod. He had more important things to do than deal with a woman that no longer worked for him. "Right. Best let you get at it then. I've gotta get that new doc off the train…"

His voice trailed off when she turned to face him. Unreasonably close, so that her breasts brushed against him. A hint of a smile curved her lips. "I heard a rumor about you."

He frowned as her green eyes peered up at him through her lashes. An odd sense of desperation in her gaze reminded him of days when she begged him to keep her on as a whore. A familiar sense of pity welled. To put distance between them, he took a step back. "That so?"

"A new brothel?"

"Yeah. What's it to you?"

"Nothing. I just find it rather interesting." She set a finger on the grip of his Colt. "Things always go in a circle is all."

"Daisy. What are you getting at?"

A knock on the door had the effect of turning her back to business. She strode across the room to pull open the door to find Mike on the other side. "Oh. What is it?"

Mike's brow furrowed at the brusque greeting. "First wagon just arrived from the settlement. It's not good."

Daisy sighed. "As we'd feared. I'd best get to work. You, Tom, and Graham keep stitching."

Mike glanced at her departing back. "All right, then."

Cole eyed the departing doctor as well, confused as hell over what had just happened. When things settled, he'd have to mention it to Jane. Something was off about the whole conversation. A train whistle pulled Cole out of his confusion. "Damn. Gotta meet the new doc and head to the settlement. You good, Mikey?"

"Hm? Oh, yes." Mike glanced around the room. "Plenty more to stitch. I imagine Daisy'll need some help if she needs to do surgery."

"Nah. Did it herself all them years."

"You helped her."

"Did not." Cole didn't flnch under Mike's sideways look. He amended, "Much."

"Exactly."

Cole chuckled, heading out into the street to grab the horses he'd tied up in front of the Inn knowing he'd have to take the new doctor out to the settlement. He managed to arrive at the depot right as the passengers began to disembark.

People of every sort emerged from the train. Cole had no idea what he was looking for in the crowd. Rather than try to seek the man out he shouted, "Hey, Doc!"

A young pup in a bowler hat like Charlie often wore, dressed fine as Leanne's wealthy clients turned at the call. He carried a black medical bag in his left hand. His hair was as black as the velvet bowler he wore, and his skin was pale, untouched by the sun.

"Doc!" Cole waved him closer. "Hurry up. We gotta ride north."

The kid rushed his direction. "I'm Dr. Cross. I was supposed to meet Dr. Young here."

"I'll take ya to him. Get on." Cole swung into Faro's saddle easily.

"Take me to—what?" Dr. Cross stared at Brag in confusion, then up at Cole. "What's going on? Why must I—ride?"

"You do know how, don't you?"

"I do…"

The hesitation would have made Cole laugh aloud on any other occasion. Now was not the time to deal with a Nancy-boy not ready for the frontier. "Well?"

"Where are—where are we going?" Brag spun away from the doctor's fumble attempts to attach his medical bag to the pommel.

"To the settlement. You're being put right to work. Stop dancing with him and get on." Cole reached to grab Brag's bridle to stop the spinning.

The doc grasped the saddle on either end, his leg lifting clumsily toward the stirrup. Once he finally got a foot on, he hauled himself upward. Halfway up his grip slipped and he landed on his ass in the dirt with a solid 'oof'.

"Doc. We don't got time for this."

Tom jogged up to them, a bag in his hand. He glanced at the man dusting off his trousers before turning back to Cole. "Some more supplies for out there. What I thought Daisy could spare now that Charlie's sending folks back here, anyhow."

"Thanks." Cole tied the bag to his pommel.

Tom jerked his thumb over his shoulder. "What's this?"

"New doc."

"Right. Buffalo. Society, highest of high class. No wonder Charlie likes him."

"Says he can ride, but can't get on the horse." Cole ignored the annoyed huff from the man.

Dr. Cross once again had a foot in the stirrup. He hopped helplessly to get into the saddle.

"I got it." Tom spun and shoved the doc into his saddle with one great push. He slapped the horse hard on the rump. A wicked grin crossed his features, the one time the man actually looked like his sister was when he grinned that way. "He's gonna be a trip. Best get on with it, before he gets lost."

"It's north. I told him." Cole watched as the man jerked about in the saddle, growing smaller by the minute. "Can't get too lost."

"Road forks. If his sense of direction is the same as his horsemanship, he can."

"Fair enough point." Cole offered a salute before taking off after the doc. By the time he caught up, the man was causing the horse to falter in its steps by keeping the reins taut. Cole pulled up beside him, bringing Faro to a stop. "You can ride, eh?"

"I can."

"Side saddle?"

The doc glared sideways at him. "No."

"Ease up on the reins."

One rein slackened, but the other tightened, leading Brag right. "Horses are my sisters' lot."

"Loosen both reins before Brag knocks you clean off his back. Then follow me." Cole spurred Faro into a good clip ahead of the doc. The ride took even longer than usual thanks to the pace of the new arrival. Still, within fifteen minutes the settlement, or what was left of it, came into view.

At least a third, if not more, of the homes were flattened. The wagon that had arrived in town would likely be the tip of the iceberg. Too many people lived out there now for the body count to not be above what it was in town.

Dr. Cross slowed to a stop beside him. "What happened?"

"Tornado."

"How many people live out here?"

"Near about five hundred these days. Miners and their families mostly."

The doc stared at the destruction another minute pale as all get out. After a second his features hardened into what Cole would only guess was determination. With more purpose than he'd used yet, he spurred Brag on toward the destruction.

"Damn. Maybe you can ride."

At a full stop near Jane, the man fell right out of his saddle on his dismount.

"Or—maybe not."

*Dionysus cut to pieces is a promise of life:
it will be eternally reborn and return
again from destruction.
—Friedrich Nietzsche*

Cole headed to the makeshift tent Charlie had set up while Jane dealt with the new doc. He hopped out of the saddle, glancing around at the scattered shouts, cries, and moans that filled the air.

Nearby several families, and a few lone souls, bent over covered bodies. Their weeping mingled with the calls for help clearing rubble behind him. The worst was the moans of pain from the injured. It was a sound he was all-too familiar with as his saloon had been the makeshift hospital during the renegade attacks several years before.

Even still, it was a sound that set an unease in his belly. The unease would linger until the nightmare was over.

Cole slapped open the flap of the tent to carry in the supplies Tom had sent. Charlie stood over a table, wrist deep in someone's stomach. Cole dropped the bag on a nearby table. "Tom sent more supplies."

"Thanks," Charlie said over his shoulder. "Can you help me with this? Where's Andrew?"

"Andrew?" Cole moved to the table. He took the end of the strip of metal Charlie thrust toward him. "What am I doing?"

"Just keep a good pull on that retractor. Now, where's Andrew? The new doctor."

"Oh, him. Where'd you dig him up? Idiot can't ride a horse."

"Perhaps not, but he is an expert surgeon." Charlie grabbed something from the tray, moving around the innards of the man on the table. "That doesn't answer my question. Where is he?"

"Right there." Cole jerked his head toward the flap when the new doc entered.

"Dr. Young?" The dapper doc walked right up to the table. He peeked into the open cavity. "Ah. Spleen."

"Bleeding like a stuck pig, yes." Charlie dropped a piece of flesh ito the bucket at his side. "I'm afraid the nurse hasn't arrived yet. It's just the two of us and whatever help we can get from the people. There are two good stitchers out there, and Jane has picked up a thing or two from being around us. I need you to triage as they find people. If anything is an immediate surgical need and I'm busy, you take it on the table over there. The rest are being loaded into wagons based on severity."

"Yes, sir." Dr. Cross took off like a shot, medical bag in tow.

"At least he's eager." Charlie relaxed as he clamped something in the man's guts. "There. That's the worst of it. You can go help the others, Cole. Thank you for the assistance."

Cole didn't have to be asked twice. He dunked his bloody hands in a nearby basin to clean most of it off, finishing the job with a towel.

Soon as he stepped out of the tent, he heard Jane cry out, "Reverend!"

Cole jogged over to where she struggled against the weight of half a wall. He got beside her and hooked his hands under the edge of wood. Muscles strained against the weight, he lifted it partway with Jane's help.

She grunted and scrambled under, pressing her shoulders against it. Together they heaved the wall up and all the way over into the road. Before it had hit the ground, she was already darting for the Reverend. "Mark!"

Cole moved through the rubble carefully, looking for the other residents of the house. Reverend Greene had a wife, Mabel, and his newest protégé, Eli Lyons. When things hadn't worked out with Eckles, Reverend Greene had taken in another young preacher to take over when he retired.

"He's alive. Where's Mabel? Reverend Lyons?" She ran her hands over the reverend's head as though looking for injury.

"No sign of Mabel yet. I think I see Lyons." Cole stepped over the remains of a baby carriage that had come from who-knew-where toward the foot sticking out from under a straw-tick. He hauled up the mattress to find Lyons underneath. "Found him."

"I don't see any—oh, Dr. Cross." Jane scooted aside when the young doc took over the task of examining Mark. "How is Eli?"

Cole flipped over the young reverend. The man groaned in response, but all was not well. Blood, scratches, glass and large splinters covered his face. "Uh, Jane."

She rushed over, kneeling beside him. Concern puckered her brow as she withdrew a towel from her belt. She held it over Eli's face for a moment, then withdrew before it touched even a drop of blood. "There's so much debris. I worry I'd hurt him worse. Doctor?"

"The older gentleman has a good bump on his head, but oherwise seems well. Oh, dear." The young doctor dug in his bag until he pulled free a vial and syringe. "He's in bad shape. We need to get him back to the tent. Let me give him something for the pain."

"He's unconscious," Cole pointed out.

"Minute we try to remove that splinter there, it won't matter how unconscious he is." Andrew pointed at a large sliver of wood that was about the size of Cole's pinky and embedded deep in his cheek near the eye.

"Good point." Cole moved aside as Jane waved over a couple of men to help Andrew move the reverend.

With that accomplished, Jane turned a circle. "No sign of Mabel. Perhaps the cellar?"

Cole followed her to the trap door. He helped her clean it off before giving the handle a good tug. Not giving Jane a chance to take the initiative, he climbed down the ladder into the low ceilinged room.

Though light was sparse from above, it was easy enough to see the small room sat completely empty. "Nobody's here."

"What?" Her wide-eyed gaze stared into the cellar, then followed his progress up the ladder. "Are you certain?"

"Check yourself, but it's not that big. There's nobody in there." He got out a grunt of protest when she scrambled down the ladder. "Good to know my word is good for something."

If it wasn't for Jane's apparent near panic, he would have snapped at her when she emerged from the cellar, but he kept his lips sealed.

"That's five missing at last count." Jane's hand sought his, even as her gaze drifted across the area where men and women continued searching and digging through the rubble. "Two of the missing are children, Cole."

Cole let the trap door fall into place. The woman was filthy. Her normally impeccable clothes were torn, soiled, and askew. Her curls stuck out in odd angles around her head. The hand laced with his held on strong. He tugged her closer to kiss the top of her head. "Deaths?"

"Ten so far—three are children. A great many more injuries. David and Archie went out to the ranches with a wagon." She wiped the back of her hand across her forehead. A smudge of dirt got left behind for her effort. "We're barely half done. So many miners moved here when the Daugherty's opened new claims for mining."

"You'll get 'em cared for." He held her tighter for a moment. Whether to reassure her, or because of his renewed relief his family had come through unscathed, he didn't know. "You always do. You, Kat, and the Rev."

Jane's gaze turned toward where Reverend Greene was accepting some water from one of those helping. There were so many newcomers to the settlement, Cole had no idea who it was. He knew Jane would, though.

"Jane?"

"Hm?" She focused on him. Her exhaustion revealed by the several slow blinks it took for her to seem to really see him. "Right. Back to work."

"But…"

"But nothing."

He knew better than to argue with her. Instead, he moved onto the next house with her. Together they worked for another several hours, only stopping to get sips of water. Along the way they recovered more injured, and a few more dead.

Cole stretched his back when they'd finished another house in the line. He'd stopped counting several houses ago. Homes, injured, dead. The numbers just kept tallying.

In the distance, motion drew his attention. A wagon rattled toward the settlement. In the seat, two forms hunched over, but still familiar. "Jane, it's Davie."

Jane scrambled over a pile of boards that had once been a wall to his side. She stared at the approaching wagon. "We're almost done here. Let's go see what he's got."

He ran with her toward Charlie's tent, as the wagon headed that way. Both doctors were intent on their work inside. Lamps were lit to afford them more light under the darkening sky. Cole nodded to David and Archie at their approach. "The ranches?"

"Keenan's was fine, still standing, all cattle accounted for. The Edwards ranch suffered a lot of damage." David barely moved when Archie hopped out of the wagon and circled around back of it. "Edwards and his wife are dead, but their foreman is alive. Matthew wouldn't let me take the bodies. He said he'd bury them on their ranch."

"Coleman? He's a pup."

"He may be, but the ranch is his now." David rubbed a hand over his face. "We found Mabel on the Keenan ranch."

Jane's features paled under the layer of dirt. She even took a step back. "You what? That's miles away!"

"I know. She was out in the middle of a field. Wasn't nothing to be done for her." David looked a little green. "Looks like she dropped out of the sky."

"Oh. My." Jane's features twisted in a bit of disgust. "Someone will have to tell the reverend his wife was lost in the storm."

"Someone will, Jane. You should get some rest." David lifted his gaze. "It'll be too dark to work soon anyhow. We'll have to come back in the morning to finish."

"The Leed's children are missing," Jane said instead of agreeing.

"You mean these two?" Archie came around back of the wagon, a young child on either side of him. The boys were disheveled, filthy, but didn't appear to have a scratch on them otherwise. "Found them out by the lake near the Edwards ranch. They haven't said a word."

"You poor things." Jane knelt before the pair of them. "What you must have been through. Do you want to see your ma and pa?"

Cole remained at the wagon while Jane led the boys away. "You're right, it's getting too dark to keep looking much longer. Lots of injuries, some pretty bad. Last count was seventeen dead, twenty with Mabel and the Edwards. Five kids. With you finding these boys, we're still missing four."

"How much is left to search here?" Archie scanned the area. "At least you had lots of help."

"Everyone healthy enough came to help dig. Only a couple more homes. I imagine that won't stop people from looking again tomorrow." Cole wiped his hands on his pants, not that the filthy garment would help clean them off much. "We need to get back to the kids."

"Alma's probably not doing well," David said sympathetically.

"No, she ain't. Now on top of it, Jane and I've been gone for hours."

"You two go back. Archie and I will see that things are handled here."

"You gonna convince her we need to go back?" Cole eyed David. "Mood she's in?"

"Nope. I divorced her, remember? She's all yours."

"She's the one that divorced you."

"She's still all yours."

*Optimism is a kind of heart stimulus,
the digitalis of failure.
—Elbert Hubbard*

Jane stretched the kinks out of her back, doing her best to not audibly groan her complaint. She dumped the water out the back door of the clinic. On her way back in, she spotted Charlie entering the kitchen. "Charles."

"What are you still doing here?" His brow furrowed even as he kissed her on the cheek. "You were supposed to return to your family last night."

"Don't you worry, I'll get plenty of complaints from them. Your need was too great here, Charles." She set the basin on the counter. "You might have gained a doctor, but there were a lot injured. Kat and I were happy to assist."

"Kat's still here, too? I swear I remember telling you both to go home last night."

"Katherine left about an hour ago. Dr. Cross discharged six souls this morning, I thought we had it covered without her."

"I'm heading to the train to pick up our new nurse Lydia. That means I am kicking you out of here." He took her arm over her protest, leading her through the clinic. "You've been here since the tornado. You have a myriad of children, a hotel to run, and duties to attend to with your auxiliary. Plenty to be done outside of *my* clinic."

"But—"

"No. I'm not taking no for an answer. You're leaving."

"Charles—"

"If I have to throw you out on your ass, I will do it."

She glared at him until she was certain he'd shut his trap. "I was going to say that my reticule is on Daisy's desk. I wanted to grab it."

"Oh. Well." His chest puffed before he released a dramatic sigh. "If you must."

"You're not as funny as you think you are." She sMaced his arm on her way past to Daisy's office. Soon as she'd secured her purse, she made it back to his side. "I'm glad you're getting more help."

"It's not enough. I need another nurse at least, perhaps another doctor."

"You aren't that busy."

"We are, plus I'd hoped to open a proper hospital. The town is growing fast, and the clinic is getting rather small. It wouldn't be bad for regular appointments, but Michael and Daisy rather jammed a clinic into a hotel. It's lacking."

"You'll insult them if you say such a thing to their face." She waited for him to shut the door behind them. "It's served us well enough the past few years. As did the saloon before that, though that was a bit more inconvenient."

"And unclean."

"I'd argue, but in the days I first arrived it really wasn't the epitome of cleanliness."

"Not by a long shot." He laughed with her, pausing at the crossroads. "I'm off to meet our new nurse. I want you to rest, Jane. You've been helping at the clinic non-stop."

"I'll do my best. I think we all know that my life does not tend to offer me time for such nonsense as rest."

"I'd argue, but then I'd be a liar. Do your best."

Jane waved him on his way. The moment she turned, she yelped in surprise. Cole and Tom stood right in front of her, both grinning like fools. "What the devil?"

"Come here. Come on. We gotta show ya." Cole tugged her hand. "It's perfect."

"What are you talking about?"

"Come on, Lou. You'll never guess what we got." Tommy pushed her onward when she tried to slow at the Inn.

"Where on earth are you taking me?" Jane's exhaustion seemed to have hit full force the second she left the clinic. Last thing she needed was the nonsense of her brother and husband up to no good. "Can't this wait?"

"Won't take long." Cole kept hauling her along behind him. They passed the Inn, moving along Main street at a brisk pace set by Cole's pulling and Tom's pushing.

They came to a stop right along the fence to the Inn's corral. They both turned her to face the empty lots across the street. Where once the library had stood on her left, and the outside café on her right, now sat open field all the way to the foothills where she'd come through five years before near dead.

Jane stared ahead, having no idea what the pair were so excited about. She heaved a sigh. "What are you two on about?"

"This!" Cole gestured toward the two empty lots. Dust swirled across the earth in a light wind. "Right here. Right close to home."

"I'm aware it's close to home, I used to work right there." Jane looked at Cole sideways. The man was awful giddy over the destruction of one of her favorite places. "In fact, it is only the grace of God that saved my books from the destruction the building faced."

"Jane." Tom half-shoved her. "Use your brain."

"My brain is as tired as the rest of me. All I wish to do is go sit with my family and relax for the afternoon. I've spent the past three days in the clinic helping the injured. I haven't the time or patience for your nonsense."

"The brothel, Jane." Cole turned her back toward the lots. "It's gonna go right there. We got the land for a steal."

"Because people died." She eyed him quietly when her words seemed to pop the bubble of his enthusiasm. "The business was a wash because Mrs. Clemens died, so the land was a steal. You want me to be excited about that?"

"Well, no. I just—"

"Lou."

Jane held up her hands to stop both their protests. "Tell me when I'm in a better mood and don't need to wash blood and death off me."

"I can help—" Cole's words died at her look. He wrinkled his nose and shrugged. "Thought I could make you smile anyhow."

"You thought wrong." She headed toward their apartment.

The moment she stepped inside chaos barreled toward her in the form of a fluffy skirt and dark curls. "Mama!"

"Hello, Clara." Jane picked up her daughter eagerly, pulling her close into a tight hug. "Oh, I missed you all so very much."

Small arms circled her legs. "Mama."

"Hello, Master Colton." Jane lowered herself to the floor so she could get her spare arm around her son. "Were you all good for Sally, and Miss Cora, and Miss Lee?"

Sally smirked from her post on the couch, where she sat reading a book. "Better for Lee than Cora. Cora spoils the twins something rotten. Jaybird and Willow, too."

"You're just mad she doesn't spoil you as much."

"She says you spoil me enough for the both of you."

"If that were true, it would merely be because I don't have a lifetime with you as I have with these two." Jane winked at Sally before getting back to her feet. The twins continued to cling to her skirts. "I really should get cleaned up."

"Go ahead. I'll keep minding them for a little while." Sally turned back to her book.

"Are you minding them? Or are you reading?"

"Both."

Jane hummed her discontent with the idea, but the children seemed happy enough. Even Jay and Willow were relaxed near the fire playing their dice game on the checkerboard. "Seems you might be right. I'll be back out shortly."

"We'll be here." Sally flipped a page.

Chuckling to herself, Jane managed to free her legs from the twins and redirect them to the blocks they'd been playing with. Once in her room, she sank to the bed, tempted to fall asleep right then and there.

She had so much to do, though. She'd been away from the Inn and her family for several days. All she could do was get washed and get back to it.

The door clicked shut, stirring her thoughts back to focus. She blinked a few times, trying to reconcile what had just happened. She'd been contemplating all she had to do and…

"Have a good nap?" Cole's rich tenor trembled with laughter.

"I wasn't asleep," She protested.

"Sally said you got home over an hour ago and said you were getting cleaned up." The bed shifted moments before he hovered over her. "Not that I mind. I'd be mad if you'd gotten in the tub without me."

"You'd suffer."

"Every time you deny me."

She pursed her lips against the burgeoning amusement. It would do him no good to let him know he was winning over her earlier upset. "You make it sound like I force you to a life of celibacy all the time."

"All the time." Though he agreed, the wicked twist of his lips proved his lie. "Ain't a man alive that's suffered like I have."

"You are not amusing."

"Then stop smiling." He settled down closer to her. His lips hovered over hers. "Or I could leave, if you want."

"I've spent three days surrounded by death and injury."

One of his brows lifted. "Is that you saying you need space, or you need life?"

"Both." She pulled him into a deep kiss.

Cole didn't waste a second in hesitation. He drew her tight against him, rolling them further onto the bed. His hands brushed along her bodice in search of buttons.

The moment he'd undone them all, Jane pushed to sit. "To that end, I need to spend time with my family. I've been gone for three days."

"That's my point. You've been gone three days." Cole didn't let her escape so easily.

"Our children missed me."

"I missed you more."

"Oh, I doubt that."

"You do, do ya?" He flipped her to her back so fast she let out a squeak of surprise. Her skirts billowed around him as he pressed her into the bed. "Let me prove it."

"Oh, that is tempting."

"Guarantee you it'll be more fun than losing dice to them kids."

"You guarantee it, hm?"

"Let me prove it."

"But—" She sighed when his lips skimmed along her jaw line. "I need to get cleaned up, and that's just going to make me all dirty."

"Not if we take a bath together."

"Now that is an idea."

"Knew you'd like that."

*Time heals grief and quarrels,
for we change
and are no longer the same persons.
—Blaise Pascal*

Jane wiped the bar for the tenth time in as many minutes. There'd been no one to mess up the surface in the casino for over half an hour, but she did hate being idle.

A week after the tornado had blown through town, the healing had begun. In that turn, she and Cole had decided to continue with their weekly horse races out by the livery. For the Centennial celebration the following week they had an even larger race planned. One that would span most of the valley and carried their largest cash prize to date. They expected some riders from outside the territory to race for the large purse.

At the moment it was a smaller race, smaller purse, and local riders only. It seemed to have drawn in a large enough crowd to keep the casino mostly empty, though.

A somber note still hovered over most of the town. There'd been at least a funeral a day, sometimes two or three. She'd attended as many as her schedule allowed and continued to visit those healing in the clinic.

In all the town had suffered thirty-four deaths in the tornado. Three souls remained missing, and countless more had been injured. Reverend Lyons was not expected to regain his vision thanks to the damage he suffered. Reverend Greene was in mourning over Mabel, and his young protégé's injuries.

Jane wiped the counter again. A movement near the door served to distract her from her melancholy. Instantly a grin split her features. "Graham Cooke. What the devil?"

The man plodded down the stairs heavily. A squirming child trying to escape his good arm, and a shirt in the hand that hung out of his sling. Incredibly the man blushed at her laughter. "Janey. It's not funny."

"It is from my way of thinking." She grabbed Joshua from him soon as he was close. "What on earth would prompt you to walk all the way down the street here without a shirt on?"

"Linh had to leave early this morning. I haven't been able to get this blasted shirt on without help yet." He held the fabric out to her. "Please."

"You poor thing. You must be absolutely desperate if you came to me for help. Especially not knowing how busy this place would be."

"You got a race going on. Why do you think I waited so late?" He offered a halfway pitiful grimace. "All right. Yeah. I'm desperate."

Jane took the shirt and draped it on the end of the bar. She set down Joshua so she might function better to assist him. With her hands free, she helped get the sling over his head. "I thought you'd have a horse in the race today."

"I'll be there next week." He slid his injured arm into the sleeve she held out, then turned in a circle to get his good arm in. "I thought I'd head out to the settlement today. You know, see how things are going out there."

Jane paused with the sling in hand. For several long seconds she remained still, eying the man across from her. "I'm sorry. You're doing what?"

Graham didn't exactly blush again, but his cheeks darkened. "You're not deaf."

"Tehnically, I am half deaf."

He paused his buttoning to glare at her. "Janey."

"What? It's true." She finished buttoning the shirt for him. When he dug a strip of fabric from his pocket, she stared at hm again. "A tie?"

"Don't pick on me, or I'll let Josh pull down those glasses."

"Oh." Jane moved quick at his words, scooping the child out from behind the bar. When the boy turned his attention to hopping through the tables, she turned hers back to Graham. Without a word of argument, she took the tie and tossed it over his head.

"What?"

"I'm just curious."

"Aren't you always?"

"True enough." She helped him get the sling in place, then set a hand on his arm. "Graham Cooke, if I didn't know any better I'd say you were gunning for mayor."

He bent to pick up Joshua with his good arm. "What if I was? Archie said he's not running again."

"I'm quite aware as he told me himself. I've also heard word Parker Krenshaw is running. Probably why he brought in workers from Pueblo to help with repairs in the town so Hammy could focus on the settlement." To that end, most of the cosmetic damage to The Hangman's Inn was fully repaired. They'd patched the roof for the moment, but all the glass had been replaced and the holes in the side of the building were fixed.

"Are you saying you're backing a Krenshaw?"

"I never said that."

"But you said he's running, and doing good."

"He's running, but the good he's done is for his own standing. Still trying to live down the nightmare that was his uncle."

"He'd do that better if he tore down that house and started fresh." Graham adjusted his tie as Joshua pulled it askance.

"Yes he would. I suppose he thought a paint job would be enough. Still, I never said I was backing him."

"You're the one that told me to run all them years ago."

"I did." She allowed a bright smile now. "Now I have far more reason to back you then I did then. You've changed for the better since you married Linh. I'd throw my hat in your ring over a Krenshaw any day."

"Thanks, Jane. Would you maybe help—"

"My speech writing days are over, Graham." Somehow she knew where he was going before he even said it.

Her guess proved right as his bright grin faded. "Aw, come on."

She pursed her lips. While he had done much better in recent years, Parker still had a leg up in the speech portion of the race. "You write it, I'll fix it."

"You're the best. Now, one more thing." He raised his eybrows. "Josh—"

"No." Jane laughed when his whole self drooped at her quick no. "I've got too much to do once the races are over."

"I can't handle him and—" At that moment, Joshua tried to climb right over Graham's shoulder. He caught his son, but not without a pained grunt for the effort.

"I'll tell you what. Sally is working at the library today, studying for her teacher's exam. I'm certain if you—"

"Hide me!" Kat ran forward, cheeks flushed near as bright as the red curls swirling about her in a state of disorder. "My mother is—she's after something, and I simply can't."

Jane couldn't even blink from her surprise at the scene. Kat's desperation was all Jane needed to hand over the keys to the cage. "I thought we were past this, Katherine."

The door to the cage slammed shut before Jane could scold further. Cuddy bellowed out a brief protest, and that's all there was to that.

Graham's brow furrowed, Josh dangling and wriggling in his good arm. "This seems familiar."

"Because it's exactly what happened the day I met Lillian."

"Right. I remember that."

"Jane." Lillian chose that moment to enter. Mere seconds earlier and she would have seen the ridiculous show of her daughter running to hide. She descended the steps into the pit without a bit of hesitation. "Where did my child go this time?"

Jane smiled brightly at the woman she now considered a friend as well. "What makes you think I'd dare hide her from you again?"

"Because you are too easy on her." Lillian returned the smile, adding some laughter to it. "I know she came through the casino."

"Kept right on going," Graham supplied as he had the day Jane had met Lillian. Of course, back then they'd been having fun at Lillian's expense. This was more good fun all around.

Jane shook her head at him, after all Lillian would never believe that. "Why don't you take Joshua to the library? Then go take your ride out to the settlement. I'll discuss your plans with you when you don't have a toddler using you like a tree."

"Thanks, Janey." He offered a nod and slipped from the room.

"Tea, Lillian?"

"That would be lovely." Lillian sighed softly. "If Katherine had allowed me to finish my thought, she might not have run, you know."

Jane gestured to a table near the cage so Kat would not be able to escape quite so easily. Still, she let Lillian take the seat with her back to the cage. Kat could leave that room, but she'd not get out of the pit without Lillian see her. Jane set down their mugs and took the seat opposite the matriarch of the town. "What in heavens name is all of this about?"

"I simply wanted to ask her opinion on something. Since it was about you, I suppose I can skip asking her to ask you directly."

"I do rather enjoy being gossiped about, but if it's a question about me, I'd prefer direct."

Lillian's brows rose as she sipped her tea. "I've heard about your plans for a new brothel. That could interfere with my hopes for you."

"Hopes? For me?"

"I wanted to ask you something."

"Please. Ask away."

"You know that Irving Callahan is leaving the Town Council."

"I do. For that matter, he's trying to sell the mercantile and planning to leave town." Jane frowned at her tea. "He's only been here two years."

"According to him it's family duty that requires him to leave. His brother passed."

"And he's taking on his brother's pregnant wife, and the farm he left behind. I've heard."

"That leaves a spot on the council, and I'd like it to be filled with a woman."

Jane paused with her cup half to her lips. Rather than speak aloud what could finish such a thought, she held Lillian's gaze.

"I think that woman should be you."

"Me?" Jane's gaze flicked toward the cage where Kat's head now peeked out of the window. "I hardly think so, Lillian."

"Why not? You are a part of this town. You have strong opinions, and people listen to you. You are a woman of business, and you helped get the government we have now."

"I helped the town form the government, but have not ever attempted a position within it for myself. I had no interest. I am not politically inclined, Lillian. I enjoy having the right to vote, and believe more women should, but I am not the one to fight for it."

"I think you are. You're a great orator. You've held your own against me, for heaven's sake."

"That may well be, but I'm far too busy to add such a thing to my schedule. I have the Inn, the library, our new brothel ventures, and together Cole and I have eight children, nine if you count Lizzie, which I do."

"Two of those children are adults, and three don't live with you."

Jane stared down Lillian, then leaned forward when the cage door opened. "Lillian, you have valid arguments, but you are forgetting something important. Rather, someone."

"What do you mean?"

"There is woman, a very strong woman, that would be perfect for the council. She's also a woman of business, she is more a part of this town than I am, seeing as she was raised here. Despite her progressive ways and trousers, she is very well liked—and she has experience in dealing with political matters that are important to women. She's been a suffragette, and a part of the Temperance League. She also knows how to talk to people when she doesn't let her fiery hair and personality escape too loudly."

"Katherine," Lillian supplied.

Jane rose as Kat approached the table. "Katherine."

Kat shook her head. "You aren't serious, Jane?"

"I am. What do you think, Lillian?"

"I believe I couldn't see the forest for the trees." Lillian turned in her seat to face Kat. "Jane has some valid points. What do you think?"

Jane slipped away to let the women talk, relieved to have avoided being pulled into sitting on the Council. Perhaps at some point in the future she'd consider it, but not with the children the age they were.

A young man wandered up to the bar, exhaustion dragging his features into lines. "Whiskey."

"Mr. Coleman. You hardly take liquor. Is all well?"

He lifted his gaze to hers, then back down to the bar. "Buried the Edwards' today. Took this long to clean up the mess so I could where they wanted."

"Then this one is on the house." Jane set the whiskey in front of him. "I heard you lost a few hands, not to mention cattle."

"We…I mean, I did." He rubbed his hand over his face. "That's gonna take some getting used to."

"I know you were close with them."

"They 'bout raised me when Ma died. My brother and sister, too." When he'd been young, Matthew's pa had abandoned them before Stephen was even born, and then died. Story was his ma had raised them down in San Antonio. Matthew had taken to ranching with the Edwards as an income, and when their ma died from a stroke, the Edwards had taken in all three children.

"How is Stephen holding up?" Stephen was twelve and still living at the ranch. Their sister, Bonnie had been in Denver for several years now learning midwifery, and then inspired by what she'd been doing had gone on to be a nurse as well.

"He ain't doing so good. That's two ma's he's lost."

"Two ma's you've lost, and two pa's."

"First pa don't count. He wasn't no pa."

Jane leaned on the counter. "You still lost him."

"Guess so." He pushed his glass toward her. "Another, please."

Jane poured. "What would Bonnie think about coming back here to work? I know Charlie would love to have another nurse."

Matthew's head popped up. "She could come home?"

"Yes. She could come home."

Relief washed over his features, and he pushed his untouched second drink away. "Would you ask him for me?"

"Soon as I'm done here."

"Thanks, Jane."

*Pleasure and action
make the hours seem short.
-William Shakespeare*

Cole carried a bundle of banners around the corner. In preparation for the Centennial celebration the following week, Jane wanted the Inn decorated. Even more so now that the street across from them was completely barren.

He draped the excess banners over the second section of railing. With a red, white, and blue banner in hand, he returned to the first section to nail down a corner of the banner.

"Pa! What are you doing?"

Cole startled at Sally's voice, and the words she'd used. Though she'd called Jane 'Ma' for near as long as she'd been their ward, and had even taken Jane's adopted last name of Spencer. Not once had she ever called him Pa. When he lifted his gaze to find her, he noted her cheeks were bright red. "Sally."

"I…Sorry…I…well…"

"That's a first." Cole laughed outright at her bold embarrassment. He sure didn't mind her calling him whatever made her comfortable. "Took you long enough."

"I didn't think you wanted…I mean, you…oh, devil."

"Ain't a problem, Sally. Call me whatever you want." He patted her shoulder before turning back to the banner. He stretched it across the railing and tried to place another nail as the drapery fell back against his hand. "Can you grab that for me? Jane wants these up today, even though the celebration isn't until next week."

"Ma said guests are coming on today's train." Sally set her stack of book on the porch. She took the banner to tug it straight for him.

"You ready for your test tomorrow?"

"I guess." With the banner nailed in place, she gathered the next and helped him stretch it out. The smile she'd worn moments before faded into a frown.

"Something wrong? Jane told me you were ready."

"I am. I mean, I know the stuff. It's just…" She tugged the third banner so hard it flew right out of Cole's hand. Another blush lit her cheeks. "Sorry."

Cole chuckled low. "It's fine. What in blazes has ya so nervous? The test?"

"I don't do well on tests, but it's not that. I don't know. I'm just not as excited about it as I think I should be. At least not as much as Ma wants me to be."

"Have you talked to Jane? Told her this?"

"No." She sighed as they lifted the last banner into place. "I don't want her to be disappointed. I want to make her proud."

"She is." One thing he knew without a doubt was how proud Jane was of all her kids. Cole hammered the last nail in. He grabbed her books for her. "She'd also rather you're honest with her, than scared to talk to her. Believe me, I know."

Sally took the books, holding them close to her chest. "I guess."

"Pa!" This time the voice that called was much younger.

Cole turned to find Kathy's daughter, Cindy, trying to run toward him. Every step of the way she dragged a dapper dandy along behind her. In the four years since he'd learned of Cindy's existence, he and Kathy had gone from begrudging acceptance that he'd get to know the girl, to the point where Cindy now knew he was her pa, and called him as such.

"Look who it is, Pa!" Cindy grinned ear to ear, still dragging the man behind her. "It's Uncle Patty! He finally came."

The pair came to a stop in front of Cole and Sally. The man Cindy tugged along laughed outright. "I would have come along without argument, CC."

Cole extended his hand to the man. "You must be Patrick."

"Patrick Warner. Good to meet you. Cole, right?" Patrick shook his hand firmly. "My darling Kat tried to convince me to come and enjoy all of the events this summer, extolling the virtues of the growth of your little town. I have to say it was little CC here that sealed the deal."

Cindy didn't stop grinning one second. Cole knew that Patrick and Kat had been close for years. By all accounts, Patrick had taught her the ways of sex, and in the process the two had become very close friends. When Kat had become pregnant with Cindy, she'd gone to St. Louis to live with the man now standing before Cole.

"I hear I've got you to thank for Kathy." He grinned as the man nodded in agreement. Movement to his side reminded him of Sally's now peculiarly silent presence. "This is Sally. Ward of Jane's and mine."

Sally blushed deep pink. After rearranging her books, and nearly dropping them, she managed to extend a hand. "Pleased to make your acquaintance."

"The pleasure is all mine." Patrick managed to sweep Sally close, despite the eager presence of Cindy. He pressed a kiss to the back of her hand. "If I'd know the town had such beauty, I would have arrived much sooner."

Sally's blush crept up to her forehead, and down her chest. "Goodness."

Cole did his best to keep his laughter at bay while Sally made her excuses and darted into the hotel. "Kathy said you were a charmer."

"And she said you were all action." Patrick didn't strut or puff up in any sort of contest or confrontation. His whole demeanor remained easy and light. "Speaking of which, would you know where I could locate my beautiful vixen?"

"In the casino with mine." Cole grinned as the man took a step toward the stairs. Much fun as it would be to let him be surprised, he thought it fair to call out some warning. "Her mother's in there, too."

"Ah, yes. Kat mentioned she lived here once again. Is it safe to go in?"

"Last I saw they were all laughing together."

"Then it was a pleasure meeting you, Cole. CC, would you show the way?"

Cole hopped onto the porch, but didn't follow them inside. He dropped the hammer on a bench when she spotted the approach of his friend, Graham. "Jane said you were gussied up. Ya don't look like it now."

Graham dusted some dirt from his chest with his free hand. "My visit turned into helping out best as I could one-armed. Think I did a better job getting dirty than helping."

"Jane said you're going for mayor."

"Thought it wouldn't try to hurt again." Graham leaned on the railing next to Cole. "Everyone's working hard to make sure the town is decent for the celebration."

"Sure are." Cole gestured across the street. "One good thing came outta that tornado. We got two lots to build the brothel. Right there where the library used to be."

"You'll have a woman at home and a brothel across the street. You're a lucky man, Cole."

"I got Jane. No need for a whore." While the town might gossip and spin tales about what he'd be doing at the brothel, he had no need to lie to Graham. The man had been Cole's business partner in his original brothel. Graham was aware that Cole hadn't touched a whore since Jane had arrived in town.

"A lot has changed in the last five years."

"Yeah. Like you aren't such a bastard."

"Same to you."

"You're gonna be mayor." Cole shook his head, still surprised such a thing could actually happen. Once upon a time, Graham had been up for the role, but he hadn't been liked enough.

"It's not for sure."

"If Parker's who you're running against, It is." Cole noticed a light tickle of fingers along his side. They danced along his thigh until her hand cupped him firmly. He groaned. "Jane."

She ducked under his arm so her back was to the railing, her smile turned toward him. "Hello there."

He welcomed her kiss, moaning into it when she massaged his length through his trousers. When she abandoned the kiss he muttered, "Evil woman."

"Am I now?" She offered him a wicked smirk, turning her attention to Graham. Her hand continued to tease him, the voluminous skirts she wore sufficing to make her actions discreet. "Graham. I have something for you."

Cole let out a low growl when her hand disappeared from its attentions just as he was getting really excited. Hs cock pulsed at the transgression of being abandoned.

Jane pulled a slip of paper from her right pocket, handing it off to Graham.

"Is that what I think it is?" Graham took the paper eagerly. "You said you wouldn't."

"I got to thinking better of it. As together as you are now, you're still a buffoon. I thought it would be best to write your speech announcing your candidacy and we'd take it from there." With a slight movement from Jane his trousers loosened. Seconds later her left hand wrapped around his shaft. Warm and smooth, her hand stroked his length.

He grunted at the sensation, meeting her gaze briefly.

She winked and leaned in close. Her lips brushed his ear in her whisper, "Stopped by the kitchen on my way out for a little splash of oil. Didn't want you uncomfortable."

His hands tightened on the railing at the shockwave that coursed through him when her hand twisted along his shaft. "Fuck."

"What?" Graham picked his head up from the paper.

"Nothing, Graham. What do you think?" Jane distracted the man while she worked Cole over with small, but sure movements.

As his balls tightened, Cole gripped her wrist. Much longer and he'd be done for. He muttered, "I don't got skirts to hide."

She pointed to the apron on her shoulder. Her tone remained low as his. "You're taking bar duty when I'm done. Relax."

"We're on the porch."

"Never stopped you from taking care of me, and that's more difficult to conceal with the skirts you mentioned."

Cole couldn't make his argument because Graham interrupted their quiet conversation with a question for Jane. He never heard what the man said as Jane continued to stroke him, her hold never consistent. Twisting, scraping, teasingly light, and brutally hard.

He closed his eyes, braced against the railing as her body remained closed to his, her breath brushing his neck with every word she spoke to Graham. His jaw clenched against the moan he wanted to make. A grunt slipped free despite his best restraint. Every muscle in his body tenses in preparation for release.

A jerk ran through him when the orgasm hit. If Graham noticed the guttural groan Cole couldn't contain, the man was good enough to keep his trap shut. Probably the man's years of experience co-owning the brothel with Cole left him immune to such things. Jane's soft, warm hand milked him dry. He leaned close against her until she was thoroughly pinned to the railing while he calmed down.

Jane, for her part, didn't seem fazed a bit by her stance. Once her hand was free from his trousers, she slipped a towel from her belt to wipe her hands. She pulled the apron from her shoulder and slinked it between them, wrapping it around his waist to tie it. All the while, her stream of chatter never slowed. "Reverend Greene is determined to see to his care by himself, but that's too much work. Until Reverend Lyons adjusts, he'll need more care than Mark can give him. I'm not quite sure what to do about that."

"Can't they hire someone to help?" Graham asked.

"With what money? They aren't exactly wealthy. What little they do make is used to care for the home, or in most cases donated to help those in need. They live a very simple life." Jane's gaze flickered to Cole's. She winked and brushed her lips across his. "Better?"

Cole returned the wink. "Was good before. Even better now."

"Good, because I want to spend time meeting the infamous Patrick Warner, and I can't do that if I'm manning the bar. It's your turn."

Cole's brow furrowed. "What about the kids?"

"Not due back for a couple of hours. What's wrong? Are you jealous of Patrick?" Jane glanced Graham's way. "He's opening a brothel and he's jealous of me socializing with a dapper fellow like Patrick Warner. Probably shouldn't tell him I had to help you dress today."

"You what?" Cole leaned back. "You didn't mention that."

"It was my shirt." Graham laughed heartily. "Can't get a shirt on without help. Don't go getting me in trouble, Janey. He just started liking me again."

Jane chuckled low. "Fine. Off with you, Graham. I need to get this man to work."

Graham nodded to them both, heading down the sidewalk.

"There's something I'd rather do than work after that." Cole kept her pinned to the railing.

"Too bad. I must meet Patrick properly, and you have a bar to man."

"Make Chauncey do it. And Patrick'll be here."

"No, sir. Chauncey is running roulette, and Cuddy has the cage. All our staff is occupied, you have work to do."

"I got plenty to do." He trailed kisses along her jaw, then nipped at her earlobe. Her small gasp let him know she was as excited as he was. "Like give you your turn."

"Oh, I'll expect my turn."

"We'll take it now."

"Can't." Swiftly, she ducked under his arm. Before he could turn to catch her, she stood behind him, leaning into his back. "Later."

He went to object, but she'd reached around him and grabbed him again. The shock stilled him long enough that she disappeared inside before he could even grab her wrist.

"Evil woman."

*All women are flirts, but some
are restrained by shyness,
and others by sense.
-Francois de la Rochefoucauld*

Jane grabbed the key for the largest room on the second floor for Patrick. Kat and Lillian had left half an hour before, and Patrick had taken to amusing himself on the casino floor. Somehow she didn't find it coincidental that he'd gone to the roulette table where Sally was working right then.

When Jane entered the casino again, Patrick still played at the table with a few others. She went to the bar where Cole was working. The man had one eye on the roulette table. Patrick's presence seemed to have gotten the crowd a little more excitable than they'd been before he joined. To that end, Sally wore a continual blush whenever the man spoke to her.

Jane carefully sidled behind Cole close enough to brush against him. Her maneuvers effectively pulled his attention off the table donto her. She smiled slyly. "Jealous of Patrick?"

"You were playing and flirting a lot, but I'm not jealous."

"Patrick is the sort that thrives on flirtation and play. Glad you aren't jealous, though. You jealous is an ugly thing."

"Only jealous when I need to be, and I know what I got."

"Hm, really? Then if I told you Al was planning on visiting for the Centennial—"

He tugged her close, eyes narrowing. "That's not funny."

"As I thought. I sent him on his way after his proposal, and he's married now." She dropped her voice low enough that no one else would hear. "And I married you."

"Told you, I'm only jealous when I need to be."

"You've never needed to be with Al Webb."

His nose wrinkled, but he didn't argue.

"As far as Patrick goes, though."

"Man can look me in the eye. I got nothing to worry about with you—now the attention he's giving Sally, on the other hand."

"It's attention she needs. That girl is starved for excitement, even if she doesn't admit it."

"She's courting Arthur."

"True, but that's all they're doing is courting. A little flirtation never hurt. Sally is a grown woman now, able to make her own choice in the matter." Jane nodded toward the table. "She's too embarrassed over the attention to act on it, anyhow. She hasn't received attention like that since she stopped whoring. That's a whole mess of something in her head."

"What?"

She chuckled low and leaned close. "To get such attention when you aren't a whore and have been working so hard to be the opposite can confuse the senses."

"If you say so." He turned his attention back to the dirty glasses. "How long is he staying?"

"At least for the summer. He stated he intends to remain for the statehood celebration in August as well. I don't have an exact approximation yet."

"What room?"

"Nine. It's the largest and has a lovely view of the thoroughfare. Perhaps if he stays on long enough we can convince him to join the gold room for a month. He's good for it."

He lifted his gaze to study the man again. "Looks like he comes from money."

"He does. Plus he earned some wealth on his own. For all he talks of business, I'm not even sure he has one at the moment outside of investments."

"Kathy said he had a girl."

"Yes, at one time. Pearl, if I remember correctly."

"You remember everything."

"Except the first twenty-seven years of my life."

"Except that." He laughed low along with her. "Pearl, then."

"They parted ways some time ago, I believe. Still friendly. She went onto San Francisco and has been heavily involved with the suffragettes there. Unmarried, much like Patrick. Of course, that's far more scandalous for a woman than a man."

Cole's brows rose when Sally let out a bit of embarrassed laughter, while Patrick leaned close to her, speaking quietly.

"Every young woman of age with appeal catches that man's eye. He charms them all. He is quite charming."

For that he cut her a look. "Do I need to be jealous?"

"You are the only man I want in my bed—or wherever we can make do."

If the man were a cat he would have been purring. The way he drew closer, pulling her near. "I'd like to make do right now."

"Oh, I bet you would."

"Shall we?"

"It's five-thirty."

"What?" Cole blinked in surprise at her reply.

"Mr. Hamm." Jane turned to greet the man that walked up to the bar right on time. "Cole was just getting your beer."

"Thank ya kindly, Lady Jane. Been busy as all get-out." Hammy wiped his hands on the towel Jane handed him.

"I don't doubt it. Between all the work from the tornado, and already starting our brothel despite your other pressing tasks. You are working far too hard." Jane patted his hand. "Though I appreciate you getting to work on the brothel so expediently."

"Me too." Cole set down the drink. "Although that might be because Hammy wouldn't mind somewhere less fancy to get his beer at the end of the day."

"Sure wouldn't. Don't care much for Tully's. Too much fightin' in there." Hammy slurped his beer. "Teddy's helping out a lot. I got him handling all the building at the settlement, while I take care of stuff here in town."

"Closer to the beer," Cole muttered as he passed behind Jane.

She cut Cole a look, but smiled at Hammy. "Well, I'm pleased you're personally handling the brothel. Your places always have a special touch to them."

Hammy's cheeks darkened at the compliment. "Aw, I don't do nothing special."

"I beg to differ." She patted his hand again. "If you'll excuse me, Mr. Hamm. I must attend to our new guest. I believe he'd like to freshen himself before supper."

Patrick had, indeed, stepped away from game play at the roulette wheel. Sally had also, as it was time for Cuddy to take over. Patrick still spoke to Sally, his charms definitely working magic on the now-flustered young woman.

When Jane approached, he nodded. "Jane. You failed to tell me what an absolute delight your young ward was."

"I had little doubt you'd learn for yourself." Jane smiled kindly at Sally. "I believe Arthur is waiting for you."

Sally looked toward the front entrance, alarm striking the smile from her face briefly. A deeper blush took over as she saw, in fact, Arthur was standing there. Jane had noticed him walk in moments before. "Oh, yes. We were going to take a walk before supper. Is that all right, Ma?"

"Of course it is. We'll see you in an hour." Jane waited until Sally had rushed off before turning to Patrick. "Give her too much flattery and she may dissolve into a puddle. She doesn't get nearly enough."

"She should get too much often. If her young man won't, what is the harm?"

"Oh, you do wish to stir trouble, don't you?"

"Wherever I can, whenever I can." He offered her his arm. "Is this the part where you allow me to get freshened up after my long journey before I run to dine with my dear vixen and her husband and children?"

"It is. I hope you'll be pleased with the room. It looks out onto First and Main, so you'll see Kat's home from there. Plus all the activity on the thoroughfare."

"I've no doubt the room will be as charming as this hotel, unfortunate though the name is."

"I rather like the name. It gives it a certain charm, and our guests something to ask—for they always wish to know how such a name came about."

"Then should I pretend I don't know the reason behind it so you might tell the story?"

"It would be gauche for me to tell a story you know." She guided him up the back steps to the second floor. "I must say, I'm pleased to have finally met you. Katherine's stories hardly do you enough justice. You are a man that needs to be experienced to understand."

"In more ways than one, dear Jane." He sighed softly. "I do wish I had been able to come out sooner. Alas, life was such that it proved impossible."

"Wooing fine women takes an awful lot of time."

"More than you would think. You are also more delightful than Kat's tales led me to believe. I do regret not meeting you before you got close to your possessive gentleman downstairs."

She laughed brightly. "Oh, believe me. You got it easy. I think he actually likes you. Four years ago, you might have gotten your nose broken."

"Oh, that would be a shame. I have a fine nose."

"Of course, four years ago I was letting Cole believe I was making time with quite a few other men. That was his peak possessiveness."

"No, no." He shook his finger at her. "I believe his peak possessiveness was when another man asked you to marry him."

"Ah, yes. Katherine told you about that as well. Yes, you might be right."

"Our dear Katherine shares all with me. I'm her family."

"My brothers are family, and I still share more with Kat than them. Perhaps it is the soul being confided in rather than the station."

"Fair point." He lifted her hand to kiss the back. "I have enjoyed your company, but for now I must cleanse the travel off me."

"I don't blame you. Enjoy your quarters. We'll see you at supper." Jane left the key with him, then moved back downstairs. When she reached the bottom, Cole hopped out of the pit to join her down the hallway. "Are you joining us for supper?"

"I am. Chauncey is working the bar."

"Horace? I thought he had tonight off."

"He did. Said his wife's going to a revival at Eckle's church, and he didn't want to go, guess he told her he had to work to get out of it."

"Don't blame him." She pushed open the door to the apartment to pure chaos—in the best way. Alma played a lively tune on the piano which had the four other children in the room hopping and dancing about.

Jay and Willow even danced, though in a strange fashion unfamiliar to Jane. The twins did some semblance of dancing themselves. Leanne sat on the bench beside Alma, tapping her toes to the music. She waved heartily at Jane and Cole, but kept her eyes on the children.

Cole pulled Jane into the bedroom, closing out most of the noise. "Forgot to tell you."

"What's that?" She crossed to the mirror to fuss with her hair. In the summer heat the curls got loose far too often for her liking.

"Sally called me Pa today."

She paused her fussing to study him in the mirror. "Did she now?"

"Yeah. Don't think she meant to, but then said…"

She abandoned her hair to face him directly. "Did it bother you?"

"Nah. Not so much." He almost looked embarrassed at the admission. She had to fight her smile at his confused brow pucker. "She's been with us two years, anyhow. Started calling you Ma right away. Guess I thought she didn't want to since I once owned her contract and all."

"But thankfully didn't indoctrinate her into that world the way you did so many before her, seeing as we were already together when Graham found her."

His nose wrinkled. "She was a child."

"Who had help putting on airs to appear the age she is now."

"Still. I wouldn't."

"Ah, but you did before I came along." She turned back to the mirror to tuck in a few more curls. "You've acted as her Pa as much as I've acted as her ma. Granted, it took you a little longer to do so because you had owned her contract."

"She's one of our kids, just like the others."

"She just waited until she was near-grown to join us. Just like Alma."

"Alma ain't our kid."

"You adopted her after her Ma passed, Leanne too. So in a way they both are."

"Let's not talk about Leanne like that. She's with your brother."

"Oh, right." Jane's nose wrinkled. "Good point."

He drew close, pulling her back against him. His gaze met hers in the mirror. "About this afternoon."

A pleasant flush warmed her cheeks at the mention of her attentions to him on the porch. "What about it?"

"I gotta make it up to you."

"Who says?"

He spun her to face him, pulling her tight against him until her body curved along the hard planes of his. "I do. You got a problem with that?"

"Not one bit."

There is no such thing as accident,
it is fate misnamed.
-Napoleon Bonaparte

"How did I get roped into this again?" Cole nailed a support plank into place. Half the town was hard at work setting up for the Centennial celebration. The meadow teemed with people moving every which way. Booths sprouted up across the green stretch of grass. The dance floor already lay complete near the church. The grandstand had become Cole and Tommy's job.

"Jane distracted you when she asked. You said yes for both of us before I could shut you up." Tommy climbed onto the stage beside him, surprisingly nimble for a man of his girth. He hauled the next board behind him to their level. "The woman plays you like a fiddle."

If any other man had said such a thing, Cole would have words with him. With Tom, Cole only chuckled. "I'd be mad, but I got a sweet deal going."

"Do *not* extol my sisters virtues to my delicate ears."

"So long as you bite your tongue about mine."

Tommy nailed the end of his board in place. A low chortle passed between them. "Deal."

Cole hopped down to the ground. Rather than going up and down now that the supports were up, he handed the long planks up to be stacked on the boards they'd already set in place. From here on out, the deck of the grandstand would be quick work.

"Jane tells me Sally finally got the gumption to call you Pa."

"Damn woman." Cole tried to be annoyed, but once again it was Tom. If she told anyone else—then again, Sally might be saying it on the regular.

"It's not like anyone will hear it if she does it again." Tom managed to point out what Cole had been thinking himself.

"Fair point."

"That's a good sign."

"Sign of what?" Cole paused with a long plank in his hand.

Tom eyed him over the edge of the plank. His features were hidden by shadow, unreadable. Not that the man ever revealed much. He was the best at keeping secrets, many of them. "Sally's a good girl."

Cole furrowed his brow at the comment. "I know."

Tom took the board from Cole, moving aside to let the man up. "She's been doing everything she can to not rock the boat. To be everything she thinks Jane wants her to be."

"Jane don't want her to be nothing but happy." Cole and Tom fell into a groove of nailing boards down in quick succession. "Never did."

"Sally's got it in her head she's got to be…"

Cole paused when Tom did. He glanced at his brother-in-law in confusion. The man had a faraway look on his face, thinking. "What?"

"No other way to say it, I guess—she's got to be the opposite of what she was when you took her in. She was a whore, a runaway, quite the troublemaker."

Cole thought back to the days before they'd taken Sally in. He remembered Jane likening her to a surly teenager. Sally certainly had been about causing trouble and pushing Jane's buttons. He definitely could see the point. "Since we took her in, she's been the best behaved of all the kids."

"Because she found she liked learning—and being part of your strange family."

"You're part of that strange family."

"I'm well aware." Tommy chuckled as he slid another board in place. "Thanks to Jane having the good sense to offer her a home, Sally's found out a lot about herself. She's smart as a whip. Good as you are with numbers, I'd bet. She has talent—can sing, and act. She's too smart for it, but she could be in your burlesque if she wanted."

"Jane wouldn't mind if she was, if that's what she wants."

"I know that. You know that. Jane knows that. Sally— has it in her head she's got to be something else."

Cole frowned as they hammered more boards into place. "Where you going with this Tom? You still haven't told me what you meant. Her calling me Pa is a good sign of what?"

"That's she's getting her gumption up. That girl has a mess of something in her head."

"Jane said the same thing yesterday when Patrick was flirting with Sally."

Tom smirked as he rose to his feet. "She was talking about a different mess of something, but then again, maybe it's the same."

"Tom."

"I can't say for sure because she hasn't even told me." Tom dragged another board forward. "Let's just say I know the look she gets sometimes. I used to wear it, or so Ma told me, and often. She said I was always looking for something else, somewhere else. I never wanted to sit still in one place for long. Sally gets that look, too."

Cole frowned and dragged another board into place. They both worked silently, which was good for Cole's racing thoughts. Tom couldn't mean that Sally wanted to leave Dominion Falls. He didn't know how Jane would take it. For that matter, he didn't know how Alma would handle it. Sally and Alma had formed an almost sisterly bond, and Alma didn't handle change well.

They finished the last board, standing together at the railing when they finished. "Sally wants to leave?"

"Don't know if that's it or not. She wants something. She just needs to get the gumption to say it out loud to someone. Once she does, maybe she'll stop looking."

Cole found Jane across the meadow, talking animatedly with Lillian for a few minutes before the older woman walked away. He took in the meadow, the booths lining the outside ready for the party and the wares they'd been filled with. Pies, lemonade, and games would abound for the party. "Town really got this together."

"The tornado threw us all for a loop, but it came out in the end. What's Jane doing?"

Cole returned his attention to his wife, who still stood near the church. The new doctor now stood with her, and the pair seemed to be having a rather intense discussion. Jane's back was to the grandstand, and she gestured about emphatically. "No clue. Looks like she's yelling at him. Poor guy. New in town, already on Jane's bad side."

"Never a good sign."

In the midst of what appeared to be a tirade on Jane's part, Dr. Cross began to laugh.

Tom looked sideways at him, clearly confused. "What the devil?"

Cole waited for Jane to retaliate in some way. When she doubled over, then straightened again wiping at her eyes, he realized she was laughing. "I have no idea."

"Let's get down from here. Maybe we can escape before we're set to work again." Tommy climbed down quick. The second he hit the ground, Leanne came around the corner.

She sidled up to Tom, batting her eyelashes at him.

Before he could find out what she was going to wrangle Tom into doing, Cole scrambled down the other side of the grandstand. He darted behind a nearby booth, sticking to the edge of the meadow to avoid detection.

When he reached the church, Jane spotted him. She waved him over.

"Damn," he muttered. So much for going back to the Inn without having another task set upon him. Rather than give her a chance to say one word, he strode right up to her and pulled her into a deep kiss.

By the time he released her, she was flushed and breathless. "Well."

The young doctor beside them cleared his throat. His gaze focused across the meadow.

"I'm so sorry, Andrew." Jane's hand rested on her chest as though she still couldn't catch her breath. "Sometimes Cole lacks the decorum God gave the simplest miner."

"Just saying hello." Cole kept his arm around her waist. He nodded to the man. "Doc."

"Of course you were." Jane offered him a chastising look. "What I was going to ask before you decided to silence me, is if you could head back to the Inn. Katherine, Lillian, and I have a bit more to do here, and it's almost one o'clock."

"Lunch time." Cole and Jane had tried altering the strict schedule Alma kept. Since the first time she'd visited, before they'd moved her in with them, lunch had to be at one, supper at six. Unfortunately, as part of the strangeness that controlled her soul, having her schedule disrupted could become catastrophic to her temperament for days.

"Sally is helping here, and the other children are…" Jane's gaze fell toward the creek behind the church. "They're supposed to be as well. Cora was kind enough to sit with Alma yesterday, I don't want to pull her from her kitchens again."

"Then why'd she hire another cook?"

"So that she might have some time for herself now and again. We aren't going to chain that woman to the stove, Cole." She laughed softly.

"Fine. I'll take care of Alma." He kissed her forehead. "Sorry to interrupt, doc."

"No interruption. Jane was sharing some stories with me while we waited on the paint to arrive." Andrew looked slightly less uncomfortable now that he'd been included in the conversation. "I'm not certain how she roped me into painting some of these booths. I don't believe I've painted a thing in my life."

"The good doctor comes from one of the wealthiest families in Buffalo. The poor thing didn't get a callous until medical school when he spent hours practicing with his instruments non-stop." Jane grinned broadly. "I told him it was high time he learned how to get his hands dirty properly. There are no servants here to do it for him."

"Careful, Andy. She'll get ya doing all sorts of helping around town if you give in this easy. You won't have time for doctoring." Cole winced when her elbow jabbed sharp into his ribs. "What? You could charm a bird off a branch."

"Flattery will get you nowhere right now, no matter how devilishly enticing you might be. I'm far too busy."

"You always are anymore." He captured her lips again. When she leaned further into him, he brushed his tongue across the seam of her lips. She opened up eager as him.

Screams echoing across the meadow made them both freeze. When his eyes flew open, he found hers staring at him.

They broke apart and spun to find the source of the screams. They seemed to be a distance off toward town, but headed toward them like a wave crashed to shore. On the heels of the screams, people scattered.

Loud bangs and rattling forewarned of the sight moments before the sea of people parted. A wagon tore across the meadow straight toward them, the horses half-wild. They bucked against the hitch, and each other. The wagon behind them flew in the air at every bump, banging back down to earth with brutal force.

Cole shoved Jane out of the way, diving for the horse's reins. The beasts wove to get away from him, heading straight for the nearest booth. He managed to grab the edge of the wagon as it passed. He ran along beside, then hauled himself into the bed, only to crash against the floorboard when it flew in the air again.

Ignoring the flash of pain in his foot, he leapt over the seat, then straight onto the back of the horse on the left. He reached for the horse on the right. His legs clamped tight to his horses' flank to facilitate his grab for the reins. Only able to find the reins for the horse he was on, he stretched toward the bridle of the other.

Both horses lifted on their hind legs before hauling forward. The booth they'd raced toward busted apart when they hit. Cole had to lie flat on his stomach to avoid the broken boards that collapsed around him.

The crash slowed the team enough that Cole was able to reach for the right horses bridle again. With a hefty pull on the halter, he distracted the horse enough to make its steps falter. He wrapped the reins in his left hand around his arm to pull tight on the left horse.

Finally they slowed to a stop.

Cole let out a breath, relaxing his hold on the beasts flank. Pain radiated through his foot like a shot the moment he did. He must have done some damage when he leapt into the wagon.

After a few good breaths, Cole realized the screams hadn't stopped when the horses did. He turned to look behind him. A crowd gathered, pointing at the wagon in pale-faced horror.

He slipped from the horse, then paused to set the brakes before swinging around the back to find Dr. Cross kneeling on the ground next to the lifeless, bloody body of Bob Keller. The man was almost completely under the wagon. "What in hell?"

Jane rushed to his side. Her arms flew so tight around him, he knew she'd been worried. After a second she pulled back to slap his chest. "What were you thinking?"

"Someone had to stop them," he said in a low voice. He pulled her against his side, turning his attention back to the doc. Jane remained silent after her initial scolding, her own gaze fixed on the body. Cole noticed the rein wrapped around Keller's ankle. He narrowed his eyes, looking from it to the snorting horse in front. When Dr. Cross reached for the rein, Cole set a hand on his shoulder. "Leave it alone unless you want them to take off again."

"He's dead," Dr. Cross said quietly. "We must untie him."

"Dead," Jane squeaked. "But, how? I mean, I know how, but how?"

Cole lifted his head and spotted Tommy heading for them through the mass of spectators. "Hold the horses for me. I'll get him untied."

Tom shook his head. "Reverse that. You're the expert on horses. I'm the expert on knots."

Cole nodded his agreement and returned to the front of the wagon. He took both halters in hand, talking quiet to the team while Tom worked. The horse on the right snuffed and stomped a couple times. Cole kept her firm in hand until the reins slackened. He took both set of reins in hand soon as they were free.

He ignored the scramble of activity at the back of the wagon to continue soothing the horses against the panic in the meadow. When Tom and Jane came around front, he glanced at his brother-in-law. "I'll take the wagon to the livery."

"On thing." Tom glanced at the dispersing crowd. He lowered his voice despite their relative solitude. "No way that knot was an accident."

"What? No." Jane shook her head firm as if it would make her words more true than Tom's. "That can't be. Bob hasn't got an enemy in town. He rivals Mr. Hamm in friendliness."

Cole frowned, turning his gaze toward the meadow. "You sure, Tom? He probably got tossed around a lot in that run."

"That wasn't an accidental knot," Tom confirmed. "It was meant to last."

"Who'd want to kill Bob?"

"I haven't the faintest idea."

*Anger, if not restrained,
is frequently more hurtful to us
than the injury the provokes it.
—Seneca*

Jane paced the length of the exam room, back and forth incessantly. The damn woman wouldn't even look at Cole. Worse—when he tried to speak, she shushed him. He might have found her fuming temper amusing if it hadn't been directed at him.

To that point, he still wasn't sure what he'd done wrong to deserve it besides shoving her too hard. He'd done it to get her out of the way of the runaway wagon, and in the process save her life, or at least from injury.

After a brief knock, Charlie entered. "Cole. How are you feeling?"

Jane scoffed over Cole's attempted answer. "Damn fool thought trying to get himself killed was a good idea today."

Charlie's brow raised at his sister. Rather than answer, he moved to Cole's feet. "Right or left foot?"

"Left. Soon as I landed in that wagon it hurt like the devil." Cole didn't bother to glance Jane's way when she scoffed again. "You mad I didn't get killed or something?"

Jane's pacing stopped short. Fists clenched at her sides; her nostrils flared as she glared him down. "You stupid son of a—"

"Jane." Charlie set one hand on the toe of Cole's boot, the other on the heel. "How about you try to distract Cole for me?"

"Let him suffer," she snapped.

"What?" Cole didn't have time to object to her remaining anger. Pain lanced through his foot and up his leg in one sudden motion. He cursed Charlie up and down before he managed to release a pained groan. "Damn."

This time when he glanced Jane's way, a whisper of concern creased her brow. The moment she caught him looking she flipped it right back to anger.

"Jane." That's all he got out before another flash of pain hit him. "Blast, Charlie. I thought you were done abusing me."

"I only took your boot off. Now I have to examine you." Charlie's amusement carried in his tone. "I promise to move fast so long as you don't kick me. You do, and I'll take my damn time."

"You won't distract me none?" Cole turned his attention to Jane when Charlie continued abusing his foot. "You're good at it."

Her arms folded across her chest. Rather than answer, she stared him down.

"At least tell me what I done wrong."

Eyes narrowed, she returned to pacing. "Charles."

"Yes, Jane?"

"I haven't seen you for a few days, and I made a promise to ask you a question."

Cole dropped his head back. Alternately he held his breath against the pain of the exam, and tried to focus on what Jane was saying.

"Go ahead, then." Charlie finally set Cole's foot back on the table. "You broke your fifth metatarsal bone."

Jane paused at Charlie's statement, only to resume pacing. Only difference is she now wrung her hands. "Do you know Matthew Coleman? The foreman at the Edward's ranch?"

"I've met the young man." Charlie leaned against the exam table. "You won't sit around with the foot up and resting for me, will you?"

"Not a chance," Cole confirmed. "We got too much going on."

"Then I'm going to plaster it." Charlie turned his attention away. "Go on, Jane."

"Wait." Cole sat. "What do you mean, plaster it?"

"I mean instead of splint and bandages, I'll use a splint and some plastered gauze to keep it immobile as possible." Charlie moved to the cabinets. "Jane?"

Jane stared at Cole for the first time since they'd entered the room. The briefest smile crossed her features. "It's a technique they've used for treating battlefield injuries. Doctors prefer splinting and rest, but you're too stubborn."

"Says the woman that walked on a broken ankle for two days straight a few years back." Cole happily pointed out the fact, but it had the opposite effect he'd hoped. Jane's smile flittered away, replaced by her temper yet again.

"Mine was necessary, yours is stubbornness." She resumed her pacing. As if there'd been no interruption, she resumed her conversation with Charlie. "Matthew's sister

Bonnie is in Denver. She's a midwife, and she's been training as a nurse. With the death of the Edwards, I'm certain the family would like to be together, if you're still looking for another nurse to help around the clinic."

"I am, actually. Before the past couple of weeks it was an extravagance. After the tornado and today, I'm beginning to wonder if it isn't necessity." Charlie moved back to Cole's foot.

Soon as the doc began to work, Cole focused on blocking the blinding pain over whatever conversation Jane and Charlie had.

For one brief moment in the midst of whatever Charlie was doing that caused more pain rather than relieved it, Jane's lips brushed across his forehead. She was out of reach before he could grab her. At least he knew her anger wasn't something she wouldn't get past soon enough.

The pain eased after a few minutes. Unbelievably, with him silent and not partaking in the conversation, Jane jabbered away to her brother. When he sat to examine the damage, Jane shut off her stream of chatter. He dared a glance her way, but her back was to him, gaze firm out the window.

Charlie cleaned his hands. "You'll need to use at least one crutch. I'd prefer two so you weren't using the foot at all."

"That won't work for me, doc."

Jane harumphed, spinning on her heel out of the office.

Charlie sighed, meeting Cole's confused look. "One crutch will do it. Take it easy on it today as much as possible. Hell, rest with it up as much as possible. As for Jane, you scared her witless. She'll come around."

"That's why she's mad?"

"How is it you two have been together so long? You didn't know that?"

"She's usually the one scaring me, not the other way around." Cole maneuvered the ungainly block his foot had become off the table.

"Good point. Let me find a crutch for you."

By the time Cole had gotten set up and able to follow Jane outside, at least five minutes had passed. When she wasn't in the lobby, he figured he'd have to hunt her down. Instead, she stood outside on the porch with two of her brothers, and her ex-husband.

David appeared harassed. "No, Jane."

"Thomas said—"

"I know what Tommy said, and I trust him." David shook his head. "No one saw anything nefarious. Last thing anyone remembers is Bob pulling up to Hammy's shop with his wagon."

"If that were the case he would be in the wagon." Jane huffed. "*Not* under it."

"Obviously something happened in the interim." Tom rubbed his hand over his beard.

"A few people thought they saw him talking to Eckles," Mike provided.

"He was what?" Jane slapped Cole's hand away when he tried to set it around her waist. "He doesn't attend Glorious Valley, and has spoken against it. Why would he speak to Eckles?"

Tom's mouth twitched in barely hidden amusement when Jane slapped Cole's hand again. "I thought it was strange, too. Perkins said it didn't look like a pleasant conversation, but it wasn't in any way heated."

"Eckles probably trying to get him to his church again." Mike sighed. "He's tried a few times with some of Greene's most upstanding members. He's only managed to pull about twenty from our church's flock. I think he wants to take over the territory with his zealousness."

"Me too." Jane shook her head, turning to David. "What does this all mean, Sheriff?"

"I'm afraid it looks like nothing more than an accident, Jane." David set a hand on her shoulder. His focus on her, he didn't notice Tommy's deepening frown at his words. "A tragic accident to be sure."

"Thank you for checking." Jane hugged the man tight. She cast a glance toward Tom. The pair nodded to each other, but said nothing aloud.

Cole moved close to Jane again while David made his goodbyes. He snaked his arm around her waist. Once again he felt the sting of her slap. "Jane."

"Thomas." Jane slipped her hand through her brother's arm and took off without him.

Michael turned a curious gaze on Cole. "What the hell did you do?"

"Saved her life. Maybe the lives of a few others."

"You are the devil, aren't you?"

"Apparently." Cole ignored Mike's departing chuckle to focus on the woman currently miffed at him.

Jane and Tommy huddled together in hushed conversation, rather intense by the look of the tense lines on Jane's face. Tommy lounged in a more relaxed fashion, leaning against the railing. He nodded in response to whatever Jane said.

With a deep breath, Cole began the arduous task of crossing the road with his foot plastered. The crutch slipped on the cobblestone, making his progress much slower than he liked. So slow, in fact, that by the time he got to the porch of the Inn, Jane had disappeared. Damn it.

"You'll never keep up with her long as you got that, and long as she's nursing her anger."

"Don't I know it?" Cole made his way up the steps. "Can you tell me what that was about?"

"What part?"

"That look Jane gave you when she was hugging Davie, and the talking here."

"She asked me my gut feeling about Keller's death."

"You two thinking Davie's wrong?"

"I know knots. That wasn't a tangle, it was a knot."

"Murder, then."

Tom nodded once. "No idea why. Jane wasn't wrong. Keller is well liked in town. Don't know a soul that would say a bad word about him."

"Hey, Pa. Tommy." Sally walked up quick. "Ma said she doesn't think it was an accident."

"Right to the point, then." Tom half smirked, but kept his gaze on the street. "What do you care?"

"It was a murder. A very public one." Sally practically buzzed with energy. "Are you going to investigate? Right here in Dominion Falls?"

"Wouldn't be the first time." Tommy cut Cole a look, but Cole was damned if he knew what the look was about.

"Davie doesn't think it was a murder," Cole supplied. "Said it's an accident."

"Oh." Sally's excitement waned. "Then you aren't investigating?"

"Don't now yet. Might." Tom was being vague as ever with his answers. A fact that seemed to frustrate Sally.

She wilted at the response, frowning as she turned her attention to the street. "Oh."

Tom straightened, stretching his arms above his head. "Welp. I've got the gold room tonight. Best get at it."

"Yeah. All right." She fiddled with the railing. "I guess I should go back to the meadow. I promised Kat and Mrs. Daugherty I'd help finish setting up the banners."

Cole nodded. "All right, then. Is something wrong?"

"No." She didn't sound at all convinced. "Everything is—as it always is. Ma's with the children in the apartment. I'll be back in a few hours."

He watched her go, wearing a small frown. When she hit the train tracks, heavy bootsteps walked up beside him again. Tom stared at the girl's back. "She's gotta get the gumption."

"For what?"

"Everything she wants."

Never contend with one that is foolish,
proud, positive, testy, or with a superior,
or a clown, in a matter of argument.
-Thomas Fuller

Jane stood in front of the skeleton of a building next to Tommy. "How many rooms did you and Mr. Hamm manage to squeeze into this footprint?"

"You're so bitter."

"I am not."

"You're mad we lost the Frost property and are looking down your nose at this. It's the same size of land the saloon had when it started. With the café and the library's land it's almost exact." Tommy nudged her with his elbow.

"We could have gone bigger with that bit there."

"Lillian outbid you, and it's for a dress shop. Stop complaining."

"A dress shop without a dressmaker."

"Bitter."

Her amusement at his poking won out with a laugh. "Fine. I'm bitter. How many rooms?"

"Ten for entertainment, three for the whores, and a good sized one for your new manager. We even are talking about adding in a small room for a safe under the stairs."

"The rooms for entertaining will be smaller than we'd planned, then."

"Don't need much for what's done in there."

"Speak for yourself."

Tom's nose wrinkled. "I don't want to hear that."

She laughed softly. "You'd be worried if I wasn't honest."

"True enough."

"You told Mr. Karlson where I'd be at the station?"

"I told him under the sign for The Hangman's Inn. He's happy to bunk in one of our staff rooms until his room at the brothel is ready. You decide on a name yet?"

"No. Not that it really needs one around here. The men will be happy to have another saloon and brothel to frequent whether it has a name or not." The distant whistle of the train pulled Jane's attention from the structure. "You were clever enough to name The Hangman's Inn, perhaps I should leave it to you."

"I'm on board with a simple saloon sign like your place once had. If you want it named, it's all on you."

"Sure. You'll help Cole name a hotel after a traumatic event in my life—but you won't name a simple brothel for me."

"You going to forgive him yet?"

She pursed her lips against the subject change. "You're supposed to be my brother first."

"He did a good thing."

"He scared the life out of me."

"It makes no sense. You're punishing him for nearly killing himself and wiping his existence from your life—by ignoring him?" He laughed into her stubborn silence. "Montaigne says that he who establishes an argument by noise and command shows that his reason is weak."

"I won't ignore him for long, but for now I'm still reconciling the events of yesterday and the sight of him crashing through the booth."

He tugged her into a one-armed hug. "He's miserable. Of course, that means *I'm* miserable because you aren't catering to his restriction to rest as much as possible."

"Don't cater to him. Let him suffer." She kissed his cheek at the next blast of a train whistle. "Off to meet the train."

Truth be told, she wasn't angry—but she had been terrified. It might not be fair to hold it against him, he'd tried to do the noble thing and likely saved lives, but she could have lost him.

The events also served a dual purpose of granting the gossipers a glimpse of their first public argument in almost a year. In deference to the children, their previous explosive arguments had faded to the relative silence of their bedroom. Of course, by doing that, the arguments were resolved nearly as quick as they were formed.

At the moment her silent treatment had led to Cole hollering at her from the Inn's porch that morning. It was all so immature and childish, but she'd stick to her guns a little longer. Most especially until the dance on Monday where he'd have to park his injured butt on a bench and allow her to dance with whomever asked it of her.

"That's a wicked grin if I ever saw one, dear sister." Michael leaned in to kiss her cheek. "What mischief have you been contemplating?"

"I was just pondering Cole's continuing suffering over the next few days. More so his pout at the dance when he's stuck on a bench and I'm dancing with half the town." She joined his laughter. "In other words, I'm being an immature beast of a woman, but it's great fun."

"Being angry with him for saving people, and the horses, is a bit odd even for you."

Given that no one knew what had set the horses off in such a manner that they'd taken off, dragging their owner behind them, there'd been some call to put them down. Cole had seen they were sent to the Inn's stables so he could work with them. As good as he was with horses, not a soul had argued with him. "I'm angry he scared me."

"In order to save you, and the rest of the crowd that were in danger."

"He scared me."

"'Arguments, like men, are often pretenders." Michael squeezed her hand. "Plato."

"Perhaps. Syrus says that in heated argument we often lose sight of the truth. Then again, this argument held little heat."

"On your end."

"I know. It's delightful."

"Terrible."

"The absolute worst," Jane concurred. "Are you ready for Ma and Pa's visit?"

"I am. Are you upset they're staying at my place?"

"For a few days, and then they're coming to the Inn. They stayed at the Inn last time, I hold no ill will. You are their child."

"So are you."

"Clara was. I am, too, but I'm different."

Michael hummed his disagreement. "Does that mean you aren't feeling like a Young today?"

"Not at all, but I'd wager a bet even Ma would concur that I am not the daughter she knew before the war. Before Clara went to Utah and was nary to be seen again."

"Perhaps." Mike took position under the sign for his hotel as Jane took the same post beneath her own. Over a year ago, as both hotels gained some real traction, Norman had installed the signs so arriving guests wouldn't have to search for their hosts. It came in handy when they couldn't be certain who would be there to meet the train. Even Michael had the assistance of Lee and his other manager, Rueben, to meet the trains when he was busy.

"Besides, I believe the main reason they stay at The Hangman's Inn so much is the children. If you would get off your duff and get married already, have some children we'd be in true competition."

"Jane." He groaned, cutting her a glare. "Leave my relationship alone."

"Years, Michael. You're as bad as Thomas—without the excuse of a previous divorce. My goodness, three of Ma's children have been divorced. Thomas and Leanne are rather sinful, as are Cole and I. What a series of scandals we've been for them. Perhaps it is better you don't get married, or live in sin. Continue being the annoying upstanding one."

"You're a terrible sister."

"I agree." She laughed with him. Before the train made it's final squealing stop, she reached out to squeeze his hand. "All I wish is your happiness. For all of you, really."

"I know. You don't have to be so annoying when you do it, though."

"It's my way."

His protest was overrun by the squealing brakes of the train. They both turned their attention to the train and the disembarking passengers to find their clients.

As the first few guests approached, Jane greeted them, and the ones after. All three couples opted to walk the short way to the Inn, which meant Jane remained alone while waiting for their new brothel manager to make himself known.

"Jane." The mature woman that was much like an older version of Jane with dark hair smiled her greeting. Beside Jane's ma stood the tall, blond man that was her pa. Eunice and John approached quickly. Eunice swept her into a tight hug. "It's good to see you."

"And you, Ma. Pa." Jane managed to break free to hug her pa as well. "The children are excited for you to visit, but I know you need to freshen from your trip and get settled in. I have business to attend to myself, if I could locate my new brothel manager."

"New brothel?" John's brows raised. "When did this come about?"

"A few weeks back. I would have written, but I knew you'd be traveling before my letter reached you. Of course, Cole nearly got himself killed trying to save my life and thus I'm not speaking with him at the moment."

"What, what?" Eunice blinked. "Could you take that slower for me?"

"I would, but Michael is loading his guests into the wagon. We'll talk more at supper." Jane kissed each of their cheeks. Over their protests, she shooed them toward her brother. To her disappointment, with them gone the platform stood near-empty.

No sign of the brothel manager anywhere, though she hadn't left her post until she'd sent off her parents. She pursed her lips, scanning the platform again, but only a few familiar faces were on the boards. Most of them appeared to be preparing to load onto the train once the engine got turned around.

Rather than stare around when there was clearly no one there, she moved toward the street. She strode down the cobblestone, eying the crowded thoroughfare for anyone that might be their new manager. Not that she had the faintest idea what the man looked like.

When she approached the crossroads, she spotted a man standing on the back steps of the Inn's porch, staring at the skeleton of the new brothel. Hidden in shadow, she couldn't be certain he was a stranger, but the form didn't appear familiar.

She remained on the street for her approach, strolling along the length of porch so recently repaired. The nearer she got, the more certain she was he was a stranger. Soon as the sun fell behind the angle of the roof to set her in shadow as well, she knew it to be.

The man had dark, shoulder length hair tied back with a strip of leather. His clothes were clean, though a bit the worse for wear. A black Stetson flipped around in his restless left hand; his right perched on the weapon in his holster.

He stood an inch or two taller than she, similar in height to her brother, Charlie. A short beard darkened his chin, with an accompanying mustache thick over his lip.

"Mr. Karlson?"

The man turned at his name. His sharp green eyes scanned her from top to bottom. "I'll be damned. It was you."

A tickle of humor rose at the comment. "If you are referring to the person you were supposed to meet at the station, then yes. It was me."

"You're the owner?"

Jane unleashed her barely contained laughter at the surprise in his tone. "I am. Why?"

"This is your hotel?" He pointed his thumb over his shoulder at the building. "This fancy place here?"

"It is, though I'd hardly say fancy. Understated class, perhaps. Cozy and comfortable. No gild on this lily."

"It's fancy," he stated again. His brow furrowed. "And you're wanting a brothel?"

"I do."

"Huh."

Her lips twitched, but this time she kept her laughter contained. She extended her hand. "Shall we begin again? I'm Jane Spencer. Welcome to Dominion Falls, Mr. Karlson. I'm pleased to meet you."

He wiped his palm along his pants before he met her outstretched one with a firm handshake. "Call me Wil, Ma'am."

"Please, call me Jane. No ma'am necessary, Wil."

"That the place?" He turned back to the skeleton of a building.

"It is. There will be ten rooms for entertaining, three for whores, one for you. You, of course, will dictate how your room is laid out, where you want it and such. There will be plumbing connected for the bathhouse and one water closet for the business, as well as fresh water at the bar for coffee. We'll provide you with your own water closet or bathhouse if you'd like, of course."

"Ain't ever had my own water closet before." He approached the building with her. Unlike the original saloon, this one would have an elevated from porch, allowing for a better vantage point for the whores to see and entice customers. "Don't need anything too fancy, Jane."

"Lady Jane!" Hammy stepped out of the hole where the front door would go. He quickstepped down the stairs. The hat fell clean off his head at his elaborate scrape and bow. "Always a pleasure."

"As it always to see you, Mr. Hamm." Jane kissed him on the cheek. She gestured to the gentleman beside her. "This here is Wil Karlson. He'll be managing the brothel for us. Wil, this is Mr. Gilbert Hamm. He is a dear friend, and an excellent carpenter. When he enters any of our establishments, his beer is always free."

"That so?" Wil extended a hand to Hammy.

"Everyone calls me Hammy." Hammy shook his hand. "Long since I remember, anyhow."

"Wonder what ya did to get such a privilege. I don't give freebies to no one."

"Mr. Hamm is very special. He's like family." Jane ignored Hammy's blushing denials. "Correction. In my world, he *is* family."

"Aw, shucks, Lady Jane." Hammy worried his hat in his hands. "I'd best get back to work."

"All right. You remember what I told you, don't work too hard." She kissed him on the cheek again before he shuffled off. "Now, Mr. Karlson."

"Wil."

"Of course. Wil." Jane indicated to the Inn. "Why don't I show you where you'll be staying while the brothel is being built?"

"Much obliged. Mind if I ask why the brothel?"

"Once upon a time The Hangman's Inn was a brothel and saloon. My business partner and lover and I converted it into a proper hotel and casino some years ago. I believe he's become bored with just the Inn and breaking horses, so I suggested another brothel."

"I'm sorry—business partner, and lover?" Wil glanced around in curiosity. "You're awful unashamed in such a public setting, ma'am."

"It's Jane, and I hold little shame. The town knows what we are, not that I much care so long as I am happy and satisfied."

"And—the brothel was your idea?"

"Of course."

"Lady, you ain't nothing like you seem."

"Oh, that's the tip of the iceberg, Wil."

How happy could I be with either,
Were t'other dear charmer away!
But while ye thus tease me together,
To neither a word will I say.
-John Gay

Jane sat in the corner furthest from Cole with her ma and all of the children. Even Jay and Willow had joined. It seemed the combined affection of Jane and her Ma had won over the pair so they were laughing with the rest.

Cole couldn't keep his eyes off her for one second. For three days she'd ignored him, and tonight was the dance. She always went to dances on his arm and danced with him first. He cast a dark look at the plaster keeping his foot immobile, but also his motion so restricted he was all but useless.

None of his best arguments or cajoling had worked their usual charms. Jane remained stoically ignorant of all his words and touches. She smiled and charmed with her usual aplomb with everyone else, but for him she offered nothing.

He should be furious, annoyed, but right then he couldn't be. The way she dealt with the children kept him captivated. When they'd finally freed her from the shackles of her past, they'd agreed they didn't need marriage or kids. Now they had both.

Jane was the better for it. Her love for her family ran deep and made her even more beautiful than the day he'd first seen her awake and talking. There was a glow about her when surrounded by the kids, whether young or old, or not even technically hers. Even Alma, from the first moment they'd met Jane had loved Cole's sister.

Though their apartment was quite full of children, he wondered from time to time if she wanted another. For that matter, he wondered if he did.

"You're staring." Tom plopped into the seat beside him.

"I always stare at her. Gets worse when she's ignoring me."

"Fair point." Tom thanked the waitress that poured him a coffee without asking. "You taking her to the dance tonight?"

"Doubt it. She still isn't talking to me. Plus, I got a bad foot. I'm ready to tear this plaster right off and be done with it."

"She'd really have your hide then."

"Only thing keeping the blasted thing there." He took a long drink of his own coffee. Jane's laughter drew his gaze again. His breath caught when she lifted Colton in the air, pure adoration making her radiant.

"Staring again."

"She loves them kids something fierce."

"No doubt. Being a ma suits her, much as being a pa suits you."

Cole pursed his lips at the compliment. Even after over two years with their odd little family, he still doubted his abilities. "Jane makes me better, always did. The kids help, too. I don't wanna do wrong by them. Still not sure I'm not cursed."

"Look at them. What am I saying? You are. Look harder. You're not cursed. Your woman is mad at you, but you're not cursed."

"Don't know I'd call it mad."

"Exasperated?"

"Nah."

"Sullen. Afronted. Chafed. Sore. Annoyed. Disgruntled. Vexed."

"That's the one." Cole stopped Tom's rambling when he hit the word. "If she were truly mad I wouldn't be getting looks, too. She's gonna cave."

"Not until she feels you've suffered properly."

"Three days without her in my bed. I'm suffering."

"You're uncomfortable, not suffering." Tom chortled loud enough to gain Jane's attention. She quirked an eye at her brother but kept her focus on the children.

"How'd you feel if Leanne cut you off at the prick?"

Tom shuddered. "Don't even say it. Just got that woman in bed, I'm not letting her out any time soon."

"Watch it," Cole cut in an undertone. Even with the harsh words, he couldn't keep the amusement from his own voice. Truthfully, he was happy for his sister, Leanne. Tom was a good guy, and he was glad Leanne finally got out of the shackles of the life he'd sentenced her to. That didn't mean he needed to hear about it.

"I've gotta hear you talk about my sister," Tom spoke in the same sort of undertone to keep folks from hearing them. Even though neither of them said aloud Leanne was Cole's sister, anyone with a brain might figure it out based on their conversation.

"Maybe we should both shut our traps."

"Probably."

Motion near the doorway to the casino drew Cole's attention. John Young entered the restaurant with as much life and humor as his daughter and wife. His head of blond curls hadn't thinned one bit in his age. The man rivaled Cole himself in height, matching what Tom said their now deceased oldest son George had reached.

Rather than approach the boisterous group of grandchildren, John headed to their table. "Gentlemen."

"John. You're not joining that rowdy lot?" Cole nodded to the table where Eunice and Jane still held the children in some measure of control.

"Aren't you?" John raised his hand to the waitress to request his own coffee.

"They're speaking to you. Jane hasn't had two words for me that weren't absolutely necessary in three days. Going over there I'd be little more than something for Clara to climb on."

John laughed brightly. "Isn't that reason enough?"

"Normally, yeah. I spent all yesterday with Clara abusing me so's Jane could work the floor. With the brothel opening, we need more help."

"You need a governess." Tom leaned forward. "It was fine when it was the six of you, but with adding Jay and Willow, Jane's got more than she can handle. She's too proud to agree, though. Even if you are flush enough."

"A governess?" Cole turned his attention back to the group. "You might not be far off. Them two new strays still won't be fit to attend school in town come fall. They came to us with no learning like school."

"I'll mention it to Eunice. Maybe Jane will listen to her." John frowned slightly. "Though I doubt it."

"Jane thinks she can handle near everything. Problem is it leaves her little time. That woman is always going." Cole dismissed his earlier thoughts of another kid. She'd never agree, busy as they were.

"Mr. Karlson." Jane's sharp tone cut through the restaurant. She rose, frustration creasing her face into stern lines. "What have you done?"

Cole turned to see what had riled her up and found their new brothel manager standing at the door. A bloodied lip and black eye, with blood dripped on the rough cotton of his shirt, made a sight to see.

Wil smirked Jane's way, apparently none the worse for wear. "Had a scuffle at the poker game over at Tully's. What of it?"

"I hope this isn't the appearance you plan on keeping when you are in charge of our place." She crossed to the man, hands on her hips.

John and Tommy glanced Cole's way as the pair got into it. Hard to believe that just the night before Jane had joined Wil, Tom, and Cole himself in a late night round of poker. Jane still couldn't get a grasp of the game and had lost spectacularly. Still, she'd laughed and joked with Wil over her poor skills. The man hadn't been anything like the ruffian he seemed to be, and neither had him and Jane had a cross word to say about each other.

At the moment they were head-to-head until Wil stormed off down the hall, Jane hot on his heels. Cole rose to follow the spectacle, Jane's frustrated bark of scolding carried back to him.

He finally caught up to them behind the door to the back stairs used by staff to get to their rooms. All of Jane's anger had disappeared, a note of concern pursing her brow. "You really should go see Charles, Wil. Get a stitch in that lip before it bleeds more."

"I've had worse, Janey. Nothing a little whiskey and a woman won't fix." Wil touched the lip. "That Mac fella thought he'd test me by cheating a hand. I'm no gull and didn't stand for it. Wouldn't let no one else see that I would, neither."

"Mac's a great lover of fighting," Jane sighed. "Probably rose to the challenge in no time flat. Unfortunately he's also got a mean pair of fists."

"I'm not the only one with a fat lip." Wil winked at her, grinning broadly enough to make his lip bleed again. "In the end I flattened him, not the other way around."

"You flattened Mac?" Cole couldn't deny he was impressed. Graham, and even Cole himself, struggled to get the bear of a man under control sometimes.

"I did." Wil nodded to Jane. "Just doing as I told you I would. If I'm gonna be in charge of that brothel, them mucks about town gotta know I don't take no guff. This won't be my last black eye. Ain't no worries here."

"Except the lack of a woman. Shall I ask Leanne to send another down? With the dance tonight, she may not have a spare." Jane had stepped closer to Cole. Her skirts brushed his legs in her proximity. It made him want to draw her close.

"Forgot about that. Nah. I'll make due with the whiskey." Wil nodded to them both before climbing the steps.

"If you're fine with it, why you yelling at him?"

"Appearances, Cole. You ought to know well enough. You were worried about them for much of our relationship early on." She turned to face him finally, her eyes flashing fire. "More worried about maintaining your reputation and forgetting your past than letting me in."

"Jane," Cole wanted to argue her accurate assessment, but she simply waved him off. "Jane. Come on. It's been days."

She brushed past him and out the door, her rapid pace leaving him and his blasted crutch well in the dust.

"Damn it." Cole moved down the hall quick as he could again. When he got to the restaurant, she wasn't back at the table with the children. John now had Clara clamoring over him, and Tom had a more sedate Colton in his lap. Eunice had the others.

Sally's attention fell on him briefly. She nodded toward the porch before turning back to Jay's vibrant conversation.

Cole found Jane on the porch, leaning on the railing with one arm. In the other she held her watch. She snapped it shut and dropped it into her reticule. He drew closer, relieved she didn't run away. It wouldn't be long now and they could make up real nice.

He leaned close enough to let his breath brush along her ear. "You're beautiful when you're with the kids. Ain't no finer woman around."

Delicate pink lit her cheeks, which twitched like she fought a smile.

"Always made me proud to be with you, but even more since we got them kids. I love watching you with them."

The blush deepened, and inch by inch she straightened her spine. For several long breaths she remained still. Even as he slid a finger down her arm.

"I've been missing you, and our bed. And you in our bed with me." For the first time in days, she didn't slap his hand when it wrapped around her waist slow as molasses.

Delicate fingers brushed along his cock, then cupped him firmly.

He groaned low, dropping his forehead to the top of her head.

Without warning the strong hold became a grip tight enough to erase his pleasure. Pain flashed through him fast enough to blind him briefly. She was gone just as quick.

By the time he got a hold of his senses enough to think to retaliate, she was on Kat's porch. He shouted across the street, "You're gonna pay for that, woman!"

She spun right before the door to face him. A triumphant grin on her features. "You'll have to catch me first. You aren't getting anywhere with that bum leg."

"Just you wait."

"Seems you're the one waiting." With a flash of petticoat, she rushed into Kat's.

Cole spoke under his breath toward the door she'd disappeared behind, "No, you wait. I'll get you back. Tonight. I know just the trick."

*I only desire sincere retaliations with
the worthiest of my acquaintance,
that they may give me an opportunity
once in a year to speak the truth.
—Henry David Thoreau*

Jane raced into the room and shut the door behind her. Her skin was flush with tingles after her brief encounter with Cole on the porch. The man was bound and determined to get back in her good graces. Using words as well as touch. Yes, she was ready to end the standoff, but not until after the dance as she'd promised herself.

She leaned against the door with a heavy sigh. "Thank goodness he can't climb stairs yet."

Both Kat and Leanne stopped rifling through the pile of fabric to stare at Jane. Leanne shook off the surprise first. "Losing your resolve?"

"I lost it two hours ago, but I'm determined to make him suffer all the way through the dance. I intend to have fun, not mollycoddle a grumpy man." Jane blew out a breath heavy enough to make the fringe of loose curls around her face fly into the air. "Thank heavens the preparations for the dance tonight gave me the perfect excuse to run away. Why? Who bet what this time?"

"I already lost. I said you'd cave last night." Leanne chuckled. "I thought you'd feel bad enough about his injury and that he'd actually attended church would be enough to make you cave. Whether it be because of sympathy, gratitude, or simple lust."

Jane smirked. "Not a chance. How much did you lose?"

"I'm out two dollars. I would have put in more, but I wasn't as sure about my bet as Kat."

"I've got five whole dollars on the dance tonight, and he caves." Kat fluffed her hair. "I have faith he'll figure out how to cave even though he isn't in the wrong this time."

"Five dollars? You're really certain about yourself." Jane crossed the room to the pile of clothes the pair had been rifling through. Long ago some of their friends had taken to betting on their worst fights over how quickly they'd make up. It wasn't anything new, and didn't bother her in the least. "Winning once nearly three years ago should not engender a confident bet."

"No, but you weren't really angry with what he did, mostly scared. I knew you wouldn't lat a full week like your brother did." Kat pulled free the grand bustle Jane had ordered from Denver.

"Which brother?" Jane took the bustle. It had a few wrinkles, but nothing she needed to use the iron warming on the stove for.

"Michael." Kat paused, the lace end of a petticoat in her hand. "Which, to be honest, is very odd for him. He can usually read your mood."

"He's been out of sorts lately." Leanne pulled an overskirt off the pile. "Oh, this one is mine. How did these get so disorganized?"

"Because you and I went through three dresses a piece before we settled on what to wear, and left the destruction piled in poor Katherine's spare room. Days like these I almost envy her constant use of trousers." Jane extracted what proved to be Kat's trousers for the evening. The sleek black silken fabric shimmered in the sunlight. "These are lovely."

"Tonight will be the closest to a skirt I think either of you has ever seen me wear." Kat held the trousers aloft. "I need to iron these."

Jane dove back into the pile of clothes to find the rest of her chosen outfit. Soon as it was gathered, she examined each piece to see if it needed ironing.

"I can't imagine what would have Michael out of sorts." Kat handed the iron to Jane to take her turn. "Truth be told, I don't see him as much as I used to. For that matter, I don't see Daisy much, either. She's been out of sorts herself."

"I noticed." Jane smoothed the wrinkles in her skirt as she ironed. "You know, when Charles set about purchasing the clinic from Michael last year he offered Daisy the opportunity to buy half. She turned him down."

Leanne paused with only one leg extracted from her skirts. "What? Why in heavens would she do that? It was her clinic first, wasn't it?"

"It was. Charles was merely a guest when he first arrived, helping Daisy with my—um, issues—primarily."

Kat snorted aloud. "Issues. Is that what we're calling being hunted by an insane man across the country? Mentally tortured, not to mention hanged?"

Jane stuck her tongue out at her friend. "I was hanged months before I even met Charles. Don't overexaggerate."

"But all of it is true and factual, even if my timeline is off." Kat flipped the bustle pad she'd tied over her trousers at Jane. "Either way, it was Daisy's. She'd gotten rather confident again back then, even though she still wore her whore's clothes."

"To this day she keeps the whore name. Heaven knows why. Caroline is a perfectly acceptable name, and she is no longer a whore." Jane snapped her skirt off the ironing board.

"What is it?" Kat's attention had turned to Leanne.

"What is what?" Jane shifted her gaze between them. "What did I miss?"

Leanne lowered her hand from her mouth, her gaze dropping to examine the length of fabric of her overskirt. "It's nothing."

"You gasped at what Jane said. Why? Do you not think Caroline is an acceptable name?" Kat's brow furrowed. "No. That would be a silly thing to gasp over."

"I didn't gasp. I inhaled." Leanne moved to the ironing board herself, back to them.

Jane picked up her grand bustle, frowning at the contraption. Though she loved what it did for the appearance of her gowns, the device with all its hoops and tapes was most cumbersome for daily activity. Most days she made do with a separate cage bustle and petticoats. When Leanne remained silent, Jane lifted her gaze to study her sister-in-law. "Leanne? If it was nothing, why are you hiding from us?"

"I'm not. Because it's nothing to tell. It couldn't be true, it's simply ridiculous." Leanne returned to her chair.

Kat perched on the edge of the bed near Leanne. Her eyes lit with mischievous curiosity. "Oh, now that is something, clearly. Do tell."

"Well." Leanne waited until Jane had situated herself in the bustle and taken a seat herself. "You remember you sent Daisy out to check on the health of the children."

"Of course." Jane waved off the obvious fact.

"While she was there, I also had her do a cursory exam on the whores." Leanne's brow pursed tighter. "I'd almost forgotten this because I brushed it off as silliness. I still believe it is nothing more than an inaccurate judgement."

"Leanne." Jane set her hand on the woman's. "Out with it."

"While she was examining Enid, Flo made a comment I believe Daisy overheard. She said Daisy was a whore."

Kat released a small guffaw. "Well, she *was*. She hasn't been for some time."

"That's what I said." Leanne leaned closer. "Then Flo said whores know whores, and Daisy was one, and I wasn't though I pretended to be."

"Oh my." Jane shook her head. The notion was ridiculous. Rumors around this town flew far too fast for such a fact to be true. Besides, Daisy had been courting Michael for nigh on two years. If she'd heard it, Daisy was likely to be offended. "You said Daisy overheard?"

"I can't be certain, but she kept to herself the rest of the trip, even refusing to join us during the trip home." Leanne shook her head. "Since then we've been so busy with preparations for all of the events this summer I clean forgot about it myself."

"Daisy hasn't joined us in any of the planning, though she's been invited." Kat pulled her shimmering satin bodice over her arms. "Honestly, she's been scarce at our weekly teas for months come to think of it."

Jane couldn't deny the truth of the statement. She dropped her petticoats over her head more on instinct than any attention. The more she thought on it, the more she could think back to when Daisy's mood toward others had changed. "The epidemic."

Both of the other women stopped their motion to eye Jane for her seemingly random statement. Kat's brow rose. "There hasn't been an epidemic in a year."

"I'm aware, but if I truly put thought to it, I'd say Daisy slowed her attendance to the teas after the epidemic was over." Jane fastened her petticoats in place. "I know having to live through another epidemic like the one that killed her husband must have been difficult."

"Because our population has grown so, her and Charlie lost many more lives this time, too." Kat sighed. "I didn't even think of such a thing. Do you think we should make it a point to check on her to be certain she's well? Perhaps that is her distraction."

"It well could be. We should, and will." Jane returned to dressing herself as it would take far more time, and Kat was already near done.

"Let's move onto a more delicious subject now that's settled." Leanne hopped excitedly, then spun to flare the bunched skirt she'd dropped over her head. "Such as that delectable specimen of a gentleman you've been hiding away in St. Louis."

"My, oh my, yes." Jane winked at her friend in the mirror. "Dear Sally is all aflutter over the handsome and incredibly charming Mr. Warner."

"Sally? But, what of Arthur?" Kat abandoned her fight with her curls to turn right around in her chair. "They've been courting for ages."

"Yes they have. Sally finds him good and kind and the right sort of man she is supposed to look forward to a life with." Jane slipped the length of fabric that comprised her overskirt over her shoulders. The icy blue satin flat panel settled into place at her front with two flaps that smoothed across the sides of her skirt to the voluminous poufs of fabric at her back that cascaded into the train. "That does not preclude a young woman from enjoying the flirtations of a charming man. That girl hasn't been charmed enough, she's been too afraid of doing wrong."

"Oh, that fabric. You'll match your man well tonight." Leanne's fingers danced along the silver threads scrolling along the edges of the fabric.

"Are you suggesting Sally wishes to part from Arthur?" Kat turned her attention back to her curls. "They went walking yesterday."

"I don't know what that girl wants. Every time we speak I feel as though she's calculating what the proper answers are." Jane scooped her bodice off the settee. "You're changing the subject, Katherine. About Patrick."

Kat turned to face them. "I've been bothering Patrick to come out for a visit for years. There is nothing more to tell."

Jane caught a twitch in her friend's eyebrow, and noted she turned her gaze away. "Liar. There is something to tell."

"Tell us." Leanne flounced on the floor in front of Kat. "We have plenty of time for a story. Tell us one, Kitty."

Kat chuckled softly, bopping Leanne on the head with the bristles of her brush. "It's not a story, per se. It's more of…a favor."

"He told me Cindy convinced him to come. That wasn't the truth, was it?" Jane moved her chair closer to Kat's side. "What is it you used to convince him to come all the way to our nothing little town for?"

"I told him I had a request I couldn't make via telegram, nor a letter. Such a thing would take far too long to get him in time for our celebrations. Him joining us for the celebrations would be reason enough." Kat's cheeks reddened. "I cannot say the reasons why, it would embarrass Norman."

"Who on earth are we going to tell?" Leanne set her hands on Kat's knees. "You know our secrets stay among us."

"I do, but I also know…" Kat let out a deep sigh. "Oh, Jane. You know—we've been trying for so long. Since before the wedding, really. Before Norman's age was too advanced, before Cindy would be too old to appreciate it, or even Lizzie now."

"*Oh.*" Jane squeezed Kat's hand as the realization dawned on her. Kat had wanted to expand their family. Jane alone knew the reason they'd hesitated to adopt Lizzie in the first place. She glanced at Leanne. "Kat and Norman second-guessed adopting Lizzie, fearing the adjustment to her and a baby would be too much should Kat become pregnant as they'd hoped."

"Pregnancy? Oh, dear. Such a thing didn't happen." Leanne rested her head on Kat's knee. "You poor dear. Four years is a long time to hope for a baby that never comes."

Kat swiped a tear from her cheek. "I've had Charlie check me thoroughly and he can see no fault. There is no cause for me to be barren, especially seeing as I've already had one child."

"Norman never had any children with Betsy, did he?" Jane was as familiar with Kat and Norman's story as her own and didn't need the confirmation, but wished to be gentle in its delivery to Leanne.

"Not a one, though they tried as well. Betsy wanted lots of children, he said." Kat fiddled with the brush in her hands. "Charlie was very delicate in suggesting the issue might be with Norman, because we all know the fault could not possibly lie with a man."

Leanne scoffed. "There is plenty wrong in the world of men that is all the fault of men. The bringing of a child is no exception, it can be their problem as well as ours."

"Ah yes, but we daren't suggest such a thing in proper company." Jane shook her head at the absurdity. "Despite our dear Katherine joining the Town Council, and ourselves women of business and intelligence, we must face that it is quite as much a man's world as it has ever been."

"Far too true." Leanne lifted her head to rest her chin on Katherine's knee. "Now that we've been properly distracted from the point, where were you leading us, dear Kat?"

Kat's attention focused on the curtained window, a few silent tears slid down her cheeks.

In the absence of an answer, Jane spoke quietly, "She is leading us to the inevitable conclusion. If the fault does indeed lie with Norman, there is but one way to resolve the matter."

"Patrick is a good man, and a dearer friend." Kat cleared her throat. "I don't even know he would agree to such a task. I haven't had the time, nor the courage, to ask."

Jane put an arm around Kat in a gesture of support. "Wat of another adoption?"

"I want to bring life again. Though I might wear trousers and play politics, I am still a woman. I am a mother, and I want to be one again, properly."

"Feeling the life inside you is quite a wonderful, and unique feeling." Jane brushed Kat's curls away from her face, swiping a few tears from her cheeks along the way. "I think you needn't worry about what Patrick will say. He adores you, has for much of your long time together as lovers, and then as friends and as the little family-of-sorts you became."

"We left the lovers portion well in the past, and were content to do so." Kat sniffled, fiddling with the kerchief Leanne had handed her. "More so when I went and married the man I love."

"What does Norman think of such a thing?" Leanne seemed hesitant to ask.

"He will not condemn me, but he wishes to not know it is happening, if it comes to that." Kat blew out a breath. "We've discussed it ad nauseum to the point neither of us can bear to broach the subject again. When I asked if I were to invite Patrick to town again, with much intent, Norman agreed."

"Enough with the pretty words." Leanne popped onto her knees. "They skirt the issue and do not declare the truth. Cole taught me that much."

"I asked him if I should invite Patrick to the celebration so we might discuss him siring a child with me. Norman agreed, but made me send the telegram. As if I hadn't sent every telegram to Patrick for years." Kat dabbed at her tears. "He is always gruff, but in the quiet times, when it is us and us alone, he desires a child as much as I do. If he knows not when it happens, he can pretend it is his."

"It will be his." Jane kissed Kat on the cheek, then began to brush aside her friend's tears. "You and Patrick began your relationship in a business deal, and now you'll return to one. Your friendship will not be harmed by this any more than it was in the past."

"I hope you're right." Kat glanced behind her. "Oh, I do look a fright."

"We all do. There isn't much time before the dance. Let's get ourselves gussied up for those cantankerous men so they can complain that we dance with other men." Jane gave Kat the tightest hug she could muster. "As for you. You are one of my dearest friends, and no matter what you decide, Leanne and I are right behind you."

"Every step of the way," Leanne concurred.

"Thank you. I dare say I thought this would be too much, even for the two of you." Kat smiled.

"Never. I've been the worst, this is nothing at all."

Think of the magic of that foot, comparatively small, upon which your whole weight rests. It's a miracle, and the dance... is a celebration of that miracle.
-Martha Washington

Cole walked awkwardly between Norman and Tom. With his crutch on his good side, Tom on his left, and Norman grumbling complaints whenever the crutch hit him on accident. "Aren't we supposed to be going to this dance with our women? How'd I get stuck with your ugly mugs?"

"Well, your woman is still vexed with you," Tom pointed out.

"Nah. She was ready to cave a few hours back. Ain't been able to get a hold of her since."

"She was with Kat and Leanne at my place." Norman jerked his thumb back to the building. "Damn women were cackling in that room for over two hours before they headed out to set up for the dance. Think I heard one of them crying once. Don't know what those women get on about."

"Do we really want to know?" Tom chuckled low. "I'm more than happy to not know what Leanne gets on about when she's with your women. So long as I get a happy and enthusiastic bedding and conversation, I'm happy."

"Watch it," Cole muttered under his breath. For the second time that day the conversation had taken a turn toward Tom and Leanne's recent closeness. He still didn't want to hear about it any more than he had a few hours before.

"Given what I've caught you and my sister doing, you can shut your hole." Tom elbowed him in the ribs. He raised his voice so Norman could hear. "What about you?"

"I gotta deal with them all in my house at all hours. You don't." Norman grumped.

"That's because of the kids, and the Inn." Cole paused his stride to adjust the crutch under his arm. It had been three days already and he was sick as hell of not being able to move about normally. "Easier to meet in your place with the extra rooms than the crowded casino, restaurant, or apartment."

"Your apartment wouldn't be so crowded if you would stop taking in children." Tommy clapped a hand on his shoulder. "Any more and you're going to kick me outta place to make room for them. Then you can put an orphanage sign on your back door. Start a new business."

Cole shoved his brother heartily. "We aren't kicking you out, and we aren't an orphanage."

"Coulda fooled me," muttered Norman.

"No more," Cole reasserted.

"I'll believe it when I see it." Tommy smirked. "In our family once you start, you can't stop. Ma and Pa had seven, Ma's got nine brothers and sisters."

"I made Jane promise no more strays or babies." Some days Cole still couldn't believe they had what they did. Taking in Alma had been necessity. So had Sally, to be honest. The new wards seemed a necessity to Jane. Then there was their kids together. The twins. Not to mention Cindy. He had kids—alive and healthy when Lydia hadn't made it to a year old.

Maybe his thoughts earlier hadn't been wrong. Maybe having kids meant he wasn't cursed. Maybe one more wouldn't hurt. Wait. What was he saying?

"Babies, hmph." Norman took on ahead of them a bit.

Cole moved to catch up. "What's the matter, Norman? Too old for babies?"

"Too old for lots of things, I suspect." Tom had come in line easily. "The question is, do he and Kat want more? By that I mean, does Kat? I'll bet you Jane does, even if she promised."

"Shut your mouth. That isn't true. We're good the way we are." He almost meant it that time, Cole was happy to realize.

They crossed the train tracks, now close enough to the meadow to see the dance floor clear. All three seemed to be of the same mind as they all slowed to a stop. On the platform built for the dance, Jane stood with her two friends. Her creamy neck, revealed by an enticingly low neckline, glowed in the light from the setting sun.

Her hair twisted in elaborate swirls over her head, laced through with shimmering silver ribbons. While he stared helplessly entranced, she had yet to spot him. She moved about the floor to give orders to those helping with the final touches. Graham stood by tuning his banjo. Something he said set Jane laughing brightly.

The noise carried across the clearing and set his nerves alight. Not to mention the way she moved, her smile, the curve of her breasts, the swell of her hips. His breath stopped for several seconds while he took her in. He let out the breath. "Damn."

"I know," Tommy agreed, though probably not about the same thing.

"I ain't seen Kat in a skirt since I don't know when," Norman said from beside him.

Cole hadn't noticed Kat wore a proper dress, and he didn't bother to look yet. He was too busy admiring the way Jane's dress flattered her tiny waist.

Someone brushed past him, laughter hitting his ears to stir him out of his reverie. Sally paused a few feet ahead. When she turned to face them, laughter still brightened her features. She herself showed her stunning similarity to Jane, though not at all related, with her own elaborate gown and updo. "By the way, Pa."

"Hm?" Cole's attention had already wandered back to Jane. At the word *Pa* he focused on the young woman. "What, Sally?"

"You've got a bit of drool. Just there. You too, Tommy." She pointed to the corner of her mouth, then spun and ran off. Her laughter carried back to them on the cooling dusk air.

"That girl is gonna cause someone such trouble. She takes too much after Jane." Cole tried to be grumpy about it but couldn't stop his grin.

"You love the trouble Jane causes you, so don't start." Tom laughed outright. "Let's get to it. Not much time before everyone starts arriving."

Together the three men made their way to the platform. By the time they got onto the dance floor Jane's cheerfulness had faded. Instead, she was rather in a tizzy.

"Well, where is he?" She paced the length of the platform. Her gaze drifted toward town, then she spun to pace again. "He's running well behind."

Cole caught her wrist when she walked past him. "Jane?"

"Hello." She leaned in as if to kiss him. Then suddenly seemed to remember her temper in time to pause an inch away. "You don't play fair, Mr. Mitchell. You're using my distraction against me."

"There's plenty I'd like against you."

"Oh, you stop." She sMaced his chest, but a pleasant flush lit her cheeks.

He leaned closer, not daring to try for a kiss. "You usually want me to not stop."

"Cole Mitchell, don't."

Her proximity for the first time in days, and the fact she had yet to pull her hand free made it impossible to stop. "You aren't walking away."

Her lips pursed in frustration. "I have to prepare for the dance, and we are short a harmonica player. I haven't time for your games."

"Oh, what I got for you isn't a game." He tugged her flush against him, but still didn't capture the pleasingly plump pink lips. Even when they parted in a delicate 'O' for him. "What do you say to us trying for another kid?"

"What do I—what did you say?" She stepped free of his hold, her eyes wide. The shock shuttered into a stern pout. "You stop that. That isn't funny. I must go see about our missing Mr. Finnigan. We need a mouth harp."

"No one'll notice it isn't there." He frowned when she turned her back on him. "And I wasn't kidding."

"You're not funny." She raced across the platform far too fast for him to follow. At the band she paused dead, then turned slow as molasses to look him dead on. A flush filled her cheeks before she turned away.

Cole made his way to the bench at the edge of the platform. She might not be talking nice, but she was talking. For the moment he'd content himself with that—and the more frequent looks his direction.

Jane huddled with Kat and Norman speaking emphatically. Norman shook his head to her and edged away. Kat nodded to Jane before she followed her husband several feet away.

Once again Jane cast a wary glance his way. Too far now for him to get a good read on what she was thinking, he remained content in the fact she bothered to look at all.

Hopefully by the end of the fool dance he'd have his wife back frustrating him so much he'd regret saying anything about having another kid.

Norman broke free from Kat to storm toward Cole. He dropped onto the bench. "Damn women."

"What now?" Cole glanced at the older man.

"Tryin' to get me to play the mouth harp. I ain't doing it."

"You'll do it because Kat asked ya. Why keep fighting?"

"You're still fighting."

"Not my choice. That's Jane's." Cole nudged him. "What harm'll it do?"

Tommy approached. "Got a deal for you, Norman. You play part of the night, I'll play part. Might even be able to convince Charlie to step in. He's pretty good on a banjo too, so we might have him spell Graham a bit, too."

Norman heaved a sigh. "Fine. If Chuck shows up, I'm done."

"Good man." Tommy hauled Norman to his feet. He urged the older man toward the band, then turned back to Cole. "What did you say to my sister? She's all flustered."

"None of your business. But I think it worked."

"Should I be worried?"

"It's me and Jane."

"That's always something to worry about." Tom let out a belly laugh that carried through the meadow on his way back to the band.

Mike flopped into the seat beside Cole. Rather than any form of greeting, he glared across the dance floor.

"Hello to you, too." Cole scanned the crowd filtering onto the dance floor. The noise level rose incrementally. A glance behind him showed some folks lingering in the meadow for lemonade or treats.

"Yeah," Mike grumbled.

Cole raised a brow at Jane's brother, but the man remained silent for several long minutes.

Mike's knee bounced so hard his heel tapped the boards in an impatient cadence. "Jane did a good job."

"Always does."

Mike grunted his agreement.

Rather than try to engage the man further, he searched through the crowd again for Jane. He caught her staring and offered a wicked grin. She huffed so hard her shoulders moved before she stalked away. He'd really thrown her for a loop.

"Where's the children?"

"Eunice has the twins and Jay and Willow. I'd wager to bet Jesse is around here somewhere, probably after the pies."

Mike didn't say anything to that, just kept glaring at the men and women now dancing around the platform.

After several minutes of silence, save for the band and Mike's incessant heel tapping, Cole noticed someone missing from the crowd. "Where's Daisy?"

"Damned if I know. She said she isn't coming."

"Ah."

"Don't get smart with me." The man bristled, his hands clenched into fists.

"Last thing I am is smart, Mike."

"You've got that straight." Mike stormed away without another word.

"What did you do to him?" Jane stood before him, cutting off his chance to wonder himself what he'd done. Though she'd approached, she remained just far enough to be out of reach. Smart woman. He'd grab her the second he had a chance, and she knew it. Her toe tapped impatiently on the platform. "Well?"

"Nothing."

"Cole."

"Really. All I did was ask where Daisy was." He held his hands aloft in surrender. "I swear. I didn't do nothing."

"Oh. Well. Hm." Her gaze wandered to locate her brother. "More oddness."

"More? What else?"

"Oh, nothing. Never you mind. Lillian has just arrived, I must go."

Cole groaned when she took off again. One of these times she would stop long enough for him to grab her. It was time for the ridiculous argument to end. She knew it, he knew it.

If only his damn foot wasn't imprisoned in plaster. It was a challenge he'd have to overcome.

By the end of the night, he'd solve it. If had to free his own foot to do it.

*We should consider every day lost on which
we have not danced at least once.
And we should call every truth false which
was not accompanied by at least one laugh.
—Friedrich Nietzsche*

Jane searched the dance platform for Michael. She found him sulking near the railing. She approached with her hand extended. "Dance with me. You get first dance since Cole is such a mudsill."

"Don't care to. I came to support you, nothing else. I'm not in the mood to dance." Michael stared into the darkening tree line surrounding the meadow. He ignored her hand completely.

"No. That isn't how this works." Jane slapped her hand into his. "You are dancing."

"Stop."

"Who cares if Daisy is here or not?" Jane held on through his attempts to free his hand. "You're apparently going through some trouble with her, though you haven't further explained in recent days. This doesn't mean you must be miserable, dear one."

The use of Clara's old endearment she'd used in so many of her letters pulled Michael's attention to her. For a moment pain and loss pulled his features into distressed lines. He wiped them away fast in a snarl. "I'll be whatever the hell I want to be."

"Oh, what a hypocrite you are Michael."

"Excuse me?"

"It was all well and good for you to yell at me constantly for handling things poorly with Cole. Then to throw in my face all the ways I might do better. To tell me how to act, and to just walk away from him when he was at his worst. When it's you, God forbid anyone say a word."

"That isn't—"

"You're being an absolute jerk to the one person you always said you could tell anything, and she to you. Why? Because the woman you're courting didn't come to a dance?"

"Because she…"

"Michael?" Jane kept his hand clasped in hers. "Whatever it is, perhaps I can help."

"You are not the epitome of a perfect relationship."

She hauled him to his feet at the first hint of a smile. "To be fair, the façade we put forward is not what is truly us. You know that quite well"

"I'll accept that argument." Michael sighed as she got him into the twirling crowd of dancers. "I'm not much in the mood for this. I do mean you, my annoying sister."

"What a shame. You are quite stuck with me for this dance at least. Perhaps after you'll be the kind soul that asks Cora. That dear woman needs to dance. Kelly died years ago."

His brow puckered and he gave her a sharp look. "You aren't trying to forge something else when I'm still in—something—with Daisy?"

"Heavens, no. I meant as an honest gesture of friendship. I want Cora to remember what fun it was to participate in a dance in some other way than providing food." Jane paused as she was spun away from him, then back. "As for Daisy, did she give a reason for not coming?"

"Probably because she turned down my proposal."

Jane stopped so fast Michael stomped on her foot. Someone bumped into her, sending both her and Michael stumbling to the side. She grabbed his hand to drag him away from the circle of dancers. She took him all the way off the platform into the meadow. "What?"

"I asked her to marry me."

"Oh dear. Not because of what I said, I hope? I was merely teasing at the train."

"No. We've been courting almost two years. I thought maybe her mood of late was because I'd waited too long to ask. I just—I wanted her to be—I don't know. She took so long to shed the whore and come into her own."

"Then the epidemic happened, and Charles bought the clinic."

"He wanted her to buy it, too. She said no."

"I'm aware." Jane sighed, clasping his hands close. "Did she give a reason for her refusal?"

"Said she didn't want marriage. Then distracted me from discussion." Even in the dim light of the lanterns she could see the ruddy hue flushing his cheeks.

"Distracted you?" Jane coughed lightly. "Ah, yes. A woman's powerful weapon, the man's near constant desire for sex."

"Jane."

"It's true. You know it, too."

"We used to court, Jane. I mean truly court." Michael pulled a hand free to rake through his hair. "I'm not the rake your man is, or was, or—whatever. I've wanted to marry her for some time. The past few months there's been a lot of—distraction."

"Wait. The past few months?"

"I wanted her to know that I wasn't interested because she was once a whore. That's what I mean—we were truly courting."

"Kissing, maybe heavy petting, but no sex."

"Jane." He cut her a glare. "Point is, ever since we first went to bed, I feel like I don't know her anymore. I don't know, maybe even longer than that."

"You started screwing around, which should have made things more intimate, but instead pushed you further apart."

He rubbed his hand over his face, a grunt of frustration leaving him. "Yes."

"You poor thing." Jane laced her hand with his to lead him back to the floor. "Before I send you off to forget about things and remember what a true conversation with real people is like, I want you to think on something."

"What's that?"

"You aren't the only soul that's noticed a change in Daisy."

"I'm not."

"No. She's all but stopped coming to our weekly teas. I only see her if I must go to the clinic. Kat has noticed the same."

Mike frowned slightly. "I didn't know she'd stopped going to the tea. She always leaves her office at the hotel at the same time she always did, is gone for a few hours like usual, and comes back to work."

Jane knew Daisy worked odd days at Mike's hotel and health spa selling snake oil and dips in the mineral rich water to wealthy visitors. Though Jane didn't approve of such tactics, it certainly was a draw for his hotel. The fact she still left on Thursdays as if going to tea was news to her. "I can't explain that, I just know she hasn't been coming. I haven't seen her for the past month, though we've kept her seat open and a cup out for her."

"I don't know what to think."

"You don't need to right now. Tonight, I want you to enjoy company, friendship, and family. You can confront your relationship tomorrow."

"Tomorrow is Independence Day."

"True enough. Wednesday, then."

"If there's anything to confront."

"Worry about it Wednesday." Jane pulled him back onto the dance floor, then pushed him toward Cora. She grabbed Charlie's hand, tugging him away from his wife Millie for a dance. After that, she danced with each of her brothers in turn. Kat's father, Henry, took a turn. Then Jesse, and David even.

The entire time Cole's gaze burned into her. While she longed to head to his side and discuss his ridiculous suggestion that had unexpectedly given her a stir of excitement, another hand reached toward her before she could make her move.

Patrick graced her with a bright smile. "Might I have a turn, my lady?"

"You are a dangerous charmer, aren't you?" She took his hand willingly and hopped into the Romany polka taking place on the floor. "You must continue to have all the women of St. Louis in a tizzy over your scandalous ways."

"I've quite calmed in my age."

"Of course you have. A leopard cannot change its spots."

"Yet, they can. Kat changed hers, and you've changed yours."

"Not so much."

"Might I ask if you know why my darling friend beckoned me here so urgently?"

Jane used a small hop and turn in the dance to school her features. "I might."

"You wouldn't dare tell me, would you?"

"Why should I spill secrets that are not mine to share?" She grinned at him. "You two are dear friends, and once there is a moment of calm, she will tell you. She cannot help herself. I do believe she is closer to you than I."

"She was once, but no longer as I live so far and have failed to visit for several years."

"She visited you."

"Not near often enough." The dance concluded, he kissed the back of her hand. "Would you be upset if I asked your lovely daughter for the next dance?"

"Not at all, but please be kind. Your charms might give a child starved for such attentions too much excitement before she is quite done being the good, proper ward she believes I wish her to be."

"You would rather she become a wicked creature such as yourself, then?"

"I would rather she live a life she dares only dream of. Much like myself." She tipped her head, then turned to search for Cole, only to have another sight distract her once again.

At the very edge of the floor, Hammy stood against the rail. His hands twisted together in the lavender gloves he wore. The outfit was infinitely familiar, as he'd worn it the evening she took him to supper for caring so well for her after she'd been shot. Cole had once told her the reason he'd caved and apologized, leading to their first coupling, had been due to his witnessing her care for the old man during their meal.

She cast her gaze toward Cole, who was taking in the same sight she had. When he turned to face her, his lips twisted in a smirk. He nodded once.

She moved toward Hammy. In front of him, she dipped into a deep curtsy. "Mr. Hamm. It would give me the greatest pleasure of my evening if you'd be so kind as to join me in a dance."

"Aw gee, Lady Jane." Hammy blushed, brushing gloved hands over his unruly hair. "Ya don't gotta be so formal."

"But you are dressed every bit the gentleman tonight, sir." Jane gazed up from her continued curtsy. "Would you honor me with a dance? I believe we can expect a polka next."

"I'd be much obliged." Hammy held out his arm for Jane to take.

She did so, eagerly following him onto the floor for the polka. They dipped and spun, and this time she didn't doubt the feeling of a heavy stare the whole time. She an inkling

Cole was as ready, if not more, for her to make time for them to apologize as proper as they might in public.

Still, she didn't allow her attention to waver once from the old man that eagerly spun her haphazardly through the couples on the floor. When the dance finished, Leanne swooped him away in another round.

Jane took the opportunity to catch her breath. On the opposite side of the platform, she could only catch glimpses of Cole as he sat, his boot tapping in time to the music. He caught her gaze, holding it strong as the dancers moved between them.

She stepped forward to cross the platform quick as possible through the midst of enthusiastic dancers. Finally in front him, she took his outstretched hand. Not a whisper of protest slipped free as he yanked her into his lap.

The kiss he gave her was filled with such heat she was breathless in moments. Her fingers laced into his hair, holding him close until they were both sated enough to separate.

"You have caused Katherine to win a good deal of money. She owes you a drink for the favor." Jane ran her finger along his jawline.

"How's that?"

"She bet that we would end our argument tonight at the dance, and you'd cave."

"Wait." He pulled his forehead from hers, brow furrowed. "How did I cave?"

"You asked me to have another child with you, of course." She raised a brow. "What a ridiculous notion to get my attention."

"What if I meant it?"

"I'd think you insane. We have eight children combined together."

"Not a one of them was on purpose, you know." He smirked. "Ever wonder what it would be like to have a kid because we meant to do it?"

"I don't think we'd know what to do with ourselves. Such planning." She slipped off his leg onto the bench. Through the smirk she caught the intensity of his gaze. The man couldn't be doing anything but gaining her attention, could he? "You aren't serious? You're the one that made me promise no more children."

"I'm not keen on getting any other strays."

"Oh, you are insane." She flew to her feet, but he kept a hold of her hand. Rather than attempt to free herself, she tugged his hand gently. "Dance with me."

"Can't." He gestured to his foot. "Remember? That's why you're mad at me?"

"Get on your feet, rest the bad one on the bench." She tugged again on his hand. After a minute, he did as he'd been told.

His hand slipped around her waist the moment she stepped close. Their clasped hands twisted into a proper embrace for the waltz that had just begun. "You said I'm insae, but this is what's insane."

"Then it will work for us." She stepped with the music, swaying in his arms.

He moved with her best as he could in place until it almost seemed they were on the floor spinning among the crowd.

She dipped into a low curtsy before him. As she rose his deep, lustful gaze added to the heat of the dance in pleasant tingles along her flesh. "There'll be none of that here, Mr. Mitchell."

"What?"

"I know that look all too well. There is nothing easy about the hoops and tapes in this unruly grand bustle. No hiding in the dark making our apologies in public tonight."

"But hat's more fun, and you wanted all the scandal."

"Scandal in this outfit is near impossible and not at all comfortable."

"So long as I'm happy, right?"

"You rotten, inconsiderate—" Her protest cut off at his kiss. "Another child?"

"Why not?"

Worrying never did anyone any good.
-Proverb

Cole leaned against the post of the grandstand, his gaze not wavering from the sight before him. Jane led the games for the children and adults alike, from the three-legged race, to a sack race, and even a game of blind man's bluff.

Her dewy skin was flush with life as it had been the night before in bed. If he hadn't seen her do it often enough he'd wonder at how she managed to function and laugh when they'd stayed up so late wrapped in each other.

He caught her glance his way, the flush deepening under his watchful eye. They'd agreed to try for another kid and had begun straight away. Though he had moments of panic if it was the right choice, deep down he knew it was. In fact, the only thing keeping him in place right then was his blasted broken foot. The plaster made every day life too difficult. He was set to rip the blasted thing off and suffer in his boot.

The games were supposed to be led by the Reverend's Greene and Lyons, but due to Eli's injuries, Jane had taken up the charge. Which meant he'd be heading up the race the Inn was running, starting right at the grandstand he stood by. In about two hours he'd be starting the largest horse race the territory had seen. They had riders come in from as far as

Wyoming for a winning purse of five thousand dollars. For the upcoming statehood celebration, they planned to offer double the purse size.

The numbers made his head hurt, but as he was the one running the betting on the races as well as the race himself, he knew they'd recoup the purse, and even more. For both events. In August they expected riders from as far as Buffalo, and even one from Boston.

Unfortunately, Jane had hinted that her old friend Al Webb would be arriving in town for the race in August. The mere thought tensed him up right good. He shook off the tensions best he could when Jane looked his way again.

Cole offered her a nod, then scanned the crowd. Dozens of children dotted the meadow in the games, adults as well. Others lingered near the booths offering lemonade, pasties, pies, and candy. There was even one giving out ice cream.

One child seemed to missing from the games, much to Cole's surprise. Jesse's blond curls so like his Ma's weren't bouncing around the crowd. A quick search had him locating the lad walking with Lizzie, who held a bouquet of wildflowers. Though nearly twelve now, Jesse seemed to be closer to courting the pale-haired girl than Sally seemed with Arthur. Odd, considering Sally and Arthur had been courting for nearly two years.

He searched for their ward as well, locating her near the popcorn with Alma. No sign of Arthur around. Tom's comments about her needing the gumption returned to his mind. Seemed odd that the girl was more distant from her beau than Jesse to Lizzie.

Speaking of Tom, the man now made a blatantly pitiful attempt for his round of blind man's bluff. Cole knew Tom to be quite quick and nimble, but the man bumbled through the crowd like he hadn't a clue where the screaming children around him were.

Cole chuckled at the sight, but immediately his mind switched to wonder where Leanne was. By all accounts she'd planned to join the celebration early. Considering her hand in planning right along side Jane and the Daugherty women, it seemed odd she hadn't arrived yet.

A shout from across the meadow drew his attention to Kathy calling over the group of children for another activity. Jane fairly pouted that the game was over, but then her gaze fell on him again. Once again she smiled, a deepening pink to her cheeks.

She took a few steps toward him, but was diverted from her progress by Hammy. As always, Jane offered the man her full attention, allowing Cole's gaze to wander. Tom and Lillian were both helping Kathy set up the children for a ball toss game. He remembered hearing something about candy prizes.

When he turned back to Jane, her focus had drifted from Hammy to something behind him. He turned to find what had managed to draw her attention from Hammy to see Leanne trotting toward the meadow at a rapid clip.

None of the usual laughter and charm that drew attention to her wherever she went lit her features. Cole pushed off the grandstand to meet her.

Jane drew close to him. "Something's wrong."

He didn't deny her observation, for he'd seen the same. At her approach, he raised his hand to grab the bridle of the beast. "Leanne. We expected you hours ago."

"I know. I've been looking everywhere." Leanne alit from the saddle, allowing Cole to take the reins.

"Looking? For what?" A whisper of amusement flickered across Jane's features. "The party has been here all along."

"One of my girls." Leanne didn't even offer her usual smiles to Jane, for whom she always had a ready grin. "Emily. Is she here? This is the last place left to look."

"Did you check with Wil? He likes her, it seems." Jane remained close, her voice low despite their relative solitude.

Cole tied off the reins. "Maybe she found someone willing."

"My girls don't do anything outside of the brothel. I don't have many fierce rules, but that is key to being able to ensure their protection." Leanne's hands wrung in her skirts. "I had several at the dance last night, including Emily, to draw business. She never made it back to the brothel."

"I haven't seen her." Jane still turned to search the meadow as though she didn't know every face that had stepped foot into the party. Cole didn't even bother asking how she knew who Emily was. Cole himself couldn't place which whore it was, but he didn't doubt Jane knew.

Tom jogged close, a bright grin on his features. "Well hey, there. What's wrong?" The smile had faded quick as Tom had sized up the mood of the group.

"Emily is missing. She was at the dance last night." Leanne stood on tip toe to search the crowded meadow.

"I remember. She danced with a fair few men, including Patrick and Mike since they were stag last night. Several of your girls took their turns." Tom frowned, hands on his hips. "Would she entertain outside of the brothel?"

"Never. She was one of my best girls." Leanne bit her lip. "This isn't like her. She likes what she does, has never expressed any desire to leave."

"The money she makes, why would she except to start her own place?" Jane took a deep breath. "We should start looking. Cole, you can spare an hour to help before you have to really start wrangling the riders, can't you?"

"Sure do." Cole didn't hesitate. "Tom, where do we start?"

"We'll talk to some of the folks she was dancing with. Discreetly. Just see if they saw where she went when she left the dance. Leanne, I'm going to talk to your girls." Tom stepped closer to her, squeezing her arm. "I'll do all I can to find her. I'm sure she's not far."

"Thank you." Leanne set her hand on his, relief seeping into her features. "The girls like you, I'm sure they won't give you any trouble."

Tom pulled Leanne close, kissing her forehead. "We'll get it figured."

"Ma?" Sally approached, Alma on her heels. She looked between the four of them. "What is it? What's happened?"

Jane took one look at Alma and moved to gather the girl away from the group. She distracted Alma with bright chatter as they moved further away.

Cole appreciated her taking Alma away from the tension, but wondered at how she didn't just send Sally and Alma away together. He turned to Sally. "Leanne lost a whore."

"Lost?" Sally's brow pursed. "How do you lose a whore, exactly?"

"She never returned from the dance last night. At first, I thought maybe she went to gamble at the Inn and didn't think too much of it. When I arose this morning, Enid told me she'd never returned last night." Leanne released a shaky breath. "Tommy, Cole, can we start looking now?"

"You've been looking." Cole set a hand on her shoulder. "You're near frantic and won't be much good. Tom can get some help in the searching. You stay here, or come to the Inn and have a drink. We'll get her found."

"A drink. Yes, I suppose." Leanne closed her eyes as she took a deep breath. "I care about my girls. I don't like her being missing."

"I know you don't. I wouldn't like it much, either." Cole squeezed her shoulder.

Sally had turned to search over the meadow. "Which one is it, Leanne?"

"Emily."

"Oh, she's so sweet. Gets men all agog over her cherubic face." Sally turned back to the group. She opened her mouth to say something, then closed it, her brow furrowed.

"Sally?" Cole eyed her. "You know something?"

"No." She shook her head. "I just...I...."

Tom kept an arm around Leanne, but a calculating gaze on Sally. "Out with it. We gotta start looking. Your pa only has an hour before he has to get the racers set in place."

Sally startled under Tom's words. After she'd straightened her shoulders, her mouth opened again to speak, before she shut it. "I suppose I should take Alma so Ma can help?"

Tom's lips twisted in a grimace before he shook his head. "If that's what you want. Let's go, Cole. Get Leanne to the Inn, I'll head to the brothel. Tell Jane to gather the troops we can spare."

Cole waited for Tom to give Leanne a parting kiss before he took her by the elbow. He guided her to the Inn at as quick a pace as he could manage with his crutch, and she seemed too stunned to protest. "You got Tom on your side. No better way to get her found."

"I know. I'm just worried. She had her eye set on being a madam herself. I can't imagine she'd up and leave. She didn't take any of her things, and I have her money in the safe. She couldn't leave without that."

"Fair enough point." He led her to a seat at the bar, then poured her a whiskey. "I'll start asking around here. Brace up or you won't be any help."

Leanne nodded, lifting her drink to her lips.

Cole moved among the patrons of the casino, asking if they knew of, or had seen Emily. A few men admitted they knew the whore he spoke of, but none recalled seeing her after the dance. He hadn't expected much out of the search of the current scant level of patrons, but he'd wanted to give Leanne a chance to get her strength back.

By the time his circuit was complete, she seemed to have it, and Jane at her side. He approached the pair. "I'll take a look along Second Street and head back to the grandstand for the start of the race. I won't be much help for a few hours, sorry."

"You take care of the race. It's too big a purse to ignore the event. We'll manage. Michael and Nicholas are helping. David will be busy with the race as well. Wil is in the race, so he can't help, if he even would given—everything."

Cole knew Jane meant Wil's intention to set himself up a reputation around town. Though he was genial and friendly to Jane and himself, Wil had already earned a reputation as a fighter and one that didn't suffer fools. "With the race there'll be men scattered through the valley. We'll tell them to keep an eye out in case she got confused and lost."

"That isn't like her," Leanne asserted.

"Stumbling into a saloon near-death wasn't much like Clara either, but here I am. Sometimes things happen, and we have no control." Jane soothed Leanne. "Let's go over to Third Street and search again. Never you worry, we'll find Emily."

Cole nodded to Jane as she led the Madam out of the casino. He didn't dare voice it aloud, but he had a bad feeling about the situation.

Wild animals never kill for sport.
Man is the only one to whom torture and
death of his fellow creatures is
amusing in itself.
—James A. Froude

Jane slowed Tempest near the creek. Even far as she was from town, she could hear the cheers from the meadow as Cole read off the status of the racers making their way through the valley. Hammy dismounted nearby.

The dear man had demanded on joining her while she searched north of town. Mike had taken south, and Tom east, while Benjamin Daugherty had sent his foreman to search the area around the mines to the west.

Hammy had insisted that she needed accompaniment on the search for the whore as she was a woman, and it might be unsafe. She'd been loathed to argue that she'd survived much worse than a ride through the territory. After all, he'd been pleasant enough company talking about his early mining days while she kept an eye out for any sign of the missing whore.

"That's when I started sugaring. Never run out of kids that wanna join the candy making fun. Cora's kids loved it." Hammy continued the conversation without missing a beat.

"Weren't no use looking for gold on the claim, so's I thought I'd have something good out of it."

Jane couldn't help but smile at his jovial tone. "You, Mr. Hamm, could make something good out of anything, I think."

"Not anything, Lady Jane."

"I beg to differ."

"Weren't nothing good when ya died."

Jane paused at his words, turning to face him fully. "Oh, Mr. Hamm."

He mumbled something under her fierce hug, but it was lost to the fabric on her shoulder. His cheeks were ruddy when she released him. "Didn't mean nothing by it."

"Of course you didn't." She squeezed his hand before turning back to the creek. "By my best estimate, we have another two hours before the race concludes and I must be there to help disperse the winnings. Let's make the best of it, shall we?"

"Why we looking in the creek?"

"Emily doesn't seem to be anywhere in town. Perhaps she got confused, or lost, or even worse—injured. I don't see any sign of her within sight line up there. The wild grasses haven't grown enough that I don't have good vision from the horse."

"Lots of places to get lost in the valley," Hammy admitted.

"Hence, why there are so many of us looking. We were going to send a search party out after Mr. Finnigan, but he was found well into far too much of Petey's moonshine early this morning. Apparently, he had much fun imbibing instead of playing at the dance." Jane's remaining frustration lingered, but not enough for her to curse him.

"Miss Emily ain't been gone that long. Why we so worried?"

"Emily wished to become a madam, was learning at Leanne's right hand. She was not one to break the rules laid out, which included being safe in the brothel every night. There are those that would abuse a woman in such an occupation for simply being without a guardian."

"Like Mac."

"Mac would abuse any woman no matter her occupation. That is one soul this town would be best off to see board a train and never return." Jane herself had suffered enough abuse at the hand of the man to know. Though she'd fortunately had Cole around to keep her free of too much first-hand knowledge, she knew there were some girls not so lucky. Daisy had needed to treat several women after the man's abuses.

"Don't need to be a woman, neither." Hammy scrambled over a felled tree. Though he stumbled, he quickly hopped back to his feet. He offered his hand to help her over the same obstacle without hesitation.

Rather than try to go around the tree through the creek, she took the offered hand. Two hours wasn't enough time to return and change before she had to make another appearance for the end of the race.

Hammy made no comment at her somewhat undignified climb over the trunk. He took the lead now, pushing through the brush ahead of them. The path he led them on kept them far enough from the edge of the creek to keep her skirts dry, though the branches tugged at the width of the fabric.

Half an hour of the struggle later they'd found nothing but more conversation. Jane was about to suggest turning back when a putrid smell hit her.

Hammy's nose wrinkled. "Probably a dead animal. Stay here."

Jane didn't listen, following behind so quick she was almost ahead of him when they came upon the sight. The scream erupted before Jane could stop it, and she turned away.

The image remained glued to her brain as much as anything ever had. Emily's sweet features contorted into a scream frozen in time. Her body torn open viciously. Memories of a nightmare long relegated to the depths of her mind rushed forward.

She closed her eyes against her internal struggle to regain her composure. As her senses returned, she became aware of Hammy's supportive hold.

His gentle, worried tone carried floated into her awareness. "Ya get Tommy, and I'll watch her. Go on now, ain't a sight for a lady to see."

"It's all right, Mr. Hamm. I'm fine. I was simply startled." She patted the hand at her elbow. "Really. Don't worry too much."

"Still say it ain't a sight ya need to see."

"I've seen enough bad, it's nothing more to see this. We do need to find Thomas. We cannot abandon her, though." Jane immediately reached for her skirts the moment her hand was freed. Fighting with the buttons and ties, she managed to free her top layer of petticoats.

Once her top layers were refastened, she hopped and twirled to tug free the underlayer. When she stood, she found

Hammy looking respectably away. She also noted his hand was on his weapon. A quick reach for her own, and she realized she'd left it off in honor of the party that day. Well, that would make it difficult to convince him to go for help.

Jane knelt next to the dead woman. A strange longing to shut her eyes came over her, but she knew better than to touch a thing before Thomas got there. Instead, she forced her gaze to study the wounds. The torn open belly almost seemed animal in nature, which wasn't unlikely.

Beyond that, she noted bruises on the arms and partly exposed chest. Most of her clothes were absent, though she saw no evidence of them in the surrounding area. Jane draped her petticoat over Emily gently so she wouldn't disturb anything.

She rose to study the area, spotting a path through the brush on the bank beside them. "I don't think she died here."

"What, Lady Jane?" Hammy drew closer.

"Wait. Stay there." Jane backed toward the man. "We must get Thomas, and Dr. Cross."

"She don't need a doc no more, Janey." He grimaced at the petticoat.

"Dr. Cross was a coroner in New York while in medical school to aid in his training. He's rather familiar with dead bodies."

"That ain't right."

"To some, no. I suppose it isn't." She braced herself for the oncoming argument. "Mr. Hamm. Lend me your spare weapon, then return for Dr. Cross and go find my brother."

"No way. It ain't safe. They may be 'round here. I ain't leaving you."

"We can't both stay."

"You're faster."

"I've also been around Thomas enough to know what not to touch or do with the area. I'm also quite skilled with a weapon. I dare say my aim is better than yours."

Hammy's brow furrowed as he worked up an argument.

"Please." Jane set her hand on his, clasping it close. "I know you only have my safety in mind, but we also have to consider that someone likely murdered this dear, sweet woman. We must be certain that Thomas has the best chance of finding who did so."

"I don't know. Don't seem right."

"I'll move up there to be further from the smell and to leave the area clean outside what I've already done. I'll keep an eye out for animals, including human ones." Even as she assured him, she worried herself that she'd be late to return to the party. He had a point, she was faster, especially on Tempest.

"Still don't seem right."

"When you get to the party, send Katherine or Sally for Thomas." The idea struck her so fast, she grasped his hands. Yes, they would be faster than Hammy, as they could have run in the race if they'd wanted, but neither had opted to. "They're the fastest ones there."

"All right. I'll get the doc and send one of them, but then I'm comin' right back."

"Agreed. Oh, and Gilbert." She smiled when he stopped short and blushed again at her use of his proper name. "Please be discreet. I don't want Leanne to see this."

"I'll do my best."

That was the best she could hope for. On a good day, Hammy was far from inconspicuous. She followed him up the embankment. Soon as they hit level ground, he raced off with surprising speed toward where they'd left their horses.

Jane paced on the spot. Nerves had her tapping the barrel of Hammy's gun against her thigh. Another round of cheers echoed through the valley, loud enough to be heard even at her current distance. She let out a sharp whistle.

Tempest appeared in the distance shortly after the sound. Another whistle brought the horse to her. Comforted a bit by the presence of her horse, she smoothed her hand along the beast's neck. "Well, Tempest. We are in a pickle until he returns. Can't move, and no idea what's going on. What shall I do?"

The horse blew out a breath, then bowed her head to nibble at the grass. Calm as anything.

"You're no help." She resumed her pacing, gaze fixed on where Hammy had disappeared. Time passed in slow and quick bursts. Right when she thought she might lose all patience, a figure appeared in the distance.

The person rushed forward quick as their horse would carry them. Sally drew to a stop before her, Agatha snorting in protest of the quick end to the run. "Ma. What happened? Hammy looked a fright."

"Drat. I told him to be discreet. Leanne didn't see him, did she?"

"She wasn't there. She'd gone back to the brothel again in hopes Emily would show up. Why? What is it?" Sally leaped from her saddle, eagerness alighting her features in a way Jane hadn't seen in what seemed ages. "What's happened?"

"I'm afraid Emily is dead."

"Oh. Oh, no." Sally turned a circle. "Where is she? Down by the creek?"

"Yes." Jane had to physically grab the girl's arm to keep her from descending. "Don't."

"Ma."

"For one, I don't think you need to see it. For another, Thomas wouldn't want us all traipsing around down there. I did enough by covering her."

"All the way out here? Was it an animal? What would she be doing out here? That doesn't make any sense." Sally's gaze slipped along the tree line. She paused on the break in the bushes several feet further north. "What's that?"

"Sally Ann. I just told you Thomas wouldn't want us messing with anything. What has gotten into you?"

"Nothing." Like a balloon, the young woman's spark diminished to almost nothing.

Jane moved to stand in front of her ward. "Is something wrong?"

"No. Not nothing important."

"Why do I feel like you're keeping something from me? You can tell me anything, you know. I don't mind." Honestly, Jane had a sneaking suspicion what was bothering the girl. After two years as their ward and doing her best to be good and follow the rules, she was fit to burst with boredom. Whether it was Tommy's stories, or the fact her courtship was rather sedate compared to Jane and Cole's, Jane couldn't be certain.

"I'm not hiding anything." Sally didn't meet her gaze, instead focusing on the break in the trees again. "That's two deaths."

"Well, this one is a bit clearer as to the cause. I doubt anyone would suspect this to be an accident of any kind."

"Why not?"

Another set of hoofbeats interrupted Jane's reply. Hammy had returned. "Miss Kathy's going to get your brother, Lady Jane."

"Thank you, Mr. Hamm. Sally here tells me Leanne wasn't present."

"Sure wasn't. I told Cole, though."

"Of course you did."

*Do your best to forget it
and if you don't succeed,
at least pretend to.*
–Moliere

Jane rode back to the meadow at a rapid pace. Soon as the trees bordering the celebration came into view, her pace grew slower. Cole's voice rang over the trees announcing the placement of the riders as they entered the second to last leg of the race.

The lingering images of broken bodies flashed through her mind until she shuddered. Tempest stopped beneath her without an order, as though the beast sensed its rider's unease. Jane did her best to school her features to hide whatever panic lingered.

Even more than that, she needed to set about putting forward a happiness her uneasy soul didn't quite feel after the days events. There was no reason to panic the crowd waiting for an exciting conclusion to the race. Especially with those from out of town wandering about.

She knew by the end of the day, Thomas would be talking to anyone and everyone that had been at the dance the night before, but for now they would allow the party to continue. Even if the pure joy of the day would be marred before the fireworks began.

Eyes closed, Jane took several deep breaths to calm herself until she was certain she would remain in full control of her faculties for the next hour.

"In the lead is Coleman on Hunter, with Mac on Bastard right behind, and in a surprising turn for some of you, Abrams on Lightning is neck-and-neck with Mac!" Cole's voice called over the crowd. A cheer went up among the women in the crowd, as Abrams was the only female rider in the race that day.

Jane drew up to the grandstand, surprised when their stable hand approached. "Bill. What are you doing here?"

"Cole thought ya might want to send Tempest back so's she wouldn't be bothered by the racers when they got here." Bill took hold of the reins she tossed him. "Had Sally get me when she came for Agatha."

"That was quite thoughtful of him. Thank you, Bill. I do believe Tempest has had enough excitement for the day. Or perhaps that's me." She offered the young man a smile. When he led the horse away, she climbed the steps to the grandstand.

Cole's fngers immediately laced with hers, squeezing tight. He leaned close. "Look like you've seen a ghost."

"My brain did."

Cole's brow furrowed as he took her in.

"Broken body torn apart. Though in a rather obviously different way, my mind immediately latched on Mr. Querney after Bingham pushed him in front of the train."

"You're gonna have nightmares."

"It is a distinct likelihood." She turned with him toward the south where the riders would appear soon after they got word the final marker had been passed. "I'll do my best not to hit you when they happen this time."

"Not worried about a black eye. Helps my reputation."

"Hurts it, more like. You're a respectable businessman now."

He shuddered dramatically. "Don't say that."

The teasing had the effect of bringing her laughter. She imagined that had been his plan. "Too bad, Mr. Mitchell. You've proven a good man of business, of charity, and even of oration when the situation is one you believe in."

"Ugh. You done ruined my reputation, didn't you?"

"As you have ruined mine. I suppose we're even."

"Not even close."

"No?" She turned away from the empty stretch of valley beyond Main Street to focus on him. "How's that?"

"I owe you everything. I'll never refinish repaying that debt."

"As I owe you, once again, we're even."

He chucked his finger under her chin. "That's a much more believable smile. Think you can hold it a while longer?"

"I've had to do worse with far less motivation."

"Don't need reminding of that."

She leaned into him, watching the distance for the flag at the final marker. Cole himself had a binocle to his eyes to see it clearer. She glanced around the crowd. "Where's—"

"Nope. We aren't discussing it until the race is over."

"But—"

"You'll keep fretting and you need to leave that to Tom. You can fret over Leanne later."

She pursed her lips when he winked at her. "Fine. Then am I allowed to ask where the children are, at least?"

"Over there with your Ma and Pa. All except Alma. The crowd's been rowdy. She went back to the apartment with Millie, who was tired from all the celebrating."

"She's tired from the weight of the child she's carrying, not that she'd ever complain about such a thing. Charles says they've been trying for years for a child with no success. This child is a great surprise and joy."

"Guess we're lucky that so far we haven't had to wait and try. Them kids keep happening whether we expect them or not." He lifted the binocles again.

"Hopefully our next will buck tradition and be well-planned and behaved."

"Would be a first." Though he kept his gaze set to the south, a broad grin creased his features. "Don't think one of them has ever behaved. Think this one will?"

"I beg to differ. Sally and Alma have both always been quite well behaved. Sally almost distressingly so. A girl her age should have some fun. At least at the age we believe her to be."

"There's the flag." Cole grabbed the bullhorn to announce to the waiting crowd the final marker had been passed by the first riders.

For the first time since she'd learned of Emily's disappearance, a stir of excitement rippled through Jane. She leaned on the railing, eying the edge of the horizon for signs of the riders. Cole took position beside her.

"Who do you think it'll be?" Jane cast him a sideways glance. "Since we can't bet and all."

"My odds were on Mac, but Coleman has been really pulling it out. Might surprise us all."

"What about Abrams?"

"Wasn't sure she could get through some of the obstacles, but then I never really saw her ride before, so I couldn't rightly guess. Only other one I'd think would be Dean Pibble. Little guy, which could work in his favor, and he's got a touch with the horses. If you'd been in it, I mighta said you."

Heat filled her cheeks at his words, but she scoffed. "I race for fun, not for real. I'm not certain Tempest and I would do well on this sort of race."

"Nah. You'd do good. Once you knew the course." He bent over as a rider came up holding up a piece of paper. "Final marker shows Mac in the lead, Pibble right behind. Abrams and Coleman are trailing by a horse length."

"Mac likely up to no good," Jane muttered under the cries of the crowd.

"Or they're pacing their horses for the final sprint." Cole lifted the binocles. "We'll know better when they make it over the rise. Here, you take these, I got a telescope here, too."

"You keep those, be easier to hold the horn with it. I'll take the telescope." She spotted the brass piece in the corner of the grandstand. By the time she had it to her eye, she could see the riders coming over the rise toward town.

She hit the railing, she rushed forward so fast. Mac was in the lead, but if she wasn't mistaken, Coleman and Abrams were closing the distance. Pibble was making an equal effort, but racing off to the side from the group, his head down and focus on town.

While Cole called off the final leg of the race to the crowd, Jane kept her focus on the riders making a beeline toward them. Coleman and Abrams crept up on Mac at an almost equal pace. Jane leaned forward as though it would get her a better view.

Right as Abrams got beside Mac, the large bull of a man made a move. He cut off the horse quick as anything. The move was so quick and sudden, Abrams horse lost its footing and tumbled to the ground with her on it.

Loud complaints came from the crowd at this announcement. Jane had a thought to declare such tactics illegal next race, but she knew it would get stomped on. After all, for most of the race no one could see the riders or what tactics they pulled to get to the lead.

For that matter, Jane was curious as to what had happened to their out-of-town racers in the course of the race. She lifted her telescope to see the rest of the riders as they came over the ridge. Several Denver riders were now pushing their beasts to the limit, leaning forward to aid the speed they'd need to catch up to the leaders.

She moved back to watch the leaders again. Coleman and Mac were right beside each other, far too close for comfort as Mac tried his best to dislodge the skilled rider beside him. Every time Coleman got himself free and swerved to run around the man, Mac pushed further forward to get after him again.

"Mac would win if he'd stop trying to best Coleman by shoving him off." Jane could hardly believe her eyes as a Denver rider gained on them all. Pibble had taken a lead, though he had to make a wide berth around the previous leaders to do so.

"It's between Pibble and Jennings from Denver now." Cole was leaning forward as well. "What's that? Mac's got something."

She'd caught the flash of metal as well. "I think it's a knife. Coleman better watch his back."

Coleman clearly didn't need telling as he yanked the reins of Hunter taut until the pair came to a dead stop. After several heartbeats, Hunter reared in the air before taking off a dead run. By taking a similar wide berth as Pibble, he managed to pass Mac and began to make gains on both Pibble and Jennings.

Jane set down the telescope to rush toward the end of the bandstand. The flags for the end of the race flapped in the breeze. With them in hand, she leaned over the railing so she'd have a clear view of the finish line from above to call the race.

Cole was yelling out placement fast and furious as the riders drew ever closer to the finish line. Out of the corner of her eye, Jane could see movement approaching fast. Unwilling to take her gaze from the finish line for fear she'd miss the winner of the close race, she lifted the flag high in the air.

Soon as the dapple-grey horse's nose touched the line she brought down the flag. A cheer went through the crowd as all the leaders tore over the finish line at a brutal pace. Jane glanced at Cole. "It was Pibble on Moonshine by a head. Jennings beat Coleman by a nose."

"Got it." Cole turned to announce the winners to the waiting crowd.

Jane's gaze got distracted by an approaching wagon from the north. Sally and Dr. Cross sat in the wagon seat talking quietly. Agatha trailed behind the wagon by her lead. Though she wondered at what Sally was still doing with the dead body, a tug to her hand pulled her back to the race.

"Let's get the horse bedecked, and deal with the fallout. We'll deal with the rest later."

"Right, later." Jane gave one more look at her young ward and the doctor before grabbing the wreath of roses to award the winners.

Curiosity is one of the permanent and certain characteristics of a vigorous mind.
—Samuel Johnson

Cora's feast spread out over a dozen tables in the meadow. The delicious smell of fried chicken and potatoes filled the air. Jane helped her parents get the children set up with their meals. Sally remained absent from the event.

Jane had expected Sally to return to the celebration quickly. Certainly Andrew had merely given her a ride home. Of course, she was also worried about the continuing absence of Leanne and who would tell her what they'd discovered.

A warm hand on her elbow pulled her from her distraction. Cole met her gaze with a sexy smirk. "You can't sit still for nothing."

"Not with so much going on, I can't. Someone needs to tend to Leanne, and I need to locate Sally. I saw her return with Dr. Cross some time ago. She hasn't returned to the party. I hope what she saw didn't disturb her too badly. I tried to keep her away from the body, but Thomas isn't nearly as careful with her."

"Quit panicking." He pulled her flush against him until her body relaxed. "I got no doubt Tommy's gonna handle

Leanne. Let him do it. Far as Sally goes, go check on her. Your parents and me got the rest of the kids."

"Thank you." She rose on her toes to kiss him gently. "Save me some chicken."

"Chicken? That all you want?"

"Oh, not at all, but as I've pointed out quite often—I must satiate that appetite before I can indulge my favorite."

He groaned low, nipping at her neck. "You'd best be quick. Maybe we can get a nibble in before the fireworks."

"Sound like a delightful plan." She pulled free with some measure of regret. The amount of responsibilities they had made spontaneity difficult some days.

Even more so when Cole took a seat by Clara, who immediately climbed into his lap. The man gave his daughter his full attention, listening seriously to whatever story she told him.

"Times like this, I see why you love him."

Jane startled at Charlie's voice. She spun to sMac him on the arm. "Charles. You scared the daylights out of me. You can't sneak up on a person like that."

"I didn't sneak. You were staring lost in thought. Not my fault you didn't hear me." Charles chuckled low. "I see my wife has returned to the party. I should join her before I get scolded."

"All the riders are patched up, then?" She knew all too well the route was difficult and tricky leading to injury to horse and man, especially when you added in dirty tactics such as Mac had displayed. There had been men posted along the route to get the injured men back to town to be cared for by Charlie and Daisy.

"Sent the last one off about an hour ago. I've merely been cleaning up the mess so I wouldn't return to it in the morning."

"Have you seen Sally?"

"I thought I saw her at the clinic, but only when Andrew first returned. I have no idea if she remained or not."

"Thank you. Enjoy your meal." She squeezed her brothers hand briefly before she took off for town.

Though she knew the reason, it was odd to walk through the town with it so silent. With so many at the celebration, the streets were almost completely devoid of life. It seemed like on a normal day the town always had a bustle about it.

As she passed the Inn, she spotted Wil on the porch. She slowed to nod to him. "Wil. You wouldn't be out causing trouble, would you?"

"With who?" He spread his arms wide to encompass the quiet street. A wicked smirk crossed his features. "I could come to the celebration, ya know. Stir up trouble there."

"Only trouble there will be the boxing matches, which you are not signed up for."

"You got them rules. Makes the fight less fun." Wil winked, then leaned closer over the railing. "Heard 'bout Em. Too bad."

"You don't remember seeing her last night?"

"No ma'am."

"I didn't think so. I know you favored her, but she is out of your price range. After all, she's top shelf, not bottom-dwelling."

He smirked at the insult, giving her a nod. "Maybe if ya paid me more."

"For what? You aren't working yet." She bowed her head as a dismissal before resuming her path to the clinic. The barbs proved amusing when they exchanged them. She knew Wil was anxious to get to his own room at the brothel. Especially considering they had asked him not to take women to his room in the casino. Then again, he hadn't seemed overly upset by the rule.

Jane paused on the porch of the clinic to turn back and study the man. Curious, for sure. She hadn't heard word of lecherous acts about town that weren't her own. Then again, Wil had only been in town for a few days. There was still plenty of time for such a reputation.

She shook off the thoughts to return to the task at hand. The door to the clinic was shut, but not locked, so Jane let herself in. "Sally? Dr. Cross?"

No answer to her calls. Jane made her way through the empty lobby. All of the exam rooms sat open, revealing no sign of the young doctor or Sally. "Sally? Are you here?"

Still nothing. She tapped on the door to surgery, and popped her head into the room at the lack of answer. Empty.

Just as she was about to call again, she heard laughter from down the hall. Jane strode down to the kitchen, but found it empty as well. When she turned, she noticed the door to the back room Charles had been debating using as a second surgery remained closed as well.

Jane knocked once before pushing the door open.

Emily's body lay on the table, splayed open like a grotesque display. Dr. Cross held something bloody in his right hand, his left inside the cavity.

The smell she'd been overwhelmed by out by the creek hit her again, hardly decreased by a sweet incense burning near the door. Jane wretched and spun so her back was to the room. "What in heavens name?"

"Ma!" Sally's exclamation overpowered the doctors. "Are you all right?"

"Yes. I believe so." Jane kept a hand on the door frame to keep herself steady. A handkerchief was pressed to her nose, the sweet scent of lavender overpowering the smell of death that had affected her ever since her own near-death.

"Breathe in this. It helps." Sally kept the cloth over Jane's nose until Jane took up the task herself. "Andrew's doing Emily's autopsy. He did them in Buffalo while in school."

"I'm aware." Jane straightened, the lavender a blessed relief to her senses. Rather than turn back to the sight of the whore on the table, she faced her young ward. Jane was surprised to find a glimmer of excitement in the young woman's eyes. "Sally. Should you be in here? It's a difficult thing to deal with."

"She's not balked once," Andrew assured Jane from the table. "She's a curious one. Nothing wrong with that."

"No, there isn't." Jane's brow furrowed when Sally moved back to a stool she'd been perched on before Jane's entrance.

Sally popped a peppermint candy in her mouth, watching intently as Andrew continued to work. "Andrew made me aware that most people faint or vomit at their first autopsy. He's been telling me stories."

"I wasn't aware you two were on a first name basis." Jane cautiously took a step further into the room. She kept the cloth pressed firm to her nose. Though her stomach churned at the bloody sight before her, she held her ground.

"Just became so. Your ward is a delight." Andrew set something on a set of scales. "Plus, being in an autopsy tends to expediate friendships."

"I'd never have guessed as much." Jane took a shuddering breath but kept steady. "Was it animals, Dr. Cross?"

"I'm not quite finished with the exam, but I'm going with no. Though her face was left pure and clean, there were signs of her being beaten on the body. Her spleen was damaged. It's possible she was alive when she was left by the creek, but bled out. Then, well, that's when the animals got her." Andrew grimaced, but made a note on a paper. The page was smeared with blood, covered in notes around the red swatches.

"When she was still alive?" Jane held in her horror at the idea, barely.

"Possibly. I don't think she could move between the bleeding and her ankle." He lifted the blanket over Emily's legs. The ankle twisted at an odd angle, bruised in a familiar way. Jane's own formerly broken ankle throbbed at the mere sight.

"Oh dear." Jane sank into a chair.

"Here, Ma. Take a peppermint." Sally held out the candy. When Jane scrunched her nose, Sally's smile brightened. "No, it helps. With the scent and the lightheadedness. I swear."

Jane took the candy doubtfully but did as she was told. While she sat there, Sally moved closer to the body, an unfamiliar light about her visage that made Jane's heart ache. This is what she'd wanted for the girl, excitement. But to find it in a dead body being pulled apart in an autopsy? How strange.

"What's that?" Sally pointed into the open cavity. "Right there."

"Oh, interesting." Andrew moved the lantern closer. "It appears to be metal. That definitely shouldn't be there. You found it, do you want to remove it?"

Sally eyed the large tweezers he held toward her, then looked down at the exquisite gown Jane had gotten her for the occasion. "I probably shouldn't."

"There's an apron and sleeves over there." Andrew gestured toward Jane before he turned his attention back to the body.

Sally glanced Jane's way, doubt clouding the burst of excitement she'd had. For a moment, it seemed as though she was asking permission. Then, her shoulders sagged and she shook her head. "No. You get it."

Andrew lifted his head in surprise, then disappointment flickered across his expressive features before he shook his head. "Don't be silly. It was your discovery."

"I—I really shouldn't." Sally took a step back.

"Sally." Jane rose from her seat. "I think I'm going to go find Leanne and see how she's holding up. Your Pa and Mams and Paps have the children handled. Andrew, thank you for doing this. I trust you'll tell Thomas what you've found?"

"Of course." Andrew didn't look up from his work at her words. "He's the one that requested this, after all. You might sit in the fresh air before you try to go anywhere. The moment you leave the cloud of the autopsy smell you're likely to get lightheaded."

"I will. Thank you." Jane got up to leave. While she wouldn't go so far as to give Sally outright permission to dive into a dead body, she wasn't going to stop her, either. She had an uneasy feeling her presence had inhibited that momentary elation. That, above all, was the last thing she wanted. Didn't Sally know all Jane wished was for her to be happy? Beyond that, there was little in expectations save for her to prove she'd finished her schooling properly by passing a teacher's exam.

Jane stepped into the fresh air, and as predicted the wave of dizziness hit her hard. She took a seat, breathing in deep. Heavy bootsteps stopped in front of her.

"You good?" Tom crouched in front of her, his brow pursed tight.

"Fine. I was in the autopsy room, just regaining my head. Made me a little—"

"Autopsies are tough." He patted her knee.

"Not for Sally. She's still in there."

"Is that so?" One brow arched into the shadow of his hat brim.

"Thomas."

"Yeah?"

"You don't believe I'm keeping Sally from doing what her heart desires, do you?"

"Nothing's stopping that girl but her own self. I've never heard you hold her back from anything. Not once."

"That doesn't mean she doesn't think I want her to be something else."

"What her mind has twisted your words into isn't your fault."

She frowned deep, looking off down the street. "She's worked so hard to shed the stigma of her life as a whore. I've done what I can to help her."

"Everyone knows that."

"Sally doesn't seem to." Jane shook off the thoughts to turn back to Tom. "What do you know?"

"Quite a lot, actually. Care to narrow it down?"

"About what Sally wants?"

"She hasn't told me anything special, if that's what you're saying."

"Thomas."

"I know you've noticed it, too. I observe, and I see her. You see her."

"That doesn't answer my question."

"I don't know. She's not said anything outright. She could be dreaming of all sorts of craziness, but I know she doesn't want marriage, kids, a good, stable life like the world tells her she should have."

Jane shuddered when Thomas did. "God forbid."

"God forbid."

A million questions flooded her brain, but she tucked them all away until they could be dealt with. A matter that would require sitting Sally down for a proper discussion. Once she felt more settled, she focused on her brother. "How is Leanne?"

Tommy's features crumpled. "A mess. Blaming herself. She's with her girls now, and I left to let them all comfort each other and discuss the situation. She'll probably be looking for her friends late tonight or early tomorrow. Don't think anyone will want to be out late by themselves for the time being."

"Are you saying I shouldn't go up the hill tonight?"

"I'll be going soon. I wanted to get some more information from Andrew first. I'll take good care of her."

"I know you will."

*Keep your eyes wide open before marriage,
and half-shut afterwards.
-Benjamin Franklin*

Cole wiped down the glasses on instinct more than need. A sort of melancholy had fallen over the town in the days after the Centennial party. Never mind that there was another big party to celebrate Colorado's statehood in three weeks.

The death of one of Leanne's whores hadn't helped matters. Especially seeing as it was murder, not an accident. Whispered suspicions ran rampant through town, but none of them seemed to hold enough weight to Tommy.

Jane had spent quite a bit of time with Leanne over the past few days, along with Kathy. When she wasn't with them, she had been in a bit of melancholy herself. She'd confided in him that she was worried over Sally. Their ward had been quiet too, but that could be because of the constant studying she'd been doing. Her test was the next week, and she was frantic over it.

John took a seat across from him. Though the man didn't know Cole and Jane were married, he'd always treated Cole like a son-in-law. Cole liked the man a lot. He'd been raised a farmer and was down to earth, but had a razor sharp wit like Jane.

Cole nodded to John. "What'll you have?"

"You know how to make a Brandy Smash?"

"I do. Jane got me a book about them fancy cocktails. I even got some Regent's Punch made back here in honor of the party." Cole grabbed the ingredients for the requested drink, dropping the sprigs of mint into the glass.

"I'm guessing it was her idea to get fancy cocktails in here."

"Sure was. Said it met with the, what was it she said? Tone of the place with the high rollers we got coming in."

"She's not wrong. Harder to get the supplies in here, I'd bet."

"Nah. Train brings most of what we need. We got plans to build a little greenhouse for Alma's butterflies since we don't got a long summer here. Jane thought Alma could start growing some of the other stuff we need. Like the mint and rosemary, and such."

"That's a little of Clara coming out, I think. Always thinking of ways around what is scarce. She's resourceful."

Though focused on making the drink, Cole didn't miss the flash of sadness on the man's face when he spoke of Clara. Odd that this group of people so like family to him, wished the opposite of what he did. They hoped Clara would return, while Cole feared what would happen if she did. If Jane one day remembered who she'd been. Would she still want Cole?

"You all right?"

"Huh?" Cole startled, then realized he'd stopped pressing the mint and sugar. "Oh, sorry. Got lost in thought. I blame Jane, she's a bad influence with all that thinking."

John laughed heartily. "Most people would think that's a good influence."

"I spent a lot of years not thinking, John. To me, it isn't good." Cole chuckled, pouring the brandy. "Thinking tends to get me in trouble. At least, it used to."

John took his drink, raising it in a toast. "To great thinking, then."

Cole nodded to the man, pausing when he spotted Jane descending into the pit. A grin tugged the corners of his lips when she caught his eye. "Speak of the devil."

"I am not the devil," Jane said in response. "I believe that has always been you."

"Can't argue that." He met her kiss easily, but pulled back far too soon for his liking out of respect for the man across the bar. "Your pa just ordered a smash."

"I told you the bartender's guide would come in handy. I hear they're creating new drinks all the time. We should consider getting a proper bartender from out east, or even from out west to come in and teach our employees some new things." Jane smiled at her father. "Even without proper training, how is your drink, Pa?"

"He did good. Just the right amount of sweet." John set down the glass. "Cole tells me you're thinking of a greenhouse."

"I am. Alma loves the butterflies so much, but our garden never lasts long enough. If we get a greenhouse we could potentially see them all the time if she kept the plants growing right." She pouted. "It's too bad I kill everything I touch. She does so beautifully I'd love to contribute. Although maybe the best I can do is offer the land behind the library for a large greenhouse. It's convenient we built the library right next to the stables."

"Well, if you're thinking of adding things for the bar, you should talk to Eunice. She has some experience with a proper greenhouse. We've got one in Buffalo. Our winters aren't quite as long as yours, but they can be no less brutal." John pulled Jane into a discussion on different herbs and berries he'd seen used in drinks out east.

Cole's attention wandered from the discussion to survey the floor again. The typical crowd was in place for a Friday afternoon. Things would really begin to pick up in another couple of hours. They had a burlesque that night that would draw big crowds.

A familiar cowboy dropped into a seat a few down from John. Cole moved to greet him. "Coleman. Tough luck at the race."

"That Mac was out for blood, literally." Matthew removed his hat. "Came to put my name in for the race at the Statehood Celebration."

"You sure? The purse is big, which means the entry fee is." Cole winced at a sharp pain in his calf. He glared at Jane, who glared right back and shook her head.

Jane slid over to their discussion. "It is a higher entry fee than the recent race due to the larger purse, but we charge more for the out of towners."

That was news to Cole. They'd agreed to a five-hundred dollar fee for entry to the next race for all riders. While they'd only charged fifty dollars for the most recent. They had two large purses to recoup from, and they wanted bigger fish for the statehood race. Which also included the future senator for Colorado. Between his horse in the race, and Lillian Daugherty's manipulations the man had agreed to come to Dominion Falls over Denver.

"I don't need charity, Miss Jane." Matthew grimaced. "Hunter and I had a real chance at winning, and I want it again."

"It isn't charity, Matthew. We have a different fee for those fancy folk coming from out east. For townies it's one-hundred dollars. Double what you paid for the race earlier this week, for double the purse. If you can't spare it, I'd bet you could find a sponsor based on your performance a few days ago. It was quite impressive."

"It really was." Sally's voice surprised them all. "I thought for sure you were going to win. Lost five dollars on my bet."

"Sally Ann, gambling?" Jane tried to look shocked, teasing Sally. In doing so, she missed what Cole saw.

Matthew flushed at Sally's words, and gave the young woman a distinct once over. He seemed to come to himself. "I guess I owe you five dollars, Miss."

"Nonsense. Just win the next one. I'll gain it back and more." Sally winked at him. Her head turned so fast, she also missed Matthew's reaction to the wink.

Cole lifted a brow, intrigued. He almost missed Sally's departure with his intense study of the cowboy's lingering glances at Sally. Cole leaned on the bar to regain the man's attention. "You in or not? Or are you interested in chasing skirt?"

"What? I—no. I wasn't." Matthew's cheeks darkened under Cole's laughter. "I'm interested. I'll be back tomorrow with the entry fee. Don't need no sponsor. I'll get it together."

"We'll see you tomorrow, then." Jane waved off the young man. She pinched Cole's side hard. "Be nice. The boy needs that money. The tornado did some damage to the ranch and he lost about twenty head of cattle. I could kill Mac for his antics in the race. That five-thousand would have rightly been Matthew's."

"I can let him enter for no dollars if you want, but it won't make him win."

"He at least needs a fair shot without losing every bit of money he's got left." She bumped his hip. "What was that about chasing skirt?"

"You didn't see him making eyes at Sally?"

"He was not."

"He was."

"Oh. Oh." Her eyes widened. "*Oh.*"

Cole chuckled softly, tugging her close. "You and Sally were properly distracted and neither noticed. Probably good for Sally since she's courting Arthur, right?"

Jane's good mood left quick as it had arrived. "Is that what she wants, though?"

"I don't know. I'm not her."

She hummed disapproval before sliding back down to resume the conversation with her pa on the garden. At least her mood seemed to be improving, even if she was currently annoyed with him for no good reason.

Cole returned to preparing the bar for the influx of people at the show tonight. With the glasses sparkling, and the bottles lined up to what he thought would meet even Jane's satisfaction, he pulled out the bartender book Jane had given him to look for another punch to make for the burlesque. They had some Regent's left, but perhaps they could offer another.

A throat cleared nearby, pulling him from his search. Arthur took a seat at the bar, glancing around the room uncomfortably.

"Arthur Turner." Cole smirked at the surprising appearance. He stepped in front of the young man. "Fancy seeing you in here. What'll ya have?"

"Nothing. I was hoping—I mean, wondering." Arthur's forehead creased.

Cole thought it would be fun to make the boy sweat. He noticed Jane move closer but didn't dare glance her way. The smirk flipped into a frown. "Spit it out, boy. I've got paying customers to serve."

"I wanted to talk to you," Arthur all but yelled in surprise to Cole's tone. "About something important."

Cole ignored the sMac Jane had given him for snapping. "Important?"

"Yeah. Regarding Sally."

Now that was interesting. Especially considering Sally now had at least two other men making eyes at her, whether she knew about them both or not. Still, Cole eyed Arthur long and hard. Then tilted his head toward Jane. "If it's about Sally, don't you want to talk to Jane?"

"No. I wanted to talk to you."

Cole leaned closer. He looked the boy up and down. "Is that so?"

"Yeah. Man to man."

"I see." Cole was definitely interested to see where this went. More so, he was curious how far he could push the boy with his fit of nerves. "Do you need a drink to follow through on your side of the man-to-man deal?"

"No." Arthur's gaze slid along the line of bottles behind Cole despite his protest. He shook his head. "No."

"You don't gotta listen to your ma anymore. If you need some courage in a glass, I'll get one for you."

"Can we just talk?"

Cole nodded toward a table near the end of the bar. "Go on. I'm getting myself a drink and I'll be along."

Jane approached as he poured not one, but two glasses of whiskey. "Cole. Cora will have your hide."

"He's a man now, don't much care." He kissed her cheek to try to soothe the temper threatening to erupt. Still, he grinned broadly when he pulled back. She kept glancing over his shoulder, her brow pursed. "Sticking close so's you can eavesdrop?"

"Considering I know what he wants, and you haven't the foggiest? You bet your sweet ass I will be doing just that."

Cole turned, pausing to wiggle his ass at her before he went to the table with the two full glasses. He dropped into the chair, setting a glass down in reach of them both. Even though it was close enough, Cole still nudged the second glass toward Arthur.

Not one to make it easy for anyone, Cole said nothing. He let Arthur stare at the glass while he nursed his own whiskey. The silence lingered so long, Cole was nearing the end of his whiskey. Impatience started to brew, but he tried to school his tone. "Well?"

"I know you aren't Sally's Pa…"

"That's for damn sure." Cole chuckled. Never mind Sally had seen to start calling him Pa recently, he still wasn't.

"But you're the closest thing to it."

"Not especially." All right, maybe he was, but it was fun to needle the nervous kid.

"You are."

In that moment it struck Cole what Arthur was after. He wanted to talk to Cole because Cole was Sally's pa, in a manner of speaking. What else did young men talk to a girl's pa for? The glass slipped from his fingers to hit the table with a thunk. He sat straighter. "I'll be damned."

Arthur didn't speak for nearly a full minute. Several times he opened his mouth, but closed it just as quick every time.

Cole pushed the still untouched glass of whiskey closer to Arthur. "I'm not jumping the gun. You want to talk, you talk. Otherwise, I've got business."

Arthur's hand trembled, but he picked up the glass. He tossed back the whiskey hard and fast. His face turned bright red, and for a second Cole thought he might vomit. Arthur coughed once, twice, then got himself under control.

Cole had to admit he was impressed he'd handled his first shot of whiskey so well. "How about that? You might have what it takes to be a man after all."

Arthur frowned, but pressed on. "I wanted to ask for Sally's hand."

For a long moment, Cole studied the young man. While he appreciated the gesture, and its significance, he didn't have the say. Not because he wasn't her Pa. He'd spent far too long around Jane to not know where the say belonged. "There's one problem with that."

"What?"

"I'm not the one you need to be asking."

Arthur glanced wildly toward Jane.

"Nope. Not her, neither."

"Huh?"

"Sally's her own woman. Has been for a long time. Mighta been, or still be, Jane's and my ward, but she can make up her own mind, I reckon. Learned a long time ago some women know their own minds."

Arthur stared at his empty glass, a frown etched deep into his face.

"You wondering if she'll say no?"

"No."

"Then what?"

"Wishing I hadn't wasted my first drink on that is all."

Cole shrugged. "Worse ways to waste it, I guess. When you gonna talk to Sally? I'd best warn Jane." As if he didn't know she'd heard the whole thing.

"You don't gotta tell her."

"Yeah. I do. You showed up in the bar and had a drink, she's gonna ask."

Arthur spun his glass. "Sally's been different."

Cole knew Jane had seen the same thing. Hell, even Cole had noticed. Still, he only nodded. "That happens."

"What if she says no?"

"Plenty of women around."

"Not like her."

"True enough, but ya never know." Cole finished off his glass. "Another?"

"Yes."

Cole headed back to the bar. He paused to kiss Jane on the cheek, muttering under his breath, "You get all that?"

She spoke just as quiet. "I'm going to have to talk to Sally."

"Why?" Cole didn't wait for the answer, instead heading to grab the bottle of whiskey. He stopped when she waved him over.

She lifted a receipt as cover. "Because I know how awful it is to be surprised with a proposal."

"That so?" He glanced sideways at her. "You'd best be talking about Webb."

"Perhaps."

*The more I see of the world, the more I am
convinced that I shall never see a man
whom I can really love.
They require so much!*
-Jane Austen

Jane finished the letter to Al in relative peace. Alma had gone for a walk with Cole, while Willow and Jay had gone with Isaac and Jesse to the lake for some fishing. Sally was sitting her teacher's examination, which left her with Colton and Clara.

The twins sat near her feet. Colton lay on his stomach, turning the pages in a children's book. Cole had said he could swear the child was reading. Jane might have argued, but by all accounts she was reading at three. With the twins now nearly two and a half, and her propensity to read to them every night, anything was possible.

Clara, on the other hand, played with blocks. Her favorite task was knocking them down. In turns she'd build a tower nearly tall as her, only to smash them loudly seconds later. The clattering had been Jane's only disturbance for a blissful twenty minutes.

As the two remained distracted by their toys, Jane pulled her journal from a drawer. The evening before Cole had sidetracked her so thoroughly she hadn't had a chance to make an entry for the day. She planned to remedy that immediately.

The door to the apartment slammed open, then shut in quick succession. Sally stomped into the room, muttering under her breath. It appeared she hadn't noticed Jane or the twins yet as she slammed her books on the stairs. "Arrogant, pretentious, bull-headed, cock sucker!"

At that moment, Sally turned. Her face went beet red for a moment. Hands flying to her mouth she half sobbed. "Ma! I'm so…I…Oh."

Jane flew to her feet when Sally burst into tears. The twins toddled after her to clasp Sally's legs in their tiny comforts while Jane pulled her into a strong hug. The girl shook with sobs, her hand pressed to her face.

After a moment her arms surrounded with a hold so tight, it took Jane's breath away.

Jane did her best to soothe Sally through the shudders. When it seemed the tears were under some sort of control, Jane breached the silence. "Sally. What happened?"

"Nothing," Sally muttered into Jane's shoulder.

"Clearly. Come on, let's sit down. Clara, Colton, why don't you return to your toys?" Jane tried to lead Sally to the sofa, but the twins kept a firm grasp on her legs.

Clara patted the skirts that puffed around her hold. Her sweet little voice kept saying, "There, there."

Sally laughed weakly at her inability to move. Slowly she extricated herself from Jane's hug to crouch down to the level of the twins.

Jane took Sally's appreciation of the twins comfort to pour some tea for them both. In case Sally needed something stronger, she added a decanter of whiskey to the tray. By the time she'd set the tray on the table, Sally had soothed the twins back to their playing.

Sally sat beside Jane silent as a church mouse. Her face still flushed from her tirade, eyes rimmed red from her tears. The absent gaze out the window seemed rather lost.

"Whiskey or tea?"

"What?" Sally turned to Jane, some life returning to her at the question. "Whiskey?"

"For that level of upset, I wondered if you'd need it."

"But you haven't let me since…"

"You are hardly a child of fifteen any longer." Jane set her hand on Sally's. "Plus, with the way you entered this room I thought something stronger might be in order."

"I don't even know if it is. I'm just so…I don't even know."

Jane poured two glasses of whiskey, along with two glasses of tea. "I suggest we start at the beginning. Your exam. How did it go?"

"I got good marks on everything. My reading was the lowest, with an eighty-five."

"Sally!" Jane turned to face her dead on. A smile formed even as Sally lowered her head. "That's wonderful news. I knew you'd do well."

"I guess." Sally stared at her folded hands.

"Sally?"

"The superintendent." Her eyes welled with tears again until a drop slipped down her cheek. "He said he wouldn't give me a certificate, and I definitely could never teach here because of what I was."

A flash of anger rose in Jane so fast, she almost stood to go give Superintendent Paxil a piece of her mind. In the face of Sally's upset, she managed to tamp down the anger quick enough. "He wouldn't even give you the certificate? Despite your grades?"

"No. Ma, nobody here would want—even if—I won't ever be seen as—"

"The superintendent is one man. He doesn't live in our town. He doesn't know you or these people."

"But he knew what I was, Ma. If he knows that, he knows something."

Jane scooted closer to Sally to wrap an arm around her shoulders. "You did well, Sally. That's all I ever asked of you, for you to be learned enough to earn a second grade certificate. Are you truly so upset about not getting a certificate?"

Sally lifted her gaze. Her lip trembled before she turned away. "I'm sorry I disappointed you. I know you wanted me to be a teacher."

"What?" Jane leaned back, unable to stop her incredulous stare. "What on earth would make you say such a thing?"

"You said." Sally sniffed, taking the kerchief Jane handed her. She dabbed her eyes and nose. "I don't think I even want to, but I wanted you to be proud. To see me as a teacher, like you wanted."

"Oh, you darling child. No. I never wanted you to be a teacher." Jane squeezed Sally's forearm in reassurance. "When we spoke about you moving in with us, I specifically said you did *not* have to become a teacher. I only wanted you capable of passing at a level wherein you could gain a second grade certificate as a measure of your learning. You did well enough to have gotten a first grade if the superintendent wasn't such a prick."

"I thought you wanted—oh. I guess I forgot that part. I thought you wanted me to teach."

"No. I want you to do whatever it is you wish. If you know what that is yet." Jane smiled when Sally met her gaze again. With her thumb, she brushed away a stray tear on Sally's cheek. "Furthermore, I am very proud of you. I have been for some time. For all your struggles, you did exceptionally well on your exam today. You've come well ahead of what you might have once been."

Sally hugged her fast and tight. After a few minutes she drew back with a sigh. She grabbed her glass of whiskey and tossed it back fast. A shudder ran through her, but her features calmed. "I'm so relieved."

"Me too. Now, have you thought of what you might want to do now?"

Once again Sally avoided Jane's eyes. A flush darkened her cheeks.

Jane pondered the meaning of the newest onset of nerves. If it were Arthur, the boy was in luck. If not, Jane wondered what had caused such a reaction. Her wonderings over Tommy's cryptic mentions of Sally needing gumption crept into her thoughts. It seemed as though the man knew something she didn't.

Then again, if she thought hard enough on it, she did have an idea. One she didn't want to entertain, for the sake of her own heart. Jane swallowed her own nerves to draw her focus back on the young woman before her. "Sally?"

"I have. A little." She spun to face Jane again, her eyes wide. "I don't think you'd like it, or you might think me crazy."

"Oh, I know crazy. I've *been* crazy." Jane chuckled softly, even if Sally's own nerves began to secure her own worries into place. "Tell me. I can handle it."

"I've always been fascinated by Tommy's stories. That life he led. He's been teaching me some about what he did. How he investigated. It's so very interesting."

Jane worked hard to keep her features neutral. The idea of Sally living a life of risk and danger worried her to no end. Having lived through risk and danger of her own, she felt no draw of excitement to his stories. Even if to this day she couldn't keep from adding her two cents to things like Keller and Emily's deaths.

"Ma?"

Jane stirred back to the present at Sally's nervous tone. She met her ward's worried features, and once again the worry tugged her heart. "A Pinkerton?"

"Or a private detective without such a tie." Sally bit her lip. Worry shone in her eyes with the remnants of tears. "You don't like it."

"I said no such thing."

"You don't look happy."

"I won't lie, the idea worries me. Pinkertons lead dangerous, lonely lives full of secrets and deception. It's not an easy life."

"I'm probably not suited for it anyhow."

"You deceived Cole and I for over a year at the tender age of fourteen." Jane sighed out her reluctance to admit the logic of Sally's thoughts. She wasn't blind, and knew that Tommy's own comments meant he wanted her to, thought her capable. "Perhaps it is something you would do well at. You simply can't expect me not to worry over you any less than I would any of my children. Rather more, should you choose such a dangerous lot in life."

"You don't mind? Really?"

"I wouldn't say I don't mind, but it's my own worries that bother me, not any doubt you could likely do this. I'm not about to stop you if it's something that truly excites you. What does Arthur think of this endeavor?"

"He, um, he really doesn't know."

"Don't you think he should know? The young man has designs on marrying you, Sally."

"He—what?" Sally's eyes widened. "What on earth would make you say such a thing?"

"Sally, be reasonable. You two have been courting for over a year. Why should Arthur's intentions surprise you? The goal for courting someone is usually to become betrothed, or at least to see if you are compatible for such."

"He hasn't started college. I thought a had time." A whole new emotion drew Sally's features into a frown.

"Time for what?"

"I, well, I." A deep flush filled Sally's cheeks. Her fingers twisted together in a fit of nerves.

"Sally. You know you can speak to me about whatever it might be."

"I just thought—with time—maybe. Oh." Her shoulders sagged.

This time Jane didn't speak, she allowed the silence to linger while Sally pondered. The girl poured another whiskey and downed it fast. Jane continued to nurse hers slow, watching Sally as she rose to pace the floor.

"I keep thinking about when you spoke of the beasts of burden."

Back when Jane had first approached Sally about becoming their ward, and no longer being a whore, she'd likened the men who paid for entertainment to beasts of burden—asses. The idea didn't jibe with what she knew of Arthur, even less to Sally's relationship with him. "You aren't saying that Arthur is—"

"Oh, no! Never." Sally chewed her lip, eying the twins playing nearby. Then she met Jane's gaze, a shimmer of tears returning to hers. "You said that one day I would know what it was like to figure out what it is I would truly enjoy. How to ask for it, and perhaps even demand it."

"That you remember, but not my determination that you needn't become a teacher?"

Sally's blush carried down to her bosom. "You said one day I would meet someone that excited me. Someone that stimulated me and…"

Jane understood at last. For as sweet as the courtship between Sally and Arthur had been, it certainly couldn't be called fiery such as herself and Cole's. "You want excitement."

"I see what you and Cole got. Tommy and Leanne. Even Kat with Norman of all people." Sally finally managed a sheepish smile when Jane chuckled. "I want such a thing, too."

"And you don't have that with Arthur. None of the passion and excitement."

"He is *good*, Ma. Kind. Sweet. He's everything I should want, isn't he?"

"David is all of those things as well. I had no desire for him." Jane smiled sadly, knowing how it still pained her to hurt him. "I agree that Arthur is a very good young man. I've always found him smart and intuitive, and as kind as his parents have ever been to me."

"It isn't fair to him to hurt him. He's been so good to me."

"Sally, it wouldn't be fair to *you* to marry him out of obligation. You'd never be truly happy, nor truly who you were meant to be."

"I could be an old maid before I find anyone."

"If you want a life of adventure and excitement as you say you do, you shouldn't settle."

Sally sank to the couch by Jane. She leaned closer and lowered her voice. "When he kisses me, I don't feel…"

Jane knew where it was going before Sally found the word. "Stimulated?"

"I don't."

"You must talk to him about this. Perhaps with kind words instead of brutal honesty."

"I'll break his heart, Ma."

"It will likely be the first of many you'll break."

27

*When we are tired, we are attacked
by the ideas we conquered long ago.
—Friedrich Nietzsche*

Cole waited until the patron walked away before shutting down the Faro table. Faro was notoriously bad for the house, but that's why they kept it. It could give someone new to gambling a sense of confidence, and Jane occasionally used it when someone had lost too much to ever recoup. Today had been a new client. Once we'd won half a dozen hands, Cole had gestured for Felicity to come urge the stranger toward another game. With the skill of the whore she'd once been, she got the man wrapped up in roulette.

The casino bustled with life, which was good for them. The brothel still wasn't open and their coffers had taken a hit with all of the initial capital it took to build a business. At least Wil was already there. Tommy had found them some leads on whores when the time was right.

If everything kept to schedule, they'd be ready in a few weeks. Wil had already picked out what room he'd use and the size, which meant he'd be moving out of their staff rooms soon as it was done.

Speak of the devil, Cole spotted Wil heading down into the pit right then. He crossed to the man before heading to the bar. Cole spoke low to avoid detection. "Don't care what sort of mess and turmoil you make at Tully's or anywhere else in town. Keep it outta my casino."

"Wouldn't disrespect Jane like that." Wil offered a smirk. "You, on the other hand."

Cole held his frown long as he could before he broke into a chuckle. "Don't blame you there. She can be scarier than me."

"Damn straight."

Still laughing under his breath, Cole went to the bar. When he'd taken Alma back to the apartment Jane had seemed on edge, on the verge of a towering temper. She'd given him no clue to the reason, instead had shooed him to the casino to work.

When he'd inquired after Sally's test that day, Jane had curtly told him she'd passed but had no certificate to show for it. Once again, she didn't bother to explain, all but pushing him out the door. Of course, that had been too bad, as he'd hoped for another go at making a baby.

Her mood showed that wasn't going to happen. Though often a great cure for her tempers, she wasn't heated enough to soothe herself in such a way quite yet.

"What's got you grumpy?" Tom circled the bar.

"Jane's in a temper."

"What'd you do?"

"Nothing. I was out walking with Alma. Came back to her in a mood. Not sure who she's angry at, actually." Cole poured drinks for those seated at the bar. "Did you do something?"

"Don't think so. I've been at Leanne's since last night. Her and the girls are still out of sorts after Emily. Couldn't get any more information out of them, though. Instead I made time with Leanne. You know, comforting her."

Cole cut him a sideways look. "You're enjoying this way too much."

"If you want to complain, you've got to come clean." Tommy grinned wickedly as he poured his coffee. "We both know that's not happening any time soon."

"Sure isn't." Cole accepted the coffee he handed him. He wanted whiskey, but Jane forbade drinking while working. A limitation he'd never much cared for, even if it did make sense when you were running a casino.

"How'd Sally do?"

"Jane said she passed but didn't have a certificate."

"What? Why not?"

"Didn't tell me."

"Maybe that's why she's in a temper."

"Could be." Movement at the edge of the pit drew his eye.

Jane stood at the top of the steps. She'd changed out of the simple dress she wore in the apartment into a stunning blue dress that matched her eyes, drew attention to her cinched waist and low-cut bosom. Her features lit with a fury he'd always found so appealing, part of the reason he'd needled her so often in the start of their relationship. Temper darkened her cheeks, and he knew her eyes were alight with ferocity. Beauty and vexation.

"Maybe you should ask her yourself." Cole pointed her out.

"Oh, she is in a temper, isn't she?" Tommy polished off his coffee, eying his sister as she descended the stares. "Why is she glaring at me?"

"Dunno. Thought you said you didn't do anything."

"I didn't know I had." Tommy greeted Jane with a smile, despite her temper.

"Thomas Eugene Young." Jane approached so fast and furious it made Tommy take a step back. "You couldn't have been bothered to forewarn me?"

Cole would have laughed at the flash of worry on Tommy's face if Jane weren't so ready to spit fire. In all his time around Tommy, he'd very rarely seen the man truly scared.

"What, exactly, am I supposed to have warned you about?" Tommy straightened; the worry gone. "What did I do? I've been gone all night."

"Sally."

"Ah." Tommy dared to smile. "She got the gumption."

"I am good as her ma, I've cared for her for two years. You should have at least told me."

"You knew."

"I did *not*." She took another step toward her brother. When he took a step back, she countered with another forward. "I was blindsided today. No time to prepare for such news, to give her a better answer to her questions, to prepare my *heart*."

"You did know. You didn't want to see it."

"What in hell are you two talking about?" Cole stared between the two, but only Tommy bothered to glance at him after the question.

"You're an ass." Jane poked a finger into her brother's chest. "You know you should have said something more than your stupid cryptic clues that mean *nothing* in the scheme of things."

"You're smart enough to figure them, you didn't want to." Tommy put his hands on his hips. "It was her secret, and she's the one that had to tell it."

"Of course she did, but that didn't mean you couldn't have prepared me. Outright, like a man. You are not the keyholder for all the secrets of the universe, Thomas."

"Fine, *Clara.*"

The word struck Jane like a slap. She took a step back, a whole new twist of emotion darkening her temper. Eyes dark as a stormy sky, she stared at her brother.

Cole stepped forward, ready to pull Jane away. The woman beat him to it, turning fast to hightail it right out of the casino. He stared after her departing back, considering if it was wise to follow right then.

No, she needed to cool her head, and he needed to find out what the hell that was all about. He turned on his brother-in-law.

The man stared the same place Cole had just been watching. Remorse pursed his brows. "Damn. That slipped out."

"I never once heard you call her Clara. All your other brothers do it all the time, you haven't done it once that I've heard." Cole poured Tommy a whiskey despite the rules. The man looked like he could use one.

Tom took it in silence, still staring where he'd last seen Jane. After he'd tossed it back, he shook his head. "She's never been Clara to me. Clara hated me, hated my secrets, hated what I did. For a minute there—that was the closest to Clara I've ever seen. And you're right, not once have I ever called her that. Lou, sure, but not Clara."

"Care to let me in on what that was all about? If I'm gonna calm her down, it'll help to know what she's on about."

"Right." Tom's hand shook imperceptibly when he poured another glass of whiskey.

Cole didn't point out he shouldn't have another, especially given the shaking. He imagined Jane was just as shaken by Tommy calling her Clara as Tom seemed to be. Instead, he nursed his coffee to give Tom a moment to collect himself. "Sally?"

"Right," Tom repeated. "Sally. Yeah. She's been real keen on what I did since after she saved my life. The past year it's gotten more so. She's asked to learn some of it on occasion. Nothing big, more about how I investigated, how I read people."

Cole remained silent. He had a feeling where it was going without being told. Then it struck him. "Jane was put off by the way she was fascinated and stayed during the autopsy."

"That was surprising to me, too. She bonded quick with the new doc."

"Did she now?"

"Friends, not friendly." Tom rubbed his hand over his face. "She was definitely curious about what he did as a coroner much as she was about being a Pinkerton."

"Tom. Spill it."

"She wants to be a detective, maybe a Pinkerton, but I don't think she wants to be tied to that group, not that I blame her. It isn't all intrigue and fun. There's some ugly."

"You couldn't give Jane a heads up?"

"I kept Clara's secrets, I keep Janes, and yours. Sally had to get the gumption to tell Lou herself, or she'd never have the gumption to go anywhere with it."

"You still coulda clued her in."

"I really thought she knew." Tommy downed his whiskey.

"You really think little Sally can do something like what you did?"

"Hell no."

"What?"

Tom settled on the bar stool across from Cole. "Women can't do what I do, but they can do some pretty ingenious stuff when it's required of them. Some of the best agents I worked with were women. You met one."

"The chambermaid in Sioux City."

"That's the one." Tom spun his glass on the counter. "Sally is clever. Given her past as a whore, she knows a bit about reading people."

Cole frowned. "She's been planning this for a while. Why take the teachers exam at all?"

"First, because it was Jane's requirement at the start of taking her in as a ward."

"Don't really think she cared by the end of it. Sally's family now."

"I know that. You know that. Sally had it in her head that Jane for sure told her she had to be a teacher. She wants Jane to be proud of her, so rather than tell her the truth, she went ahead and went for it."

"You sure she's clever?"

"Cleverer than you." Tom chuckled. "She made that promise when she was young, scared, and injured. Since then she's gotten a lot more confidence. There's just one thing holding her back."

"She was a whore."

"She was a whore," Tom concurred. "Jane and I both have been working on reminding her she isn't that person anymore."

Cole straightened, thinking over the whole thing. "A Pinkerton? Sally?"

"With the right training. Proper training, not the piecemeal lesons we've had until now. She'd be one of the best, I reckon."

"Huh." Of all the things he'd imagined, Sally as a Pink hadn't been one of them. He supposed he hadn't much thought of her beyond being their ward. She'd always been so good to, and with, Alma. The pair had formed a bond, and Cole wondered how this new development might affect that.

"I should go apologize."

"Not sure it's safe yet." Cole blinked away the stray thoughts. "She was pretty upset."

"Wounded, more like."

"You know they say it's not safe to corner a wounded animal."

"I know. Pray for me."

*There is only one way to happiness
and that is to cease worrying about things
which are beyond the power of our will.
—Epictus*

Cole stopped by the barn on his way back to the apartment. He and Wil had been looking over the progress on the brothel when he'd spotted Jane returning on Tempest. He'd been sure the woman had gone to the library as she often did when upset.

Inside Jane brushed down Tempest. Still dressed in her good gown, though the bustle looked off balance now. Easy, strong strokes slid along the horse's flank. All the while Jane kept a steady stream of quiet talk to the beast.

He leaned on the doorframe to watch her while she worked. Once Tom had left the casino, he'd not seen hide nor tail of either of them. Part of him wondered if Tom was still hunting her down. The man was usually pretty good at finding people.

"I don't know what he wants. Sitting there with that scowl about his features."

Cole focused on Jane when her now louder words hit his ears. He lifted a corner of his lip. "Not scowling. Didn't know you knew I was here. I was just enjoying the view."

"Looked like the view made you miserable." She resumed brushing the horse without another pause. "Grumpy as hell."

"You're one to talk."

"Yes. Well. I have rights to be."

He wrapped his arms around her waist, nestling his chin against her throat. "You make up with Tom?"

Tension ratcheted through her quicker than a bolt of lightning. "I haven't seen him."

"He left here looking for you."

"I went for a ride. He didn't find me. I didn't care for him to."

"Jane. He felt right bad after he said it. Haven't seen the man that upset in…" He straightened, thinking hard. "Ever."

"Good for him." She scooted under Tempests neck to her other side.

"Jane."

"I don't want to hear you defend him." Her gaze lifted to lock him in place. "I'm justified in my upset, and I care not what his defense is."

"Fine. Fine." Cole lifted his hands in surrender. "Now come back over here. I was right comfortable with you where you were."

Finally, her lips curved into a delicious smirk. "What if I don't care for your distractions, either?"

"Oh, but you do." He winked. "Remember, you don't lie if you can help it."

"Even in my temper, hm?"

"It's better with your temper. Why do you think I like riling you right up?"

"You always did."

"Still do. Let the hand finish up Tempest. We can make quick work of soothing your temper."

"We could, but it would rile me in another way."

He wagged his brows. "I won't complain."

For that she offered him a deliciously warm laugh that tingled right through to his toes. "What of Clara's parents? They leave tomorrow. We're supposed to spend time with them."

For a moment Cole was too distracted to realize she'd come back to his side of the horse. Then her body pressed into his, and his gaze flicked down to her. "Clara's parents?"

"They are today."

"Tom really threw ya."

"Are you going to ruin the moment? I mean, after the ride, my bustle is already dislodged."

He dropped the subject faster than a bad bet after the suggestion. Tugging her close, he closed his lips over hers, drawing her in deep until her moan rumbled against his.

They made it two steps toward the loft ladder when an ill-timed booming voice reached into the barn. "Janey! Archie saw you ride back to town. I know you're in here."

Jane's lip curled at her brother's voice. She glared toward the door when a shadow darkened it. "Not talking to you. Get out, we've got business."

"If I tried to catch you not in business, I'd be waiting for years."

"Then wait." She clutched Cole's shirt when he tried to slip away. When her glare cut his way, he lifted his hands in defense again. "Don't even think of it. You wanted my temper, you got it."

"Jane," Cole started.

"Leave him out of it." Tommy interrupted him. "You're going to hear me out for once."

"I don't have to. More so, I don't want to. I'm going to sit in my anger."

"Stop being such a brat." Tom offered Cole a nod as if to release him.

Too bad Jane still had a fistful of his shirt. Cole moved to close his hand over Jane's, but her grip released a second later. Tom had grabbed her arm, and she turned her full ire on him. While she yelled at her brother, Cole slipped free.

Though frustrated by the interruption, he knew they'd make up for it soon. Still, he had to adjust himself before he stepped foot into the apartment. When he pushed open the door it was onto quite a load of chaos.

All of the children cluttered the apartment, along with Jane's parents, her brothers Nick and Mike, along with his own half-sister Leanne. The resulting scene was anarchy. The twins vied for Eunice's attentions, while Jay made quite a show of it with John.

Sally sat with Leanne and Jane's brothers, all four sipping on whiskey or bourbon and laughing loud at some story Leanne shared freely given the general noise level in the room. Whether to add to the noise, or distract from it, Alma pounded away a gay tune on the piano with aplomb. The second the last note landed a round of cheers went around, and she launched into another lively number.

Willow was the sole stone of quiet in the mess. She sat at the table Jane had stowed in the corner for lessons. Quite alone. Watching the room in utter silence.

Cole headed her way. Though he took the seat beside her, he didn't speak. Rather, he watched the revelry as silent as she. Over his years he'd been an onlooker near as much as a carouser. If she wanted to talk, so be it. Otherwise, he'd just sit there with her observing the show for what it was.

Too bad Jane was fired up and fighting at the moment. She'd rather enjoy mixing in with this nonsense. Even more if Jesse was a part of it. Cindy and Lizzie too, for that matter. More than anything, she loved having all of the kids in one place.

"I'm forgetting them." Willow's words were quiet under the gaiety.

Cole didn't bother to look her way, wondering if it would make her clam up. "You mean your ma and pa?"

"He is, too." Out of the corner of his eye, he saw her nod to her brother. "He gets mad. We don't want to forget. You made us."

"Not us." He frowned. Jane was better at this sort of stuff than he was. The two had been with them for a year already. In all that time, Jane had never forced them to forget, rather she'd asked them questions. "Jane would never make you."

"We're forgetting what we are. You are making us."

Cole chewed his lip while he watched Jay attacking his checkers game with John. "If we are, it's not on purpose. Anything we can do? Jane doesn't want you to forget. That's why you get to wear your clothes at home. She's even seen to getting bigger sizes for Jay. Boy's growing like a weed, he is."

"We want to see them."

For that, Cole turned to face her. She leaned back as if intimidated, but her brows furrowed her intensity. He sighed deeply and leaned on the table. "Don't know that it's possible. It's a journey to Utah, and the reservation isn't likely to allow it."

"She doesn't want us to."

"I repeat, Jane doesn't want you to forget. Never did. I just don't think we're gonna be able to take you there. Maybe we can get word from them, though. We can ask Tom."

Her stubborn gaze wavered, then sank to the floor. When she started blinking rapidly as if to keep away tears, Cole turned away to give her a minute.

"I'll talk to Tommy. Meantime, think of something you can do that helps you remember. Jane just doesn't know what to do to help. If she doesn't, I sure don't. She's better at this than me. Always was."

The door opened, letting in a flushed Jane. She took one look around the room, pausing on him and Willow before turning her attentions to the twins when they ran up.

The chaos seemed to reach new levels with Jane's arrival. Cole wondered where Tom was, and what she'd done to him. With her temper, and the gun still strapped in her holster, it could have been anything. He didn't hear a shot, but it was really loud in there.

Silence lingered beside him. Cole wasn't about to push the girl. He figured she was twisted up tighter than a drum and needed to figure some stuff out. He'd been there a few times in his life. Most of them revolving around the creature across the room joining in the revelry as if she hadn't been close to fisticuffs when he'd left her.

"Beads." Willow spoke the word so suddenly, it startled Cole's attention back to her. "And string. I'd like beads."

"I'll mention it to Jane. If they don't got them at the store, she'll see to it."

"They do. I saw them."

"Fair enough. I'll let Jane know. If it helps, I'll bet she don't mind."

Willow nodded once, then turned her attention back to the floor.

When Cole turned, Jane headed straight for him. She leaned in to whisper *coward* in his ear before acknowledging Willow. He slid his hand along her waist, tugging her onto his lap. "Willow was just saying—"

Willow's head snapped up, her eyes narrowing in suspicion.

"That she'd like some beads and string from the store. Said she saw them there."

"Yes. I remember." Jane smiled at Willow. "You were looking at them two weeks ago. I'm happy to pick them up for you. How much do you need? I think he does it by weight."

Willow shrugged.

"Hmmm. Well, I'll get you some. String as well, do you mean like sewing thread? Oh, how about we go together? You can show me what you need." Jane set her hand on Cole's where it sat on her hip. "We'll go tomorrow after the Young's are on the train."

Willow nodded, then slipped away.

Jane sighed softly. Her words carried on a whisper with heavy weight in the cacophony. "She stubbornly resists us at turns."

"She said we're making them forget her parents, and what they are."

"Oh, dear. That isn't my intention."

"Asked to visit them."

"Simply not possible. I hope you were able to say as much."

"I did. Thought we might try to get them messages, though."

"That's an idea." She nodded. "We'll see if that's possible."

"What about Tom?" He patted her hip, pulling her close. Glad he had her good ear he spoke low, "Do I need to clean up a body? You got your gun. Shoulda taken it when I ran."

Her lips pursed, narrowed eyes turning on him. "I have some restraint, thank you very much."

"Not always."

"He lives. Pouting because I gave him an earful and am not ready to forgive yet."

"No?"

"No. Now, we should join the festivities so we might retire sooner rather than later. I'd like to finish what we were discussing in the barn."

He nipped at her earlobe. "You mean how I like your tempers?"

"That's the one."

"Bully for me."

*Marriage is like a cage;
one sees the birds outside desperate
to get in, and those inside equally
desperate to get out.
-Michel de Montaigne*

The picnic wound down in the late afternoon sun. The children quieted as parents called them to return home. Sally lazily helped clean their three blankets from the remains of a hearty lunch. Once again Cole hadn't joined them, as Sally had come to expect. In the years she'd been living with Jane and Cole, she'd only seen Cole attend church on a handful of occasions.

His absence didn't seem to have any effect on Jane's enthusiasm for the day. She'd spent an hour playing with all the children. The amusement she'd carried all day had only been marred by one thing that Sally could tell—Tommy. The pair returned to the blanket along with Kat and Leanne but didn't speak to each other directly. Jane had only made perfunctory comments to her brother as decorum and conversation had dictated.

Jane sank to the blanket, sipping her water delicately. "What a beautiful day. After the sweltering heat of our crowded church, I'm pleased the day isn't quite so intense."

"I still wouldn't mind a dip in the swimming hole." Tom stretched out on the blanket, resting his head in Leanne's lap. "Especially after that round of games."

"Perhaps we can find a way to cool you down." Leanne poked his belly. "Once I've seen you properly overheated, of course."

Heat flooded Sally's cheeks at the inuendo. She ducked her head to hide her grin over Cora's shocked exclamation of the day. She found Jane eying her with matching amusement making her lips twitch.

After another sip of water, Jane's attention wandered back toward town where the Inn sat in clear view. Sally wondered if Jane could actually see Cole on the porch, or just imagined him there. With a sigh, she turned back to the crowded blanket. To have the sort of love that it seemed you could sense your lover. What would that be like?

She found Jane had turned back to her, an eyebrow arched. Jane's head tilted; her voice low. "Is everything all right? That was a rather deep sigh."

"It is. I think. I suppose. Oh." Sally blew out her frustration while Jane chuckled softly. Rather than face the question, Sally leaned closer. "Are you upset with Tommy?"

"I am."

"Is it…" Sally hesitated to say the words aloud. "Because he's been teaching me?"

"No." Jane offered a smile that she'd shown Sally often, one so akin to motherly affection, Sally drank it in like water. "It isn't your fault Sally. He's my brother. Siblings fight.

Even you and Alma have had a tiff or two, as well as Jesse and yourself. It happens. It'll pass when I'm ready for it to pass."

"If you're sure."

"I rarely say anything I'm not certain of." Jane chucked her under the chin before turning to reach for a biscuit still sitting on a plate.

Sally glanced around and spotted Jesse sitting with Lizzie. The girl had a handful of flowers, and the two were speaking rapidly with their hands, almost talking right over each other. She was sure Jesse had learned to speak with his hands because of his affection for the girl. They'd been sweethearts near as long as Lizzie had lived with Kat. She wondered if she could master the language as Jane, Jesse, Kat, and Lizzie had. She'd even seen Norman using it a few times. If she wasn't mistaken, a few of Jane's brothers had as well. "Ma?"

"Hm?"

"Do you think you could teach me hand speak?"

"Well, I certainly can try." Jane licked some jam from her fingers rather indelicately. "We'll see if you can't learn it. I imagine Lizzie would be glad for another soul that understands her."

"Thanks. Maybe French, too."

"French, too? Goodness, you are feeling ambitious."

"You know them both."

Jane laughed. "Fair point, although I don't remember learning French, and despite the Young's telling me we learned German as youths, I remember not a word."

"That's not entirely true. You read von Goethe in German."

"I suppose I do. Perhaps because I remember the English words so well, it's easy to translate." Jane finished her water. "I suppose we ought to clean properly. The hour is getting late for lazing about."

A throat cleared behind her. "Sally?"

Sally froze with her hand outstretched to grab a plate. In the days since Jane had told her of Arthur's intentions, she'd avoided him as much as possible. It was tough to avoid someone on Sunday, though. She turned to find him fumbling nervously with his vest.

He cleared his throat again. "Would you accompany me for a carriage ride? Mike said we could borrow his since he's heading to his resort after this."

"I need to help Ma with the children," Sally protested. Arthur's fit of nerves raised her own. Though they'd shared a few walks and carriage rides in their courtship, Arthur hadn't been nervous for any but the first few.

"Nonsense," Jane objected. "I have four blankets full of people to assist me with the children. Go." Jane squeezed her hand. A serious look on her face, she gave Sally a reassuring nod. "Have your carriage ride. We'll be at home when you're done."

"I—if you're sure." Sally'd hoped Jane would help her avoid the ride, but she was clearly out of luck. She pushed to her feet, brushing grass from her skirts.

"Of course. We're fine here." Jane turned her attention away to Clara as the child ran up to the blanket, arms outstretched.

Sally walked with Arthur to the carriage, glancing back once more in hopes of assistance. Instead, she found Tommy staring her down. He gave her ne deliberate nod before his own attention wandered back to those on the blankets.

She accepted Arthur's help into the carriage, then tucked the dust robe around her skirts. Given the sheer amount of events over the summer, Jane had allowed her several new dresses. She was taking great pains to ensure none of them got mussed. Though Jane had never once complained of the cost of raising so many extra children, Sally didn't dare squander such generosity.

"You all right?" Arthur's voice interrupted her thoughts on clothes. "You look like you'd rather not go."

"It's not that, really." She did her best to not wince at the small lie. "I'm just distracted. Did you know Ellis didn't come to church today?"

"I did notice, so did Ma. It's not like him to not come to church."

"Has every Sunday for years, even after his wife died."

"I think I heard Kat say something about going to check on him tomorrow. They want to make sure he's not sick."

Sally frowned. "Last time Jane did that, she got the scarlet fever. They'd best be careful if they go. Who knows what they'll find."

"I'm guessing they learned their lesson the first time. Don't seem to take them but once or twice to learn, anyhow."

She laughed softly. "No, it doesn't. I hope I'm that quick a study. I have a lot to learn."

"Seem pretty smart to me."

"There's so much more to learn, though." Sally's eagerness blew away her nervousness. Imagining all she could learn under Tommy always brought that excitement forward. "There's a whole world outside of this place, after all. You know that. You're going to Denver for school. One of the first students in the university. It must be so exciting."

"It's just Denver. You've been there."

"I suppose." She sighed, leaning on the carriage with her elbow. Off in the distance the mountains stood, a barrier to the outside world she longed to cross. "Imagine what else is out there, though."

"You want to leave home?" He slowed the carriage by the edge of the lake. "Really?"

"I've thought about it. Quite a bit lately, actually. Home is something I can always return to. Ma isn't going anywhere if she can help it."

"I can't imagine leaving home."

"But you are." Sally turned to face him. "You're going to Denver."

"For school," he reiterated as if that made any difference. "I'm not leaving. I'm gonna work with Rusty at the newspaper like I've been doing for a while."

She let her gaze drift away toward the streak of color as sunset took hold of the valley. There was no way around it, she had to tell him. "I like hearing Tommy's stories. The adventures he had, the dangers he's faced. Everything is always the same here, even as it changes."

"Sally?"

"Hm?"

"What about me?" When she turned to face him, he stared at his hands. In his hands sat a small box that hadn't been there moments before. He twisted it through his fingers. "You wanna leave me, too? Like you do Dominion Falls?"

"I…" Her flash of courage faded into sorrow. He'd been so kind to her, so sweet, and at times rather charming. Still, they'd never truly talked in depth. A barrier had always existed between them. A barrier comprised of his need to help her be as good as him after her unseemly past as a whore. A barrier she hadn't truly seen until recently. Always she'd tried to be good for him, too. At the sacrifice of her own excitement. To be what was expected, or what she'd thought had been expected of her. Jane had proved it was the opposite.

Arthur said nothing in her silence for a long few minutes. He lifted his head toward the colors she'd just been admiring. After a deep breath, he seemed to regain his own strength. "Dominion falls is my home, always has been. I wanted to raise a family here like my Ma and Pa did. Like your Ma and Pa are."

"I know. I want something more."

"Something more than me?"

"No. Yes. I don't know." She turned to face him fully, desperate for him to understand this was about her, not him. "Don't you understand? I can never be more than what I was here. I'll always be the whore Pansy gone good…but *never* good enough. That's why Paxil wouldn't give me a teaching certificate, you know."

"That's not true."

"It *is* true. He told me as much. What with the history I had at the saloon, he couldn't in good conscience allow me to teach the children of the good people of this town, all of whom know what I once was."

"Then we'll find something else for you, if you want to work."

"*If* I want to work? Why on earth wouldn't I?"

"But as a wife and ma, you wouldn't have to."

"Kat does. Ma does. Your ma did and does. You expect me to be less?"

"I expect you to want the same things I do."

Sally stared at him for a few minutes, too stunned to speak. "You want a meek and quiet wife doing nothing but raising babies?"

"I mean, no. Not exactly."

"Besides," she cut him off. "Who says I want babies?"

"You don't want babies?" His features went slack. "But—your family."

"I'm my own person. I'm not my ma, much as I admire her."

"I thought you wanted to spend your life with me. We've been courting for over a year. I told you I wanted a family of my own. A big one."

"You did, and when I thought I had to be something expected of me, that was fine." Her cheeks grew tight at the well of tears threatening to erupt. "I didn't know your dream would be at the expense of my happiness."

"It ain't! I mean, it's not. Of course I'd want you to be happy. I want that life of a whore far behind you, just like you do." He held up the box for her to see. "I'm doing this all wrong. Sally, I want to marry you."

"No. You don't." Sally pushed the box back into his lap. "You are so focused on saving me from my whore past. You wanted so bad to do right by me, *for* me, loving me despite what I have been."

"I do love you."

"I know you believe that. I want to believe that. But can you love a soul you don't truly know? I mean, if you loved me, if you saw me as more than the poor wretch you had to save would you be surprised by anything I said tonight?"

"Sally."

"I don't want my past to go away, I don't want to bury it deep so no one can see. I don't want to be this town's next Martha Starbird. Angry, bitter, being obscenely proper to hide what I'd done in my past I'd rather everyone forgot."

Arthur's eyes were wide, his mouth moving in silent protest.

"I was a whore. It's a part of me, and always will be. It's the part of me you can't love. You don't want to think of the men in town you know that I serviced under contract."

"I—wait—stop. This is all wrong. How did this go so wrong?"

"You never want to talk about it, and I understand. It's not polite conversation. I've done all I can the past two years to be all I thought I had to be." Sally pulled the dust robe off her lap. "Paxil did one good thing by me. He made me see that I don't have to be something I'm not to make the world happy, because they will never be happy."

"Please, wait." Arthur scooted to her side of the carriage when she climbed out. "This went wrong in so many ways. Come back, so we can talk."

"I do want to talk to you, and tell you everything I want out of life. But not tonight." Sally took a step back. "I can't marry you Arthur. Not when we spent so long lying to each other."

"I never lied."

"No. Not intentionally. If it helps, I didn't mean to, either." She moved closer when he took her hand. She leaned in and kissed him softly. His desperation pulled her closer still, but she withdrew before he could pull her into the wagon. "I'm going to walk home. I need time to think."

"It's getting dark. Let me take you home. We can talk on the way."

"No. Go home, Arthur. I need to think. There's so much I want to tell you. Not right now. I need some time. Please."

Arthur sat there staring so long she had to turn her back on him. She walked with her back straight, head held high as she curved around the edge of the lake in silence. When the brake clicked open and the horses began to move again, she let out the breath she'd been holding.

She knew she'd overreacted to Arthur's statements. Bullied her way in charge of the conversation in order to say all she needed to. She wondered at how she hadn't realized his thoughts on what he'd wanted for a wife.

Over the course of their courtship, so much of their time had been spent around family. Siblings, parents, half the town that their parents considered family. Their true alone moments had been few and far between.

They'd talked about themselves, sort of. His plans for working with Rusty until he could take over the newspaper himself. She'd skirted mention of her past before Dominion Falls. No one wanted to hear about a mother that didn't want her, never had. It was as indelicate as her past as a whore to mention.

She'd been so wrapped up in following the rules and being the perfect ward, she hadn't wanted to rock the boat. Disrupt the burgeoning relationship, but she hadn't encouraged it, either. If she'd truly wanted alone time with Arthur, she would have found a way.

Perhaps it was all her fault. So much time being the good ward for Jane, the proper girl for Arthur. If she'd been honest from the start. Marriage, children, they weren't what she'd pictured in all of her wildest imaginings.

Then again, she hadn't really known what she wanted. What she'd dreamed of, certainly. Dreams she'd never thought possible.

Once Jane had freed her of the notion she had to be a schoolteacher, a whole world of possibilities now seemed possible. Best part was, she had time to explore them. She wanted time for that, not marriage. She wanted passion, not propriety.

Could she have those things with Arthur once she stopped being what she thought was expected of her? Did she dare to try?

A rustle in the tree line distracted her from her musings. She halted the inane task of tearing blades of grass to toss in the water to scan the nearby tree line. Could have been an animal, likely was.

After a shrug she plucked another blade of grass to tear apart.

Another rustle drew her gaze back to the tree line. Two dark shapes emerged. Not animal. In the dimming light of day, she didn't recognize them. "Hello?"

The pair waved to her greeting with simple hello's of their own.

Sally returned to shredding the grass, pondering what she'd do. It wasn't until the pair had circled closer that she thought to pay them mind again.

"Whore," the woman shrieked.

Sally saw movement to her right and raised her arms before she was hit so hard white pain flashed across her eyes.

Out of this nettle - danger -
we pluck this flower - safety.
-William Shakespeare

Jane paced the porch in front of Cole. Most of her brothers had gone home hours before as night fell over the town. Kat lingered, along with Cindy, Lizzie, and Jesse. They entertained the children back in their apartment. Leanne and Tom had remained in the apartment as well.

When Sally hadn't arrived home by nightfall, Jane's nerves began. Arthur had returned during supper, saying Sally wanted to walk home. The boy had seemed awfully glum about the whole situation, which led Jane to the conclusion Sally had turned down his proposal.

Several hours later Jane couldn't contain her nerves. In part, Cole understood. It didn't take hours to walk back from the lake. Thirty minutes, maybe an hour if you dawdled.

The later the hour grew, the more frantic Jane became. Cole didn't know what to do to calm her down, except finding the girl. He stood, leaning on his crutch. "I'll go out after her."

"You can't." Jane gestured to the blasted plaster still encasing his foot.

While he managed somewhat normal activity, he was still limited due to the size of the block of plaster. He'd threatened to take it off often and just wear a boot. He didn't really hurt that bad anymore, anyway. "I'll rip this off and get a boot on, then be on my way."

"No, you won't." Jane's pacing paused to face north again, though it was so dark you couldn't see past the light of the last street lamp near the train tracks.

"You're fretting. You hate fretting."

"Of course I'm fretting. Sally isn't one to stay out so late. Arthur returned with the carriage before we'd finished supper."

"She told him she was walking back. They were out at the lake, it takes some time. Especially if she stayed there thinking. You taught her to think too much."

"It still wouldn't take this long." Jane paused her pacing to stare north again.

Cole crossed to her side, wrapping his arm around her. "She'll be all right."

"Tell that to my nerves. Something's wrong."

He didn't argue with her. She'd had plenty of experience knowing when something was wrong. For that matter, he didn't feel to good about Sally's extended absence either.

Horseshoes clipped along the pavement slow and steady, stopping nearby. They both turned to find Tommy standing there with Brag and Bluff.

"Thomas?" Jane moved forward a half-step before tucking back in against Cole.

"Come on, Cole." Tommy nodded to Jane. "We'll go find her. Bring her home."

"Cole's foot," Jane objected.

"He's not about to sit around if he can help it. Let him do this." Tommy threw the reins over the hitching post. "Got Brag for you. Easier to get on than Faro."

"Thanks." Cole stepped aside when Tommy tugged Jane into a hug.

"I'm sure she's fine, Lou. You worry too much." Even as Tom said it, Cole could see concern lining his brother-in-law's features.

"I'll feel better when she gets back here." Jane pushed Tom away to face Cole. Rather than the scolding or warnings he expected, she wrapped her arms around his waist. "She likes to walk Tanner Lane when she goes to the lake."

"We'll take Tanner Lane on the way, and Settlement Road on the way back to be sure." Cole kissed the top of her head. "We'll get her."

Jane released her tight hold on his waist. She stepped back to give him room to maneuver his crutch. At the bottom of the steps, he leaned the crutch against the rail to get onto Brag's back. With a little maneuvering, he made it up with only a flash of pain in his bad foot.

He nodded to Jane once more before spinning Brag around to head down the road. Brag kept an easy pace until his brother Bluff got beside him with Tommy on his back.

"Wait," Jane called after them.

By the time Cole turned in his saddle, she'd gone from the porch. He glanced at Tommy with a furrowed brow. "She's not joining us."

Tommy shrugged, then shook his head. "No. There she is."

Jane jogged down the street, two lanterns dangling from her hands. "The moon is near full, but the cloud cover might be too much. Take these."

Cole hooked his lantern to his saddle. Once Tom had done the same, he met Jane's outstretched fingers with a quick touch. "We'll be back soon."

She nodded, stepping back as they took off toward the edge of town.

After they crossed the tracks, they took the east fork toward Tanner Lane. It was the long way to the lake, but they set an easy pace. Quick enough the ride wouldn't take too long, but slow enough to keep an eye out for Sally.

"Sally," Tom called into the night. "Where you at, girl?"

No response came. Wind rustled through the grass, a few crickets, but otherwise nothing. Cole called out for Sally as well minutes later, but the same nothing response came.

The moonlight guided them well enough for a while. Then as Jane predicted, it slipped behind a cloud. Cole paused to light his lantern. He lifted it high to shine along his side of the lane while they moved. After a while of silence, they both called for Sally again.

In the quiet absence of a response, he glanced at Tom. "Thanks. Jane wasn't going to let me go without a push."

"No thanks necessary. I wouldn't tell Jane, because it would make it worse, but I'm worried as well. It's not like Sally, Jane's right about that. I know she's upset about her boy, but she wouldn't stay gone too late. Besides, I figured now that she got the gumption to call you pa, you were all in."

"I've been all in for a while." Cole lowered his lantern when the moon breached the clouds. "Sally!"

They continued along Tanner Lane for half an hour without any sign of Sally anywhere. In the distance, the smooth surface of the lake reflected the moonlight. From where he sat he saw no sign of anyone near it.

"Check the lake first, then head back?" Tommy glanced his way.

"Jane'd kills us if we didn't take a closer look, even if we don't see anything from here." Cole spurred on Brag for the remaining quarter of a mile of open field. The grass grew taller the closer they got to the lake. He slowed so he didn't miss anything.

Tommy circled toward the east edge of the lake, so Cole moved along the opposite path. He brought brag close as he could to the shoreline, slowed him down to an easy walk.

Gaze fixed on the lake, the grasses, the tree line in the distance. No sign of her anywhere. Worry began to edge up stronger. They should have found her already if she was on the way to or from the lake. Sure there was still Settlement Road, but she didn't like to walk that one as it was busier than Tanner Lane.

"*Sally,*" Cole bellowed, not caring if he disturbed anyone else.

Tommy's voice echoed back from across the lake. "Sally!"

Halfway around the lake, Brag paused. The horse stomped, snorting out a huff of air.

"What's your problem?" Cole raised the lamp to look through the grass for something that might have spooked the horse. "Was it a snake? I don't see anything."

He urged the horse forward. They took two steps before something caught his eye. The tall grasses that rimmed the waters edge had a break in them. A swath of empty space.

At the same time he swung to dismount, Tommy's voice rang out. "Cole! Right in front of you. There's something in the lake."

"On it," He called back. Moving slow because of the blasted cast, he waded through the weeds. Water splashed over his feet before he finally spotted it. The bright green dress with gold trim Sally had been wearing at the picnic was nearly black in its soaked state. "Shit. Sally!"

Without further care to his foot, he rushed through the water to her side. He was knee deep by the time he reached her.

Sally lay face down at the edge of the water. Her nose sat barely above the edge of the water. Cole rolled her over, panicking at the blood and bruising he could see in the moonlight. "Sally!"

Hoofbeats stopped suddenly nearby. Cole hefted Sally into his arms, carrying her out of the water fast as he could manage through the choking weeds.

Tom met him the second he breached the edge of the tallest grasses. "What the hell happened?"

"No idea. Hold her a second." The sodden remains of his cast sloshed to the ground as he swung his leg over the saddle. "Give her here."

Tommy handed off the young woman without argument. He stepped back to allow Cole the room to race away.

Cole pushed Brag toward town fast as the horse could run with both of them in the saddle. Once in town, he tore around the clinic. He yelled to anyone in hearing distance. "Get the doc!"

By the time he hauled to a stop at the clinic, someone was at his side pulling Sally down from the horse. He followed her down, taking her back from whomever had grabbed her. He rushed into the clinic, his wet feet slipping on the floor. A set of hands caught him and pushed him heartily toward the exam room.

The hands turned out to belong to Jane. As she went to the other side of the exam table, tears streaked along her cheeks. Her hand shook as he smoothed back Sally's damp curls. "Oh, Sally. What happened?"

"Found her nearly all the way in the lake like this." Cole adjusted the way Sally lay on the table. The sodden dress and bulge of her bustle made it tough to get her on properly.

Jane dashed around turning up the lamps. As she did, a dark bruise blossoming across Sally's cheek shone in stark relief to her pale skin.

Cole grabbed Sally's cold hand, frowning as he realized something. "I don't think she's breathing."

"What?" Jane rushed forward. She dipped her left ear close to the girl's mouth. After a few seconds, she let out a breath. "She is…just not well. Cut her out. Charles should be here any second."

A pair of scissors were shoved in his hand. Jane worked at the bodice with a set of her own. Her hands shook so much they slipped on the soggy fabric. She kept at it until the garment came loose.

Cole snipped through the layers of skirt until they broke loose enough to yank off. Before he could continue, Charlie was at the bedside. "You both need to leave. Lydia will be here in short order, as will Andrew. We'll take care of her."

"Charles," Jane protested.

"Go, Jane. Let me work."

Cole set his hands on Jane's shoulders. "Let the docs do what they do. Charlie's got enough help, and your shaking, you won't help him none."

"I…" After a second, her shoulders sagged. She clutched her shaking hands tight together and nodded.

Cole led her from the room toward the waiting room. The second they got there, she spun into his hold. He sighed, pulling her tight against him. His shirt was soaked from carrying Sally, but neither of them cared. "Don't know what happened to her out there. If we hadn't thought to check the lake better…"

"But you did. You found her." She trembled in his hold. Her shaking fingers clutched his wet shirt. "Who could have done this to her?"

Cole frowned, shaking his head. Sure, the last person to see her was Arthur, but he couldn't imagine the boy doing something like this. "Surely not Arthur."

"No. It couldn't have been. It simply couldn't." Jane stepped back, her trembling hands smoothing over her hair.

Andrew and Lydia dashed into the clinic at nearly the same time. They didn't hesitate to run to the room with Charlie when Cole pointed to it.

Cole kept a hold on Jane's hand to keep her from following. "You gotta let them work. Ya know it."

"I do." Jane collapsed into a chair. Her gaze remained fixed on the door.

Millie entered, glancing around. Spotting Jane, she rushed to her side. She took a seat, out of breath from her travels. "What's happened?"

"Sally's been hurt." Jane blinked back to life. "She was at the lake with Arthur. She, um, told him she wanted to walk home, but never came. Cole and Thomas just—where's Thomas?"

Cole shook his head. "Don't know. I ran back here quick as I could. I suspect he'll be along in short order."

Jane clutched Milli's hand in hers. "She didn't look well at all, and I only saw her face. Who could have done such a horrible thing?"

"We'll figure that out in time. Most important thing is that we help Sally." Millie wrapped her arm around Jane's shoulders. "You know Charlie will take care of her, and he has excellent help in there with him."

"Reminded me of you when you first got here, 'cept you wasn't drowning." Cole shook off the memory of the first time he'd ever seen Jane—bruised, bloody, near death. He focused on the aftermath. "You survived all right. Sally's tough like you. So will she."

"She doesn't have to malinger in her wounds like I did, either." Jane sniffled, swiping at errant tears. "She'll be fine. She will be."

"'Course she will," he agreed.

A ferocity took over Jane's features. "And whoever did this will pay."

"You bet your ass they will," Tommy said from the door. He crossed to Jane to kiss the top of her head. "We'll see to it. We take care of our own, right Lou?"

"Right." Jane nodded once, short but strong.

"Millie. Oughtn't you be in bed?" Tommy took in his sister-in-law. "Resting for that baby?"

"The baby is what keeps me awake." Millie chuckled. Her hand swept over her stomach. "I heard the calls before Charlie did. This little one doesn't like his mama to sleep."

Jane set her hand on Millie's swollen stomach. "You be nice to Millie. She's a good one, and going to be a good ma…but I make no promises if you never give her any sleep."

Tom laughed quietly. At a look from Cole, he stepped away from the women. "I found a tool handle floating in the lake, a trail into the woods. It's too dark to follow now, but I will tomorrow."

Cole frowned. "If it doesn't rain tonight and wash it all away."

"It's still dry right now. We'll hope it holds."

Jane's quite undertone carried from the chair. "It makes no sense. Sally wouldn't hurt a fly."

"Doesn't always make sense, Lou."

"Well, it should."

"Maybe so, but it doesn't."

The worst thing you can possibly do is worrying and thinking about what you could have done.
-George Christoph Lichtenberg

Cole's legs were asleep, all except for his broken foot. The offended limb throbbed and ached from his abuse. Still, he didn't dare move a muscle.

Jane had drifted off to sleep nearly half an hour ago. Far better than pacing and worrying, he'd let her lie there all night if he needed. Then again, he figured she'd be up soon as one of the docs emerged with news.

Millie half dozed across the room, her head propped on her hand. The other hand running over her stomach absently. Tom had taken off fifteen minutes before assuring Cole he'd check on the rest of the kids.

When the door opened, then clicked shut, Jane stirred a moment before settling back down. Tom crept into the room, eying her, then Millie. In his hands he had a pair of boots. He held them up. "Figured you could use these."

"Yeah. Good foot is still soaked, bad foot is killing me."

"She'll kill you if you don't get it plastered again."

"Maybe. She's got plenty of other things to worry about, though."

Tom set down the boots. "Kids are sleeping. Leanne and Kat just managed to get the older ones settled in, though. Jesse is real worried about his sister."

"We all are. Haven't seen Charlie since before you left."

"They've been working nearly three hours. Won't be much longer."

"Took Daisy and I six hours to fix up Jane." Cole's gaze fell to the woman sleeping in his lap. "Then again I wasn't that good at helping."

"My skull was fractured," Jane whispered softly.

Cole and Tom both startled at her voice. Tom frowned. "You should be sleeping."

"When you have a child nearly killed you tell me the same." Still, Jane didn't open her eyes. "Daisy once told me it took you an hour to clean my hair so she could get to the wound."

"It did. She wanted me to clean it 'til the water ran clean. Took ages. So much blood and dirt." Cole brushed his finger along her cheek. "Sally isn't hurt near as bad."

"She's hurt bad enough." Her eyes fluttered open to meet his. "Andrew said her spleen and kidney were damaged, though he thinks the kidney will heal. She has broken ribs, and was bleeding in her belly. They were looking for the source, though it might have been the spleen."

Tom lifted a brow. "Stop reading medical texts."

"I get bored when I've read everything in the library."

"New library isn't even a month old. There's plenty of new material there." Tommy chuckled. "Should take you a good six months to get through busy as you are these days. Longer if you keep ordering new books."

"Doesn't mean I'll forget the medical texts I've read already." She clasped Cole's hand. "They'll give us word soon, right?"

"They sure will. Before you know it. No sense worrying now." Cole squeezed her hand in reassurance. "She's gonna be fine."

"Your lips to God's ears." She shifted, then pushed herself to sit. While Cole stretched out his tingling legs, she slid closer to him on the sofa.

Cole folded her close when she rested against him. His hold didn't last long as a door opened down the hall.

Jane flew to her feet at the noise, her hands wringing together. The second Charlie stepped around the corner, she all but pounced on him. "Charles. How is she?"

Cole took a moment to slip his boots on while Jane's focus was elsewhere. He winced his way into his left boot, but got it on.

"Jane." Charlie took her elbow and led her to a seat. "I know Andrew gave you an update earlier. We had to remove the spleen. We managed to stop the bleeding. I'll be keeping an eye out to see if she shows any sign of continued bleeding."

From what he could tell, Jane had a tight grip on her brother's hand. She offered a brief nod. "She's going to be all right?"

"I believe so. It may take a few days for her to come around, though. Her body has a lot of healing to do." Charlie managed to free his hand with a small wince. He set his hands on hers. "Her arm is broken, as well as a couple of ribs. She was hit pretty hard in the face, so her brain might be a little addled when she does wake."

"Not like mine," Jane whispered. "Please, not like mine."

"I won't know until she wakes. Andrew should have her nearly settled now. I put her in your favorite room. Go see her, and we'll go over all of this again when you're of sounder mind." Charlie nodded to his wife when she took Jane's arm to walk her upstairs. As they left, Charlie let out a deep sigh.

"Charles." Tom rose at the same time Cole did.

"Someone beat her within an inch of her life." Charlie turned to face him. "More than fists did that to her. The bruises…"

Cole eyed Charlie quietly. "What?"

"Some of them looked like boot marks, ladies boots at that." Charlie turned to his brother. "As well as men's. Then there were contusions like I've seen truncheon's make."

Tom frowned. "Found a tool handle in the water. Might've been from a rake or hoe."

"She's definitely heavily concussed. With the chloroform and the concussion, I doubt she'll wake for a few days. Likely for the best. She got some water in her lungs, too. It's a small amount, but such things can progress quickly." Charlie rubbed a hand over his face.

"We found her in the water. Her nose was an inch above the water at most." Cole felt his stomach twist in a sickening knot. "Guessing they wanted her to drown."

"I think she pulled herself out before she lost consciousness." Tom's frown lined his face into deep creases. He played with his beard. "Saw what looked like claw marks in the mud where you pulled her out."

"She's strong, just like her ma." Cole took a deep breath, unwilling to think what might have happened if Sally hadn't had the strength to pull herself out of the water.

"I'm going to help Lydia clean up surgery, then take my wife home. Andrew will watch over Sally tonight." Charlie extended his hand to Cole. "We're going to do everything we can to see she comes out of this. I know Jane knows this, but remind her for me."

"I will. Thank you." Cole shook his hand. After he left, he turned to Tom. The man still fiddled with his beard. "Tom?"

"Can't figure it. Who would even know she was there? Why attack her?"

"Tom."

Tom shook off his thoughts. "You go take care of Jane. I'm going to get some rest so I can head out at first light to find any further clues."

"Thanks. For all your help."

"Sally's family. I'm going to do everything I can to solve this thing, to find out who did this to her. Don't you worry about that."

"Never doubted."

Tom freed a small notebook from his pocket. The whole way out the door he mumbled to himself as he flipped the pages.

Cole climbed the steps to the second level. Muted voices echoed out from an open door at the front of the building. A room far too familiar, as Jane had stayed in it several times. When she'd had scarlet fever. When he'd accidentally punched her. When the twins had been born.

At least not all memories of the room were terrible. This would be another bad one, though.

Inside the room Jane sat on the edge of the bed. She smoothed Sally's curls back. Even as she fussed, she spoke to the doc quietly. "She asked to see more, did she?"

"She did. I hope you don't mind." Andrew closed his medical bag. He sat on the chair beside the bed. "Sally has a keen mind, very curious. It's also startling how well she handled her first autopsy."

"I agree on all points." Jane smiled at their ward, though she remained unconscious. "I've always thought she was smarter than she gave herself credit for."

"Still, watching a dead body get cut up?" Cole kissed the top of Jane's head. "That's not something I want to see."

Andrew chuckled softly. "Most don't. Even doctors that need to use dead bodies to practice and learn on struggle with it. My father made me get a job with his coroner friend before he'd allow me to enter medical school. I was fourteen. Had nightmares for weeks after my first autopsy, truth be told."

"Fourteen?" Jane's surprise carried in her tone.

"I finished school much earlier than most. I was actually twelve. Spent two years apprenticing at my father's side before I was able to begin with the coroner." Andrew didn't even blush at the boasting. "I always preferred books and learning to anything else. Lisabeth preferred horses."

Cole glanced at the young doctor. "Lisabeth?"

"My sister. My twin, actually. Drove my mother crazy with her ways. She forever climbed the tree in our backyard, well into her teens. School never interested her as much as a horse, or a needle and thread."

"Those are two rather disparate things." Jane chuckled softly.

"That's my sister." Andrew straightened in pride. "As for Sally, I'm happy to show her whatever she asks. We had talked about learning how I tested for chemicals, poisoning, if you will. It's very interesting to those inclined to such things."

"I'm sure Sally will enjoy learning whatever you want to show her. I have a feeling she's just beginning to find herself." Jane's voice cracked. Her head ducked to the side.

Cole set his hand on her shoulder when she blinked rapidly as if to stop tears. He turned his attention to the doc. "Charlie said you're watching for signs of her bleeding again. What do we gotta watch for? I'm sure Jane would feel better with something to do."

"Of course." Andrew explained quickly and succinctly what they needed to watch for. After a few more minutes, he rose from his seat. "I'll be downstairs if you need anything. Even if you need a break to grab something to eat, I'm happy to sit with her."

"Thank you, Andrew." Jane let out a shaky breath when he left.

"Do you want to try and rest? I'll keep watch first."

"Yes. We're supposed to head out to Ellis' farm tomorrow to check on him. I should try to be somewhat rested."

"You're still going?"

"Yes." She straightened her shoulders. "This isn't her deathbed, she's going to be fine. Besides, she has no shortage of folks that will want to sit with her."

"She sure won't."

"Cole."

"Yeah."

"Hold me until I fall asleep?"

"You didn't have to ask. I always will."

Life and death are one thread,
the same line viewed from different sides.
-Lao Tzu

Jane settled into Tempest's saddle, but didn't urge her forward. Her gaze landed on the clinic where Sally lay still unconscious. Guilt nagged her. They'd spent two hours already speaking with Arthur. Now they headed out to Ellis'. She'd need to spend time with the children as well. It was likely she wouldn't get back to the clinic until after nightfall.

"Nick's with her now." Tom sidled alongside her on Bluff. Why the man didn't get his own horse, she didn't know. "Then your boy wants to sit with her for a while."

"Jesse said he wants to keep an eye on his sister," Jane acknowledged. "All by himself."

"He may be barely eleven, but he acts like he's much older." Tom nudged her shoulder with the tips of his fingers. "Plus, he loves his sister."

"He does." Jane took a deep breath, then nodded. "Let's go. We're already running late. Katherine is likely waiting on us."

"You got it, Lou."

Jane clicked her tongue. Tempest set off at a brisk pace through town. The pouding hooves of Bluff followed behind.

Kat sat waiting for them at the crossroads a little past the railroad tracks. Jane slowed Tempest as they got close. "Morning."

"Morning." Kat nodded to Tom as he caught up. "How is Sally doing?"

"Still unconscious. Charles said it could be days before she wakes." Jane wrapped the rein tight around her hand, the only allowance she made for her distress.

Kat smiled sadly. "She'll come back spitting mad."

"Of that I have no doubt," Tom concurred.

"Thank you for joining us," Kat said to Tom.

"After what happened the last time you fools went to check on someone that didn't show up for church, you bet I'm coming. Last time I almost lost my sister—again." Tom winked. "We're not taking any risks, especially after what happened to Sally."

"I would not be such a fool to do the same thing twice," Jane protested. "I learn my lessons in their due time."

"Some of which take more than one failure." Tom grinned, then pulled his reins tight. "Shall we head out to Ellis'?

"Let's. The man hasn't missed a church service, even though Mrs. Ellis passed away thread years ago and hadn't been there to make him attend." Jane nudged Tempest forward.

Kat took the lead, racing off down the road toward the settlement. They passed the lake at such a pace, Jane didn't have time to malinger in thoughts of Sally. Before they neared the settlement they banked right to head northeast toward the Ellis homestead. The ride would have taken them well over an hour in a wagon, so they'd agreed riding separate was the best thing. Worse came to worse, Ellis had a wagon they could use.

As the homestead came into view, they all instinctively slowed together to search for signs of life. Two horses stood tethered some distance from the house. They grazed on the short grass their leads let them reach.

Tom sidled up next to Jane. "Nothing looks out of place. Ellis doesn't have a cow. He'd tether the horses during the day and shelter them at night."

"What?" Kat glanced his way. "How on earth could you know that?"

"He's a regular at the casino. Likes the nickel ante. Talkative sort. Just how we like them to be." Tom frowned. "He's got a weakness for moonshine, though. We'd best check and make sure he isn't lost in the sauce."

Jane followed suit when Tom urged Bluff forward. Keeping the casual pace Tom set, if a little slower, she waited until he'd moved on to turn to Kat. Reassured by the signs of life at the homestead, she took the chance to ask Kat a question she'd been wondering since the dance. "Have you talked to Patrick?"

"I did. Though unseemly to have such a conversation on a Sunday, we were already talking in the sitting room. Norman had gone to bed, so I broached the subject with him." Kat glanced sideways at Jane. "He's thinking about it. He worries that Norman will resent me. I do appreciate his concern as I have the same one."

"As you said, no one will be the wiser so long as your relationship with Norman doesn't change. He never has to know it's even happened. Not that I encourage lying on a regular basis, of course. This situation is…unique."

"To say the least."

"Norman gave his blessing. Truth be told, if you are careful and smart, not even you will know who the father is unless the child shows evidence." Jane slowed to a stop beside the first horse. "We should move these picket lines. There's hardly food left for them, and no water."

"If they've been put up at night there's water in the barn. I can see the trough from here." Kat frowned at the grass. "It seems as through they've been in this spot for some time, though. The grass is rather short. They've both eaten through the breadth of their tethers."

"Tom?" Jane caught his attention before he got too far. "It looks as though they've been tied here for a couple of days. There's hardly grass left for them to graze on."

Tom turned back toward them, a frown settling on his features. "Why not tie them up by the lean-to where they can have some water? We'll move the tethers when we're done."

Jane swung out of her saddle. She got hold of one horse while Kat grabbed the other. They walked toward the lean-to that served as the horses barn together. Kat nudged Jane, a secretive smile lighting her features. "What of Cole? Have you given him your answer?"

She had, but Jane decided to tease her friend first. "How can I have? I'm not even certain what to think. Together we have eight children, between our natural children and wards. How can we add another child now? Even if Sally is an adult, and Cindy and Jesse don't live with us, it's still overwhelming on good days, near impossible on the worst."

"Jane."

"Plus, Willow and Jay have yet to properly adjust. They've been exceptional considering the life they came from and what they've been forced into. This world is foreign to them, even after a year. Those poor children still cry themselves to sleep some nights."

"Jane." Kat finished securing the horse she'd led into its stall. Her hand rested on Jane's arm. "There will always be many reasons not to do this, and only one good reason to do it."

"We've never planned for a child. They've always been quite the surprise."

"Do you want another child with the man you live in infinites amount of sin with?"

Jane bit her lip, making a split-second decision to end the charade. At least with her best friend. "We don't live in sin, Katherine."

Kat studied her with a hard look. "What?"

"I feel horrible for not telling you sooner. At first it was because we agreed with didn't want anyone to know. We also rather enjoyed the scandal. I always felt bad for not telling you sooner, though. Only a few people know, but…oh."

"Jane Spencer, you'd better use your words far better than this."

"Cole and I will have been married three years as of the Statehood Celebration."

"Three years!" Kat clasped her hand over her mouth when it came out as a yell. "You are joking. Aren't you?"

"No." Jane clasped Kat's hands in hers. "Please don't hate me for not telling sooner."

"You're really married?"

"Really, truly. We were married in Denver right after I became a partner in The Hangman's Inn. After Al's unfortunate proposal."

"I'm so happy for you." Kat hugged her tight as could be. When she pulled away, she punched Jane's arm. "I could kill you for not telling sooner."

"Ow." Jane rubbed her arm. "That hurt."

"Good. You horrid friend." Kat laced her arm with Jane's as they returned to their own horses. They both grabbed the reins to walk to the house rather than ride the short distance. "You haven't distracted me from my original question. Do you want another child?"

"Yes. Cole and I already agreed."

"Oh boy, what fun. Perhaps we'll be blessed at the same time. Then our husbands will have to suffer by our sides while we labor."

Jane laughed with her friend, striding toward the homestead in a much better mood. She knocked on the open door before she stepped inside. Tom leaned on the door leading out the back of the house. "Thomas? Any sign of him?"

"Nothing." Tom didn't move from his vigil, eyes narrowed on the horizon. "Both of his horses are here. Where in hell could he be?"

Jane stepped around him to the back yard. To her right sat a long-gone to waste garden. He'd likely let it die when his wife passed. After a few more steps, whimpering pulled her attention to the wagon off to the left.

She approached, spotting shadows wriggling behind a wheel. When she bent down for a better look, four puppies clamored over each other to sniff her. "Ellis have a dog, Tom?"

"Sure did."

"There's puppies here by themselves Where's the dog?" Jane straightened and shielded her eyes against the sun.

Tom whistled sharp and loud. A howl erupted from over the ridge. All three of them headed toward the sound. As the crested the small hill, the dog howled again. She sat parked by the well.

"Damn." Tom ran down the hill at a breakneck speed, hauling to a stop at the edge of the well. He circled for a minute before dropping to his knees. "Ellis! Can you hear me?"

Jane and Kat flew down the hill behind him. Kat overran the well by several feet before she managed to come to a halt. Jane managed to teeter to a stop right by the hound whimpering at the edge of the well. She took note of the fresh, smooth wood lying broken in the well's lid. "The top broke? But this looks new."

Kat crouched down to peer in the hole. "Ellis!"

Jane spun and ran. She got halfway to the door before she heard Tom holler for her to go back for help. She leapt into her saddle and tore back to town fast as Tempest could run. The ride took forever and no time at all. Before she'd hit First Street, she put her fingers in her mouth and blasted a whistle.

At the boarding house, she repeated the whistle. By the time she stopped the horse at the Inn, Cole sprinted from the front doors. Michael had run out of the jail, as had Charlie with Nick hot on his heels. "Ellis fell in the well! We need help!"

Tempest spun beneath her as a crowd formed. Cries went up around her, and in no time a group had gathered with tools and rope piled on saddles. Jane didn't wait or them to organize, just took off toward the homestead again.

By the time she arrived, Kat paced in front of the homestead. They moved to the side as the group tore around the back of the house. Jane dismounted. "Did he ever respond to your calls?"

"Not once. He didn't seem to be moving tall. I don't think this is a rescue." Kat wrung her hands. She paced in front of the door. "It makes no sense. Those boards weren't rotten. Ellis might have liked his sauce, but could he have been that drunk?"

"I honestly have no idea. I don't know what happens in a person's home when they're alone. I myself have never seen him drunk, but that doesn't mean in private he wasn't." Jane tried to not pace Kat was. If she went back to the well, she knew they'd be in the way. "The wagon. We can get the horses hitched to the wagon. That will give us something to do."

"Thank you." Kat moved with Jane eagerly. "I needed something to do."

"I have no idea what to do about those pups. We let them run free and a mountain lion will have them for a midday snack." Jane pulled the horse around the back of the house. She could hear the shouts of instructions and worry from over the crest of the hill.

At the wagon, she bent down to scoop the pups out from under the wheel. With no better place for them, she set them n the wagon bed.

"I'm sure someone will take them." Kat lined her horse up to the hitch. Yells over the hill increasing in panic pulled both their attention. Kat worked faster at getting her horse secured.

"Probably," Jane agreed rather than face what they'd heard. She got her horse secured to the hitch as well. Once the beasts were set, she moved to the back of the wagon and hopped up on the lip. "It's going to take ages to get him out. If they even can."

"Don't say that. They'll get him out."

"What is going on? Mr. Keller, now Mr. Ellis, not to mention Emily, and what's happened to Sally."

"What a bad run of luck right before we reach statehood."

"Thomas would say there is no such thing." Jane stared at the crest of the hill, waiting for someone to appear. "Coincidences often are no such thing."

"Bob's death was an accident. David said so. I can't imagine Ellis will be any different."

"I'm certain it won't be. That's what so odd."

"Don't anticipate trouble, Jane."

"I do my best not to. However, it always seems to show up to surprise me when I don't." Jane sighed when Rusty Piper, the owner of the newspaper, rushed over the hill and promptly bent over to vomit. "Oh dear."

"Let's go get some blankets from the house, get him covered proper for the ride back into town." Kat hopped off the wagon and headed inside.

Jane walked toward Rusty. "You all right, Rusty?"

He remained bent over, but waved and nodded.

At that, Jane followed Kat into the house. They gathered what blankets they could find. Jane grabbed the hand-stitched quilt at the last second.

Kat frowned. "We probably shouldn't…"

"Not for the ride. For the burial."

"We'll put it in the front of the wagon, then."

Jane made it halfway to the wagon before David and Nick ran over to take the blankets from them. "What are you doing?"

"Ride on back to town, Jane." David stepped back. "You don't need to see this."

"Don't be ridiculous—"

"Ride back to town," Nick repeated. "Trust me. We'll take care of Ellis."

"There's puppies in the wagon, and that quilt is for burial not for transport." Jane took a step forward, but Nick's sharp look stopped her. "You have it handled, then."

"We've got it handled. It's not a sight you need to see." Nick turned toward the wagon.

Jane glanced at David. "Was it an accident?"

"Looks like. Charlie said his legs were broken, must have went straight down the well. Been there for days near as we can tell, so he's—it's…"

"Not a sight I need to see. Got it."

And in that town a dog was found,
As many dogs there be.
Both mongrel, puppy, whelp, and hound,
And curs of low degree.
—Oliver Goldsmith

Jane sank onto the sofa with a heavy sigh. She'd returned home to find Jay in a tizzy. He screamed loud for all the world to hear that he wanted to go home, wanted his real parents. With no idea what had set him off, it had taken nearly an hour to get him and Willow settled. For the moment they talked quietly in their room in the Ute language. About what, she didn't know.

Because of Jay's temper, Alma had been in a fair snit of her own. At the moment she still pounded away on the piano to vent her otherwise silent frustration. Jane buried her face in her hands, taking several deep breaths.

As she'd pointed out to Katherine, at times it all seemed impossible. She exhaled heavily against the frustration in hopes of helping to calm Alma. After she'd set the teapot on the stove, she settled onto the bench next to the young woman.

Alma didn't say a word, but her music softened a touch. Though she wanted to hug her, Jane knew that could likely make the situation worse. Instead, she lowered her tone. She spoke deliberately, with an attempt to match the pace of the music. "I know you're worried for Sally."

Alma grunted in response.

"If you would like to visit, we may. You must know first that Sally is wounded. Her face is swollen and bruised. She will not appear as you always have known her until healed."

The music stopped. Alma's figures hovered over the keys.

"If you would rather, Cole can take you."

"You." Alma's fingers drifted down to rest on the keys.

"Then we will visit Sally after we have had our tea."

Excited shrieking echoed through the door before it burst open. Jesse walked in, one of the hound puppies squirming in his arms. "Look, Ma! His name's gonna be Barnaby."

"Jesse Michael, did your pa say you could have a puppy?" Jane rose as Alma began to play again. At least time the song wasn't frantic in its tone.

"Sure did, and look!" Jesse grinned toward the door as both Clara and Colton, their arms full of puppy as well, entered.

The puppies were enormous in their tiny arms. Jane shook her head. "Oh no."

Cole limped through the door, a grin splitting his features. He pointed to each pup in turn. "Whiskey, and Bourbon."

"Oh no. No no no, Cole Mitchell! What have you done?" Jane looked between her three children and sighed. "Dogs?"

Clara shrieked over top of her squirming pup. "*JayJayJay.*"

"Clara, please. Jay is not having a good—"

Jay peeked out of the room, his sister right behind him.

Jane did her best to force forward a smile as Jesse drew near with his dog. Jesse held him up high as he could. "Ain't he cute?"

"Isn't he. And yes, all the puppies were adorable, are adorable." Jane sighed, scratching Barnaby's head. "Your pa is really fine with this?"

"He said I'd have to keep it here. You don't mind, do you ma?" At her sharp look, he laughed loud. "Just kidding, Ma. Cole told me to say that. He'll stay with us."

"Cole has some explaining to do." Jane hugged Jesse. "Why don't you take Barnaby home? I'll see you tomorrow at the clinic."

"Pa said I can watch over her by myself tomorrow since Uncle Charlie's gonna be there. That all right with you, Ma?"

"Yes. I'll be there when you come for your watch." She chucked her finger under his chin. "You be careful with that pup. Don't let him run off before you get home."

"I won't ma. I'm not a kid, ya know. Nearly a man now."

"You're eleven. Don't you grow up too fast on me." Jane kissed his cheek and hugged him again. "Go let poor Lee know that she has a dog now."

"See you tomorrow, Ma." Jesse darted from the room.

Cole's joviality lessened at her sharp look. "What?"

"Children, why don't you take the puppies out back? Willow, please see they are put in the chicken coop. Thankfully we haven't gotten the chicks from the Mortells yet to fill it for Alma. We'll have to have Mr. Hamm build a place for the dogs." Jane wasn't too surprised when Alma rose as the children darted outside. "Go ahead, Alma. I want to have a talk with Cole before we go to the clinic. The puppies have the softest ears ever."

Alma drifted outside with the others.

Jane rounded on Cole. "Colton James Spencer, what the devil were you thinking?"

"What?"

Jane closed her eyes against the rush of temper that had her seeing red. "Our lives are so chaotic that I was wondering if we were being smart to bring another child into our lives. Somehow you thought bringing home two puppies was the way to fix things?"

"I just…I thought…"

"You didn't think." Jane groaned her way back onto the sofa. "It's been a horrible day. Your timing is awful. Sally is terribly off. Ellis is dead. Emily is dead. Jay still screams he wants his real parents after a year with us. Willow isn't much happier. You throw Whiskey and Bourbon in the mix, and I don't know what to do with you anymore."

He scooped her off the couch so fast she couldn't protest. Over her strong fight, he carried her toward their room. Halfway there he hollered, "Tom!"

"I told you," Tom called back as he traipsed down the stairs. "Leanne will be along soon to help out."

"Cole!" Jane grabbed the door frame when he tried to tug her into the bedroom. "You put me down this instant."

He managed to wrestle her into the room, and kicked the door shut behind him. He blocked the door with his frame. "Settle down."

"Settle down? You want me to *settle down*?" She let out a frustrated scream and turned away. "The day I've had."

"It'll pass. It always does." His hands settled on her shoulders. "You haven't really been thinking we shouldn't have a kid."

She jerked free from his hands to cross to the window. "Bob is dead. Ellis is dead. Emily is dead. Sally is injured, unconscious…and I come home to Jay screaming how he wanted to go back to his real parents. Alma was nearly inconsolable from the chaos. Then you walk in with those damn puppies."

"Cindy and Lizzie took one, and Jesse got one. The twins didn't want to give them up. I didn't think it would do any harm." Cole stepped behind her until his body was flush to her back. His hands settled on her hips. "Don't be mad."

"I'm not mad. I'm frustrated and overwhelmed."

"You once had a maniac try to kill you repeatedly, along with everyone you knew. Someone nearly destroyed our business…and you're worried about a couple of dogs?"

"Those things pass. Our children and those dogs aren't going away."

"You had a rough day."

"I've had a rough life." She relaxed against him, her temper fading fast as it had risen. "It happens when you marry a large idiot of a man. Damn fools don't know when they're being cute and when they're being moronic."

"Don't gotta be cute." Lips brushed her neck, sending tingles down her spine despite her best intentions to remain angry. "Or smart, even. Just gotta know how to handle my woman."

"You'd think so." Somehow she found the strength to shrug off his lips. "I never said I was done being upset."

"Figured it would take a bit. That's why I had Tom at the ready." He spun her to face him. "We'll make it work with a new kid, just like we always do."

"Changing the subject will not win you points."

"The dogs are my responsibility, not yours." A hint of a smirk tugged his lips out of his frown at her rebuff.

"See, you say that, and yet…I don't believe you. Something will arise to cause trouble or distraction and it will fall on me."

"Promise."

She leaned against the window to distance herself from the distraction of his proximity. "Don't think I won't make certain you keep that promise. You will regret it one day, probably soon."

"Forgive me?"

"No."

He took her hands in his, setting them on his chest. "Not going anywhere until you do."

"But the dogs are your responsibility." No matter how strong her temper and nerves still railed against complacency, she couldn't stop the teasing. No, this argument wasn't over. In fact, she'd ensure it lingered. She leaned into him. "You can't stay here if that's true."

"I made arrangements." His smile told her he thought he'd won. "We can talk."

"Of course." She had to be careful, or he'd sense her deception. As she leaned further into him, she slipped her arms around his neck. "How about a bath? We always talk well in the tub."

"Talk, eh?"

"Yes. Talk." She allowed the kiss without argument. She let her lips dance across his. With practiced skill, she scratched her fingers along his neck with enough pressure to draw a deep moan from him. "You get the water ready."

"Yes ma'am."

The second he disappeared into the bathroom to fill the tub, she turned to the window. The door would be faster, but he'd see her pass by on her way out, as would Tom who was likely in on this conspiracy to supplicate her.

Quiet as possible, she opened the window wide. One ear on the next room, she listened for him to pour another bucket before she swung her legs out of the window. She tugged the window back down quick as possible and took off down the alley toward the street.

The question was, where to hide? He'd expect her at Kat's or Sally's without question. She turned left and raced toward the road to head south of town toward Michael's hotel.

At the edge of town she stopped short. With what had happened to Sally, did she really want to make such a trek on foot? They had no idea what had happened to Sally, and any travel by oneself could be dangerous.

She rushed up to the back door of Graham's shop and pounded on it. Graham flung open the door. For a second he stared at her like she'd lost her mind. "What in blazes do you want, Jane?"

"I need to borrow your horse."

"My horse?"

"Yes. Quickly." Jane heard the first call for her name, and turned away. "This was a statement, not a request. I'll return it. Don't tell Cole you saw me."

"Why in hell not?"

"He's in trouble."

"What? Again?"

Jane swung into the saddle, grinning at Graham. "Isn't he always?"

Without another word, she took off toward Michael's at a quick pace. It wasn't until she pulled up in front of the Sage Brush that she felt some measure of guilt. As she'd realized herself, they were worried over who might have attacked Sally, and her disappearance would worry Cole needlessly.

Michael stepped out of the hotel as Jane dismounted. "Jane?"

"Michael. I need to send a quick telegram for the simple purpose of letting Cole know I'm safe. After that, we can relax."

"What's going on?"

"Cole is going to suffer for a bit."

"Again? So soon?"

"Yes. Would you mind if I remained here tonight until I had to go watch over Sally?"

"Of course." Michael folded her into a hug. "Are you all right?"

"I've been better." She pulled back to study his features. "You look tired. Sad. Maybe even angry. What's going on?"

"Nothing."

"Michael."

"It's Daisy."

"Oh dear." She clasped his hands in hers. "Did she ever give you a real reason for turning down your proposal?"

"She got mad when I brought it up again. Told me to leave things as they were. Didn't speak to me for days after."

He flushed as he looked over her shoulder toward town. "Next time I saw her, we didn't really speak."

"Oh, Michael."

"What can I say? I'm—"

"A man?"

"Weak."

"Well, we are a happy pair tonight, aren't we?"

"The happiest."

The thing about performance, even if it is only an illusion, is that it is a celebration of the fact that we do contain within ourselves infinite possibilities.
-Sydney Smith

A knock on the door startled Jane awake. After spending most of the night at Michael's, Jane had immediately come to the clinic for her shift to sit with Sally. To be honest, she wondered at how Cole hadn't appeared to yell at her yet. Alma had come to visit, but she'd been brought by Leanne, not Cole.

Blinking to clear her head, Jane yawned. A second knock caused her to lift her head from Sally's hand. "Come in."

"Good morning." Lillian bustled in; a dress draped over her arm. "I brought a fresh dress for you to wear for our meeting. Arthur should be here shortly for next watch. I believe your brother Nick will be due after him."

Jane glanced at her ward, taking in the bruised features. She rose to lift each lid. As it had been the day before, Sally's right eye was blood red. Jane knew Charles worried the eye had suffered permanent damage from the blow.

"Nothing yet?" Lillian set the dress behind the privacy screen.

"No. I don't think Charles expects much yet. They had to remove her spleen, she bled quite a bit into her belly. Plus how concussed the blow made her. I just pray her brain isn't rattled as mine was when I woke."

"Your brain is far from addled, child." Lillian turned Jane to face her. "Did you sleep at all?"

"Some." A huge yawn emerged with the simple word. Jane chuckled at herself. "Clearly not enough. Must we do this today?"

"Yes. Life continues on, even in times of great turmoil. There are mere weeks until we officially become a state. There are plans to be finalized."

"We only recently celebrated the Centennial and now another event. The town will tire of such things."

"Nonsense. Everyone appreciates a reason to celebrate. Even those with a sick child."

"I suppose that's true." Jane accepted Lillian's hug. "I'll get dressed, you needn't yell at me, which I'm certain Katherine told you to do if I was being stubborn."

"She might have mentioned something of the sort. Fortunately for you, my Katherine is far too busy ordering people around to give long-winded speeches about how to handle you."

"Thank heavens for small blessings." Jane moved behind the screen to change in case Arthur arrived before she'd finished.

"Did your brother find anything of import in regard to Sally's attack?"

"I'm afraid not. The trail circled about, then headed toward the settlement. Once whoever it was hit Settlement Road, they could have gone anywhere. Nobody he's talked to knows a thing about it. Most of them were settled in with their families for the night."

"Such a shame. This poor dear." Lillian straightened from fussing over Sally when Jane emerged from behind the screen. "Lavender suits you well. I don't think I've seen you wear it before."

"I haven't. There was a lovely lavender dress donated after the fire, but it didn't fit. Without a proper dressmaker in town, I left it aside. I thought I'd try when we ordered dresses for the events this summer." Jane returned to Sally's side. "Sally has a few new dresses as well. Her dress for the celebration is a lovely turquoise. I do hope she gets to wear it."

"Of that, I have no doubt. She'll be awake and enjoying along with everyone else, if a little sore for the excitement." Lillian turned to the door at a light knock. "Hello, Arthur. Perfect timing. I was just about to drag Jane away."

"Hello, Mrs. Daugherty. Jane." He ducked his head. "I hope you don't mind. I mean, I'd understand if you don't want me to…"

"You didn't do this to her, Arthur." Jane set her hand on his arm. They'd gone over the whole ordeal with Arthur, and Jane trusted the young man when he said he left and returned straight home.

"I left her there, though. I was so mad and hurt." He blew out a long breath. "I should've waited. Stayed there, even though she told me to go."

"It's not your fault. If you'd remained, she might have been more upset."

"She might not be hurt."

"Sit with her. Talk to her. I know you're still hurt, but she does care for you. It's nice to hear a friendly voice when you are like this. Believe me, I know. I remember two young men chattering away when I was unconscious." Jane gave him a quick hug. She turned her attention back to Sally and placed a kiss on her forehead. "If she wakes, send for me straight away. I believe our doctors and nurse are taking shifts as well."

Arthur nodded, "I saw Lydia downstairs."

"Perfect." Jane smoothed the hair from Sally's forehead. She hated to leave her, but she had the rest of her family to care for. Plus, Sally wouldn't be alone for a second. "Wake up today, Sally. Please. We'd all like to see you."

Lillian extended a hand, which Jane took gladly. As they walked down the steps, Lillian tucked Jane's hand in her arm and patted it. "You've been good to that girl. You gave her something to fight for. We all need that."

"Yes we do, Lillian. We certainly do."

"While I'm thinking of it, Arthur mentioned Lydia. I thought I heard Charles was taking on another nurse."

"He is. Bonnie Coleman, Matthew's sister. Her return home has been delayed as she wanted to see her final patients through their births. I believe she'll be along in August."

"If all of her patients deliver on time."

"Of course." She smiled at Lillian as they emerged onto the bustling street. "Now to put on my performance that I'm not struggling with quite so much."

"A performance you've perfected." Lillian glanced her way. "I saw Cole struggling with a large group of children all on his lonesome this morning."

"Did you now?"

"I believe Clara was missing a shoe."

Jane snorted at the image of Cole's struggle that passed through her mind. "I'd say something about his poor suffering if he hadn't earned it."

"What on earth did he do to warrant your temper this time?"

"He let the twins bring home two of those puppies."

Lillian chuckled softly as they turned the corner to head to the meadow. "I've never known Cole to be particularly forward thinking. Instinct wins over true thought."

"His instinct was to spoil those children, nothing less. It was incorrect. Now there's nothing to be done. The dogs are there, and I'm not about to kick them out."

"You'll adjust. Your family seems to have an enormous capacity to do that."

"By force of circumstance, we've had to." Jane slowed as they approached the meadow. The bustle of activity drew a smile. "I see Katherine is already hard at work."

"I appreciate both of you taking over the celebration while Henry and I try to get some persons of influence to come to our town."

"It cannot be an easy task to undertake. I imagine most of Colorado is attempting to draw anyone that might be important to their town. As for the party, it's no trouble." At Lillian's quiet scoff, Jane demurred, "All right. It is some trouble. I don't mind, though."

"I appreciate you saying as much."

"I am always honest."

Lillian chuckled softly. "Too true. Now, I do have some good news for you."

"Oh?"

"There will be a dressmaker moving into town in a week."

"Thank heavens. Leanne's dressmaker is wonderful, but it will be nice to not have to send out to Denver for a dress any time something strikes my fancy."

"Something always strikes your fancy."

"I'd argue, but it's the truth." Jane laughed as they made it to the meadow. They parted ways, Lillian going to meet her husband, and Jane heading toward Katherine. "Am I running late?"

"Not at all. I got an early start." Kat gave her a warm hug. "How are you holding up?"

"Well enough, I suppose." Jane sighed softly and glanced around. "Seems like you have everything well under control."

"As under control as can be expected with our gaggle of children insisting on playing the games in the midst of it." Kat gestured toward where a small throng of children played with the hoops, another group played tag around the booths lining the meadow.

Though she saw Kat's two children and Jesse, she noticed the rest of her family remained missing from the apparent festivities. "I suppose they must occupy themselves somehow while the adults tend to business."

"Except they're getting in the way of business." Kat cringed when Teddy got one of his legs swept out from under him as a child ran past. The stack of boards he carried toppled precariously as he did. "Oh dear."

Jane chuckled softly as her friend darted off to attempt to save the man from falling over. She turned in search of Cole, but another voice drew her attention right back to the children.

"Ma!" Jesse ran toward her at a full tilt, the gangly limbs of his twelve years moving precariously. He all but tackled her in a hug.

Jane accepted the hug happily. "Good morning to you, too. How are you doing?"

"How's Sally?"

"Still unconscious. I'm praying she wakes soon." Jane smiled as David approached with Lee on one arm, a baby in the other. She offered her cheek for a kiss, then hugged Lee. "It's good to see you both. You've been rather sequestered since this little one was born."

Lee sighed, dark rings under her eyes a testament to how little sleep the baby was allowing her to have. "Marjorie doesn't appear to enjoy sleeping very much. I'm quite tired."

Jane nodded. "I remember when Clara went through a phase where she never wanted to sleep either. I'm glad to see you, though. We miss you at tea."

"I miss going. I'm quite happy to have Marjorie, but I miss being able to join you ladies. Hopefully soon." Lee squeezed her hand. "We're praying for Sally."

"Thank you." Jane turned to Jesse. "You children try not to knock over any more adults. Billy nearly toppled Teddy back there."

"That's why I'm not playing tag. Besides, Lizzie can't play it so well." Jesse's ears turned red at the mention of

Lizzie, much like his pa's did when embarrassed. "I should get back. Don't want her to get lonely."

Jane managed to contain her laughter until Jesse was out of earshot. "Never mind that she's surrounded by friends, Jesse can't let her be alone."

"They're adorable. Young sweethearts." Lee glanced over Jane's shoulder, her brows pursed. "Is that Cole? With your other children?"

Jane turned to see her family crossing the meadow. Oddly enough, Cole seemed to have the situation well in hand. "It certainly is. Here I thought he'd need rescuing."

"Appears to have things in hand," David said with as much surprise as Jane felt in his tone.

"True. How strange. Excuse me." Jane approached the group, eyebrows raised as Cole caught her eye. She picked up Clara as the girl ran to her. "Hello, Clara. I heard you lost a shoe this morning?"

"I hides it."

"You hid it, did you?" Jane's lips twitched when Cole drew closer. She noted that despite his laughter, he appeared a bit the worse for wear. His hair stuck out in all directions thanks to Colton's tight hold on it. In general, his entire demeanor came off a bit bedraggled. "Cole."

He leaned in to kiss her gently, then withdrew just as quick. The man knew all too well she liked to keep up appearances when they were in an argument. Blessedly, he wasn't certain of her mood enough yet to claim victory with a proper kiss.

"Are you all having fun?"

Jay tugged her hand enthusiastically. He pointed across the field toward where the children were rolling hoops across the grass. "Hoop. Hoop."

"You want to play?" At his nod, Jane smiled. For the moment it seemed the boy was in good enough spirits. His mood was unpredictable at best, but she didn't see the harm in letting him roam free in the meadow where there were plenty of people about. "Go on ahead. Jesse is over there with Lizzie and Cindy. Willow? Would you like to join them?"

Willow nodded, lowering her gaze almost shyly.

"That's fine. Do you have your medicine pouch?" She nodded when the girl pulled it free of her pocket. "Wonderful. Go ahead. You two have fun."

The pair rushed off, leaving her with the twins, Alma, and Cole. Cole eyed her quietly. "You still mad at me?"

"Perhaps." Jane moved to his free side, opposite of Alma. "I heard you had some struggles this morning getting everyone ready."

"Wasn't so bad. Missed you, though."

"Me? Or my assistance?"

"Yes."

She laughed softly. "Good to know."

"Talked to Hammy. He said he'd build a run for the dogs. I'll get 'em trained up real good."

"They aren't horses." She nudged him with her elbow. "Are you certain you can handle two dogs nearly as well?"

"I will. Promise."

She set down Clara when she girl spotted Cora and squealed for her. Cole did the same with Colton. The twins ran to Cora, who swept them into her booth. Though it wasn't even time for the celebration, she'd loaded the booth with food and desserts for those working to change the setup from Independence Day to the Statehood celebration.

"Cole," Alma spoke quietly. Her eyes darted around the general chaos of the meadow. Much like at Independence Day, the general air of celebration led to lots of noise and an air of excitement that made the air fairly buzz.

Cole drew his sister closer. "I bet we can find a quiet place. Maybe by the creek."

Nick approached before they could discuss the matter further. Jane hugged him tight. "Nicholas. It's lovely to see you."

"Kat's had me hard at work the past couple of hours." His words were clearly rather true, for the man wasn't looking nearly as dapper as he usually was. The bowler he usually wore was nowhere to be seen, nor was his jacket. His shirt sleeves were rolled up, and his tie and shirt buttons were lose.

"So I see. Haven't seen you this unkempt, well, ever." Jane chuckled softly.

"I was looking for a reason for a break. Miss Alma, would you like to tinker on the piano in the church? It's nice and quiet in there." Nick extended a hand.

Jane smiled gratefully at her brother, then turned to Alma. "I'm about to put Cole to work, so feel free."

Alma glanced sideways at Cole quietly.

He nodded. "If Jane says she's gonna put me to work, I'd bet it'll be true. I'll catch up with you when it's time for my break. Or Jane will."

Jane remained silent as Nick guided Alma toward the church. "You planned this."

"What?"

"The utter disappearance of the children. You wished to get me alone."

"I did want to get you alone, but I didn't plan the twins or Willow and Jay. That was pure luck for me."

Jane hummed, but didn't argue when he slipped his arm around her waist.

His next words were low. "Near three years married, and you can still frustrate the hell outta me."

"Feelings mutual. Wait. You remembered?"

"It's same day as the statehood. Hard to forget."

For that, she granted him a kiss. Of all things she expected, it wasn't that he would remember their anniversary. Especially not with everything that had been going on. "I'm impressed you would remember. Or were you reminded?"

"Little of both."

She wrapped her arm around his waist. "Well, I'm pleased either way."

"Did you really escape out the window and steal Graham's horse?"

"Didn't steal, borrowed, and do you not understand the ridiculously difficult day I had yesterday?"

"I was drawing you a bath."

"You were drawing a bath for your own selfish pursuits."

He groaned loud. "Damn frustrating woman."

"You like a challenge."

Rather than answer, he steered her away from the crowd toward the tree line that surrounded the meadow. With each step his limp grew worse. "Are you done?"

"I am."

"Good." He pulled her into the shade of the trees, and tugged her close.

"Wait." She placed her finger over his mouth before he could kiss her.

"You said you were done," he spoke around her finger.

"Why didn't you get your plaster replaced?"

"It was getting in the way."

The frustration she'd brushed aside welled again. "I don't care. What would you do if I did the same thing?"

"You did do it."

"I was trying to rescue Arthur, I had no choice, and I continue to suffer for it all these years later. Why on earth would you—"

Warm lips closed over hers, effectively shutting off her tirade. A yell rented the air, and them apart with its panic.

"*Jay*," Jesse's voice rang through the meadow.

"*Jay*," screamed Willow.

Jane and Cole's eyes met. Panic coursed through Jane's heart like a stampeding bull. Neither of them spoke, but they both turned and tore back into the meadow. They nearly collided with Jesse, who was pointing behind him. "Willow. She's…"

Jane raced toward Willow, who was breathing harshly into her medicine bag. Strong wheezes carried through the air. She knelt before the girl, brushing her hand slow along her back. "That's it. Breathe in, breathe out. Charles? Where's Charles?"

A hand settled on her shoulder. She turned to meet Cole's intense gaze, and another wave of panic sped her heart rate. Cole grimaced. "The boy's disappeared."

"Jay?" Jane turned to study Willow and the tears in the girl's eyes. "Oh no. Cole."

"We'll find him."

"Hurry."

*I roamed the countryside searching for things
I did not understand.
—Leonardo da Vinci*

Cole drew Faro to a stop. They'd been searching for nearly two hours. The boy had left on foot, but raised by Indians, he knew how to hide his tracks. He spun the horse in a circle, trying to best guess where the boy might have gone.

Hoofbeats drew near, pulling his gaze back toward town. He'd ended up deep in the foothills north of town. One group had gone north, another south. The sun would be setting far too soon, and they'd have no chance of finding him in the dark.

Tommy rode up on Brag, his gaze scanning north. "He can't have gone any further than this on foot."

"Fast as he is, I doubt it." Cole lifted his hat to scratch his head. "All he had to do is find a crevice to hide in and we'd never find him."

"He had a bit of a head start."

"I know." Cole frowned back toward town. "Jesse said it was Jay's idea to switch to hide and seek. Probably had an eye on running. Again."

"One of these days he'll be gone for good he keeps this up."

"Don't say that to Jane. Damn woman got attached, even if the kids didn't so much."

"Of course she did. She has an affection for lost souls. Fell for you, didn't she?"

Cole sMaced his brother-in-law on the arm. "Watch it."

"Don't hate me for telling the truth." Tommy chuckled, but his eyes kept scanning the area. "I say we go another couple of miles, then head back. Looking the whole time."

"Until it's too dark," Cole agreed. He turned Faro back west, but a loud whistle echoed through the hills. Both of them turned back east. He recognized that whistle. All the Young's made the piercing sound to get the attention of their family. Usually, it didn't mean anything good. "Danger or success?"

"Could be either."

"Guess we head back now to find out."

"Hopefully it's good news." Tommy urged Brag back toward town.

Cole followed suit, moving much faster than he'd planned on for heading back. Neither of them bothered to stop to check any hidey holes they passed as another whistle rented the air, followed by another more distant.

Tommy placed his fingers in his mouth and blasted a response whistle. They picked up their pace until they were fairly tearing over the hills. They rode for near half an hour. As they tore over the last hill, the creek came into view, and they both veered south to avoid the traps set by McKinnon near the water.

The second they got south of his trapping area, Cole turned back toward the creek. With a squeeze of his legs, the horse leapt over the creek. They landed on the other side without a stumble. He turned toward town where he could already see a group of people gathered on Main, even from his current distance.

He leaned over the neck of Faro, urging the horse faster with a few simple words. He'd been riding the horse so long, it knew his moves and the words were hardly necessary. Faro even slowed as they drew close to the tracks where the road turned to cobblestone.

As he drew close enough, he spotted David near the midst of the crowd, standing next to his friend Black Moon. They were both looking down, but Cole couldn't see what at due to the small crowd around the scene.

Then Jane rose from where they were staring. She wrapped David in a one armed hug, then stepped toward Black Moon. She paused, then extended her hand to shake the Indian's. That made Cole draw up short. "Did she just shake Black Moon's hand?"

"I saw it, too." Tommy drew to a stop beside him.

Cole stared on as the crowd thinned. Jane remained speaking to Black Moon. Through the dispelling crowd he saw she had one hand holding onto Jaybird's even as the boy sulked enough to be leaning away from her grasp.

Even more stunning than the handshake, Jane seemed to be gesturing for the Indian and David to move with her to the Inn. As they stepped away, Jane glanced over her shoulder. She waved for them to follow.

Cole remained still for several minutes. "What in tarnation?"

"We're going to have to follow to find out."

"Right." Cole didn't move a muscle. The odd scene of Jane walking side-by-side with an Indian kept him frozen. He startled when Faro nickered. "Right. Follow."

Tommy moved before he did, making it to the Inn before he'd gotten a good start. By the time he hitched Faro to the post, the man was inside with the others.

Cole hopped up the steps much quicker and went inside. As he came in, Willow burst into the restaurant. She glared daggers at her brother, then shouted at him in what Cole assumed to be Ute. When she stopped to catch her breath, Jane sidled up to her, one hand still holding onto Jay's arm. She touched Willow's shoulder, but the girl turned and ran back toward their apartment without another word.

Jane sighed, but on spotting Cole offered a weak smile. Cole glanced at the Indian, certain he'd never seen the man inside their business before. He raised a brow as he turned back to Jane.

"Black Moon," Jane grimaced through the words. She straightened her features quick enough. "Found Jaybird in the woods south of town. He was kind enough to bring him back, where he met up with David during the search."

Cole looked down at Jay. The boy snuck glances at Black Moon, something Jane caught onto. Cole turned his attention to the man. "Thank you."

"I am glad I could help." Black Moon had a deep, sonorous voice that carried through the restaurant.

"Well." Jane led them all to a table. She didn't make Jay sit, but she didn't let him go, either. Instead, she pulled him close to her side. Her attention on him. "I don't know how to help you, Jaybird. I've tried allowing you to wear your skins at home, even figured a way to make more as you've outgrown them."

"We can't keep watch on him all the time. If we let him lose, he might run again." Cole kept his frown when the boy gave him an indignant stare. "Won't even stick around for his sister."

For that, Jay hung his head. Jane gave Cole a reproachful look, her arm running along Jay's upper arm. "It's been a year, and you're still so angry, Jaybird. I know you miss your old home, your old life, but I'm afraid it's long gone."

David frowned. "When's the last time you heard from your parents, Jaybird?"

Jane's gaze dropped to the floor. In her silence, as well as Jay's, Cole spoke. "It's been months. Jane has sent quite a few letters to the parents, and to the sergeant in charge of the reservation. There's been no response."

Jay's head snapped up to Jane at that. He spoke in rapid-fire Ute, wrenching his arm free to hit her shoulders.

Jane stared at him as if she understood everything the boy said. Her eyes brimmed with tears that spilled onto her cheeks. "I don't know what's happened. I wish I did. I've asked Tommy to look into it, he was friends with the soldier, but we've gotten no response. I wish with all my heart I could help you."

Jaybird hit her shoulders one more time, then flopped into her arms.

She held him close against her, but her gaze fell on Black Moon. For a long time she stared at the Indian in complete silence. Turmoil rippled across her features for many long minutes before it became calm again.

Tommy spoke low, "I've got a few other connections that might be able to tell me what happened, but it's taking time to reach them. I'd go, but it's not a good time."

Jane peeled Jaybird off her. She cupped his cheeks, brushing away tears subtly with her thumbs. "I promise we aren't keeping you from them. We don't know what's going on."

Jaybird muttered under his breath, still in Ute.

Rather than acknowledge Jay's latest complaint, whatever it might be, she glanced at Black Moon again. After a moment, she took a deep breath. "Thomas. Would you be so kind as to take Jaybird back to the apartment? Perhaps he can make a start on apologizing to his sister."

Tommy got to his feet right away. Before he took the boy, he leaned down close to Jane. The pair shared a hushed exchange Cole couldn't hear. Tommy straightened, extending his hand to Jaybird. "Let's go."

While they walked out, Jane turned back to face the men at the table. Once again she stared at Black Moon, then turned her gaze to David.

"What are you thinking, Jane?" David stared her down, his brow furrowed.

She stared down at her hands. Several deep breaths rose and fell. She shook her head then lifted it with a familiar stubborn set to her chin. Like she didn't want to do something, but knew she must. "Black Moon."

Cole was impressed that Jane managed to keep her features straight. No hint of disdain or fear in her tone.

"I know he is not of your tribe, you do not speak their language, or know their ways. I don't know any other way to help him." She set her shoulders and lifted her chin. "Perhaps if you could spend time with the children. Let them live free sometimes. David, if you would join them it would ease my mind some. I know you better."

The last words were rushed like she feared offending the Indian in the midst of her request.

Black Moon remained silent, but David spoke up. "Jesse and I go camping in the woods with Black Moon once a month so he can learn as I did."

"Yes, like that. Jaybird and Jesse get along well enough. As well as Jay gets along with anyone." Jane's chin trembled slightly. "I never expected them to see us as parents, they have parents they love dearly. I simply want to help them. Everything I've done—it's not been enough. He still runs."

"He is searching for something," Black Moon's deep voice was quiet.

"I know what he's searching for, but I…" Jane's voice trembled so much, she fell silent. "I care for them as my own children. Every time I think we make progress, he turns tail."

Cole rose when Jane did. She waved him off, rushing out onto the porch. He hesitated a moment, but before he could follow, Black Moon walked past.

David approached when Cole remained standing. "He's not about to hurt her."

"I'm not worried about him hurting her. I'm worried about Clara coming out and doing something stupid."

"Clara doesn't come out much anymore."

"You still can read her moods." Cole hated admitting as much. He hated being reminded of their long-dead marriage.

"That's because Jane is an open book. Can't hide her moods for nothing. It's akin to lying." David chuckled quietly. "She can be pleasant enough to people she doesn't like when she has to be, and put on airs when she must. Doesn't mean you still can't see what she's thinking underneath. Well, for those that know her at all."

The man had a point. Jane was an expert at people, and reading them, but it seemed to make her as easy to read. How early in their relationship had he been able to tell what she was thinking after all? Days? Minutes?

"I'll check on them." David moved to the door. Before he'd crossed the threshold, Jane appeared. A few tears still shimmered on her cheeks as she spoke quietly to her ex-husband. After a few minutes the man went outside, and Jane approached Cole.

She folded into his arms easy as anything. Her soft sigh seemed to course right through him. "He said he would do it. They're to leave tomorrow for two nights."

"You're doing good with them, Jane. Don't be so hard on yourself."

"I don't know what's got into me. I'm so emotional anymore." She swiped at her tears.

"There's been lots going on. What with Sally, and Jay, the tornado."

"The deaths."

"The deaths."

Jane sniffled, then straightened.

"I was so scared when he was gone. He doesn't see me as his Ma, but he's every inch my boy. I share him with his mother, just as I do Lizzie."

"I know that. Maybe one day he will, too."

"I doubt it." She squeezed him tight before releasing him. "Shall we go tell the children about their forthcoming adventure?"

"Sure. Maybe it'll cheer them up."

"At least someone will be cheered."

He tugged her close. With a finger, he tilted her chin to draw her gaze to him. "Maybe once we're done talking with them kids, I can find some way to cheer you up."

"I like the way you think, Mr. Mitchell."

The eternal in woman draws us on.
-Johann Wolfgang von Goethe

Cole locked the puppies back in the chicken coop. Hammy had only half finished the pen for the dogs, but expected it done soon. Considering the man was working five jobs at once with his crew, Cole wasn't about to complain.

Cindy and Lizzie had taken the twins over to their house, and Alma was taking a walk with Arthur. For the moment Millie was sitting with Sally, but it would be Cole's turn in another hour.

A hand rested on his shoulder, pulling him from his distraction. He turned, surprised to find Willow there. She took a deep breath. "Thank you."

He remained crouched on the ground. "What for?"

"Letting us go."

"This was Jane's idea." Cole wouldn't have ever thought of it, that was for sure. To be honest, he was surprised Jane had. The old prejudice against Indians of Clara's hadn't faded, and had likely been cemented by getting shot by the renegades herself.

"He doesn't understand." Willow's previous begrudging English flowed much smoother after a year in their company.

The same couldn't be said for her brother. His stubborn clinging to their old life, and likely the fact he'd been an infant when the Ute took them, left him speaking Ute more than English. Willow looked off toward the East. "That we can't go back."

He eyed the young woman quietly. "I'm thinking you don't, either."

"I understand. I don't like it or know why this had to happen."

Cole rose, leading Willow back inside. David and Black Moon were due to arrive soon. "Jane's better at answering questions than me, Willow."

"She tries." Willow fiddled with the straps of her medicine bag. "Maybe this one can help my brother."

"That's the hope." Cole sat on the arm of the sofa. "You'll make sure he doesn't run again?"

"He ran without me." Her brow furrowed. She stared at the ground. "He left me here."

"He was mad and not thinking right. I'd bet if he planned ahead he would have." A knock on the door saved him from trying to figure out a way to placate the sibling trouble. "Come in."

Jesse burst through the door with his usual bright smile. He hugged Cole tight, then looked around. "Where's Jay? We're gonna have so much fun."

"We hope. Jaybird isn't in the best of moods right now. Remember?" David planted his hands on Jesse's shoulders to keep him still. Hard to believe the boy had first arrived in town he'd been mute and sedate. The boy had been so excitable since Jane had rescued him from Bingham and returned him to his father. Four years later and there was no sign of him calming into adulthood. "Cole. Willow."

"Davie." Cole stood when Black Moon entered behind David. Jane had wanted to be there, but she'd been pulled away by responsibilities. Perhaps it was best. Two days in the Cheyenne's presence might've been too much for her. Cole turned back to David. "I appreciate you going with them. Jane'll feel better knowing someone she trusts is with them, especially after what happened yesterday."

David nodded. "Millie will be going to our place when she's done sitting with Sally. She'll help with Marjorie."

"Hope Lee isn't too mad," Cole offered by way of apology.

"If she didn't like Jane, she might've been madder. Besides, like I said, Jesse and I go once a month anyhow." David's attention turned over Cole's shoulder. "Jaybird. Are you ready?"

Jay nodded, clutching an animal hide bag over his shoulder.

Willow waved him over. She didn't speak to him, but took the bag onto her own shoulder.

A deep voice came from the door where Black Moon still stood. "Shivering Willow, Jaybird. I am Black Moon."

The pair stared at him wide-eyed. Willow broke the staring contest first to glance at Cole. He nodded to her. "You two go on. We'll see you in a couple of days."

The ragtag group gathered at the door. Words of greeting and explanation passed between them as they made their way outside. Once the apartment was empty, Cole sighed out some exasperation. He wasn't sure it was a good idea, but Jane seemed at a loss for anything else to do. Hopefully some time around Black Moon would help them. He just hoped it wouldn't make things worse.

With some time left before he had to head to the clinic, he went out to the casino in search of Jane. He found her working behind the bar, pouring drinks and cleaning. As always, her bright mood lightened the moods of the folks filling the room.

Cole headed around the bar toward her. With her back to him, he set his hands on her hips and leaned down to nip her earlobe. "The kids are gone."

Her body arched into his eagerly. Clearly his enthusiastic apologies last night had done the trick to rid her of any lingering anger over the dogs. Her head tilted to one side to give him glorious access to her neck. She hummed as he kissed along her neck. "I thought you had somewhere to be."

"Not for an hour."

"I see." She turned in his arms, wrapping hers around his neck. "We've already been making regular efforts for another baby. You want to squeeze more in during your last hour?"

"Sure wouldn't mind."

"Fun as it would be to continue our efforts, I have work to attend to."

Rather than waste words in argument, Cole crushed his lips to hers. She responded eagerly, tugging at him with a desperation that lit a fire in him down to his toes. All too soon the heat cooled, and she withdrew. Lips swollen, eyes heavy with lust, she cleared her throat.

When he went in for another kiss, she set a finger to his lips. "Hold that thought."

"You're joking."

"Damn. I wish I was, but I'm not." The hand on his chest pushed him back a step. "A few minutes is all I need."

"What for?"

She slipped under his arm and went to the beer tap, pouring a tall glass. The glass hit the bar soon as Hammy's ass hit the stool. She offered the man a warm smile. "Good afternoon, Mr. Hamm."

"Much obliged, Lady Jane." He slurped on the beer, a little light on the smiles and blushing he usually offered.

"Is something wrong, Mr. Hamm?" Clearly Jane had picked up on it as well.

"Nah. Been busy as all get out. Your place is coming along swell. Should be ready 'afore the Statehood party."

"Really? So soon?"

"Woulda been sooner, but Mrs. Daugherty wanted the dress shop built, too." He rubbed a hand over his face. "Everybody wants something doing."

"You are working far too hard. You don't look well." Jane patted his hand. "You need to let Teddy take control of some of the projects. That's why you hired him. He's no Gilbert Hamm, but he isn't too shabby with a hammer."

This time Hammy did flush under Jane's compliment. "Aw, Lady Jane."

"You'll take better care of yourself for me, won't you?" Jane gave the old man a stunning smile. "I can't imagine a day without you stopping by."

"I'll do what I can." Hammy turned bright red under Jane's smile. "I'll let Teddy take some jobs, but I won't let no one else work on your projects."

"You'd better not. I deserve the best, after all."

Cole chuckled under his breath when Hammy slurped his beer in reply. "All right, Jane. You've flattered Hammy enough."

"There isn't enough flattery in the world for him." Jane winked at Cole. "You, however, get far too much."

"Oh, I do—do I?" He tugged her toward the end of the bar. Unfortunately, she stopped short when someone else sat at the bar.

"Mr. Warner. I'm pleased to hear you're gracing us with your presence for a while longer." She tugged her hand free of Cole's. "What can I get for you today?"

"Do you happen to have any sherry? I haven't had one since I left St. Louis."

"Considering the wide variety of folks we serve; you doubt I have any?" If Jane got any more flirty with the man, Cole might start to get jealous.

"I beg forgiveness for my rudeness. It is obvious that you would have only the finest, oh Jane of the Hangman. I mean, Hangman's Inn."

Jane pulled a ring of keys from her belt to unlock the cabinet with their most expensive liquor. She laughed all the way through pouring the drink. "Be careful, Mr. Warner. You don't want to upset the woman that pours your drink."

"Fair point. As to my staying, I have decided to remain for three months."

Jane's smile faded. "Three?"

"That's the best I can do. I cannot linger too long. It would be inappropriate." An odd look passed between the pair of them.

Jane opened her mouth to speak, then inhaled sharply with hesitation. When she spoke, it was a cryptic, "Of course. We musn't be unseemly."

"Friendship endures."

"And shall remain as such."

Cole had to admit total confusion over the turn of the conversation. "What's going on?"

Jane shook off whatever melancholy had taken over at Patrick's words. The smile returned to her face. "Three months, then. Well, allow us to offer a discount for such a lengthy stay."

"Oh no. I'm happy to pay full price for your comfortable room and various services."

"You didn't allow me to finish. I was going to offer a discount if you would join one of our exclusive rooms for your stay." Jane leaned on the counter, a too-bright smile once again crossing her features. At least this time Cole knew she was working over the man. "There are some very exhilarating games that happen in both our Silver and Gold rooms."

"You are a temptress. No wonder that man glowering at us snatched you up so quick." Patrick took a sip of his sherry. "I accept your offer. I wouldn't mind some entertainment while I remain in town."

"Excellent. Let's work out the details over supper. You may join Cole and I, and whatever other souls decide to join us."

"It's a deal." Patrick patted her hand. "Thank you for your understanding."

"You have business to return to, and..." Jane hesitated as if to search for words which was unusual for her. "Your kindness can only extend so far before it becomes wickedness."

"Precisely."

Cole glanced at Jane askance when she took his hand to lead him away. "Mind telling me what in tarnation that was about?"

"What?"

"You and Patrick. You were talking in circles."

"There were no circles."

"There were. You were talking in circles like you do with Kathy and Lil."

Jane laughed softly as she pushed open the door to their apartment. "How about if I tell you it's not something discussed in polite conversation?"

"I ain't polite."

"You'd better not be." She spun to face him as the door closed. "Because I'm looking to get real impolite right about now."

"You are, are ya?"

"Care to get impolite with me?"

"Always."

*The same thing is happening to me as happens
to people in dreams when they see and feel
a wound but can't remember having
received it.
-Alexandre Dumas Père*

"Easy, Sally." Jane's kind voice entered her awareness quiet and steady. "It hurts to come awake after such a thing, but you are a strong woman. We're here with you."

Pain reached through every muscle in her body. Each breath hurt so bad she wanted to stop breathing altogether.

A soft hand brushed along her hair. "That's it. Breathe slow, easy. It won't hurt so much after a bit. Until then you need to be strong."

"Are you sure she's waking up?" Tommy sounded farther away than Jane.

"She'd know better than you. She was worse off than Sally when she got here," said Cole.

"Hush, you two," Jane scolded. "She's right here, listening to your jabber."

Sally tried to open her eyes to see the three people talking about her. After a few tries, her lids fluttered open. First thing in her sight line was Jane, smiling.

"We've missed you this past week. It's so good to see you again." Jane squeezed her hand, which blessedly didn't hurt. "Take your time. We're not going anywhere."

"What happened?" The words came out hoarse. Her mouth felt as though stuffed with cotton. "Why?"

"We aren't certain what happened to you, other than you were attacked out by the lake." Jane disappeared from view. Behind her, both Cole and Tommy leaned on the end of the bed. When she reappeared, Jane held a glass of water to Sally's lips. "Drink slow. You don't want to upset your stomach."

Sally took a couple slow sips of water. Her parched mouth soaked it up eagerly. She released a small sigh. "Everything hurts."

"It's like a nightmare." Jane spoke with the surety of someone who'd suffered through the same. Of course, she had when she'd first come to Dominion Falls. "Within a day or two you'll feel more capable of handling it."

Sally's mind spun with the effort of remembering what had happened. The carriage with Arthur. Then…what? "I…the last thing I remember…Arthur. Is he all right?"

"He's fine. Only worried about you. He feels terribly guilty for leaving you by yourself, though he couldn't have known such a terrible thing would happen." Jane glanced behind her. "One of you oafs help the girl sit. It's incredibly dehumanizing to be lying flat while people are fretting over you."

Cole came around the side of the bed. When he picked her up to move her, she did her best to not voice the pain the motion left her in. Through it all, Jane held her hand, not reacting a lick when Sally squeezed it hard.

"That better?" Cole readjusted her sheets.

"Yes." Sally found she could breathe easier sitting. The pain of being moved to sit eased with each breath. "I was at the lake."

"You don't have to go over it right now, Sally." Tommy's voice remained calm and reassuring. "You just woke up."

"I'm trying to make sense of it." Sally took as deep a breath as her lungs would allow her. "What day is it?"

"Monday." Jane leaned over to grab the soup steaming on the bedside table. "Charlie believes the blow to the cheek concussed you enough to leave you unconscious for so long."

"That…" Her hand trembled on the way to her cheek. Shadowy memories pressed against the cloudiness in her mind. So much was muddled. "I remember that. She screamed."

"She?"

"She screamed…whore."

Jane sat straighter, a frown drawing her lips down. After a moment, she went back to stirring the soup.

Cole dragged a chair closer to the bed. "She? Who was she?"

"I don't know who she was. She wasn't alone, though." Sally sipped the soup while silence lingered in the room. After she'd managed a few spoonfuls, her stomach turned. She waved off the next spoon Jane offered. "I don't think I can."

"That's fine. You need to take everything slow, Sally. Nobody expects you to go over it all now." Jane's eyes remained downcast.

"What have I missed?" Sally hated to see Jane so worried. A change of subject seemed to be in order. Especially since she couldn't remember worth a damn yet, anyhow.

"Jay ran away again," Cole supplied while Jane busied herself with setting the soup down. "Jane sent him and Willow off with Davie's Indian friend."

"She what?" Sally glanced at Jane. "You did?"

"I didn't see any other choice in the matter. Jaybird is not adjusting to life here, not even after a year. I thought maybe if he had some time…" Jane's voice trailed off. The worry Sally'd tried to abate with a subject change grew deeper instead of lessening.

Tommy set a hand on Jane's shoulder. "Your pa made your ma mad all over again."

Sally grasped at the humor in Tommy's tone. "Again? But he just did when he broke his foot. How could you mess up again so fast?"

"I'm talented like that," Cole said with a grin.

Even Jane managed to smile now. "Well, Cole decided the twins weren't spoiled enough and gave them both a dog. Whiskey and Bourbon. Jesse got one as well that he named Barnaby, and Cindy and Lizzie got the last puppy, named her Nellie."

"Puppies?" Sally raised her brows at Cole. "Ma didn't kill you?"

"She sure tried." Cole's grin broadened when Tommy laughed outright. "She really did try."

"He's not wrong." Jane winked. Sally was glad to see her mood had sufficiently lightened. "I wasn't thrilled at first. He'll pay for his mistake slowly over time."

"It's already started. Whiskey didn't get taken outside fast enough this morning. Jane put his shit in my shoe." Cole grimaced.

Sally had to put a hand to her rib when her own laughter brought the aches to the forefront. "Ma, you didn't?"

"I most certainly did. I had to make certain he knew I meant it when I said they were his responsibility." Jane laughed along with Sally and Tommy. "That's what happens when I find feces on my floor. Imagine what will happen if any of my fine clothes or furniture are chewed upon. There will be hell to pay."

"On that note." Cole cleared his throat and rose. "We should let Sally rest. Let's head back, Jane. Tom's got the next shift anyway."

"Next shift?" Sally looked between them confused.

"Of course. You don't think we left you alone for one second this week, do you?" Jane kissed Sally's forehead. "Rest. Eat when you can, drink water slow. Let your mind rest best you can, even if it does want to find out what happened."

Sally's lip trembled when Jane said exactly what was going on in her brain. It raced and raced, trying to find the answers, trying to push through the fog. Even the distraction of humor hadn't stopped it for a second. "Thank you."

"Lucky for you, there's no one better to understand. At least you remember who you are. That gives you a strong advantage over me when I awoke." Jane squeezed her hand warmly before she moved to Cole's side. Cole limped out the door with her.

"Why isn't Cole using his crutch?" Sally turned to Tommy, who offered a look of frustrated amusement. "Ah."

"The plaster came off when he was rescuing you. He said it was a waste to put it back on. He couldn't do anything with it. The crutch is just a pain."

"How angry is Ma that he refuses to use it?"

"Jane's plenty frustrated, and they've had a fight or two over it, but they always make it work." Tom sighed. "It's frustrating to deal with them half the time."

"You don't live under their roof."

"Fair point."

"How did Pa come upon four puppies?"

A frown flickered across Tommy's features.

"Tommy?"

"Ellis died. Fell in his own well. Your ma found the pups on the property same time as I found him."

"Wait. Ellis died?"

"He did."

Sally stared at the man for a long time. "Did you say he fell in his own well?"

"I did."

She pondered over that. "Tell me more."

"Like what, specifically?"

"How did he fall in the well?"

"No one knows."

"Tommy!" She hit the bed in frustration over his vague answers. Immediately, she winced and pressed a hand to her ribs. "Oh. Ow."

"Fine. Since you're hurting, I won't make you ask specific questions, though that's how you would learn."

"How I learn?"

Tommy eyed her. "You want to know about Ellis, or you want an explanation?"

"Yes."

He chuckled low. "Fine. Jane said you could learn."

Hope rushed up through her chest with a heady warmth. "Really?"

"Yes."

A thousand more questions blossomed in her head, making it pound with the sudden exertion. "Oh, my goodness."

"Ellis?"

"Yes. Ellis first. What happened?"

"We found him in his well. The top was broken like maybe he'd fallen through."

"Maybe?" Sally sat up a bit straighter. "You don't think so?"

"As your ma pointed out, the boards were new. It looked like he'd recently built a new one. Had to be less than a year old."

"Then how would it get broken apart unless it was intentional?"

Tommy sat back, smiling at her. "Very good."

"Then who would want Ellis dead? He was a good man. Liked his moonshine a little too much sometimes, but was at church every Sunday. Even after his wife died."

"I know."

She stared out the window at the clear blue sky. Between Ellis and Keller, not to mention Emily and herself. "What is going on?"

Tommy craned his head to look out the window. "What are you talking about?"

Sally turned so suddenly her head spun. She groaned, placing a hand to her head. "Oh dear."

"You all right?"

"Turned too fast. Give me a moment." She took several deep breaths until her head stopped spinning. "What did you find out?"

"About?"

"What happened to me."

"Not near enough. You not remembering who it was is another stumbling block."

"I want to help."

"With what?" He arched a brow.

"All of it. Ellis. Keller. Emily. Me."

A genuine, warm grin broke across his face. "I figured as much. Jane was right, though. You need rest. We'll start your training now, then. The physical training will have to wait until you can breathe without wincing."

"Then what do we train?"

"Your mind."

"Tell me what to do."

To be able to enjoy one's past life
is to live twice.
-Marcus Aurelius

Jane stood outside the freshly completed brothel, examining the fresh painted sign which read 'The Golden Touch'. With the exception of the stairs leading to the elevated porch, the exterior stood eerily similar to Cole's original brothel. She'd said as much to him, but he'd laughed off the suggestion.

For the past two weeks Cole and Tommy had conspired against her seeing the progress. They'd staunchly refused to allow her inside. The best she'd had was Hammy's vague updates about how close to completion it was. To that end, the whores had been in town for two days and she hadn't had a chance to meet one of them.

Over the past week Sally had left the hospital and been forcing her healing, despite Jane's urging to take it easy. The attack had lit a fire under her ward, and she was now soaking up every bit of knowledge Tommy could give her. Despite Jane's requests to keep to mental exercise, she had a sneaking suspicion her brother had been endeavoring in some physical training.

Jane shook off the concerned turn her thoughts had taken to focus on the brothel again. With the statehood celebration in a few days, they were set to open the following day. Cole had finally agreed to allow her to see the place. He'd said he wanted to make it *just right*. Whatever in the hell that meant.

Jane climbed the steps to the front doors. The tall doors stood closed behind the swinging doors that would stand open during business hours. She pulled aside the swinging door to push open the tall inner door, and stepped into what could only be the past.

Not only was the outside of the building similar to the original Hangman's Inn, the inside held a nearly identical layout. Jane walked further in, taking in the familiar layout of the tables, the balcony above the circled the saloon floor, the rooms on her left, the bar on the right.

She had no doubt that the door beside the bar would lead to the storeroom, and an icehouse beyond. The whores' rooms would be behind the stairs leading up to the second floor balcony, and a bath house in the back as well. Only thing she felt certain would not be the same was the room above the bar, which had been Cole's in the original building.

The absurd perfectness of the idea to recreate the saloon left her unsure whether she should laugh or cry. Cole stood silent behind the bar while she turned in a circle to take it all in. She strode over, the laughter winning the battle, and she struggled to keep it at bay. "You, sir, are quite insane. You're aware of this?"

"Says you." He poured her a glass of whiskey. "I liked the way it was. It worked real well until some crazy dead woman fell in my place."

"It worked after that, too." Jane took the drink in hand, but spun to rest her elbows on the bar. She took in the saloon again, every inch of it bringing her back in years. "I feel as though I stepped back in time. With the exception of one thing—the room up there isn't yours."

"Ours. And nah. Wil isn't even up there. He's back there." He pointed to the top of the steps. "Like we had, he's got two rooms worth of space, and a water closet. He wanted easy access to the stairs in case of trouble."

"Smart. Surprised you didn't do the same back then." She paused to drink her whiskey down. "This is either brilliant, or stupid."

"Old regulars'll like it. It'll remind them I ran a good saloon. They'll tell the newcomers."

"Your words? Or Thomas'?"

"Mine. Was my idea." His breath brushed the back of her neck. "You like it?"

"I really do."

"You ain't seen the half of it yet."

"Is that so?" When he circled the bar, Jane met his kiss eagerly. "Well, then. Where is our manager hiding?"

"Not hiding, I'm right here." Wil hopped down the steps two at a time. For the briefest of moments a smile crossed his features when he bowed to Jane. By the time he straightened, his features were quite stoic, almost angry. "What do ya think, Janey?"

Jane wasn't put off by the shifting attitude. Her interactions with Wil in private were always pleasant. The man was quite funny, and he knew his business. That meant he'd already been establishing quite a reputation around town as a rake, an ass, and a fighter. "I think we're going to do well, so long as we don't allow certain parts of history to repeat themselves."

Wil offered a wicked smirk. "You can fall down dead in my saloon any time, Janey. If ya need rescuing from that worthless sod."

Cole chuckled darkly. "Watch it."

Jane sighed. "No pissing contests gentlemen. Fun as they never were."

Cole laughed outright for that. "Fine. You ready to meet the girls?"

Wil blew a sharp, sing-song whistle. At the sound a dozen girls spilled from the back rooms. They lined up as Wil told them to. "Time for ya to meet your madam."

"You didn't say nothing about a madam," whined a short whore near the end.

"You don't need to know nothing until it's time to know it." Wil circled to face her. "I run the place, they own it."

Several curious eyes turned her direction. Jane straightened under the unspoken queries.

"Jane, I'd like you to meet," Wil gestured down the line as he began, "Rose. Lily. Poppy."

Unable to hold it any longer, Jane burst into laughter in the midst of the introductions. She held up a hand to stop Wil. "Wait. Did you really, Cole?"

"You bet I did." Cole winked her way. "Did you think I wouldn't?"

"Well. Are there certain names that are off the table, at least?" Jane ignored the whores' curious glances at each other, Wil, and herself.

"Of course. Iris, Pansy…" Cole leaned close, then paused. Seeming to realize he was on her right side, he pulled her in front of him to dip his lips to her left ear. "And Azalea."

Jane snorted, but pleasant heat flooded her cheeks that he remembered he'd offered her the name of Azalea when she'd first awoken in Dominion Falls. She cleared her throat to try to cease the chuckles that continued bubbling up. She waved at Wil. "Please. Go on."

"Right. That's Rose. Lily. Poppy. Violet. Narcissus. Jasmine. Aster. Peony. Dahlia. Honeysuckle. Snowdrop. And Buttercup." Wil said the last name with a flourish as he presented by far the prettiest girl on the floor. He winked at Jane.

Jane met each girls' eyes as she ran over the names again, committing them to memory. As she did, she allowed all amusement to drain from her so she might impart the rules with as firm a hand as ever. "My name is Jane Spencer. I will not be here as often as Wil, or likely as often as Cole, but make no mistake, I will always be kept apprised of whatever you believe you can get away with."

Wil backed away toward the bar as Jane moved forward.

"Our rules here are quite simple. We run a clean brothel. There will be no opium, no cocaine, no libations of any kind outside of alcohol." She paused at Peony, the one who'd sneered about having a madam. "There is no tolerance for disobeying."

Peony raised her chin in defiance but remained silent.

Jane continued her walk down the row. "You will take the time to clean yourself between every john."

A scoff down the line drew Jane's attention. Lily shook her head. "Ain't no way."

Jane stepped in front of Lily, staring her down. "Between servicing you will clean your pussy until it shines, is that understood?"

"That's pointless. Never done it before. Those men don't care none." Lily set a hand on her hip, not showing any indication of backing down.

Jane noticed movement out of the corner of her eye, likely Wil. Something stopped him, thankfully. Probably Cole, if Jane had to guess. Jane allowed her lips to curve into a smile and took another step closer to Lily. "You *will* do as you're told, or your scantily clad ass will be on the next train out of town without a penny to your name. Believe me, your contracts are very specific and well-thought out. If you don't like the rules, you shouldn't have signed."

"I told ya they don't care."

"I do."

"You just said you ain't gonna be here, so what's it matter?"

This time Wil did move closer, but Jane held her hand up to him to stop him. She got so close to Lily, the girls' breasts heaved against her own corset. "I also said I would be apprised of all rule-breaking. Wil has my full permission to evict you as I've said I will."

Lily snorted. "I'd like to see you try."

"Then so be it." Jane grabbed the girls' arm and hauled her to the door. She shoved her outside without a word, then slammed the doors behind her. A few pounds came on the door, then silence. She heard a male voice arguing with Lily until their bootsteps faded down the stairs. The male voice had been exceedingly familiar, as it belonged to Thomas.

When she turned back to the group, she noticed and ignored the surprised raise of Wil's brows. Jane dusted off her hands, then approached the girls again. "We don't ask much. You will be clean, and clean yourself between servicing. You'll meet with a doctor once a week to ensure you didn't catch anything from your johns."

She perched on a table and scanned the line of girls who now had their full attention on her. "Womb veils will be used, and you will tell me your bleeding schedule so I can set a schedule of when you cannot work. Pregnancies can happen by accident, but we do everything in our power to prevent them."

She hopped off the table to walk down the line again. "If you do become pregnant even though you followed the rules and schedule, your options will be discussed. We will not throw you out for an honest mistake that can happen to the most careful soul."

There was a snort, or a cough, behind her. She didn't dare look, though she wondered if it wasn't Cole trying to cover a laugh. Considering the two of them were well versed in surprise pregnancies, she might have had trouble keeping a straight face if she weren't dealing with the lot of women in front of her.

"For those of you who can't read or didn't bother to care what was in your contract, there is a stipulation for every one of you if you wish to get out of the game. You have the ability to work off your contract and learn a new skill. We own the Inn across the way and are well-situated in this town to get you any training or learning you might want. If you wish to be a whore and remain so, we're fine with that. If you don't like it here, we will find you a new place."

Jane paused her pacing to face the women dead on. "We run a strict, clean establishment, but so long as you follow the rules you will be treated well. We don't hit our girls, and we don't let the clientele hit neither. If you are injured, we will take care of it by expelling the man and treating your injuries."

She took a deep breath. "Follow the rules and you'll all do well here. Break the rules and you'll end up like Lily. Understood?"

Down the line there was a wave of nodding. Jane turned her back on them to approach Cole, who wore a smirk that promised much debauchery. While Wil took control of the women and got them back to their rooms, Jane paused a foot from Cole. "What?"

"I mention lately that you're my kind of woman?"

"Not in the past week, no."

"Get over here, woman."

"But…why?"

"You know why."

Jane took a step back, rather than draw closer. When Cole took a step toward her, she took another one back. The door opened, the beam of light spilling between them like a solid barrier. Even Cole paused his stalking at the interruption.

"Ma?" Sally's interruption couldn't have come at a better time. "Woah. This is so strange."

Jane laughed at the frustration that creased Cole's features. "I know, Sally. It's like stepping back in time, isn't it?"

"Sure is."

"Sally!" Jane had turned and immediately took notice of Sally's garb. "What on earth do you think you're doing?"

Sally flushed red. She tugged at the men's shirt she wore, then brushed her hands along the trousers. "What?"

"You are still healing, young lady. You are *not* supposed to be doing any sort of physical training yet. We just discussed this yesterday."

Sally's brow furrowed, the red in her face seeming more out of anger than embarrassment now. "Tommy won't let me get hurt, Ma. It's fine."

"We agreed you would wait."

"No, *you* ordered, I didn't agree. I don't wanna end up in that clinic again. I wanna know how to fight, how to protect myself. I ain't gonna learn it sitting at home with books like a good girl. You should know that well enough, you never sat home."

"Sally Ann!" Jane was nearly as stunned at the rough vernacular that had slipped back in at Sally's upset as she was by her words. "I was—it was—"

"Different," Sally all but sneered the words out. "No it wasn't, and you know it. Your life was in danger, well so is mine. They didn't kill me so what if they try again? Should I let them?"

"I never said that."

In her distraction, Cole had managed to reach her side. His hand slid around her waist. "Jane. Sally."

"It was mostly running anyhow, not that you care." Sally spun on her heel and stormed back to the door. She stopped at the threshold and turned to face Jane. "I wanna find out who did this, Ma. I can't keep sitting around. You've done plenty of stuff when you weren't healed right. I'm tired of healing."

"Sally," Jane called after her. The door slammed instead of a response. She sighed deeply.

"I'm sure they're being careful." Cole rubbed a hand on her back. "You worry too much."

"I'm her ma, of course I worry." She leaned into Cole. "I do hate when we argue."

"You'll make it right. Now, where was I?"

Jane darted out of his arms before his lips made contact. "You behave."

"That ain't no fun."

*The holiest of all holidays are those
kept by ourselves in silence and apart;
the secret anniversaries of the heart.
—Henry Wadsworth Longfellow*

Jane walked arm in arm with Alma through the crowd. Near the grandstand she could see Lillian and Henry Daugherty speaking with the senator who had kicked off the celebration with a long-winded speech. So long, in fact, she feared the crowd would forget it was a party.

Fortunately, the festivities had kicked into gear pretty quick. She'd tasked Cole with keeping an eye on Jaybird this time, which left her to help Alma navigate the crowd. Sally, who'd barely spoken to her in several days, was playing with Tommy and several children.

As if thinking of Cole had brought him into being, the man appeared before her, dragged by Jesse. Along with him came Jay and Willow, both seeming in good spirits. Willow even pushed on Cole as Jesse tugged him forward.

"Ma! Hey, Ma!" Jesse gave her a brutal hug, then glanced at Alma. "Hiya."

"Jesse," Alma said quietly. A smile lit her delicate features. "Hi."

"Hello to you, too. What are you three doing with Cole?"

"We're going to play Hucklebuck, and the shooting gallery. You get prizes if you win."

"I'm quite aware." Jane chuckled softly. "Maybe you should let Cole play the shooting gallery. He'll win all the prizes."

"Good idea." Jesse grinned up at Cole. "We got an hour until the three-legged race."

"You're awful keen for that race." Cole leaned down to eye Jesse. "Isn't a particular reason for that, is there?"

"Lizzie asked me to be in the race with her." Jesse's ears turned red as his pa's when embarrassed. "She asked me last week. Don't wanna let her down."

"I see." Jane did her best to keep her smile in check. "Well, then you mustn't be late for that, although it seems you're keeping an eye on the time."

"Asks me every five minutes." Cole rose, offering her a wink. "We'd best get on with it."

"Have fun." Jane waved them on, turning back to Alma. "I do believe you mentioned popcorn, and if I remember right, it's right next to the lemonade stand."

"You remember everything." Though her head was ducked, Alma wore what could only be called a sly smile.

"Alma May, I do believe you are teasing me."

"Maybe."

Jane laughed outright. "For that, I ought to let you have two lemonades."

"Maybe even three." Alma smiled at the grass.

"Perhaps." Jane walked with her toward the stands. Before they arrived, another familiar face approached.

Nick smiled brightly at them both. "Good afternoon, ladies. Are we having fun?"

"We are." Jane kissed his cheek. "We were heading for the popcorn and lemonade. Alma made a joke, so I'm buying her two lemonades."

"I'll join you. Perhaps then Alma would like to go see the calliope? It plays loud music. I bet you'd like it." Nick paused at the popcorn booth. He refused to allow Jane to pay, buying her and Alma both a bag.

Alma glanced at Jane once she had the popcorn. "Music?"

"Yes. It's delightful. Would you like to go with Nicholas?" Jane paid for the lemonade before Nick could, handing him one as well as Alma.

"Music. Loud music." Alma nodded. "I'd like to go."

"Then you both go on ahead. I'll buy you another lemonade when you're done." Jane nodded to Nick as they left. She scanned the crowd with a happy sigh. Everything seemed to be going well. Despite everything else going on, it was so nice to have the chance to relax and have fun.

After a few bites of popcorn, she took a sip of lemonade. The flavor was delightful, with just the right amount of sweetness, but her stomach turned unexpectedly after she'd swallowed. Grimacing, she set down the cup.

After a moment, the sensation passed. She lifted the glass again, but this time the mere smell made her stomach churn. "Oh. Dear."

"Jane?" Mike's voice entered her awareness. When she turned, the bright smile he wore faded. "Are you all right?"

"Yes." It wasn't a lie, for the sensation had passed quick as it had come. She left the lemonade behind as she approached her brother, though. That's when she noticed the woman on his arm. "Daisy! How delightful."

Daisy smiled pleasantly enough, but something was off. The smile didn't quite reach her eyes. "Jane."

"I feel as though it's been ages since I've seen you." Jane gave the woman a warm hug. "You've been missed. You work far too hard."

"Jane," Mike chided. He accepted her hug. "Don't tease her when she's come out for a pleasant day."

"Not teasing. Stating she's been missed." Jane smiled at Daisy. "I hope everything is well with you. Charles says the practice is flourishing, that you're talking about building a proper hospital and everything."

"I'd rather not discuss business today." Daisy leaned closer to Mike. "I'm going to get some popcorn for us to share."

Mike gave her a quick peck on the lips before she slipped away. He turned to face Jane, and his smile faltered. "What?"

"What's going on with you?" She studied him hard. "Something is up. Is it simply because you have your woman on your arm for a change?"

"Jane." Mike groaned. "Leave it be. We've talked she's really making an effort."

"Is she now?" She took a step back to study him further. "Wait. How much of an effort?"

"Will you drop it? She's coming back. Some things are best kept private for a while."

"Wait—are you two engaged?"

"What's this?" Charlie approached with a bag of candy, a smile on his features. "Engaged?"

Daisy stopped short, then cut a glare to Mike.

"I didn't tell them," Mike started.

"He didn't. I guessed. Sorry." Jane stepped forward to placate Daisy. "I didn't realize Charles was so close. Are you?"

Daisy's face flushed red, but she nodded. "Just. We wanted to keep it quiet. Personal-like. Didn't need the nosey nellie's butting in."

"Of course, it's my fault, not Michael's. I just know him too well, I guess." Jane clasped Daisy's hand before she could storm off. "If you want to be mad at someone, be mad at me. This is happy news, but Charles and I will keep our mouths shut until you're ready. Promise."

Daisy's shoulders sagged, but she nodded. "Fine. Long as you promise."

"We do, right Charles?" Jane glanced her brother's way. "Not a word."

"Not a word," Charles agreed. He shook Mike's hand. "Congratulations, and I won't say another word on it."

"Thanks." Mike shook his brother's hand, then moved to Daisy's side. He offered Jane a glare of his own before leading Daisy away.

Jane frowned after them, pondering the seeming lack of excitement on Daisy's part, and the fact she knew Daisy had turned her brother down before.

"Jane?" Charlie touched her shoulder.

"Sorry. Sorry, hello." She turned to hug her brother. "Where's your wife?"

"Resting. We've already walked and played games for an hour. She's rather tired. I bought her a bag of sweets, and she is talking with Lee while she feeds Marjorie." He held out the bag to Jane. "Care for a taffy?"

She eyed the bag, pondering her recent sensitive stomach. The taffy was too appealing to not at least attempt. "Yes, please."

He walked with her through the various booths. "You seem distracted?"

"Why wouldn't I be? There's so much going on."

"The party is done, all except your horse race, you have little to do now."

"Yes, but as we know my life tends to never be good, calm, and quiet."

"True enough. How are the puppies?"

She pursed her lips. "I'm loathed to say that even young as they are they seem intelligent enough. Cole's training efforts are already making their mark."

"You're upset you have one less reason to be mad at him?"

"Perhaps." She nudged his shoulder, but set free her rising laughter. "I've no doubt he'll find another way to make me angry in short order. The man does have a talent for such matters."

"I believe he has such talent because you two enjoy the spark of fire that comes from your rather frequent arguing."

"That isn't the only thing that allows for that spark of fire."

"One does not discuss such matters in polite company."

"Ah, but one must 'be polite to all, but intimate with few'."

"Jefferson." Charlie smirked her way at her nod of ascent. "True, but Goldsmith was known to say that 'the wise are polite all over the world, but the fool only at home'."

"Good for me I'm impolite everywhere, then."

He snorted. "Fair point."

"Besides you are the farthest thing from polite company. You are a Young, after all."

"Touché, dear sister."

Jane laughed softly, but it faded when Sally ran by on her way toward where they were setting up for the games. "She hasn't spoken to me in near three days."

He followed her gaze with a frown. "It will pass. Always does. She seems to have learned something from you on how to handle her anger. Ignore the person until they apologize."

"I won't apologize for worrying for her. She is trying to do too much too soon. Acting as if she's not been grievously injured and lying in a hospital bed."

"I repeat, she's learned something from you." He held the bag of candy out to her in response to her brutal glare. "Taffy?"

She pursed her lips, doing her best to maintain her glare. "Oh, you. Go coddle your wife. You're annoying me again."

"I always annoy you."

"You aren't wrong."

He kissed her forehead. "Behave yourself."

"That's no fun."

"I'm aware."

She laughed at his departing wave. Somehow she caught the piece of taffy he tossed back toward her, stuffing it in her mouth happily.

When she spotted Sally speaking with Reverend Lyons, she decided enough was enough. She crossed the meadow quick as she could through the crowd, approaching just as Sally excused herself. "Sally, wait."

Sally's sigh made her shoulders drop. "Yes, ma?"

"Don't give me that attitude." Jane circled her to meet her gaze. "I won't apologize for worrying, if that's what you're waiting for. It's my job to worry about you. It will never change, even when you are grown and out from under my roof. You are my daughter, and I warned you when you said you wanted to pursue this that I would worry for you. All the time."

Tears shone in Sally's eyes. "I know, Ma. I just can't sit around, though. I've gotta find out who did this and why. And…"

Jane's brow rose when Sally's gaze wandered, the sentence trailing off into nothing. "And?"

"Why these people keep dying."

Jane frowned, pondering the meaning. "People die, Sally."

"Emily was clearly murdered. I mean, her attack was like mine, except she didn't live."

"Clearly."

"The menfolk, though. They both could have been accidents, but it's so odd."

"You aren't talking to me at all, are you?"

Sally's gaze drifted back to Jane. "It's bothering me. Seems like a puzzle I want to find all the answers to. You get that?"

"I do. I felt the same way about my past." Jane set her hands on her shoulders. "Won't stop me worrying one bit. You need to accept that. I won't tolerate you ignoring me any longer."

"I know. I'm sorry, Ma." Sally hugged her.

"Promise me you'll mind your injuries. My ankle still hurts me often because I didn't mind mine the way I should."

"I'll try."

Jane's lips twisted in a smirk at the words. "That's the best I'm going to get, isn't it?"

"Yeah, pretty much."

"I'm going to have to take it, then. I don't have much choice in the matter." Jane cupped Sally's cheek gently. "I trust you, and I believe you'll try. I'm going to hope you'll succeed."

Sally ducked her head, then looked out over the meadow. "Everything's going good, Ma. You and Kat did great."

"We had a lot of help." Jane set her arm around Sally's waist. She noticed, though Sally's gaze was directed elsewhere, that Matthew Coleman was looking their way. When Jane caught his eye, his face grew ruddy and he looked away. "Will you be attending the race? Matthew Coleman entered again."

"I know. I placed a larger bet. I think he'll win this time."

"How's that?"

"He learned his lesson last race, he'll give Mac a wide berth." Sally set her hand on her hips. "No chastising about betting?"

"None at all. Considering I run a casino, I'd be remiss."

"You did last time."

"I did not. I was merely surprised seeing as you hadn't told me." Jane laughed softly. "Come now. Let's get ready to watch the three-legged race. Jesse is going to be tied to Lizzie."

"Rate he's going, he'll be tied to her forever."

"Don't I know it?"

A cowboy is a man with guts and a horse.
-William James

Cole stepped onto the porch of the Inn. A glance across the street showed that Wil was also lounging on the porch of the brothel. Several whores stood point with him, enticing passers by with their wares.

He turned back to survey the street. As usual they were bustling with people and horses. One familiar face rode up to the Inn. Cole headed to greet them. "Coleman. Congratulations again on the race. Never seen a better competition."

Matthew shook his hand in return. "Thanks. It was a good race."

"Lucky for all, Mac got knocked out early."

"There was a lot less people knocked off their horse this time." Coleman chuckled with Cole. "Abrams put me through my paces, though."

"Abrams is good on a horse. She's got spunk. Gonna make some man a fun wife." Cole grinned and nudged Matthew when he noticed the man staring inside the doors. "Women of strong opinions make fun wives."

"I'll, uh, take your word for it." Matthew adjusted his hat on his head. "Not looking for a wife, though."

"No? With that brother of yours, and the ranch to handle?"

"Keeps me plenty busy."

"I see." Cole looked out over the town. "After a win like that, you're likely to get some fresh ogling from the ladies about town."

"Not many I'd care to court."

"Never know unless you try."

"Any I'd be interested in don't seem likely to court." Matthew's gaze drifted back toward the Inn again.

"I'd repeat myself, but seems unnecessary." Cole withdrew a cigar from his pocket, offering it to Matthew. "Cigar?"

"Don't smoke, but thanks."

"Sure. So, with the impressive feat of winning that race—"

"It sure was, and I'm grateful." Sally stepped outside, a wide grin on her face.

Cole looked her up and down. "Sally, what are you wearing?"

"Clothes, Pa. Does Ma need to teach you English again?"

Matthew snorted beside him, unsuccessfully covering the sound with a cough.

Cole would have been upset, but it was a little funny. He raised a brow, looking Sally over from top to bottom. Wearing trousers over a men's shirt, suspenders holding them up, even though Jane had seen to it they were well cut. "Thought them was your training clothes."

"I'm meeting Tommy later. Working on defensive moves only." Sally slung her thumbs through the suspenders.

"First, I'm heading over to the clinic. Andrew's performing another autopsy this morning."

"Autopsy?" Matthew couldn't seem to cover his surprise. "Ain't that when they cut into a dead body?"

"Yes, it is. Why?" Sally set a hand on her hip, lifting her chin in defiance. "You do it with cows all the time."

"I just—I didn't—well…" Matthew's cheeks ruddied.

"Yes, well, anyway. Thank you for winning that race. Won me fifty dollars. Put it in my fund for a gun." Sally spun on her heel, hopping down the steps.

"Didn't mean to offend," Matthew squeaked, too quiet for her to hear.

"Speaking of women that make for a fun marriage," Cole teased.

"I…"

Cole decided to spare the young man any further embarrassment. "That was a hefty purse you won. What do you plan on doing with it?"

"Big chunk is going to repairs and replacing cattle lost in the tornado. Some is going to bring Bonnie back so's she can work at the clinic." Matthew lifted his hat to adjust it again, an apparent nervous habit as his gaze remained fixed on where Sally had disappeared. "She's due back in a couple weeks."

"Jane mentioned she was coming back. And cattle, eh? The run due here any day gonna give you any?"

"I know the boss, and worked a deal with him. Speaking of," Matthew checked his pocket watch, "they're due any time, and I wanted to eat before they arrive. Excuse me."

Cole let him go without any further teasing. Jane would frown on it, she imagined. Especially if she got wind the boy was eying Sally. Speaking of, Jane headed toward him. She offered a smile when she stepped outside, but turned her attention to the street.

He stepped up behind her. "Looking for something?"

"Sally. She left her notebook behind."

"Went to the clinic for that autopsy Andrew's doing. She'll miss it soon enough, I imagine."

"Well, she'll have to miss it. I'm not making the mistake of walking in on another one of those autopsies." She turned to face him, smiling softly. "How are you this afternoon?"

"Spiffing."

"Oooh, what has you in such a good mood."

"Our Sally has an admirer."

"I'm quite certain she has several. Are you speaking of one in particular?"

"Coleman."

"Ah yes." Jane glanced back toward the Inn. "That boy is never in town to make his intentions known."

"If he'd even have the guts. Seems a bit yella'."

"Oh, I don't know. I think there's more to him than meets the eye." She stepped even closer, her skirts billowing around his legs. "I know the look of a man with far more than meets the eye. They're often good for courting when they aren't making fools of themselves."

"Fools, eh?" He spun them to press her against the railing.

She hummed low and deep, a sound that got him excited so easy, he could have taken her right there. However, they'd need a little privacy.

"How long does it take us again?"

Her breath rose and fell, her breasts straining against the confines of her top. He sure did appreciate her leaning more toward low cut bodices over the high collars she'd been so keen on in the past. "Latest record was two-hundred twenty-nine seconds, but we were quite raring to go at the statehood celebration, and we had children to think of."

"You raring to go now?" His lips hovered near hers. "We can go for a new record."

"Oh, well, I'm…"

They both stared at each other as a low rumbling carried through the town. Not thunder, thunder paused. This was constant.

Jane sighed softly. "Apparently, we are going to have to wait. It sounds as though the trail run is arriving in town."

"We got four minutes to spare, I'd bet." He grinned and leaned closer. "I'd make it worth your while."

"You always do." She yelped when he tugged her hand and rushed down the porch toward the back. "Cole! I didn't agree."

He pulled her into the lean-to by the barn, ignoring the barking pups nearby. "Don't tell me you're saying no."

"I didn't—well." She glanced over her shoulder as hoofbeats of horses raced over the cobblestone. "We should be out there."

"They gotta get the cattle settled north of town, and them that don't will have the sheriff minding them." He spun her, planting her hands against the wall. He leaned down to brush his lips along her shoulder. "Unless you wanna go."

She whimpered softly. "You don't play fair, Mr. Mitchell."

"That's what you like about me, Mrs. Mitchell." He gripped the hips that had been wiggling against him.

"Without a doubt."

He tugged up skirts and petticoats, then the blasted hoops until he had access. One brush of his finger told him she was ready for him, and her low purr of approval blew away any hesitation he might have had.

His hand slipped along her thighs, grabbing on and tugging her back the slightest amount. A quick flick of his finger loosened his trousers so he could free himself. Slow as molasses he entered, until she whimpered with impatience.

Fully engulfed in her moist heat, he paused. Promises of breaking their record flew away as he held her there. Her fingers clenched against the wood, but neither moved for nearly thirty seconds. Her whisper of his name drove him to action.

He withdrew almost completely before driving into her again, her moan of pleasure had him going again and again. With each stroke, the pressure built. She moved with him now, the friction of their meeting stoking the fire.

Right when he thought it would get too much for him to enjoy, he slowed his rhythm. Each slow glide inside of her sent another wave of pleasure through him. His tip felt every bump of flesh, every contraction of muscle around it.

The impulse to touch her, to kiss her took over. The damned hoops hindered him. With a low growl, he gripped her hips tight again, driving in harder. He moved with the beat of his own pulse, until he had to finish it so he could get to her again.

He thrust once more, the orgasm taking over until he shuddered against her. When he came down enough to feel the first aftershock, he wasn't even certain she'd gotten her release. Keeping his cock buried deep to ride out the aftershocks, he slipped his hand around to her clit.

She whimpered when he touched the sensitive flesh. With his finger he swirled the tender spot. Her back arched in response, and the damnable bustle moved enough he wasn't face to face with it anymore.

Her hips shifted, sending another shockwave through him. Not one to give up, he continued stroking and swirling her clit until she cried out. He gave a final stroke to ensure he was dry before withdrawing.

Before she could collect herself or straighten her skirts, he spun her and pinned her to the wall to claim her lips. Her tongue met his in a brutal battle as they clung to each other while the high of their coupling faded.

A gunshot rang through the town, startling them apart.

She stared up at him, her eyes still dark with passion. "I think that's our signal to stop playing and get to business."

"Playing's much more fun."

"Don't I know it?" She sighed softly, arms draped over his shoulders. "This is our first trail run with the brothel open. I guess you'd best go see to making sure the place doesn't fall apart at its first big night."

"You're bound and determined to make me get to work."

"Oh, believe me, I'd much rather get you to bed. However—" Another crack of gunfire interrupted her. "Sounds like we have a rowdy bunch this time. It's best we get moving."

"Fine." He nipped at her lower lip. "Let me help straighten your skirts."

"Not on your life. We'll never leave this lean-to. Go on now, get." She forcibly turned him around. "Go."

"Let me get myself presentable first, woman." Cole chuckled softly, straightening his trousers. "You aren't the only one out of sorts."

"All you have to do is button up and be on your way. Now, go."

He winked over his shoulder. "I'll see you tonight."

"You'd better. I'd hate to have to get too friendly with my own hand."

He groaned, but let her push him out of the lean-to. "You don't play fair."

"You like that about me."

"Damn straight." He let her laughter carry him back out to Main Street.

Already a crowd filled the brothel, spilling onto the porch. The gunfire didn't seem to be coming from there, or he suspected the place would be cleared out more. Another gun fired off, drawing his attention to a lot south of town chasing each other in circles.

"They're restless." Tommy walked up beside Cole. "Heard they got run out of Gardner before they'd been there a full night."

"Which means it's been near a week since they got to stop and let off steam proper."

"Lucky us."

Cole nodded toward the saloon. "So long as they don't kill no one, it will be. Look at that place. Jane was right smart to suggest it."

"I have been known to have good ideas from time to time." Jane sidled up beside him. "One of you had best get in there. We can't let Wil deal with this raucous lot all on his lonesome. I'll see to the casino. I'll go back this way through the apartment and get my gun to be on the safe side."

"Good idea." Tom nodded to her. "I'll be in soon. I need to help the Sheriff a while."

"Thought you were training Sally today."

"Plans change."

And the devil did grin,
for his darling sin is pride that apes humility.
—Samuel Taylor Coleridge

Cole entered the latest numbers in the ledger, pleased with what he saw. Though they'd lost capital by building the saloon, paying for contracts, and their manager before the place had opened, the first month of business showed good enough returns he knew they'd be able to make it up within a year. Of course, the recent trail run, plus the statehood celebration had boosted that first month's numbers quite a bit.

Then again, he also had to give credit to Jane. She got Patrick paying for their Gold Room for three months, which really added to their coffers.

A grumbling growl drew his attention away from the numbers. While playing checkers with Jesse, Jay was also playing tug of war with Bourbon. Jesse had Whiskey on his lap. The two boys had gotten even closer since they'd begun their expeditions into the wood with Black Moon. Though she'd been nervous about the idea, Jane's prayer that it would settle the boy appeared to be panning out.

In truth, for the first time since they'd joined their family the previous year, Willow and Jay were not spending every minute protecting each other. Jane saw that as progress. Cole only hoped she was right.

The back door opened abruptly. Sally stumbled in, her hand at her ribs. She straightened when she saw Cole. A bright smile plastered across her face. "Oh, hey there, Pa."

"Sally. What did you do?"

"Nothing."

Cole frowned. "Jane'll be upset if you hurt yourself again."

"It's nothing, really. It just smarts is all." Sally straightened further but winced at the motion. "I mean it. It just needs some ice. Don't tell her."

"You know I can't lie to your ma. She's too smart for that. She'd find me out in a hot minute and then we'd both be up to our necks in it." Cole shut the ledger. He dropped it in the drawer, then locked it up. "Get some ice. I'll head over to The Golden Touch and see if I can't calm her down before she gets back."

"You'll never guess who I saw heading in there." Sally raised her brows expectantly.

"Who's that?"

"Mac."

"No kidding. Mac? I ain't seen him since the tornado. Wonder what brought him back."

"No idea. He looked awful grumpy."

Cole snorted. "Doesn't he always? I'll head on over. You'll keep an eye on the boys?"

"Cole," Jesse protested. Cole hadn't even realized he was listening what with the dogs and the game. "We're not babies."

"Never said you was, Jesse." Cole grinned his way. He nodded to Sally. "Hurry up and get back so's I can head over. You're lucky that last I saw her she was in a good mood."

A great mood actually. Cole was convinced she had some secret she wanted to tell him. She'd even tried once or twicw, but they'd hardly been in the same room all day.

Right as Sally made it to the door a scream rented the air. Sally threw open the door to look toward the casino, but Cole yanked open the back door. He knew it had come from outside somewhere. Yells echoed through the streets followed by a loud crash.

Cole tore out the back door toward the street, more specifically the saloon. A crowd piled right in front of where the pathway to the saloon met the street, with no clear way out. He could hardly see through the swarm of people.

"*Succubus*," screamed Mac. A crack like a whip carried through the air.

More people screamed, one man turned to wretch into the corral. At that, Cole shoved his way through the crowd. When the last soul parted his way, he found a sight to chill his blood.

Mac sat on top of Jane, squeezing the life out of her. Her legs kicked helplessly behind him, her delicate hands grasping the man's wrists.

For a moment, he stood frozen. Hands like ice, legs numb. He couldn't see her killed again. Not again. "*Jane*!"

Wil appeared on the other side, weapon raised. "Back off!"

The men trying to pull Mac off Jane scattered. Wil fired without further ado.

Mac toppled on top of Jane. She wheezed, then released a hacking cough. Her hands scrambled to get Mac's now slack hands off her throat. Several men hauled Mac off her.

Feeling rushed back to his limbs and he rushed forward. He skidded along the ground beside her. "Jane."

She rolled to her side hacking, sucking at air with her hand at her throat. Her face beet red, twisted in pain. When she turned toward him and old, familiar horror turned her blue eyes almost black.

"Easy." Cole pulled her close against him, careful not to squeeze too hard. That's when he noticed the blood on her back. "Fucking hell."

Wil guffawed behind him. "I didn't kill him, Sheriff. I just shot him."

"What happened?" David's voice was dark as he'd ever heard the Sheriff. When he raised his head, he realized the sheriff was looking at them, not the man he questioned.

"Easy," Cole repeated in low tones when Jane panic-grabbed him again. "You're alive. I promise. You're alive. You're not being put in a coffin again."

"Jane seemed to know him, gave him his drink without him asking. She remembers things like that, ya know. Figured she knew him from before." Wil stood relaxed, arm resting on the weapon he'd fired minutes before.

"She did," Cole and David said at the same time.

Wil's smirk returned. "Anyhow. All's she did was touch his shoulder and he went berserk. Saying we were all gonna burn, callin' her a succubus, screamin' at the whores, hollerin' at us all about damnation and the devil."

Cole lowered his gaze to Jane. She gasped at the air like a fish out of water, tears spilling free. He brushed his fingers along her hairline. "I've got you."

"Ba…ba…" Her fingers fluttered to her throat as pain creased her brow.

"Don't try to talk," he hushed her. "Doc'll be here in a minute, I'd bet."

Wil cleared his throat. When Cole looked up, the man blinked a few times before lowering his gaze to the ground. "Ain't a person in there that didn't try to stop him. He whipped her once inside, then tossed her out like a rag doll. Managed to throw off everyone that came at him."

Cole scanned Jane's body for signs of damage beyond the obvious. "Anything broken?"

She panicked again, thrashing, trying to scream. Her fingers scraped along her throat, her legs kicking.

"Shhhh." She looked so much like she did the first time he'd seen her after her hanging, his heart seized. "You're alive. Nobody's gonna put you in a pine box. You're alive."

"When he finally stopped fighting everyone off and focused on her, I took my shot," Wil finished.

"Jane!" Charlie dropped to the earth beside Cole. "Dear God in heaven. Get her to the clinic. Straight away. Hurry."

Cole didn't wait to be told twice. He raced through the town with her, setting her gingerly down in the first exam room he came to. Her hand clamped on his wrist when he tried to pull away. "I'm not going anywhere. Try to relax."

Charlie bustled about the room. He came to a stop near Jane's head. A small square of cloth was set gingerly over Jane's mouth and nose. Charlie put a drop of chloroform on it. "He's right, Jane. Try to relax. You know what to do. Unfortunately, you've been here before."

The chloroform did the trick. She relaxed enough Cole could pry her nails from his wrist. He brushed his hand along her hair. "From what I heard, Mac got her twice with a whip, then tried to choke the life out of her. Bastard should have stayed gone or been hanged for horse thieving long ago."

Jane's eyes fluttered back open when Charlie moved to her back. A sharp intake of breath when he peeled the fabric from her wounds sent her into another attack.

Charlie handed him the chloroform. "She'll hate me, but she needs to stay under while I tend to these. She won't be able to keep calm enough to breathe well in her condition. A drop every thirty seconds. Here, use my watch."

Cole took the watch and chloroform. He let another drop fall on the fabric. Relief flooded him when Jane's eyes closed again. In between drops he helped Charlie strip Jane down to her chemise. While Charlie worked on fixing up her wounds, Cole focused on her face. He couldn't bear to see the wounds. It would set him off into anger, and Jane needed him calm.

It seemed to take forever, but Charlie finally finished with the wounds. He rolled Jane carefully onto her back. "Cole. I need you to listen to me, and listen good. Most importantly, I need you to remain calm. You can stop giving her chloroform for a few minutes."

Cole tensed the second Charlie told him to remain calm. He bit back every biting retort that came to mind. When he felt calm enough, he spoke, "What is it, Charlie?"

"I'm going to get Andrew. It looks like Mac dealt her a couple of good blows, and she's bleeding a little. She only got confirmation of the pregnancy yesterday."

"What?" Cole blinked away from his staring at Jane. The words sank in slow as molasses at first. Then it burned through him like wildfire. "What did you say?"

"She hasn't told you yet, then?"

"We've hardly seen each other today. We were gonna meet for dinner, she wanted it real private like. I knew it had to be good news, she's been all happy…she's really…I mean, we've been trying."

"She said the same thing. It was a surprise, but you've been trying."

"But she's bleeding." Cole's mind latched on that fact.

"Yes. A little. Hopefully it's nothing." Charlie took a shaky breath. "Andrew will take a look for us."

Cole glanced down to see Jane's eyes flutter open. He held her hand gently, and leaned in to kiss her forehead. "Andy's coming to check on the baby. Easy, Jane. Breathe slow. I know you hate being knocked out, so don't make me do it again."

Charlie leaned over Jane. "I'll get Andrew to do the exam. I'm sure everything is fine, but we'll watch you for a few days. The stress is not healthy."

Jane rolled her eyes, but remained calm. Her gaze drifted back to Cole. One delicate finger flicked at the cloth over her mouth until it fell away. A weak smile graced her lips. Her mouth formed the silent word, 'surprise'.

"You always gotta be so dramatic. You couldn'ta told me normal-like."

Her silent laugh led to a coughing fit. He slid the cloth back into place and let another drop fall. When she calmed again, her lids were heavy with sleep. Still, her hand remained clutched tight in his.

There was a quiet knock on the door a moment before Andrew entered. "I'm going to do a quick exam, Jane. Then we'll get you up to a room. Dr. Young and I agree you should remain here for a few days to rest and ensure you will remain with child."

Jane nodded silently. Tears filled her eyes as she stared up at Cole. She closed them, tucking her head into his arms. Her shaking fingers danced at her throat. Cole knew this would bring back the nightmares she'd never truly escaped from. In recent years they'd been few and far between. Without a doubt being choked would have the blasted memories of her hanging too close to the surface.

Her exacting memory could be fun, and beneficial in so many ways—but he knew it was also her biggest curse. Some of her memories were too dark for anyone. Shaking deaths hand is something he wished every day she could forget.

After a splash of water, Andrew cleared his throat. "You are still with child. The bleeding seems to be minimal at best. Why don't you take her to room three, Dr. Young said she likes that room. We'll get some food for you both in a little while."

"Thanks, Doc." Cole pressed his forehead to Jane's. "The baby's fine. Promise me you'll stay calm as you can."

She squeezed his hand gently.

"Dr. Young says you know what to do with the chloroform if she has problems." Andrew placed the bottle on Jane's stomach once Cole had picked her up. "Ring the bell if there are any problems whatsoever. Someone is always here."

Cole nodded, carrying Jane from the room and up the stairs. Without a doubt there'd be an influx of visitors before the evening was through. Before that happened, he wanted her settled and he needed to make sure she was still with him, not lost in memories.

He got her situated in bed, then kicked off his boots to slide in beside her. The fact that she curled tight against him immediately eased his nerves. "You're alive. Death ain't taking you so easy. I won't let him. You're mine."

All evil is like a nightmare;
the instant you stir under it,
the evil is gone.
—Thomas Carlyle

Cole stepped out of the Gold Room after another successful round of poker and twenty-one. Behind the bar stood Jane, leaning close to Hammy in conversation. He figured it was because her attack had only been a few days prior. She still could only whisper. Topped with Hammy who, after working all morning, probably couldn't hear much of anything.

Jane finished whatever she was saying and rubbed her throat. Only days before he'd been pondering his gratitude over her lower collars, but there she was wearing high necks again. He knew all too well that under the collar lingered ugly bruises she preferred hidden.

Truth be told, she should still be in bed resting. Soon as she'd been cleared to leave the clinic, she'd gone right back to work. Mac still sat in jail, though his fits of temper had been heard throughout town. He didn't bother to say why he'd done what he'd done, and Cole couldn't care less. If it had been him instead of Wil, he would have outright killed him, not merely wounded him.

Cole descended into the pit. Along the way to the bar he greeted patrons and friends as Jane had taught him. When he got to the bar she was pouring a drink for Carl. He nodded to the man, then leaned close to Jane. "How are you doing?"

"Fine." The whisper barely carried under the general din of the casino. She winced at the simple word.

"You need to rest."

She shook her head adamantly. Her brows puckered as she met his gaze. The lightest touch of her fingers brushed along the bruise around his eye. He caught her hand, holding it to his chest.

"It wasn't on purpose," he reassured her in a low voice. As expected, her nightmares had returned with a vengeance. Two nights before she'd clocked him good before he managed to get a hold of her and calm her down.

Frustration pursed her lips. She set to washing glasses with enough force he worried she'd crack one. He ran his hands down her arms to still them. After a deep sigh, she relaxed back against him.

"You keep pouting like this and I don't get to enjoy the fact you can't yell at me proper."

The sMac to his hand was weak enough he knew she didn't mean it. A whisper of a smile teased along her lips.

"That's better" He kissed her cheek. "I know you don't like the restriction, but your three hours are up. It's time to rest."

She huffed out her frustration. After shrugging off his arms, she threw down her towel. Stomping down the bar like a petulant child, she paused to give a warm hug to Hammy.

She tossed Cole a dark look, then stomped off to their apartment.

Cole chuckled softly, shaking his head. Damn woman got so testy when on restriction. Little did she know what he had planned for her.

He followed her back to the apartment, grabbing her hand soon as they got inside. "How about this? We'll take a carriage ride. You can't race your beast of a horse, but I can take you out in the carriage."

Her eyes narrowed to slits. Lips pursed, she stepped closer. "I'm already pregnant."

He laughed heartily, tugging her close. "So? Don't mean I can't enjoy making time with my wife. I plan to, often as I can."

Her fingers danced up his chest, a whisper of a smile still ghosting across her lips.

"I'll get us a supper basket from Cora's, then we'll head out." He kissed the tip of her nose gently.

She hugged him gently enough that her hands coursed down to his ass.

"Wait 'til we're on our picnic, wicked woman."

Her groan drew another laugh from him on his way out the door. He grabbed the basket he'd asked Cora for before going to the Gold Room. By the time he got back to the apartment, Jane was nowhere to be found.

He discovered her outside by the stables, already in the carriage. The bright smile she wore lifted his mood enough he didn't yell at her for going ahead of him. He hopped into the carriage without argument. She took off so fast he toppled back against the seat. "Why don't you let me drive, woman?"

She shook her head. Fortunately the crowded street made her slow enough, Cole had a minute to right himself and the basket. The moment they crossed the train tracks, she slapped the reins to speed them along. They rode in comfortable silence for a while, and it wasn't until they passed the Settlement that she began to slow.

He frowned slightly. This wasn't where he'd planned to take her. He'd had a thought to go to the hot springs. "Where are we heading?"

"Hidden swimming hole," she whispered hoarsely. She turned the wagon toward the creek. They kept going for a couple of miles. Finally, she drew them to a stop.

"Ain't we on McKerney's land?"

"We are."

"We shouldn't stop here, then. He's a trapper, you know."

"I do."

"Jane." He grabbed her arm before she got too far. "We could get caught up in one of his traps. We'd be in for a world of hurt."

"He doesn't trap this side of the creek." Her whisper had become so hoarse, barely any sound escaped. Without waiting for any further argument, she hopped from the carriage to head down the bank.

Cole moved the carriage deeper into the shadows of the tree line and put on the brake. Once he'd grabbed the basket, he followed her down to the water. When he got there, he was surprised to find her standing still, fingers on the pin at her throat which held the lace in place.

He dropped the basket on a tree stump. . Once in front of her, he brushed her fingers away from the pin. He quickly released the pin and tugged the lace free. Once he'd begun the process, she undid the buttons of her bodice quickly.

As she pushed the bodice from her shoulders, he brushed his fingers along the angry bruises still circling her neck. "Bastard's gonna pay for this, you know that."

"I do." She turned to give him access to her ties.

He needed no further encouragement to free her of her skirts and corset. In a few minutes she stood in her new-fangled one piece chemise. While she dropped to the ground to remove her shoes, he stripped off his own clothes.

The water was bracingly cold despite it barely being September. Jane shivered while she swam in his arm. "I didn't think this through."

"Stop talking so much."

"Yes, sir."

He pulled her into a kiss as they floated through the cold water. When fire burned through his veins, he slowed the kiss down. They swam for a while. Jane's mood improved until she was splashing him and ducking under water away from his chase.

Nearly an hour passed before Cole tugged her toward the shore. He wrapped her in her own petticoats before he jogged up to the carriage to get a blanket and some matches.

By the time he got a fire going, she was shivering. He carried the basket over and pulled her onto his lap. "Charlie'd kill me if he knew I let you swim in cold water."

"Charlie can stuff it." She chuckled, drawing a few coughs out along the way. "It was fun."

"Plenty fun we could have had warm and dry."

"Still can." Her fingers danced along his jawline, then his lips. She followed them with a kiss that sent warmth through him he couldn't get from the fire. He laid her back on the blanket, stretching over her. The damp chemise clung to her and counteracted the burgeoning heat with cold in a tantalizing conflict of sensations.

He undid one button to kiss the cool skin below it. Her soft sigh washed over him. The next button popped free and a low moan followed the action. No, wait. That was *not* a moan, and it wasn't Jane.

She tensed beneath him. Quick as a cat, she flipped onto her belly, gaze fixed across the creek. Cole flew to his feet, yanking his trousers back on.

Another weak groan echoed through the trees. Jane clamored to her feet beside him.

"Who's there?" Cole stepped in front of Jane to prevent any peeper from a free show. Jane rustled around behind him. A few seconds later the solid handle of his Colt Walker was pressed into his palm. "Show yourself or I'll shoot."

No response came for a long time. So long that when Jane stepped into place beside him she was fully dressed, sans lace. Her own weapon poised in her hand, ready to fire.

Cole tried to spot a good place to cross. Problem was, if he found one he'd have to leave Jane behind. He didn't want to leave her alone.

She beat him to it, taking the path beside the creek south toward where the creek grew narrower. He hesitated to follow, not wanting to lose his vantage point of where they'd heard the noise from.

He tried to keep an eye on Jane as well, but in no time she disappeared behind a bend in the path. "Jane."

Cole leveled his Walker on the opposite shore. "Damn it, Jane. Why didn't you stay where I could see you?"

A quiet rustle of leaves several minute later preceded Jane emerging into view on the opposite side of the creek. Her weapon raised, trained steady as a rock on the same place as his. As she moved along the trail slow and steady, his breath caught at the impressive sight of her. Unwavering strength, all in that small form, like nothing could cross her and win. In that moment he understood what Tom meant when he said the lady Pinkertons could be more formidable than the men.

Jane halted in her trek, her head tilted. Slowly her weapon lowered. Disgust creased her features for the briefest moment before her eyes widened. She waved frantically at Cole to join her on the opposite bank.

Cole tore down the trail she'd taken and found a felled log that stretched the creek. He crossed it careful not to slip on the damp bark before running back up toward the swimming hole. Jane wasn't anywhere in sight at first, then he spotted her skirts peeking out from the bushes.

He came up behind her, and had to stop short at the sight. Keith McKerney was lying there pale, near lifeless. His leg was clamped tight in a large bear trap, blood soaking the clothes and the ground around him.

"He's alive," Jane's whisper barely hit his ears. "Barely."

"He's not gonna make it back. Who knows how long he's been out here."

Jane brushed the man's thinning hair back. "Mr. McKerney. Someone's here now. Stay with me."

Cole was sure the man couldn't hear her, Cole himself barely could. He moved around to the man's other side. "Head back to town and get help."

Jane shook her head, pointing to her throat. She had a point, she couldn't yell properly for help. "You go."

"I'm not leaving you out here alone."

Jane held up her gun. "Go."

"No."

"Go, before he dies."

"He's already dead, Jane."

"I'll be fine. I promise."

Cole groaned, glaring at the trapper dying near them.

"If he dies, we still need to get him back. We can't leave him to the animals."

"Stop talking. Your throat."

"Then stop arguing. Do as I say."

He set his hands on her shoulders. "You don't set that gun down for one second. I won't be gone long."

"We'll be here. I'll be fine."

"You damn well better be."

What greater grief
than the loss of one's native land.
—Euripides

Jane shut the apartment door quiet as she could. With a heavy sigh she leaned back against it. After two days of fighting the blood loss and infection, Keith McKerney had succumbed to his wounds earlier that day.

Charlie and Andrew had done everything they could, down to removing the infected leg. Andrew told her the infection had gone to his blood, and there was nothing they could do after such a turn.

Another senseless loss. There'd been so many in recent months, plus Sally's attack. Not to mention the attack on her own person. Some days it felt as though a giant target sat over the town.

She pushed off the door to head inside. At the desk she plunked her reticule on the table. After the solid thump, a loud gasp sounded behind her. Willow stared at her wide-eyed from the sofa, her hands paused in midair over something.

"Willow. Goodness, I didn't know anyone was home." The words emerged as barely a whisper. Her throat was still raw, and grew worse when she used it too much. She rubbed her neck, then cleared her throat to speak again. "I thought you went to the library with Sally."

"I was, but I wanted to finish…" Willow's words trailed off. Her gaze drifted to her lap, red seeped into her cheeks.

Jane drew closer to see what sat half hidden in Willow's lap. A long wooden frame with threads stretched taut like a loom sat there. From the farthest end from Willow, halfway along the length of the frame was an intricate pattern of colors. "Oh my. Willow, how beautiful."

Willow gave Jane a sideways glance when she sat beside her.

"Is this why you wanted the beads? To create such beautiful pieces?" Jane ran her fingers along the colorful lines of the design. Somehow Willow had created a tapestry of sorts out of string and beads.

"M-Ma used to…I…didn't think you'd like…"

"Oh, Willow. You darling girl. Did you think you had to hide this?"

Willow's cheeks darkened further and she ducked her head. "I thought you'd be mad."

"Why do you think I send you with Black Moon? I know he isn't Ute like your parents, but I thought it would give you both time to be away from all the restrictions of this new life as a non-Ute." Jane smoothed her hand over Willow's dark locks. "And as for this beadwork? It is beautiful. If it makes you happy, then you should do more. I never want you to hide where you came from. It's part of who you are."

"I have more." The blush seemed to have taken up permanent residence on the girls' cheeks. She set down the loom and darted into her room. When she returned, she carried another strip of intricately patterned color, as well as a piece of leather with a complex beaded flower upon it.

"You are quite talented, Shivering Willow." Jane admired the flower for several minutes. Her throat was on fire from all the talking, but she couldn't stop yet. "You know, I'm friends with the Kilmurry's. They run the leather smith over on Second Street. I can see if they have leftover scraps of leather for you to use."

"You'd do that? For me?"

"Of course I would. Art like this should be encouraged." Jane shifted to face her more directly. "I imagine they would pay you if you wanted to put some of this beadwork on their pieces. If you added something like this to a reticule it would bring you some nice money."

"Pay? Money?" Willow blinked several times. Her brows knit together. She looked from the flower in Jane's hand to the loom. "Why?"

Jane kept her laughter quiet so as to not set off another coughing fit. "Because the white man thrives on money, Willow. I'm happy to buy you what you need to create whatever you wish. If you then want to sell some to the Kilmurry's—then whatever you earn will be yours to keep for whatever you like."

Willow stared at the piece she'd been working on. "I don't know."

"You don't have to decide now. Take your time. In the meantime I'll see if I can get some more leather for you to work with. All right?"

Willow pulled the loom closer. After a moment, she nodded. "Thank you."

Jane wrapped an arm around Willow's shoulder. "You don't have to give up what you once were to become something new. I'd never ask you to forget your parents or the life you had. I only ask that you try to adapt into this new life. I'm trying to help you embrace them both."

"I miss them. All the time."

"I know. Your brother does, too." Jane sighed softly. She wished she knew what to say to make things better. A year wasn't enough time, but she'd hoped for much more progress. Willow strung more beads on the thread. "I can't take you to see them, I wish I could. You can talk about them any time you want to. I don't mind."

Willow nodded weakly.

"I'll leave you to your beading. We'll see about ordering more beads tomorrow." A door opened and closed upstairs. After another hug to Willow, Jane rose as someone headed down the stairs. A few seconds later, Kat stepped into the room.

She stopped short the second she saw Jane. A deep red flush flooded her cheeks. "Oh. I didn't know anyone was home."

Jane quirked a brow at her friend. Rather than argue or point out it was her apartment, she waved Kat toward the table. She set the teapot on the stove.

"Sorry. That wasn't polite."

Jane offered her a pointed look. "I told you to use our apartment so you weren't walking through the lobby every time. I don't mind."

"What did you tell Cole?"

"Nothing. He isn't one to ask question, you know that." Jane sat beside her friend. When the silence lingered, she set a hand on Kat's. "Have you gone to see Charles yet?"

"No. I—I don't want to know." Kat's voice trembled. "Patrick is only here for another month. I don't want to know if I only have a month left. I'll wait until he's gone. Then the pressure and worry will be over and it will have happened—or it won't."

Jane squeezed her friends hand. "I can only imagine."

"I think, perhaps, it has happened. I might be with child…but what if I only wish to be so badly that I'm imagining things."

"Then see Charles. Put an end to your torment. If you are, then you can stop the pretense and truly visit with your friend."

Kat stared at their clasped hands. "I don't know."

"Wouldn't you like to be able to enjoy your last month with your friend?"

"What if I'm not? What if everything relies on these last few weeks?"

"Oh, my dear Katherine. You are in a conundrum." Jane rose to pour their tea. She settled Kat's right into her hands. "Drink your tea, and we'll take a walk. I told you, I'm here to support you every step of the way."

"I want it to be over. Did I make a mistake?"

"No. I don't believe you did." Jane moved closer as her voice grew ever weaker. "You'll see, and know, when you and Patrick are close as ever when all is said and done."

"I do hope you're right."

"Willow?" Jane glanced toward the couch. Though she knew the girl had been in the apartment by herself for at least a couple of hours, she didn't want to run off. "Will you be all right here if Katherine and I go for a walk?"

Willow nodded. "I want to finish."

"Wonderful. Come along Katherine. We are going to take a stroll." Jane pulled her friend to her feet. She set a casual pace as she led Kat toward the clinic. "Would you like to hear Cole's and my latest idea?"

"Please. I'd be happy to hear of anyone else's problems right at the moment."

"I certainly have a bevy of them, but you are rather wrapped up in yourself right now you didn't bother to ask." Jane nudged her friend in her teasing. "Anyhow, you know Bill Banks had those two claims by the hot springs, yes?"

"Of course. Father's been keeping an eye on the claims for some time. He swears there's more under the surface Bill isn't bothering to mine for."

"Your pa is wrong according to our surveyor. Maybe he found that out, which is why we were able to buy the claims ourselves."

"You got the Banks claims? Whatever for? You aren't miners."

"Oh, goodness no. However, we have visitors that come to look for gold. We'll give them a place to search. It's adjoining our claim with the hot springs, so Landon will watch all three, and we can expand his shack into a small cabin."

"Jane?" Charlie rose from the desk in the waiting room of the clinic. "What are you doing here? Your appointment isn't until tomorrow."

"Katherine was hoping you had fifteen minutes to spare. We had something we'd like to discuss with you."

Kat looked surprised to find herself in the clinic. Of course, that had been Jane's intention by distracting her with the news of the claims. "Oh, dear. Jane. I don't know."

"Too late. We're already here. We're doing this. Charles?"

"Of course. Right in here." He led them into the closest exam room. When they were all in, he shut the door. "Might I inquire what this is about now?"

"After so many years of trying, Katherine believes she is having some pregnancy feelings. However, due to her eagerness, she's concerned she might have wished herself into this state. Could you do an exam to settle her mind one way or the other?"

Charlie smiled brightly. "Of course. I know you've been wanting this for a while, Katherine. Remove your trousers and I'll do your exam."

Kat kept a tight grip on Jane's hand. "But if I'm not…I can't…"

"'Tis foolish to fear what you cannot avoid'." Jane smiled at her friend. "Remove your trousers, Katherine. It's best to know. This way you can stop worrying."

"Syrus, Jane? A fair fitting quote." Charlie set about getting ready while Kat removed her trousers. Once Kat was on the table, Jane draped a sheet over her legs.

"Katherine needed the distraction and assertion." Jane took Kat's hand in her own. She held her friend's gaze. "Now. Where was I? Oh, yes. We'll allow folks to pay for a pan or a pickaxe. There are a couple of good surface veins, and some flake in the creek."

"Would you be speaking of the claims you just purchased?" Charlie set to work, taking part in the conversation Jane used to distract Kat easily. "Tom said you were going to offer the chance for gold to your customers."

"Yes. They'll sign an agreement and pick a pan or a pickaxe, along with a stretch of time."

Kat frowned. "If they get gold, they'll have more than what they paid."

"Which is why we'll offer gold exchange at the Inn. The agreement they sign stipulates we keep ten percent of the gold's value. We'll make money coming and going. I'm certain some will opt to keep their gold, but in the end, we'll still get the value out of it." Jane glanced toward Charles to see if he was near finished. "Nicholas is quite handy when it comes to drafting such things."

"He's a crafty sort." Charlie patted Kat's knee before he moved to wash his hands.

Jane helped Kat sit. "Get your trousers back on."

Charlie met Jane's gaze as Kat did as she was told. After a long moment, a smile broke his features. He nodded the affirmative.

Jane clasped Kat's cold fingers in her own. "Katherine. We will have our babies together. As you'd hoped from the beginning."

"What? What are you saying?" Kat's head shot up. Color flooded her cheeks. "You don't mean—Charlie, am I really?"

"Yes, Katherine." Charlie chuckled softly. "You really are pregnant. It isn't wishful thinking. Congratulations."

"Oh." Kat hugged Jane so tight every unhealed wound smarted. "I need to go tell Norman."

Kat darted from the room so fast, Jane stumbled from the loss of the embrace. She sighed in relief. "I'm so pleased. That poor thing has been terribly worried."

Charlie offered his arm. "How are you feeling, Jane? Are you healing well enough?"

"My appointment isn't until tomorrow, Charles," Jane scolded him playfully. "How about you act as my brother, not my physician."

"Fair enough." His grin took on a wicked air. "How are you feeling, Jane?"

"Oh, you." She nudged his ribs. At the porch railing they both paused to lean. "I'm doing well enough, I suppose. Cole and I are so busy we hardly see each other during the daytime any longer. That isn't making me happy."

"The addition of the brothel and the puppies really took quite a bit out of your already cramped days."

"You don't have to tell me."

"You'll figure things out, I'm sure. You are one determined woman when you need to be."

"I do try. However, that's precisely why I had Lillian look to Katherine fill Mr. Callahan's seat on the Council instead of myself. For one, I wasn't interested. For another, I'm far too busy."

"About to get busier with another little one on the way."

"Which was my biggest argument against us trying for another child. However, the idea of having a child on purpose for a change? It was too tempting." Jane's gaze flickered through the familiar faces traveling up and down the street. "It's all so strange."

"What is?"

"First, Mr. Keller."

"That was an accident."

"Thomas said that knot could not have been an accident."

"That's Thomas." Charlie sighed deeply. "All those years as a Pinkerton, he sees guilt before innocence and suspicious circumstances everywhere."

"Then Emily, which we all know was not an accident. Plus, Mr. Ellis."

"That was—"

"Don't tell me it was an accident. That well cover was brand new, not rotted in the least, yet it was smashed open. I don't care if Ellis was drunk, he couldn't have done that, could he?"

"I'm not certain."

"And now Mr. McKerney. That bear trap should not have been anywhere near that creek." Jane turned her back to the street, resting her elbows on the railing. "He told Hank he sets his bear traps up in the mountains away from people. He's more likely to trap a good-sized bear up there, away from the mines and the town. He only sets traps for small animals near the creek. It makes no sense."

"Are you certain you shouldn't be training with Sally to be a Pink? You've been pondering this an awful lot."

"One thing I did learn from Thomas is coincidences are rarely that." Jane sighed heavily. "To answer your question, no. I have no desire to be a Pinkerton. I've had more than my share of danger and death."

Charlie frowned when her hand fluttered to her throat "You're pushing yourself far too hard, talking too much. You won't heal that way."

"I'm well aware of how my throat can and will heal. It's not the first time I've nearly had the life choked out of me."

"At least this time it wasn't the gallows."

"It's no less terrifying."

A liar should have a good memory.
-Quintilian

Jane pushed open the clinic door. She couldn't wait to see the look on Charlie's face when he saw her arriving early for her appointment.

Instead of her brother, she found an empty waiting room. "Charles? Are you here?"

One of the exam rooms stood closed, but the rest were wide open. She peeked in the open rooms briefly. "Charles?"

Well, it was no fun gloating that she'd been early for once without her brother to boast to. With no sign nor sound from her brother, she took a seat to wait for him. Occasionally a noise came from the closed room. Otherwise, she was quite alone to wait for Charles.

It wasn't like him to miss an appointment. She wondered at what might have kept him from the chance to scold her for doing too much. Especially seeing as the whip marks on her back were showing little improvement according to Cole. The pain was bad enough she'd taken to sleeping on her stomach. Fortunately, her stomach had not yet grown too large for such a feat to be impossible. Although, she already had a small swell growing.

The exam room door opened, pulling Jane from her reverie. Hushed voices preceded the appearance of Artie Graves. He paused at the door, speaking to whomever was inside. A sly smile crossed his features. When he spotted Jane he tipped his hat to her, then departed the clinic.

Jane frowned at his departing back. When Daisy emerged from the room next, Jane did a double take. Confusion brought her to her feet to confront the doctor. "Daisy?"

Daisy stopped short. Her hand ducked quick into her pocket. "Jane. What are you doing here?"

"I have an appointment with Charlie."

"You're early. You're never early."

"I'm aware. Do you know where Charles has gone to?"

"No idea. Davie called him away."

Jane studied the woman that had once been almost a rival. After her freedom from Cole they'd become friends over time. Now the woman avoided her gaze. Shouldn't they be celebrating her engagement? Making plans? Jane looked back at the now closed front door, pondering the man that had stopped in. "That was Artie Graves, yes?"

"You never forget a face. You know it was."

"I'm confused."

Daisy braced her hands at her hips. "What are you on about?"

"I thought you didn't want to doctor any of your old regulars. You said it made you uncomfortable. Artie always favored you at the saloon, and then at the Silver Saddle."

"How does it matter?" Daisy's eyes flashed as she met Jane's gaze dead on. "I have things to do, Jane."

"Daisy." Jane set a hand on the doctor's arm. "Is everything all right? I'm not trying to pry, but you've not seemed yourself lately. I'm worried about you."

"I'm fine and dandy."

"You don't have to talk to me, but ever since the epidemic."

"I said I'm fine."

"Do you at least talk to Michael? He loves you—"

"Enough." The angry lines faded briefly from Daisy's features. Her gaze drifted off in an almost tormented grimace. "That's none of your concern."

"I beg to differ. You're my friend, at least I thought you were. He's my brother. I'd like to be happy for you, but you don't seem happy yourself." At the lack of response, Jane moved closer. "Did you say yes to appease him? If so, please be kind enough to end things. You're torturing yourself as well as him."

"I'm so tired of your judgment. From the day you met me you've assumed everything about me and my life. It's not any of your concern. It never was."

"I'm not—"

"Leave me alone."

Jane stared at Daisy's retreating back in confusion and a bit of guilt. Maybe she had been assuming things when Artie came out of that room, but still, she'd tried to be kind. Rather than linger where she was not wanted, Jane headed for the door.

Outside she found Charlie walking her way. His features were creased in a scowl under his bowler. "Charles?"

Charlie lifted his head, a brief smile crossing his mouth. "I'm a few minutes late and you're ready to run away?"

"I came outside because Daisy doesn't care to have me anywhere near her apparently. I was curious about the fact she was tending to Artie when I'd thought she didn't care to see any of the men she once serviced."

"She was what?" Charlie's frown returned, his attention now on the door to the clinic. "That is odd. Artie is my patient, and he didn't have an appointment today. I wonder what brought him in."

Jane linked her arm with his. Honestly, she had no clue what to make of the situation. If it had been about her, or Daisy. "Well, she gave me a dressing down for judging her and her life. Thus, I thought I'd make myself scarce."

"I'm rather glad I caught you before you completely vacated the premises, then."

"I wouldn't have left unless you'd taken much longer. What did have you running so late for a chance to berate me?"

"Mac is dead."

Jane stopped short, though Charlie continued his pace. Her arm stretched out as he made it further away until it dropped completely.

At that, Charlie turned to face her. "Jane?"

"What do you mean, dead?"

"I mean that he will no longer be harassing women, nor stealing horses. He is dead."

"Dead."

"As a doornail."

"But—how? He was in the jail. All reports indicated his gunshot wound was healing."

"Jane. Come inside so I can perform your exam."

"Charles Emerson."

"He killed himself. Crafted a noose from the sheets and hanged himself."

Jane leaned against the wall, the shock of the statement numbing her limbs a moment. "I don't—I can't—what?"

"Michael was on duty last night."

"You aren't saying Michael sat there and let him."

"Of course not. He'd been in a prickly mood for some time. I don't think he bothered to check on the prisoner too often."

"Why would Mac do such a thing? You can't tell me he held any remorse."

Charlie shook his head. "I can't begin to imagine what provoked such a thing. Now, dear sister. Enough avoidance. Let's get your examination completed so you might go on about your life."

"Right. Of course." Jane followed him into an exam room, too stunned to pay any mind when Daisy stormed past them booth. Once seated, she shook off her silence. To facilitate the exam, she removed her bodice and the underlying chemise to reveal her wounded back.

Charlie peeled away the bandages Cole had placed over the seeping wounds that morning. "I'm surprised you can function with this wound right over your scapula. Your corset is cutting into it. You should abandon your corset for the sake of healing."

"With the bandages it isn't all that bad. Besides, you'd be surprised at the amount of pain I can work through."

"I've heard the stories. No, I wouldn't."

"You haven't heard all the stories." Jane winced as he examined the wounds closer, tugging on the sensitive skin. After a moment she noticed the cooling touch of the salve. "I never knew how horrifying a pain a whipping could be. The terrors the slaves must have lived daily. I can't begin to imagine."

"You've been so close to death twice you've been nailed in a pin box and *now* you're sympathizing with the slaves?"

"You make it sound as though I approve of slavery."

"I didn't mean that."

"Good. I don't, never have. I don't imagine Clara did either."

"She didn't. Our biggest argument was when I went South to doctor during the war."

Jane did her best to hold still while he worked. Pain lanced through her entire body when he moved to the second wound. She had to hold her breath for a moment to let it ebb before she answered. "I've never been whipped before. It's a completely different thing to be hanged or thrown off a train. Then again, I don't truly remember being thrown from a train."

"You do remember being on a train that fell into a ravine, though."

"Oh, stop." She hissed out her pain, unable to keep her back from arching from his touch at the wound.

"Sorry. I need to make sure there's no infection."

"I know. That's the worse of the two, though." She cleared her throat. "I wonder at how it could be that you went turncoat to support the south."

"I already had this argument with Clara. I won't have it with you."

"I'm simply curious." She all but sighed in relief when the cooling salve eased the pain. Soon as he'd set the gauze in place, she lifted her chemise back in place. "Did you go with the intention of becoming a spy? Perhaps you didn't bother to fill Clara in on that bit of information."

"Actually, that's precisely what happened." Charlie washed his hands. He circled around to examine her neck soon as they were dry. "I had good enough arguments of needed medical care and the horrors of battle. Clara had little to no sense of decorum and would not have kept her mouth shut over my true intention."

"You went to war against your own brothers, all while secretly working with them." Jane set her hands on his to bring his attention to her instead of her injuries. "I've heard plenty from Nicholas about how Clara abandoned him. You two last saw each other after such an argument. Did she ever make things right with you?"

"She did. We exchanged letters on occasion, and she often worried for me in them. I hold no ill will toward Clara. I thought you knew that by now."

"You've accepted me from the start, we didn't struggle as Nicholas and I have, and continue to do sometimes."

He sat next to her. "You, Jane, are a frustrating, infuriating, fascinating, and incredibly strong woman. You're easy to love, even when you're impossible to love."

"Cole would agree."

"I bet he would."

"What does this have to do with Clara?"

"Unlike you, Clara was quick to forgive. Tales of her stubbornness have been exaggerated over the years. She forgave me before I got on the train. Our argument was not the last we saw of each other. I never held malice toward her as Nick did, because I knew she didn't have my whole story and forgave me anyway."

"Do you think Nicholas will ever truly forgive me?"

"I think he has." Charlie pulled her into a hug. "You must realize by now that it isn't so much a person Nick is mad at so much as he's mad at the world. It's ended friendships, and a marriage. It's easier to be angry at Clara alone than the whole world."

"He can be angry at my past self all he wants, but I'd prefer some leeway."

"Ah, but you committed a sin of your own."

"What's that?"

"You failed to tell us you were alive, even after Mike found you."

Jane slipped off the exam table to don her bodice. "The entire family believed me dead. Considering someone had tried to kill me and I had no idea who it might be, I thought it was best to not tell anyone until that little problem was solved. I didn't know at the time that I had a Pinkerton and a spy as brothers."

"You would have if you'd let Michael tell you anything about us beyond our names."

"I want you to read something." A sudden urge for him to see it all, all the truths she'd lived prompted her to push forward. She turned to face him dead on. "Though the originals burned in the fire, I've rewritten my journals from my first years as my own person. Word for word. They might explain better what I was going through."

Charlie studied her a long minute. A slow nod came as his first response. "I think I would like to read some of that, though not all."

"I'll mark the passages it's best for you to skip, as I'm certain you don't care to hear of my feelings and wonderings about Cole."

"Those are the ones, yup. Definitely not."

Amusement tickled her at his uncomfortable grimace. "The rest, though. I still find it hard to describe some days. It's gotten easier now that I've been here for so long that I truly feel like my own person. I don't even use the words of others as much as I once did, because I have my own."

"Ma would be proud to hear that."

"Maybe it will help you understand. Maybe it could help Nicholas."

"One more question."

"Go ahead."

"I never asked. What precipitated you reaching out to me in Buffalo? You were so convinced for so long we shouldn't know. What changed your mind to allow us in?"

"George's death." Jane fiddled with her shawl. The day Michael had told her of George's murder as clear in her mind as they day it had happened. "When I knew that he was going after all of you because of me, or her. For the first time, I told Michael that we could tell the truth. I left it up to him to lead the way on how to respond to Ma's letter. He was the one that decided to wait then, because he knew I was leaving to find Alan and could easily die."

Charlie thankfully held his silence when she took a shaky breath.

"When I arrived in Buffalo and knew I was mere hours from possible death, I knew I couldn't leave without something left behind. I was terrified we'd fail."

"You would have."

"I know. I realized it then. The plan wasn't good enough. With what had happened to George and James, it was clear Alan would never stop. Even if Cole succeeded in his initial task, we could not do it alone. I left the note, not knowing of a Pinkerton and a spy, but of a family that would fight for their own. I only hoped I wasn't too late."

"You always were a bully."

Of all the responses Jane might have expected, that wasn't one of them. "I'm sorry? What?"

"With Michael. As the only brother younger than you, you could manipulate and bully that boy like no other. If it had been any of the rest of us, the whole family would have been involved long before we were." Charlie chuckled softly. "Honestly, if you hadn't left the note, Thomas was set to initiate a plan of his own, with or without Michael. I'm just glad you trusted us enough in the end."

"I didn't even know you."

"Then it took more than trust."

"I believe it's called fear, Charles."

"Fair point. That, too."

Jane slipped her shawl over her shoulders. "What's the verdict on my condition? Cole will want the news."

"You're healing remarkably well. We can't expect the whipping marks to heal fast, they just don't. You're doing quite well all things considered. You have better medical care than the men and women I've seen with them in the past, of course."

"That's little comfort in this lingering pain." Jane let him lead her to the door. "When do you wish to see me again?"

"When is your next appointment with Andrew?"

"I'm to see him next week, Tuesday."

"Then I'll expect to see you then as well. If you need more salve, drop by any time."

"Oh, speaking of my appointment with Andrew. When is Bonnie due to arrive? Nothing against you doctors, but I'd prefer a midwife."

"She's completing the terms of her final two patients. We expect her at any time. Don't worry, you and Katherine have first dibs."

"Good to know." Jane hugged him tight. "I'll see you Tuesday, then. Probably sooner for a social visit."

"I do hope so."

Jane headed across the street, then around the corner to the saloon. She hadn't returned since Mac's attack. However, she wasn't one to let something like that stop her from checking on her business. After a deep breath, she climbed the steps to head inside.

Several patrons called out greetings before her eyes adjusted. When they did, she returned the greetings with names. Many of the former saloon patrons that didn't visit the casino as often had begun to frequent The Golden Touch over the ramshackle saloon in town, she was pleased to see.

Wil nodded to her from behind the bar. "Need something, Janey?"

"I simply wanted to check in and say hello to our patrons." She approached the bar. "Whiskey, please."

"You got it." Wil poured the drink, along with one for himself. He scanned the patrons once before returning his gaze to Jane. "Doing better?"

"I am. Thank you for shooting him. Mac's a bull on a normal day. I don't know what got into him that night. I don't think anything else would have stopped him."

"Word on the street was he'd been getting cocaine on the regular."

"That could do it."

"I hear he's dead now anyway."

"So it would seem."

"Good riddance."

"Pleasant."

"Ain't heard a man that'd say different."

"True enough." She tossed back her whiskey. "How are the girls behaving?"

"They've all been followin' your rules."

"Good to hear." Jane sought out the whores on the floor. A few were lounging, but most were seated with, or enticing, men.

"Gotta say." He leaned closer on the bar. "That doc is odd."

"Doctor?" She turned her attention back to the bartender. "Which doctor do you mean? Andrew? He's not used to frontier life."

"Nah. That lady. She was luring my customers."

"She was—what?" Jane straightened at the information. "That doesn't make sense."

"Acted like she was just being friendly, but I know when a woman's looking for something. She was lookin' awful hard."

She tried to process that information. The discussion with Leanne weeks ago came to mind. Flo saying that Daisy was a whore. It couldn't be. "Damn. I really need to talk to Michael."

"How's that?"

"Oh, it's nothing." Jane released a breath. "We'll see that only Andrew or Charles attend to the whores from now on. We don't want anyone drifting to a woman that isn't under contract."

"Definitely not."

"Didn't expect to see you here," Cole's voice drifted down from above.

Jane tilted her head to find him on the balcony. "What are you doing up there?"

"Why? Worried?"

"Coming out of a room we use for entertainment? Should I be?" A murmur went around the room. Though Jane teased, not truly worried, any hint of argument always stirred the pot.

"What do you think?"

"I think it would be best if you answered."

"Relax, woman. I'm showing Aster and Dahlia how ya really want the rooms cleaned." Cole circled around to descend the steps. "They don't appreciate the extra work."

"Too bad for them." Jane glanced at Wil. "I thought you said they were following the rules."

"They are. Didn't say they weren't grumbling about some of them." Wil flashed a grin before he tossed back another whiskey. His gaze drifted to the door when it opened. "Teddy. Step right on up, I'll get your beer."

Jane pulled Cole toward the storeroom while Wil dealt with the new arrival. "Question."

"We gotta come in here for it?"

"Most definitely."

Soon as the door closed behind them, he folded his arms across the chest. He studied her face for a long minute. "Seems serious. Let's hear it."

"You mentioned a while back something about Daisy acting odd."

"During the tornado. Seemed real interested in knowing we were opening a brothel."

"Wil just told me that when she came to check on the girls, she was luring customers."

"She was what?"

"You heard me, don't be obtuse." Never mind she'd had a similar reaction. "She was interested in the fact we were opening a brothel. She's luring customers."

"When she was talking about the brothel, she had that look about her."

"Which look?"

"The one she had when she was trying to get me to keep her contract." He leaned back against the shelves. "I've seen it a few times since."

"Look at you, telling me Daisy is trying to entice you in such a casual tone. I was joking before, but do I need to be concerned?"

He scoffed. "I ain't wanted her since you dropped dead in my saloon. I guess it's just familiar."

"Tell me this, do you pity her?"

His brow furrowed. "What?"

"When you see her? When she acts like that? Do you pity her?"

"Ain't really thought about it much."

Jane chuckled under her breath at the renewed frequency of his rough vernacular. "You really get into character over here."

"What?"

"You talk differently over here than you do at the casino."

"Old habits."

She hummed. "That's what I'm worried about."

"If I do pity her?"

"That's trouble."

"Why?"

"It means she's a whore again."

I thoroughly disapprove of duels.
If a man should challenge me,
I would take him
kindly and forgivingly by the hand
and lead him to a quiet place and kill him.
—Mark Twain

Sally pushed Agatha into a harder run across the open fields east of town. The only clue Tommy left behind was a cryptic 'Ma came from'.

She'd heard enough stories to know they'd followed Jane's trail in from the east when she'd first arrived. That's why she headed now to the foothills on the other side of the valley. The night before Tom had ordered her to wear proper clothes instead of her training clothes. He'd warned her to be prepared for anything.

Already she was tired of the restricting corset and skirts. That was likely Tommy's point. Up until then all her physical training had been done in comfortable trousers and shirts with nary a corset in sight.

In order to learn to do the moves properly, the lack of restriction had been necessary. Tommy had put her through her paces over and over again until the moves were near instinct. Something he called 'muscle memory' so she'd know to do them even in proper ladies clothing. At least, that's what she'd be tested on today.

Sally slowed as she neared the property line of the new homestead nestled against the foothills. The entire town had been curious about the appearance of the homestead. The location chosen was also curious as their land went back into the hills, none of it into the flatland for cattle.

According to Jane, the home sat situated practically right on top of where she'd emerged from the hills five years prior. Whether intentional or not was anyone's guess. Whomever lived there rarely came to town, or if they did, no one was sure who they were.

Sally circled to the south of the homestead to seek out any sign of a trail. If she didn't find one, she'd swing north. She walked Agatha at an easy, but fast pace along the edge of the woods. If Tommy had left a trail at all for her to follow, it would be minimal.

Twenty minutes later she thought she'd turn back. That's when something caught her eye. Sally slipped from her saddle to look closer.

A rock lay innocuous, the soil to its right still fresh and moist as though the rock had been lying there instead. She grabbed the rock and found dry soil beneath. Clearly the rock had recently been moved. She replaced stone to its original home.

Agatha snorted nearby. Sally threw her reins around a tree and patted her neck. "Have a rest, girl. I'm not sure how long I'll be."

Sally gathered her skirts to edge into the woods with as little noise as possible. With every step she kept an eye out for any further marks of a trail. Problem was, Tommy was good at not leaving a trail. The rock at the bottom of the hill had been her last intentional clue, she was certain of it.

In a turn of good luck, the wind blew strong enough that she thought the occasional rustle of her skirts remained well hidden. Unfortunately, it also blew quite cold. The wool cape she wore hardly blocked the biting gusts.

Still, she pressed up the hill. Every few moments she paused to scan for a trail. Now and then she'd spot small signs a human had passed. A broken branch here, a disturbed bit of ground that revealed damp ground. For over an hour the trail took her in circles. Three times she had to double back to figure the right way.

The whole endeavor was taking far too long. She knew Tommy would be disappointed. To that end, she had a sneaking suspicion he sat somewhere nearby spying on her. Always a damn step ahead.

On her fourth double back, she stopped on the spot. She huffed out a breath of frustration. Her nose was cold, her toes weren't much better, and she'd been out there for at least a couple hours already. That also meant she was hungry.

She crouched low to the ground to study that last hint of a trail she'd found. A flattened patch of weeds. Sally thought back to everything Tommy had taught her already.

Logic puzzles and scenarios ran through her head. Over top of it all was the key he'd always stressed the most.

Instinct.

Above everything else, instinct would win.

Sally rose to face the woods before her. She straightened her shoulders. This was something she could do. She closed her eyes and took a few deep breaths. Her gut instinct. What did it tell her?

North. Without allowing room for doubt, she headed toward the border of the lands that belonged to the homestead she'd passed earlier. Then turned east again, back up the hill. At the top, she ducked back south, following a line of trees over the open clearing that could lead her down. She slowed near the bottom, sliding deeper into the trees when tension ratcheted through her stomach.

Tucked into the trunk of a tree, she scanned the branches above her. A dark shape tucked into the crook of some limbs of a cottonwood. The second she spotted it, the form moved, and Tommy swung down from the heights.

Sally did the opposite, jumping to catch a branch of the fir she'd tucked into. Branch by branch, she clamored up until she was out of his reach. As he made for the lowest branch, she swung down and caught him in the shoulders, knocking him to the ground.

She landed a few feet away, spinning toward him. The man hopped to his feet in an elegant turn, but a flash of metal caught her eye. Sally spun, unhooking her cape on the way around, swinging it in the path of the knife, and spinning it around his arm to wrench the weapon away.

The knife and her cape flew a few feet away as she ducked under whatever retaliating blow he might deliver. He must have anticipated because a boot headed right for her face. With a squeak, she barely managed to duck out of the way.

The dodge left her rolling down the hill until she crashed into a tree trunk. She grunted at the impact to her still aching ribs, but swung around the back of the tree. The urge to peek to check what Tommy was doing was strong, but she remained still. Deep breaths brought back calm.

No sound touched her ears, which meant the distraction of the fall had left her without a clue where he was again. She muttered under her breath, "Damn."

She scanned the woods around her, wondering what her next move should be. A scattering of lodgepoles meant no easy climbing for a better vantage point. She'd have to get back up the hill for that.

Gravity from the downhill slope could work against her, but also to her advantage. With another breath, she launched herself from behind the tree to head down the hill. With the increased speed, even Tom couldn't hide his rapid footfalls behind her.

At breakneck pace, right before she got out of control, she grabbed onto a young, narrow lodgepole trunk to swing back around. Although her momentum slowed, she was still at a good clip when she reached Tommy. She dove to the forest floor and flipped onto her back to kick out the back of his knees.

He tumbled down the hill this time. Sally leapt to her feet and skidded down the hill after him, grabbing her knife from her boot as she slid down at an increasing pace. When his tumble slowed, she crouched to leap over him. On landing, she used her free hand to stop her descent.

The flash of his knife was countered with her own, and she dipped away from the swing of a fist. She spun to get behind him, cutting one strap of his suspenders before swinging around to his front. "That was your kidney. I win."

He broke into a big smile. "It was, and you did. Impressive. I think you fight better in your skirts and corset than you ever did in pants. You're like your Ma."

The praise pleased Sally more than she dared to admit. "That was fun, but I swear my ribs are never gonna heal at this rate."

Tom laughed, offering her his hand to climb back up the hill. "It'll heal. It won't all be like this all the time. It's just good to have it. You never know what sort you're going to come across."

At the top of the hill, Sally paused to slide her knife back into her boot. "I just wish we could start on firearms."

"You need to know how to fight first. That's more important."

"No it's not. Ma can't fight, or she's just now learning, but she's a crack shot."

"Fair enough point, but I'm the one training you, and I say fighting's more important. As well as your mind."

"Can we please start?"

"Next week." Tom led her back toward where her horse was. "I saw when you stopped trying to think your way through and went on instinct instead."

"You *were* watching me."

"Of course I was." Tom laughed as they wove through the trees. "You didn't think it was all about the fight?"

"No. I just had the feeling you were watching and getting frustrated with me."

"It did take you longer than I'd hoped. We'll try again in a few days."

"Can we make it tomorrow?"

"I've got an even better idea. You won't know when the next one is coming."

"I like it."

I show you doubt,
to prove that faith exists.
–Robert Browning

Cole laughed obligingly when Clara knocked over the block tower she'd just built, again. The relative silence in the room struck him as odd. Alma was off with Sally seeking some sweets before Cora abandoned the kitchens.

The twins played in their own ways. Colton lay flat on his belly, tongue sticking out in concentration as he drew on some paper. Clara towered blocks taller than herself, then knocked them down flat.

Jane stood at the doorway where she'd been for nearly ten minutes. They'd sent off Willow and Jay with Black Moon again. Since their departure Jane had remained staring out into the night.

Like a statue she stood, her gaze unmoving from where the children had disappeared beyond the barn. Maybe even into the darkened shadow of mountains where the children would soon be with their Cheyenne guide.

Cole rose to check on her. She leaned into him soon as he set his hands on her hips. He kissed her neck. "Anything wrong?"

"I fear one day he'll go, and never return." Jane sighed deeply, her fingers tangling with his. A sadness deepened her tone, a soft warble belied tears he knew she wanted to hide.

"Jay?"

"Yes. Shivering Willow has come leaps and bounds, though she certainly has her moments of melancholy. Jaybird—he is so resistant."

"He's seemed better since you started letting him go on these trips."

"It doesn't seem enough." Her fingers brushed across her cheek. "Oh, what you must think. It's the baby making me emotional. That's all there is to it. I need to gather myself before I make a complete fool of myself."

"Nah. You're no fool, not even close." He brushed his lips along her throat again. "You're just a ma. Their ma, even if they never say the same. You love them much as the rest of the brood."

"I do."

He pulled her back inside. Before he could do anything else, Colton wrapped his arms around Jane's legs, effectively stopping her in her tracks.

Colton leaned his head against Jane. His small hands patted her skirts. "It's all right, Mama."

Jane smiled down at their son, crouching down to his level. She brushed her hand along his dark hair. The tears that had lingered in her eyes faded under his tiny comforts. "Thank you, Colton. You're right. It is all right."

Colton folded into her hug easily. He continued patting her shoulder.

Not one to be outdone, Clara raced toward the pair, nearly bowling Jane over in her enthusiasm. "Me too, Mama."

Cole laughed along with Jane. "Little rascals."

"Loving rascals, perhaps." Jane kissed each of them on the top of their head. "Bedtime, little ones. Come along. We'll read a little story before you sleep."

Cole managed to catch a kiss from her as she rose. He waited until they were in the bedroom before he moved. Jane's voice carried out in soft tones, even while Clara squealed excitedly. When he peeked in the room, both children were already changed, but Clara was scrambling around the room grabbing different toys to try to play.

He couldn't stop his smile as Jane calmly managed to restore order with their rambunctious child. In mere minutes she had both of them snuggled on a bed, reading to them.

The apartment door opened, a high pitched giggle filtering into the room. Cole tugged the twin's door almost shut in hopes of keeping Clara focused on her ma.

Alma practically skipped into the room, still laughing. Cole held his finger to his lips. Alma stopped making noise, but her body shook with laughter. Sally rushed into the room moments later. Her hands raised as if to suppress Alma, but her lips bit in a containment of her own laughter.

Cole folded his arms across his chest when Sally came to a dead stop upon spotting him. He lifted a brow, glancing at Alma's quaking frame.

"Sweets might have been a bad idea." Sally winced an apology. "Isaac was there, too."

"Nah. Isaac don't get people riled up. He's the best behaved boy I ever met." Cole allowed his amusement to show with a slight twitch of his lips.

"I thought maybe I'd take her for a walk, but it's late. Ma doesn't want us out late any longer, leastwise not alone."

"Maybe take her—"

"I get chickens tomorrow." Alma spun in a circle. "Mrs. Mortell says. Chickens."

"Oh yeah. Um, we ran into the Mortell's." Sally sighed, giving up the battle against her smile. "Mrs. Mortell says the chickens are ready. Good thing the dog run is done so Alma has her coop back."

"Jane got chicken feed for me. We get chickens tomorrow." Alma grinned at Cole.

"That's great, Alma. Maybe you and Sally can make sure the coop is ready, and check on the dogs for me." Petting the dogs often helped calm Alma down when she got excitable. "I bet Whiskey and Bourbon would like the company. They've been out there a few hours."

Sally urged Alma toward the door at the suggestion. "Good idea, Pa."

Cole chuckled under his breath. He loved seeing Alma so happy on any given day, but the timing was awful with Jane trying to get the twins asleep. He crossed to their room, leaving the door open so Jane would know where he was.

He stoked the fire and set her tea kettle on top. Part of him wanted to draw a bath for them, but he figured she'd think he was out for one thing. He was, he always was, but he also wanted her to relax. Last thing he wanted was her too worried what with the baby and all.

"What was all that noise?" Jane pushed the bedroom door shut behind her. "It took all I had to keep Clara in the room."

"Alma's a bit excitable. Between the sweets, Isaac's encouragement, and Mrs. Mortell telling her the chickens are ready, she's in a state."

"Oh dear. The chickens. The dogs. We are going to be overrun."

"Don't forget the cats."

"They're barn cats for the mice. They take care of themselves." She pushed off the door. A glance toward the bathroom drew a smirk. "Interesting."

"Figured a bath would annoy you. Make you think I only had one thing on my mind."

"You do only have one thing on your mind." She draped her arms around his neck. "Not that I mind. It's often on mine as well."

"I still could, you know. Draw a bath."

She hummed softly, leaning until their bodies were flush. "That would take too long."

"I agree."

The tea kettle rattled slightly as the water began boiling. She glanced at it. "Oh, you were making me tea."

"I was."

"That sounds delightful. Would you continue?"

He pursed his lips, narrowing his eyes at her. "Get me riled up and ask me to finish making your tea? You're evil, woman."

"Ah, but I never leave you disappointed."

"Can't argue that."

*To be kind to all,
to like many and love a few,
to be needed and wanted by those we love,
is certainly the nearest we can come
to happiness.
-Mary Stuart*

Cole thanked every man as they left the silver room. When Henry approached last, Cole offered him a grin and extended his hand. "Congratulations, Mr. Daugherty. You did well tonight."

"Perhaps I should have Lillian in the next room more often when I'm gambling." Henry shook his hand heartily. "She seems to bring me good luck."

"Sure does. I was surprised to see you tonight. You usually stick to the Gold Room, even with the Silver Room option available any time."

"Lillian got it in her head she wanted to see the burlesque tonight. I thought I'd steal the opportunity for an extra night of gambling." Henry stood by while he closed the door. "I believe our daughters' fine mood attributed to our evening out."

"Kathy's been in a fine mood of late."

"Having a baby can do that to a woman."

Cole couldn't stop his grin at the words. He knew exactly what the man meant. Jane's mood had been vastly improved since they'd also found out she was pregnant alongside her friend. "Don't I know it?"

"That's right. You and Jane are also expecting another child."

"Sure are. And on purpose this time."

Henry laughed heartily. "Well, congratulations to you. If you'll excuse me, I spy my lovely bride and daughter."

Cole scanned the casino floor, and the cubbies on the level surrounding the floor. The place teemed with life, and was all the more noisy for it. On stage Sally sang to warm the crowd before the burlesque began. He knew in their private cubby Alma would be sitting, for even with the crowd and noise, she always enjoyed watching Sally sing.

Despite the crowd, and Kathy's presence in it, he saw no sign of Jane. Right as he was about to go in search of her she appeared on the other side of the pit. On Patrick's arm she carried on a lively conversation. If he didn't know better, he'd think she was eying him rather endearingly. Though the idea of such public display rankled him, he knew he could trust Jane not to stray. He'd learned his lesson long ago, the hard way.

Still, his possessive side urged him toward the pair.

Jane descended the steps with the dandy, leaning in to speak to him before releasing him to the floor. The man crossed to Kathy's table, greeting Norman warmly before placing a kiss to Kathy's cheek and Lillian's hand.

Jane remained at the base of the steps. Her gaze swept the floor before returning to the stage where Sally sang. A pleasant smile curved her delicious lips.

Cole moved down the steps to her side. "There you are."

Jane didn't respond to his greeting. Her shoulders swayed with the music, smile unwavering.

"Saw you all cozy with Patrick. Do I need to be worried?" Her continued lack of response confused him. Normally she would mock argue, or even truly argue in annoyance over his possessive side. "Jane?"

Still nothing. Her eyes fluttered shut."

"Jane?" Cole poked her in the side.

Jane jumped at the poke, spinning on him fast. Her eyes wide, a hand to her chest as she took several quick breaths. "Cole Mitchell. You startled me."

"Startled you? I've been standing here talking to you."

"You have? Oh." Laughter lit her features; a pink hue warmed her cheeks. "You're on my right side, you buffoon."

"I wasn't whispering," he protested. Sure, he knew her right ear was almost completely deaf, had been since her bout of scarlet fever. Still, it really only mattered when he was whispering.

"With the noise in this place, and Sally's singing? I couldn't hear you, or if I did I thought it was someone in this lot." Her fingers laced into his. "Did you need something?"

"You."

"Oh, well, that you have." She tilted her lips up for a kiss he all too happily granted her. Her soft lips danced with his. Too soon for his liking she withdrew. Rather than turn back to the show, she pulled him up the stairs.

He followed willingly as she led him all the way out to the porch. When she leaned on the railing, he did the same. Lacing their fingers together, he let the silence linger for a while. His thumb traced along the back of her hand. A gesture he'd once reserved to private moments. That had changed in the past few years since they'd gotten married.

Hell, a lot had changed since he'd met Jane. Alma and Leanne both lived in town now, and though he didn't claim them as what they were, they were a part of his life. Miraculously, his friendship with Graham was restored, a feat he'd never thought would happen.

Then there was Jane. He'd married her three years before. She'd once worried that life would be boring once they'd killed the madman out for her. Instead, every day proved interesting. The worst days were the ones he didn't see her as much.

A sigh from her direction led him to speak. "You all right?"

"I am. I really, truly am." She turned toward him. "I am very happy right now. Seems as though we get so little time to enjoy such a thing, I'd like to revel in it for a while."

"Revel away." He switched hands so he could wrap the one closer to her around her waist.

Too soon, she was gone as someone approached. "Charles, Millie."

Charlie returned Jane's hug. "Hello, Jane. How are you feeling?"

"Wonderful." Jane hugged Millie tight before moving back to Cole's side. "Did you come for the burlesque?"

"Of course." Millie's hand slipped over her well-swollen abdomen. The woman was due any minute now. "We're trying to enjoy all of the time alone we have left."

"As well you should. Just remember what I warned you about, Millie. Once you have one, it's hard to stop. As if the Young family wasn't evidence of that enough on its own." Jane laughed quietly. "Although I believe I outstripped Ma and Pa by a few children."

"Only one for the moment, although it'll be two soon." Charlie chuckled. "At least you only have six with you right now, and two of them are adults."

"The age difference between my children is rather extreme," Jane acknowledged. "There will be so many babies around here soon. Little Marjorie is going to have so many playmates."

"Lee is already talking about another." Millie winked. "Then again, that may just be her inability to ignore the handsomeness of her husband."

Cole instinctively tugged Jane closer upon her agreement with Millie's sentiment. Sure, she'd divorced David years ago, but old jealousy clung on. Even though he knew she'd never granted the man more than a few kisses. "If you wanna catch Sally, you'd best hurry. I'd wager a bet she's only got a couple songs left."

Jane swatted his hand as they left. "You are hopeless sometimes."

"You like that about me."

"Unfortunately, I believe you're right." She laced her arm with his. "The Inn is well covered for the evenings show. The children are all taken care of. Would it be too much trouble to request a walk with my…"

Cole glanced around when she did to make sure they were alone.

Her voice dropped, even in their privacy, the husky note sent a whisper of excitement through him. "Husband."

"Definitely not too much trouble." He brushed his lips across hers before he took a proper step back to offer her his arm. They strode along the boardwalk in silence for a while. The occasional clop of horseshoes on cobblestone the only interruption to the quiet.

"You know," she said, effectively breaking the comfortable silence. "Some days I find it hard to believe this is the same town I woke in five years ago."

"A lot has changed. My saloon isn't there anymore."

"And yet, you've rescued it from the grave with The Golden Touch."

"Had to. Couldn't have made it any other way."

"Sentimental fool."

"Nah." He leaned closer. "If I were sentimental, I woulda saved the corner room for us."

"An escape from our children, perhaps?"

"That was a tempting idea." He winked at her laughter. They neared the end of the street and slowed.

"Cobblestone, plumbing, two more full streets and the hints of another." Jane sighed. "It truly looks like a real town now. No carts in the street, though they're no less busy during the day. I love it now, but I miss the way it was sometimes."

"I was here longer, imagine what I think." Cole frowned. "Never thought I'd stick around when it got all fancy. Now I'm one of the fancy ones."

"Pish posh." She turned to face him. "You're still a devil, you're just in sheep's clothing."

"Ya think so, do ya?"

"Look at you, sinking right back into that rough vernacular with such ease." She kissed him softly again. "Now, what was that I was saying about you being a devil?"

He eyed her mischievous grin. "What are you after?"

"I think you know."

He grunted as her fingers circled his shaft through his trousers. "I think you already got a handle on things."

"Do I?"

"Oh yeah."

"Is that a problem?"

He crushed his lips to hers, resisting the urge to tug her close as he liked the handle she had on him at the moment.

She gasped suddenly, her teasing touch gone in that heartbeat. "What was that?"

"What? Last I checked, it was my—"

"No. That flash of light."

"I didn't see nothing."

"I swear, I saw a—oh my god. Fire!"

*Neither fire nor wind, birth nor death,
can erase our good deeds.
—Buddha*

Jane raced behind Cole toward Second Street. The second they turned the corner, they both called out. "The livery!"

Cole ran toward the fire, but Jane backtracked, racing toward the newly reinstalled emergency bell. By the time she got there, her lungs burned with the need to breathe deep, but she didn't pause a second.

She yanked on the rope to set the bell clanging. Over and over she pulled as people poured into the streets to find out what was going on. Jane wasn't certain how long she'd yanked on the rope before Mrs. Kilmurry arrived and brushed her aside.

Jane paused long enough to take a few decent breaths. Then she ran toward the scene. By the time she got there, the fire was mostly contained, thanks to the pipes that helped send water through the town.

On her way through the crowd, she searched for Archie. The town's mayor owned, and lived in, the livery. She hoped against hope he was all right.

At the fence she spotted him and Cole trying to calm the horses that had poured into the corral at the fire. Jane leaned on the fence to admire Cole working with the horses, his strong arms gripping reins or raising when a horse reared up. The two men whistled, wrestled with reins and bridles, and called to the horses and each other.

"Jane," Nick's voice distracted her from her enjoyment. "You all right?"

"Fine. I was at the bell. What about you?" Jane turned away from the show, noticing the lingering crowd. "Perhaps the bell was overdone. The fire was settled faster than I'd expected."

"They're not done yet. Those haystacks are still smoldering, as is some of the hay in the stalls inside." Nick wiped the back of his hand across his forehead, dark streaks of soot left behind by the action. "We're taking it in shifts."

Jane climbed on the fence to search over the top of the crowd. "Where is Graham?"

"Graham?" Nick set a supportive hand at her waist. "He's over by the barn. Why?"

"Well, he wants to be mayor, he needs to take charge and get this crowd out of here."

"You're really helping Graham Cooke become mayor?" Nick shook his head. "Wonders never cease."

"Hush. These days he's a good fit." She pushed her way through the crowd, Nick right on her heels. Once they got to the barn, she noticed there was still a bit of heat in the air. Nick wasn't kidding about the smoldering haystacks. "Graham!"

The large man turned from shouting instructions, a pitchfork in hand. "Janey. What can I do for you?"

"You can get this crowd dispersed. You only need a couple dozen men, don't you?" Jane squeezed Nick's hand when he returned to the cleanup.

"Probably. The rest are just curious."

"Exactly. No one was hurt, were they?"

"Nah. The horses all got out, too. Looks like the stacks lit up first." Graham scanned the crowd. "Why do they need to go?"

"Graham, you want to be mayor, take control. Send them back to the businesses they were frequenting, or their homes. Reassure them that all is well, and you only need some men to finish taking care of the fire. A good mayor is reassuring, and takes control, thanks those that have helped, and ensures businesses lose as little income as possible."

"You're talking about your businesses."

"There's two other saloons and another brothel. It's not just mine." Jane slipped away through the crowd. In a few minutes Graham's voice boomed over the crowd. As he did as Jane suggested, reassuring that everyone was fine, no lives lost, Jane smiled.

By the time he'd finished and she'd made it back to the corral, the crowd had already begun to disperse. She stepped back up on the fence and swung her legs over the edge to wait as Cole and Archie finished with the horses.

Only a short time later both Archie and Cole walked toward her. Jane nodded to Archie. "Glad you're all right."

"I was heading to your place for the show. The light caught my attention." Archie used his hat to dust off his pants. "Got the horses out first, by then the bell was ringing and someone was attacking the fire."

"Graham said all the horses were saved."

"Yup. I should go check the damage and help finish putting out the fires. Plenty of hay in there to catch."

Jane smiled. "Next burlesque you're welcome free of charge."

"Much obliged." Arche replaced his hat, then jogged toward the barn.

Cole stepped closer, in between her legs. "So much for our walk."

"I guess so."

"And your happiness?"

"Still here. Everyone is safe, even all the horses. People have returned for the show, so the Inn is full again. Only dark spot now is that I know you're going to stay and help."

"I'll make it up to you."

She wrapped her arms around his waist to pull him flush against her. "You'd better believe you are. Thoroughly and completely."

His lips brushed across hers. "All night if I gotta."

"Bully for me."

"Nah, bully for me."

She chuckled softly. "Go. Be a good man and help. I'll be waiting for you."

"Be there soon as I can."

Jane sighed as he jogged toward the scene as well. She remained as she was, watching the settling horses wander the corral.

"Ma." Sally leaned on the fence next to her. "What happened?"

"A fire, of course."

"But, how?" Sally climbed onto the fence beside her. "Doesn't make much sense, does it?"

"It doesn't. I thought I saw a flash of something before it took, but my eyes were closed, so I can't be certain." Jane turned her attention to the bustle of men working to put out the remaining hot spots inside and out of the barn.

"It's not just Tommy and I, is it?"

"Hm?"

"That think all of this is odd."

Jane didn't see any reason to lie to Sally, the girl was learning to look at everything with suspicion. Something Jane had realized long ago Tom did, and she had a tendency toward after all she'd been through. "No, though we are among the few that do."

"Keller, Ellis, McKerney, Emily, me, now this."

"Have you and Tommy thought of a common thread yet?" Jane pulled her gaze away from the working men to focus on Sally fully. "Seeing as you are in complete suspicion about it."

"Nothing that's really made sense." She frowned deeply. "There is something that ties me to Emily. Also to…well you; but yours was Mac and he's long had an issue with you so that may just be coincidence."

"What's that?"

"Mac was calling you a succubus."

"And a whore." Jane rubbed her throat subconsciously as she remembered the attack. "Nothing new from him. His decent moments were far less common than his indecent ones. He was a whoremonger himself and saw every woman as something he could use how he saw fit. The man didn't visit the saloon once that he didn't make a pass of some sort."

"The woman screamed whore at me as well. Again, I was one once, and like everyone knew, Mac had it in for you. Ever since you first met him, if the stories are true."

"Quite true. He groped me as I was walking down the boardwalk. Instinct had me trip him, and then step on his hand. If Cole hadn't gotten in the way, I might not have come out of that without significant injury."

"You think it's a coincidence?"

"I think it's all a puzzle, and if you don't question, you could miss a piece."

"Now you sound like Tommy." Sally laughed under her breath. "Guess no matter which side of the law you train on, you learn the same stuff."

"I don't remember my training, but that's what caused me to be suspicious and seek out puzzles where I might not have before."

"Are you still upset with me?"

Jane pondered the question, but shook her head. "I was never upset with you, Sally. I worry over you. That's different than being upset. I know you're doing well, Thomas has told me as much. That doesn't mean I won't worry for you."

"We're starting with teaching me to shoot soon."

"Good. Having a weapon nearby has saved me on a few occasions."

"I told Tommy that I thought learning both would be good. I've been training for a while for a physical fight, but not on how to use weapons. I pointed out you're a crack shot and don't know how to fight much."

"Learning how to fight proper could have saved me in other ways." Jane shuddered at the memory of Joe, a Pinkerton that had raped her. Her Remington had been within reach, but he'd beat her to it. "Thomas isn't wrong. You can't always have a weapon on your person, and sometimes they get theirs first. You have to know how to fight."

"Ma? What is it?" Sally squeezed her arm. "Why are you crying?"

"Oh, goodness. Am I?" Jane swiped at the tears that she now realized dampened her cheeks. "I didn't even realize. Must be the baby making me emotional over old memories."

Sally's head dropped to Jane's shoulder. "I'm glad you worry for me, Ma. Even when it frustrates me."

"That's good because I won't stop. Even when you're off on your own, I'll worry over you."

"Good. That means I always got a home."

"Yes. You'll always have a home right here."

To Be

Continued...

In Book 8 of the
Dominion Falls Series

Chasing the
Red

About the Author

Sarah Cass, author of over twenty novels in 4 series, is devoted to giving her readers well-crafted, emotional stories, with depth to even her secondary characters—to give readers a full world to explore. Stories that explore not only the labyrinths of the heart, but the nightmares of the soul. A RONE finalist, she is also owner and creator of Redefining Perfect. By day, she's a nurse, a mother, wife and cat-mom to 4 mischievous beasts. By night she crafts stories that take her across centuries. From the old west of Dominion Falls, to the small town of Lake Point for the holidays, and even into the paranormal land of Shifters and Magic in The Tribe. She loves hearing from her readers. Visit her at www.authorsarahcass.com

Other Books in
The Dominion Falls Series

Independent Brake
Changing Tracks
Derailed
Dark Territory
Green Eye
Runaway Train
Home Signal
Red Zone

Coming Soon in
The Dominion Falls Series

Chasing the Red
Blizzard Lights
Dead Man's Switch
Bird Cage
A Highball Arrangement
Douse the Glim
Blood
Grave Digger
Bad Order

Books by Sarah Cass
The Tribe Series
The Tribe
The Wolf
The Chief
The Raven
The Lake Point Series
Santa, Maybe
Deep-Fried Sweethearts
Stalled Independence
Witch Way
A Thorough Thanksgiving
Eve's New Year
Heartstrings & Hockey Pucks
Luck of the Cowgirl
Stars, Stripes & Motorbikes
Free Falling
Love for Hire
Haunted Hearts
Stand Alone Novels
Masked Hearts
Leap